Praise for *The Pact* and Jodi Picoult

'You will find this novel impossible to put down – and if you take it on holiday with you, just don't plan on doing any sightseeing until you've finished it!' *Daily Mail*

'The novelist displays an almost uncanny ability to enter the skins of her troubled young protagonists.' *New York Times*

'It's riveting . . . This is a brilliant read, filled with twists and turns' *Woman Magazine*

'Engrossing . . . Picoult has a remarkable ability to make us share her characters' feelings of confusion and horror . . . *The Pact* is compelling reading' *People*

'Impossible to put down' *Observer*

'There is a lot of intellectual kudos attached to reading Jodi Picoult but there is an awful lot of enjoyment to be had . . . you know you are going to get a roller-coaster ride of a plot.' *Sunday Express*

'Picoult's pitch and pace are masterly and hardly conducive to a good night's sleep' *Financial Times*

'This is Picoult's greatest strength; her ability to inhabit other people's feelings, relishing the bits that are complex and contradictory . . . She is a master of her craft . . . and humanity is what Picoult does best' *Sunday Telegraph*

'Picoult is an amazing storyteller and as she weaves you deeper into the lives of her flawed families you'll be gripped by their traumas . . . enthralling' *Heat*

'There are many aspirants to her throne, but nobody in commercial fiction cranks the pages more effectively than

Also by Jodi Picoult

Songs of the Humpback Whale
Harvesting the Heart
Picture Perfect
Mercy
Keeping Faith
Plain Truth
Salem Falls
Perfect Match
Second Glance
My Sister's Keeper
Vanishing Acts
The Tenth Circle
Nineteen Minutes
Change of Heart
Handle With Care
House Rules
Sing You Home
Lone Wolf
The Storyteller

Jodi Picoult & Samantha van Leer
Between the Lines

Jodi Picoult grew up in Nesconset, New York. She received an A.B. in creative writing from Princeton and a master's degree in education from Harvard. Her novels include *The Storyteller*, *Lone Wolf*, *Sing You Home* and *House Rules*. She lives in New Hampshire with her husband and three children.

Jodi's UK website is www.jodipicoult.co.uk and she can be found on Facebook and Twitter at facebook.com/JodiPicoultUK and twitter.com/jodipicoult. She also has a YouTube channel www.youtube.com/user/JodiPicoultOfficial.

JODI
PICOULT
The Pact

HODDER

First published in Great Britian in 2004 by Hodder & Stoughton
An Hachette UK company
First published in America in 1998 by William Morris & Co,
A division of HarperCollins US

This paperback published in 2013

1

A CIP catalogue record for this title is available from the British Library

ISBN 978 1 444 75435 3

Typeset in Berkeley Book by Palimpsest Book Production Limited,
Falkirk, Stirlingshire

Printed and bound by
CPI Group (UK) Ltd, Croydon, CR0 4YY

Hodder & Stoughton policy is to use papers that are natural, renewable
and recyclable products and made from wood grown in sustainable forests.
The logging and manufacturing processes are expected to conform to the
environmental regulations of the country of origin.

Hodder and Stoughton Ltd
338 Euston Road
London NW1 3BH

www.hodder.co.uk

THIS ONE'S FOR MY BROTHER, JON,

who knows the cost of the Space Toilet,
the spelling of *Tetris*, and the way to find a
chapter accidentally lost in the bowels of my computer.
I hope you also know how terrific I think you are.

ACKNOWLEDGMENTS

Every time I spoke to someone during the research for this book, it changed a little, until it was something entirely different from what I expected and far, far better. So for their individual expertise and fictional input, I'd like to thank the following: Dr Robert Racusin, Dr Tia Horner, Dr James Umlas; Paula Spaulding, Candace Workman, State Trooper Bill McGee, Alexis Aldahondo, Kirsty DePree, Julie Knowles, Cyrena Koury and friends; Superintendant Sidney Bird of the Grafton County Correctional Facility; Detective-Sergeant Frank Moran, Patrol Sergeant Mike Evans, and Chief Nick Giaccone of the Hanover, New Hampshire, Police Department. Thanks, once again, to my first critics: Jane Picoult and Laura Gross; and to Beccy Goodhart, who, with her cohorts at Morrow, is giving me back my faith in the publishing industry. And finally, a toast to my Dream Team for working late, under pressure, and *pro bono*: attorneys Andrea Greene, Allegra Lubrano, Chris Keating, and Kiki Keating.

I

The Boy Next Door

Who ever loved
that loved not at first sight?
– CHRISTOPHER MARLOWE
Hero and Leander

Let us embrace, and from this very moment
vow an eternal misery together.
– THOMAS OTWAY
The Orphan

Now

November 1997

There was nothing left to say.

He covered her body with his, and as she put her arms around him she could picture him in all his incarnations: age five, and still blond; age eleven, sprouting; age thirteen, with the hands of a man. The moon rolled, sloe-eyed in the night sky; and she breathed in the scent of his skin. 'I love you,' she said.

He kissed her so gently she wondered if she had imagined it. She pulled back slightly, to look into his eyes.

And then there was a shot.

Although there had never been a standing reservation made, the rear corner table of the Happy Family Chinese restaurant was always saved on Friday nights for the Hartes and the Golds, who had been coming there for as long as anyone could remember. Years ago, they had brought the children, littering the crowded nook with high chairs and diaper bags until it was nearly impossible for the waiters to maneuver the steaming platters of food onto the table. Now, it was just the four of them, blustering in one by one at six o'clock and gravitating close as if, together, they exerted some kind of magnetic pull.

James Harte had been first to arrive. He'd been operating that afternoon and had finished surprisingly early. He picked up the chopsticks in front of him, slipped them from their paper packet, and cradled them between his fingers like surgical instruments.

'Hi,' Melanie Gold said, suddenly across from him. 'I guess I'm early.'

'No,' James answered. 'Everyone else is late.'

'Really?' She shrugged out of her coat and balled it up beside her. 'I was hoping I was early. I don't think I've ever been early.'

'You know,' James said, considering, 'I don't think you ever have.'

They were linked by the one thing they had in common – Augusta Harte – but Gus had not yet arrived. So they sat in the companionable awkwardness caused by knowing extremely private things about each other that had never been directly confided, but rather blurted by Gus Harte to her husband in bed or to Melanie over a cup of coffee. James cleared his throat and flipped the chopsticks around his fingers with dexterity. 'What do you think?' he asked, smiling at Melanie. 'Should I give it all up? Become a drummer?'

Melanie flushed, as she always did when she was put on the spot. After years of sitting with a reference desk wrapped around her waist like a hoop skirt, concrete answers came easily to her; nonchalance didn't. If James had asked, 'What is the current population of Addis Ababa?' or 'Can you tell me the actual chemicals in a photographic fixing bath?' she'd never have blushed, because the answers would never have offended him. But this drummer question? What exactly was he looking for?

'You'd hate it,' Melanie said, trying to sound flippant. 'You'd have to grow your hair long and get a nipple ring or something like that.'

'Do I want to know why you're talking about nipple rings?' Michael Gold said, approaching the table. He leaned down and touched his wife's shoulder, which passed for an embrace after so many years of marriage.

'Don't get your hopes up,' Melanie said. 'James wants one, not me.'

Michael laughed. 'I think that's automatic grounds for losing your board certification.'

'Why?' James frowned. 'Remember that Nobel laureate we met on the cruise to Alaska last summer? He had a hoop through his eyebrow.'

'Exactly,' Michael said. 'You don't have to have board certification to create a poem entirely out of curse words.' He shook
out his napkin and settled it in his lap. 'Where's Gus?'

James checked his watch. He lived by it; Gus didn't wear
one at all. It drove him crazy. 'I think she was taking Kate to
a friend's for a sleepover.'

'Did you order yet?' Michael asked.

'Gus orders,' James said, an excuse. Gus was usually there
first, and as in all other things, Gus was the one who kept the
meal running smoothly.

As if her husband had invoked her, Augusta Harte rushed
through the door of the Chinese restaurant. 'God, I'm late,'
she said, unbuttoning her coat with one hand. 'You cannot
imagine the day I've had.' The other three leaned forward,
expecting one of her infamous stories, but instead Gus waved
over a waiter. 'The usual,' she said, smiling brightly.

The usual? Melanie, Michael, and James looked at each other.
Was it that easy?

Gus was a professional waiter, not the kind who carried
food to tables, but the one who sacrificed time so that someone
else would not have to. Busy New Englanders solicited her
business, Other People's Time, when they didn't want to wait
in line at the Motor Vehicles Division, or sit around all day
for the cable TV repairman. She began to tame her curly red
hair. 'First,' she said, an elastic band clamped between her
teeth, 'I spent the morning at the Motor Vehicles Division,
which is awful under the best of circumstances.' She bravely
attempted a ponytail, something like leashing a current of
electricity, and glanced up. 'So I'm the next one in line – you
know, just in front of that little window – and the clerk, swear
to God, has a heart attack. Just dies on the floor of the
registry.'

'That is awful,' Melanie breathed.

'Mmm. Especially because they closed the line down, and
I had to start from scratch.'

'More billable hours,' Michael said.

'Not in this case,' Gus said. 'I'd already scheduled a two o'clock appointment at Exeter.'

'The school?'

'Yeah. With a Mr J. Foxhill. He turned out to be a third-former with a lot of extra cash who needed someone to sit in detention for him by proxy.'

James laughed. 'That's ingenuity.'

'Needless to say, it wasn't acceptable to the headmaster, who wasted my time with a lecture about adult responsibility even after I told him I didn't know any more about the plan than he had. And then, when I go to pick up Kate from soccer practice, the car gets a flat, and by the time I change the spare and get to the playing field she's already found a ride to Susan's house.'

'Gus,' Melanie said. 'What happened to the clerk?'

'You changed a tire?' James said, as if Melanie hadn't spoken. 'I'm impressed.'

'So was I. But just in case it's on backwards I want to take your car downtown tonight.'

'You're working again?'

Gus nodded, smiling as the waiter delivered their food. 'I'm headed to the box office for Metallica tickets.'

'What happened to the clerk?' Melanie said more forcefully.

They all stared at her. 'Jeez, Mel,' Gus said. 'You don't have to yell.' Melanie flushed, and Gus immediately gentled her voice. 'I don't know what happened, actually,' she admitted. 'He went off in some ambulance.' She spooned lo mein onto her plate. 'By the way, I saw Em's painting today in the State building.'

'What were you doing in the State building?' James asked.

She shrugged. 'Looking for Em's painting,' she said. 'It seems so . . . well, professional, with that gilded frame and the big blue ribbon hanging underneath it. And you all made fun of me when I saved the crayon pictures she used to make with Chris over at our house.'

Michael smiled. 'We laughed because you said they were going to be your retirement income one day.'

'You'll see,' Gus said. 'A statewide art champion at seventeen; a gallery opening at twenty-one . . . she'll be hanging in the Museum of Modern Art before she's thirty.' She reached for James's arm, and twisted the face of his wristwatch toward her. 'I've got five more minutes.'

James let his hand fall back into his lap. 'The Ticketmaster's open at seven at night?'

'Seven A.M.' Gus said. 'Sleeping bag's in the car.' She yawned. 'I'm thinking I need a career change. Some position with a little less stress . . . like an air traffic controller or the prime minister of Israel.' She reached for a platter of mu shi chicken, began rolling the pancakes and passing them out. 'How are Mrs Greenblatt's cataracts?' she asked absently.

'Gone,' James said. 'Chances are she'll wind up with twenty-twenty vision.'

Melanie sighed. 'I want cataract surgery. I can't imagine waking up and being able to see.'

'You don't want cataract surgery,' Michael said.

'Why not? I'd get rid of my contacts and I've already got the name of a good surgeon.'

'James couldn't operate on you,' Gus said, smiling. 'Isn't there some kind of ethical law against it?'

'It doesn't extend to virtual family,' Melanie said.

'I like that,' Gus said. 'Virtual family. There ought to be a statute . . . you know, like common-law marriage. If you live in each other's pockets long enough, you're related.' She swallowed the last of her pancake and stood up. 'Well,' she said. 'That was a sumptuous and relaxing dinner.'

'You can't go yet,' Melanie said, turning to ask a busboy for fortune cookies. When the man returned, she stuffed a few in Gus's pockets. 'Here. The box office doesn't offer take-out.'

Michael picked up a cookie and cracked it. '"A gift of love is not one to be taken lightly,"' he read aloud.

'"You are as young as you feel,"' James said, scanning his own fortune. 'Doesn't say much for me right now.'

Everyone looked at Melanie, but she read the thin strip and

pocketed it. She believed that if you spoke it aloud, your good fortune had no chance of coming true.

Gus took one of the remaining cookies from the plate and cracked it open. 'Imagine that,' she said, laughing. 'I got a dud.'

'It's missing?' Michael said. 'That ought to be worth a free meal.'

'Check the floor, Gus. You must have dropped it. Who ever heard of a fortune cookie without a fortune?' Melanie said.

But it was not on the floor, or beneath a plate, or caught in the folds of Gus's coat. She shook her head ruefully and lifted her teacup. 'Here's to my future,' she said. She drained the tea, and then, in a hurry, she left.

Bainbridge, New Hampshire, was a bedroom community populated mostly with professors from Dartmouth College and doctors from the local hospital. It was close enough to the university to be considered attractive real estate, and far enough away to be deemed 'country.' Interspersed between old holdout dairy farms were narrow roads that branched off into the five-acre parcels of land that had settled the town in the late seventies. And Wood Hollow Road, where the Golds and the Hartes lived, was one of them.

Their land, together, formed a square; two triangles meeting along a common hypoteneuse. The Hartes' land was narrow at the driveway and then opened up; the Golds' land did the reverse, so that the houses were only about an acre apart. But they were separated by a small thicket of woods that did not completely block out the view of the other home.

Michael and Melanie, in their separate cars, followed the gray Volvo that belonged to James as it turned onto Wood Hollow Road. A half mile up the hill, at the granite post that announced number thirty-four, James went left. Michael swerved into the next driveway. He turned off the ignition in the truck and stepped out into the small square of light liberated from the passenger compartment, letting Grady and Beau leap up against his hips and chest. The Irish setters danced circles around him as he waited for Melanie to get out of her own car.

'Doesn't look like Em's home yet,' he said.

Melanie stepped out of the car and closed the door in one fluid, economical motion. 'It's eight o'clock,' she said. 'She probably just left.'

He followed Melanie through the side door into the kitchen. She set a small stack of books on the table. 'Who's on call tonight?' she asked.

Michael stretched his arms over his head. 'I don't know. Not me. I think Richards, from Weston Animal Hospital.' He went to the door and called to the setters, who stared at him but then made no effort to stop chasing leaves in the wind.

'That's a travesty,' Melanie said. 'A vet who can't control his own dogs.'

Michael stepped aside as Melanie came to the door and whistled. The dogs barreled by him, bringing inside the brisk scent of night. 'They're Emily's dogs,' he said. 'It makes a difference.'

When the telephone rang at three in the morning, James Harte was instantly awake. He tried to imagine what could possibly have gone wrong with Mrs Greenblatt, because she was potentially his emergency case. He groped across the bed, across where his wife should have been, for the telephone. 'Yes?'

'Is this Mr Harte?'

'This is Dr Harte,' James amended.

'Dr Harte, this is Officer Stanley of the Bainbridge police. Your son has been injured, and he's being taken to Bainbridge Memorial Hospital.'

James felt his throat working up sentences that tangled around each other. 'Is he . . . was there a car accident?'

There was a brief pause. 'No, sir,' the officer said.

James's heart twisted. 'Thank you,' he said, hanging up, although he did not know why he was thanking someone who had brought him such horrible news. The moment the receiver was back in place, he had a thousand questions to ask. Where was Christopher hurt? Critically or superficially? Was Emily still with him? What had happened? James dressed in the clothes he'd already thrown into the hamper and made his way downstairs in a matter of minutes. The hospital, he knew, would take him seventeen minutes to reach. He was already speeding down Wood Hollow Road when he picked up the car phone and dialed Gus.

'What did they say?' Melanie asked for the tenth time. 'What did they say exactly?'

Michael buttoned the fly of his jeans and stuffed his feet into tennis shoes. He remembered, too late, that he didn't have on socks. Fuck the socks.

'Michael.'

He glanced up. 'That Em was injured, and that she'd been taken to the hospital.' His hands were shaking, yet he was amazed to find himself able to do what was necessary: push Mel toward the door, find his car keys, plot the fastest route to Bainbridge Memorial.

He had hypothetically wondered, what would happen if a phone call came in the middle of the night, a phone call that had the power to render one speechless and disbelieving. He had expected deep down that he'd be a basket case. And yet here he was, backing carefully out of his driveway, holding up well, the only sign betraying panic a tiny tic in his cheek.

'James operates there,' Melanie was saying, a soft, slurred litany. 'He'll know who we should contact; what we should do.'

'Sweetheart,' Michael said, groping for her hand in the dark, 'we don't know anything yet.' But as he drove past the Hartes' house he took in the absolute quiet of the scene, the peaceable lack of light in the windows, and he could not help feeling a stab of jealousy at the normality of it all. *Why us?* he thought, and did not notice the brake lights of a car at the end of Wood Hollow Road, already turning toward town.

*   *   *

Gus lay on the sidewalk between a trio of teenagers with spiked green hair and a couple that was coming as close to sex as possible in a public venue. *If Chris ever does that to his hair,* she thought, *we would* . . . Would what? It had never been an issue because, for as long as Gus could remember, Chris had had the same slightly-longer-than-crew-cut hairstyle. And as for Romeo and Juliet here, on her right – well, that was a no-brainer also. As soon as it had begun to matter, Emily and Chris had started dating, which is what everyone had been rooting for in the first place.

Four and a half hours from now, her client's sons would have prime seats at a Metallica concert. She'd go home and sleep. By the time she got back there, James would have returned from hunting (she assumed something was in season), Kate would be gearing up for a soccer game, and Chris might just be rolling out of bed. Then Gus would do what she did every other Saturday that she didn't have plans or an invasion of relatives: she'd go to Melanie's, or have Melanie come over, and they'd talk about work and teenagers and husbands. She had several good female friends, but Melanie was the only one for whom the house didn't have to be cleaned, for whom she didn't have to wear her makeup, and around whom she could say anything without fear of repercussions, or of looking truly stupid.

'Lady,' one of the green-haired kids said. 'You got a smoke?'

It came out in a rush, *Yagottasmoke,* so that at first Gus was stunned at the audacity of the statement. *No,* she wanted to say, *I do not gotta, and you shouldn't either.* Then she realized he was wagging a cigarette – at least she hoped it was just a cigarette – in front of her face. 'Sorry,' she said, shaking her head.

It was impossible to believe that teenagers such as this existed, not when she had one like Chris, who seemed another breed entirely. Perhaps these children, with their stegosaurus hair and leather vests, only happened to look this way on the off hours, transforming themselves into scrubbed, well-mannered adolescents during the time they spent with their parents. Ridiculous, she told herself. Even the thought of Chris having an alter ego was out of the question. You couldn't give birth to someone and not sense that something so dramatic was going on.

She felt a humming against her hip and shifted, thinking that the amorous couple had gotten a little too close. But the buzzing didn't stop, and when she reached down to find the source she remembered her beeper, which she'd carried in her purse ever since she'd started up Other People's Time. It was James who insisted; what if he had to go back to the hospital and one of the kids needed something?

Of course, in the way that most preventative medicines work, just having the beeper had managed to ward off emergencies. It had beeped only twice in five years: once, when Kate called to ask where she kept the rug-cleaning supplies, and once when the batteries were low. She fished it out of the bottom of her purse and pushed the button that identified the caller. Her car phone. But who would be in her car at this time of night?

James had driven it home from the restaurant. After crawling out of her sleeping bag, Gus walked across the street to the nearest phone booth, graffitied with sausagelike initials. As soon as James picked up, she heard the hum of the road beneath the tires.

'Gus,' James said, his voice catching. 'You've got to come.'

And a moment later, leaving her sleeping bag behind, she started to run.

They wouldn't take the lights out of his eyes. The fixtures hung over him, bright silver saucers that made him wince. He felt at least three people touching him – laying hands, shouting directions, cutting off his clothes. He could not move his arms or legs, and when he tried, he felt straps lacing across them, a collar anchoring his head.

'BP's falling,' said a woman. 'It's only seventy over palp.'

'Pupils dilated but unresponsive. Christopher? Christopher? Can you hear me?'

'He's tachycardic. Get me two large-bore IVs, either fourteen or sixteen gauge, stat. Give him D-5 normal saline, wide open for a liter to start with, please. And I want to draw some bloods . . . get a CBC with diff, platelets, coags, chem-20, UA, tox screen, and send a type and screen to the blood bank.'

Then there was a stabbing pain in the crook of his arm and the sharp sound of ripping adhesive tape. 'What have we got?' asked a new voice, and the woman spoke again. 'A holy mess,' she said. Chris felt a sharp prick near his forehead, which had him arcing against his restraints and floating back to the soft, warm hands of a nurse. 'It's okay, Chris,' she soothed. How did they know his name?

'There's some visible cranium. Call radiology, we need them to clear the C-spine.'

There was a scurry of noise, of yelling. Chris slid his eyes to the slit in the curtain off to his right and saw his father. This was the hospital; his father worked at the hospital. But he wasn't in his white coat. He was wearing street clothes, a shirt that wasn't even buttoned right. He was standing with Emily's parents, trying to get past a bunch of nurses who wouldn't let him by.

Chris flailed so suddenly he managed to rip the IV out of his arm. He looked directly at Michael Gold and screamed, but there was no sound, no noise, just wave after wave of fear.

'I don't give a fuck about procedure,' James Harte said, and then there was a crash of instruments and a scuffle of footsteps that diverted the attention of the nurses enough to let him duck behind the stained curtain. His son was fighting backboard restraints and a Philadelphia collar. There was blood everywhere, all over his face and shirt and neck. 'I'm Dr Harte,' he said to the ER physician who was barreling toward them. 'Courtesy staff,' he added. He reached out and firmly grasped Chris's hand. 'What's going on?'

'EMTs brought him in with a girl,' the doctor said quietly. 'From what we can see, he's got a scalp laceration. We were about to send him to radiology to check skull and cervical vertebral fractures, and if they report back negative, we'll get him down to CT scan.'

James felt Chris squeeze his hand so tightly his wedding band dug into the skin. *Surely*, he thought, *he's all right if he has this strength*. 'Emily,' Chris whispered hoarsely. 'Where'd they take Em?'

'James?' a tentative voice asked. He turned around to see Melanie and Michael hovering at the edge of the curtain, horrified, no doubt, by all that blood. God only knew how they'd gotten past the dragons at triage. 'Is Chris all right?'

'He's fine,' James said, more for himself than for anyone else in the room. 'He's going to be just fine.'

A resident hung up a telephone receiver. 'Radiology's waiting,' she said. The ER doctor nodded toward James. 'You can go with him,' he said. 'Keep him calm.'

James walked beside the gurney, but he did not let go of his son's hand. He began trotting as the ER staff wheeled it more quickly past the Golds. 'How's Emily?' he remembered to ask, and disappeared before they could answer.

The doctor who'd been attending Chris turned around. 'You're Mr and Mrs Gold?' he asked.

They came forward simultaneously.

'Can you step outside with me?'

The doctor led them to a small alcove behind the coffee machines, decorated with nubby blue couches and ugly Formica end tables, and Melanie instantly relaxed. She was a professional expert when it came to reading verbal or nonverbal clues. If they weren't being led to an examination room on the double, the danger must have passed. Maybe Emily was already up on a patient ward, or off to radiology as Chris was. Maybe she was being brought out to meet them.

'Please,' the doctor said. 'Sit down.'

Melanie had every intention of standing, but her knees gave out from beneath her. Michael remained upright, frozen.

'I'm very sorry,' the doctor began, the only words that Melanie could not rework into anything but what they signified. She crumpled further, her body folding into itself, until her head was so deeply buried beneath her shaking arms that she could not hear what the man was saying.

'Your daughter was pronounced dead on arrival. There was a gunshot wound to the head. It was instantaneous; she didn't suffer.' He paused. 'I'm going to need one of you to identify the body.'

Michael tried to remember to blink his eyes. Before, it had always been an involuntary act, but right now everything – breathing, standing, being – was strictly tied to his own self-control. 'I don't understand,' he said, in a voice too high to be his own. 'She was with Chris Harte.'

'Yes,' the doctor said. 'They were brought in together.'

'I don't understand,' Michael repeated, when what he really meant was *How can she be dead if he's alive?*

'Who did it?' Melanie forced out, her teeth clenched around the question as if it were a bone she had to keep possession of. 'Who shot her?'

The doctor shook his head. 'I don't know, Mrs Gold. I'm sure the police who were at the scene will be here to talk to you shortly.'

Police?

'Are you ready to go?'

Michael stared at the doctor, wondering why on earth this man thought he ought to be leaving. Then he remembered. Emily. Her body.

He followed the doctor back into the ER. Was it his imagination or did the nurses look at him differently now? He passed cubicles with moaning, damaged, living people and finally stopped in front of a curtain with no noise, no bustle, no activity behind it. The doctor waited until Michael inclined his head, then drew back the blind.

Emily was lying on her back on a table. Michael took a step forward, resting his hand on her hair. Her forehead was smooth, still warm. The doctor was wrong; that was all. She was not dead, she could not be dead, she . . . He shifted his hand, and her head lolled toward him, allowing him to see the hole above her right ear, the size of a silver dollar, ragged on the edges and matted with dried blood. But no new blood was trickling.

'Mr Gold?' the doctor said.

Michael nodded and ran out of the examination room. He ran past the man on the stretcher clutching his heart, four times older than Emily would ever be. He ran past the resident carrying a cup of coffee. He ran past Gus Harte, breathless and reaching for him. He picked up speed. Then he turned the corner, sank to his knees, and retched.

Gus had run the whole way to Bainbridge Memorial clutching hope to her chest, a package that grew heavier and more unwieldy with every step. But James was not in the ER waiting room, and all of her wishes for a manageable injury – a broken arm or a light concussion – had vanished when she'd stumbled upon Michael in the triage area. 'Look again,' she demanded of the triage nurse. 'Christopher Harte. He's the son of *Dr* James Harte.'

The nurse nodded. 'He was in here a while ago,' she said. 'I just don't know where they've taken him.' She glanced up sympathetically. 'Why don't I see if anyone else knows something?'

'Yes,' Gus said as imperiously as she could, wilting as soon as the nurse turned her back.

She let her eyes roam over the serviceable Emergency entranceway, from the empty wheelchairs waiting like wallflowers at a dance to the television shackled to the ceiling. At the edge of the area, Gus saw a swatch of red fabric. She moved toward it, recognizing the scarlet overcoat she and Melanie had found for eighty percent off at Filene's.

'Mel?' Gus whispered. Melanie lifted her head, her face just as stricken as Michael's had been. 'Is Emily hurt too?'

Melanie stared at her for a long moment. 'No,' she said carefully. 'Emily is not hurt.'

'Oh, thank God—'

'Em,' Melanie interrupted, 'is dead.'

'What's taking so long?' Gus asked for the third time, pacing in front of the tiny window in the private room that had been assigned to Christopher. 'If he's really all right, then how come they haven't brought him back yet?'

James sat in the only chair, his head in his hands. He himself had seen the CT scans, and he'd never looked over one with such a fear of finding an intracranial contusion or an epidural hemorrhage. But Chris's brain was intact; his wounds superficial. They had taken him back to the ER to be stitched up by a surgeon; he would be monitored overnight and then sent for additional tests the next day.

'Did he say anything to you? About what happened?'

James shook his head. 'He was scared, Gus. In pain. I wasn't going to push him.' He stood up and leaned against the doorframe. 'He asked where they'd brought Emily.'

Gus turned slowly. 'You didn't tell him,' she said.

'No.' James swallowed thickly. 'At the time I didn't even think about it. About them being together when this happened.'

Gus crossed the room and slipped her arms around James. Even now, he stiffened; he had not been brought up to embrace in public places, and brushes with death did not alter the rules. 'I don't want to think about it,' she murmured, laying her cheek against his back. 'I saw Melanie, and I keep imagining how easily that could have been me.'

James pushed her away and walked toward the radiator, belching out its heat. 'What the hell were they thinking, driving through a bad neighborhood?'

'What neighborhood?' Gus said, seizing on the new detail. 'Where did the ambulance come in from?'

James turned to her. 'I don't know,' he said. 'I just assumed.'

Suddenly she was a woman with a mission. 'I could go back

down to Emergency while we're waiting,' Gus said. 'They have to have that sort of information logged.' She strode purposefully toward the door, but as she went to pull it, it was opened from the outside. A male orderly wheeled in Chris, his head swathed in thick white bandages.

She was rooted to the floor, unable to connect this sunken boy with the strong son who had towered over her just that morning. The nurse explained something that Gus didn't bother to listen to, and then she and the orderly left the room.

Gus heard her own breathing providing a backbeat for the thin *drip, drip* of Chris's IV. His eyes were glassy with sedatives, unfocused with fear. Gus sat down on the edge of the bed and cradled him in her arms. 'Ssh,' she said, as he started to cry against the front of her sweater, first thin tears and then loud, unstoppable sobs. 'It's all right.'

Within minutes Chris's hiccups leveled, and his eyes closed. Gus tried to hold him to her, even after his big body went slack in her arms. She glanced at James, who was sitting in the chair beside the hospital bed like a stiff and stoic sentry. He wanted to cry, but he wouldn't. James hadn't cried since he'd been seven.

Gus did not like to cry around him, either. It was not that he ever told her she shouldn't, but the plain fact that now he wasn't as visibly upset as she was made her feel foolish rather than sensitive. She bit her lip and pulled open the door of the room, wanting to have her breakdown in private. In the hallway, she flattened her palms against the cool cinder block wall and tried to think of just yesterday, when she had gone grocery shopping and had cleaned the downstairs bathroom and had yelled at Chris for leaving the milk out on the kitchen counter all day so it spoiled. Yesterday, when everything had made sense.

'Excuse me.'

Gus turned her head to see a tall, dark-haired woman. 'I'm Detective-Sergeant Marrone of the Bainbridge police. Would you be Mrs Harte?'

She nodded and shook the policewoman's hand. 'Were you the one who found them?'

'No, I wasn't. But I was called in to the scene. I need to ask you some questions.'

'Oh,' Gus said, surprised. 'I thought you might be able to answer mine.'

Detective Marrone smiled; Gus was momentarily stunned at how beautiful that one transformation made her. 'You scratch my back, I'll scratch yours,' she said.

'I can't imagine I'll be much help,' Gus said. 'What did you want to know?'

The detective took out a pad and a pen. 'Did your son tell you he was going out tonight?'

'Yes.'

'Did he tell you where he was going?'

'No,' Gus said. 'But he's seventeen, and he's always been very responsible.' She glanced at the hospital room door. 'Until tonight,' she added.

'Uh-huh. Did you know Emily Gold, Mrs Harte?'

Gus immediately felt tears well in her eyes. Embarrassed, she swiped at them with the backs of her hands. 'Yes,' she said. 'Em is . . . was like a daughter to me.'

'And what was she to your son?'

'His girlfriend.' Gus was more confused now than before. Had Emily been involved in something illegal or dangerous? Was that why Chris had been driving through a bad neighborhood?

She did not realize that she'd spoken aloud until Detective Marrone's brows drew together. 'A bad neighborhood?'

'Well,' Gus said, coloring. 'We know there was a gun involved.'

The detective snapped shut her notebook and started for the door. 'I'd like to talk to Chris now,' she said.

'You can't,' Gus insisted, blocking the other woman's way. 'He's asleep. He needs his rest. Besides, he doesn't even know about Emily yet. We couldn't tell him, not like this. He loved her.'

Detective Marrone stared at Gus. 'Maybe,' she said. 'But he also may have shot her.'

Then

Fall 1979

From the way Melanie hefted the small brick of banana bread in the palm of her hand, her husband was not sure if she was planning to eat it or to throw it. She closed the front door, still shiny with new paint, and carried the loaf to the two cartons that were substituting as a makeshift kitchen table. With reverent fingers she touched the French-wire ribbon and untangled a card decorated with a hand-drawn horse. "'Welcome,'" she read, "'to the NEIGH-borhood.'"

'Your veterinary reputation has preceded you,' she said, handing the card to Michael.

Michael scanned the brief message, smiled, and tore open the cellophane. 'It's good,' he said. 'Try some?'

Melanie paled. Even the thought of banana bread – of any food really – before noon made her queasy these days. Which was odd because every book she'd read on the subject of pregnancy – and she'd read many – said that by now, her fourth month, she should be feeling better. 'I'll call to thank them,' she said, retrieving the card. 'Oh. My.' She glanced up at Michael. 'Gus and James. And they sent baked goods. Do you think they're . . . you know?'

'Gay?'

'I would have said "embarking on an alternative lifestyle."'

'But you didn't,' Michael said, grinning. He lifted a box and started up the stairs.

'Well,' Melanie diplomatically announced, 'whatever their . . . orientation, I'm sure they're perfectly nice.' But as she dialed, she was wondering again what kind of town they had moved to.

She had not wanted to come to Bainbridge; she'd been

perfectly happy in Boston, and even that was a stretch from her native Ohio. But this town might as well have been on the edge of nowhere, and she had never been very good at forging friendships, and couldn't Michael have found large animals to minister to somewhere farther south?

A woman answered on the third ring. 'Grand Central Station,' the voice said, and Melanie slammed down the phone. She redialed more carefully, this time getting the same voice with a smile in it, crisply saying, 'Hartes.'

'Yes,' Melanie said. 'I'm calling from next door. Melanie Gold. I wanted to thank the Hartes for the bread.'

'Oh, great. You got it. Are you all moved in yet?'

There was a silence while Melanie wondered who this person was and what protocol was in this part of the country; if one went about revealing one's whole life to a housekeeper or nanny. 'Is James or Gus there?' Melanie asked quietly. 'I, um, would like to introduce myself.'

'I'm Gus,' the woman said.

'But you're not a man,' Melanie blurted.

Gus Harte laughed. 'You mean you thought – wow! Nope, sorry to disappoint, but last time I checked I was female. Gus, as in Augusta. But no one's called me that since my grandmother died trying to. Hey, do you need a hand over there? James is out and I've cleaned my living room to within an inch of its life. I've got nothing to do.' Before Melanie could demur, Gus made the decision for her. 'Leave the door open,' she said. 'I'll be there in a few minutes.'

Melanie was still staring at the receiver when Michael came back into the kitchen, carrying a large carton of china. 'Did you talk to Gus Harte?' he grunted. 'What's he like?'

She had just opened her mouth to answer when the front door burst open, slamming back against its hinges on a gust of wind to reveal an extremely pregnant woman with a festival of wild hair and the incongruously sweet smile of a saint.

'*She*,' Melanie answered, 'is a hurricane.'

* * *

Melanie's new job was as a staff librarian at the Bainbridge Public Library.

She had fallen in love with the tiny brick building the day she'd arrived for her interview, charmed by the stained-glass panel behind the reference desk, by the neat yellow piles of scrap paper waiting atop the card catalog, by the worn stone steps that decades of use had smoothed into curves, as if each one was smiling. It was a lovely library, but it needed her. The books were jammed pell-mell in the stacks, crushed against each other with no breathing or browsing room. The spines of some novels had cracked down the middle; the vertical file was littered with minutiae. Librarians, to Melanie, were somewhat on a par with God – who else could be bothered with, and better yet, know the answers to so many different types of questions? Knowledge was power, but a good librarian did not hoard the gift. She taught others how to find, where to look, how to see.

She had fallen in love with Michael because he stumped her. Michael had been a student at Tufts Veterinary School when he had come to her reference desk with two queries: Where he might find studies on liver damage in diabetic cats, and whether she'd like to have dinner. The first question she could have answered with her eyes closed. The second left her speechless. His neat, short hair, a prematurely bright silver, made her think of riches. His gentle hands, which could coax a newly hatched bird to drink from a dropper, made her aware of her body in entirely new ways.

Even after their marriage and during the first few years of his small-animal practice, Melanie had continued to work at the college. She advanced through the library system, figuring that if Michael woke up one day and decided not to love a stuttering wren of a girl, he might still be impressed by her mind. But Michael had gone to school to tend to cows and sheep, to breed horses, and after several years of neutering pedigreed puppies and giving rabies shots, he told Melanie he needed to make a change. The problem was, there weren't very many farm animals in a big city.

With Melanie's credentials, it had not been difficult for her to secure a position at the Bainbridge Public Library. However, Melanie was used to intense young men and women, to scholars bent into question marks over their texts, to kicking people out at closing time. At Bainbridge Library, the biggest draw was toddler story hour, because free coffee was served to the mothers. There were entire days when Melanie would sit at the reference desk and see only the mailman.

She longed for a reader, a true reader, like she was. And she found it in the unlikely form of Gus Harte.

Gus came unfailingly to the library on Tuesdays and Fridays. She would waddle through the narrow arched doorway, dumping off whatever books she'd borrowed days before. Melanie would carefully open them and match up the drawn cards and set them on the dolly to be reshelved.

Gus Harte read Dostoevsky, and Kundera, and Pope. She read George Eliot and Thackeray and histories of the world. Sometimes all in a matter of days. It amazed Melanie. And it terrified her. As a librarian, she was accustomed to being expert in her field – but she'd had to work at it. To Gus Harte, this sponging up of knowledge, like everything else, seemed to come too easily.

'I have to tell you,' she said to Gus one Tuesday, 'I think you're the only person in this town who appreciates the classics.'

'I am,' Gus said soberly. 'I do.'

'Did you like 'Le Morte d'Arthur'?

Gus shook her head. 'I didn't find what I was looking for.'

And what was that? Melanie wondered. Absolution? Entertainment? A good cry?

As if Melanie had spoken aloud, Gus looked up shyly. 'A name.'

Inside, Melanie felt something snap with relief. Was it challenge she'd felt from someone like Gus, who devoured intricate historical novels as if they were pulp fiction? To find out that she was only skimming through, looking for something strong and classic to call her baby . . . well, it should have depressed Melanie. But it didn't.

'What are you going to name yours?' Gus asked.

Melanie started. No one knew she was pregnant; she wasn't really showing yet and she was superstitious enough to leave it a mystery for as long as possible. 'I don't know,' she said slowly.

'Well, then,' Gus announced brightly, 'we're in the same boat.'

Melanie, who had been too bookish in junior high school to have much of a social life, suddenly had a seventh-grade friend. Somehow, instead of Gus's exuberance overshadowing Melanie's reserve, they complemented each other. It was not unlike the mixture of oil and vinegar – neither of which one wanted alone on one's salad, but which together seemed such a natural twosome it was easy to believe they'd been made with each other in mind.

She would get calls from Gus first thing in the morning. 'What's it like out?' Gus would ask, although the same weather was visible out her own window. 'What should I wear?'

She would find herself sitting beside Gus on the big leather couch, looking at Gus's wedding album and laughing over the helmetlike hairstyles of her relatives. She would argue with Michael, and telephone Gus just to be told unequivocally that she was right.

Gus became comfortable enough to walk into the Gold household without knocking; Melanie borrowed baby-name books on interlibrary loan and left them in Gus's mailbox. Melanie started to wear Gus's maternity clothes; Gus bought Melanie's favorite brand of decaffeinated coffee to keep on hand; they grew able to finish each other's sentences.

'So,' Michael said, accepting the gin and tonic that James Harte had mixed for him. 'You're a surgeon.'

James settled across from Michael in a wing chair. From the

kitchen, he could hear Gus and Melanie, their voices high and sweet as robins'. 'That I am,' James said. 'I'm finishing a fellowship over at Bainbridge Memorial. Ophthalmological surgery.' He took a sip of his own drink. 'Gus tells me you took over Howath's practice?'

Michael nodded. 'He was one of my professors at Tufts,' he explained. 'When he wrote to say he was retiring up here, I started thinking there might be room for another vet.' He laughed. 'I couldn't find a Holstein within twenty miles of Boston, but I saw six just today.'

The two men smiled uncomfortably and stared down at their glasses.

Michael glanced toward the women's voices. 'They've hit it off,' he said. 'Gus is over so much, I sometimes think she's moved in.'

James laughed. 'Gus needed someone like Melanie. I have a feeling she gets more support complaining about stretch marks and swollen ankles to your wife than she gets from me.'

Michael didn't say anything. Perhaps James was ambivalent about pregnancy, but Michael wanted as many details as he could get. He had taken books out of Melanie's library showing a blastosphere reconfiguring into a tiny human. He had been the one to sign up for natural childbirth classes. And as ashamed as Melanie was by her burgeoning body, he found it lovely. Pomengranate-ripe and lush, it was all he could do to refrain from laying hands on his wife whenever she breezed by him. But Melanie undressed in the dark, pulled the covers up to her chin, batted away his embrace. Michael had, from time to time, watched Gus move about his house – five months more pregnant and unwieldy, but with a confidence and a vigor that lit her from within, and he would think, *This is how Melanie should be.*

He looked toward the kitchen, caught a glimpse of Gus's swollen stomach preceding her. 'Actually,' Michael said slowly, 'I kind of like this whole pregnancy thing.'

James snorted. 'Trust me,' he said. 'I did an obstetrics rotation. Messy business.'

'I know,' Michael said.

'Mmm. But pulling calves has to be different,' James insisted. 'A cow doesn't scream out that she's going to kill her husband for doing this to her. A cow's placenta doesn't shoot across the delivery room like a silver bullet.'

'Ah,' Gus said, suddenly there. 'You're talking shop again.' She put her hand on James's shoulder. 'My doctor husband is downright terrified of childbirth,' she teased, speaking to Michael. 'Would you like to deliver my baby?'

'Sure,' Michael grinned. 'But I'm most comfortable operating in a barn.'

Gus took a cheese tray from Melanie's hands and set it down on the coffee table. 'I'm flexible,' she said.

Michael watched Gus settle on the arm of her husband's chair. James made no move to touch her. He leaned around her toward the cheese tray. 'Is this the *pâté*?' he asked.

Gus nodded. 'Homemade,' she explained. 'James goes duck hunting.'

'Really?' Michael said. He took a cracker and tried the spread.

'And deer hunting and bear hunting and once, sweet-little-rabbit hunting,' Gus continued.

'As you can see,' James said, unruffled, 'Gus isn't a big fan of the sport.' He looked up at Michael. 'I guess you wouldn't be, either, as a vet. But there's a real beauty to it – you're up before the rest of the world, and it's absolutely quiet, and you're putting yourself into the mind of the prey.'

'I see,' Michael said, although he didn't.

'James is being an idiot,' Gus said one snowy afternoon when Melanie called. 'He told me if I don't stop walking down Wood Hollow Road I'm going to have the baby under a telephone pole.'

'I would think you'd have more time than that.'

'Try telling him.'

'Use a different tactic,' Melanie said. 'Tell him the better shape you're in before the baby is born, the easier it will be to get your old body back.'

'Who said I want my old body back?' Gus asked. 'Can't I pick someone else's? Farrah Fawcett . . . Christie Brinkley . . .' She sighed. 'You don't know how lucky you are.'

'Because I'm only five months pregnant?'

'Because you're married to Michael.'

Melanie didn't answer for a moment. She liked James Harte, with his cool New England looks, his effortless charm, the thread of Boston accent in his speech. Many of the characteristics that Melanie possessed James possessed also, but with a positive twist: She was reserved, he was level-headed; she was shy, he was introspective; she was obsessive, he was exacting.

He was also right. Gus's water broke three days later, half a mile down Wood Hollow Road, and if a passing telephone company vehicle hadn't stopped to ask if she was all right, she might very well have delivered Christopher on the edge of the street.

The dream went like this: Melanie could see Michael's back as he crouched down in a stall, his silver hair glinting with the early sunlight, his hands moving over the heaving belly of a mare that was trying to foal. And she was standing overhead somewhere – in a hayloft, maybe? – water dripping down her legs as if she'd wet herself, yelling for him although no sound came out of her mouth.

That was how she knew she was going to have her baby alone.

'I'll call every hour on the hour,' Michael assured her. But Melanie knew how Michael functioned: once he got wrapped up in a colicky horse or a ewe with mastitis, time fell away for him; most of the roads he traveled as a country vet didn't have a luxurious string of telephone booths.

Her due date came and went at the end of April. Then one night, Melanie heard Michael answer the phone beside the bed. He whispered something her mind did not register, and disappeared in the dark.

She dreamed again about the barn, and woke up to find the mattress soaking wet.

Pain made her double over. Michael must have left a note somewhere with a telephone number. Melanie walked through the bedroom and the bathroom, periodically stopping to sweat out contractions, but she couldn't find it. She picked up the phone and called Gus.

'Now,' she said, and Gus understood.

James was operating at the hospital, so Gus brought Chris along in his car seat. 'We'll find Michael,' she assured Melanie. She placed Melanie's hand on the gearshift, telling her to squeeze when it started to hurt. At the Emergency pavilion, she parked the car. 'Stay here,' she said, grabbing Chris and running through the sliding doors. 'You have to help me,' she shouted to a triage nurse. 'There's a woman in labor.'

The nurse blinked at her, at Chris. 'Looks to me like you're too late,' she said.

'It's not me,' Gus said. 'It's my friend. In the car.'

Within minutes Melanie was in a delivery room, wearing a fresh johnny and writhing in pain. The obstetrics nurse turned to Gus. 'I don't suppose you know where the father is?'

'On his way,' Gus said, though this was not true. 'I'm supposed to stand in for him.'

The nurse looked at Melanie, who had reached out to hold Gus's hand, and at Chris, who was asleep in a plastic bassinet. 'I'll take him to the nursery,' she said. 'Can't have a baby in delivery.'

'I thought that was the point,' Gus muttered, and Melanie choked out a laugh.

'You didn't tell me this hurt,' Melanie said.

'Of course I did.'

'You didn't tell me,' she amended, 'it hurt this much.'

Melanie's doctor had also delivered Chris. 'Let me guess,' she said to Gus, reaching beneath the johnny to check Melanie's cervix. 'You had so much fun the first time you couldn't stay away.' She helped Melanie sit up. 'Okay, Melanie,' the doctor said. 'I want you to push.'

So with her best friend bracing her shoulders and shouting in strident harmony, Melanie gave birth to a girl. 'Oh, my,' she said, her eyes damp. 'Oh, look at that.'

'I know,' Gus said, her throat tight. 'I see.' And she left to find her own child.

The nurse had just finished packing ice between Melanie's legs and drawing the covers up to her waist when Gus returned to the room with Chris in her arms. 'Look who I ran into,' she said, holding the door so that Michael could pass through.

'I told you so,' Melanie chided, but she was already turning the baby so that Michael could see her.

Michael touched his daughter's fine blonde eyebrows. His fingernail was larger than her nose. 'She's perfect. She's . . .' He shook his head and looked up. 'I don't know what to say.'

'You owe me,' Gus suggested.

'I do,' Michael said, smiling from the inside. 'I'll give you anything but my firstborn.'

The door of the room swung open again, and James Harte stood there in scrubs, holding aloft a bottle of champagne. 'Hey!' he said, pumping Michael's hand. 'Rumor has it that you've had quite a morning.' He smiled at Gus. 'And I hear you're a midwife.' He popped open the Moët, apologizing as some fizzed onto Melanie's blankets, and poured the champagne into four plastic cups. 'To parenthood,' he said, lifting his glass. 'To . . . does she have a name?'

Michael looked at his wife. 'Emily,' she said.

'To Emily.'

Michael lifted his glass. 'And, belatedly, to Chris.'

Melanie glanced at the baby's translucent eyelids and slack bow mouth, and reluctantly transferred her to the plastic bassinet beside the bed. Emily barely took up a third of the space.

'Do you mind?' Gus asked softly, pointing to the bassinet and then to Chris, snoring softly in her arms.

'Go right ahead.' Melanie watched Gus lay her son beside Emily.

'Look at that,' Michael said. 'My daughter's an hour old and she's already sleeping with some guy.'

They all looked at the bassinet. The baby startled, a reflex. Her long fingers flailed open like a morning glory and curled back into fists, grabbing for purchase. And although she was completely unaware, when Emily Gold again settled into sleep, she was holding tight to Christopher Harte's hand.

Now

November 1997

There was very little that shocked Anne-Marie Marrone. She would have thought that her ten years with the Washington, D.C., metropolitan police could offer more surprises than the subsequent ten years in the sleepy town of Bainbridge, New Hampshire, but she'd been mistaken. In D.C., she'd never known her perps. Somehow, domestic abuse was more unnerving when it came at the hands of the legendary, beloved Bainbridge Elementary School principal. A Mafia-run drug ring was less disturbing than a field of pot lovingly tended alongside the basil and marjoram at old Mrs Inglenook's house. Finding a mortally wounded teenage girl, a bleeding boy, and a smoking gun might not have been a routine occurrence in Bainbridge, but that didn't mean Anne-Marie could not have seen it coming.

'I'd like to speak to Chris now,' she repeated.

'You're wrong,' Gus Harte said, folding her arms over her chest.

'Maybe your son can tell me that.' She would not offer the mother the truth: that although she didn't yet have grounds to arrest Christopher Harte as a suspect in a homicide, the case would be treated as one until proven otherwise.

'I know my rights—' Gus began, but Anne-Marie held up her hand.

'So do I, Mrs Harte. And if you'd like, I'd be happy to read them to you and your son. But he's not under suspicion now; he'd just be helping us put together an investigation. And since he's the only living eyewitness to what happened, I can't see why you'd object to my conversation with him.

Unless,' she said, 'he's told you something you feel a need to hide?'

Gus Harte's cheeks burned; she stepped back and let the detective enter the hospital room.

Although the woman wasn't wearing a uniform or visibly carrying anything more threatening than a notepad, there was a self-righteous scent about her that swept into the room with her arrival, causing James to rise and sidle closer to Chris's bed. 'James,' Gus said quietly, hoping that her son would sleep through it all, 'Detective-Sergeant Marrone would like to speak to Chris.'

'Well,' James said, 'as a doctor, I can tell you he's in no condition—'

'With all due respect, Dr Harte,' Detective Marrone said, 'you aren't the attending physician. Dr Coleman's already cleared my entry.' She sat down on the edge of the bed and rested her notepad in her lap.

Gus watched this woman sit where she was supposed to be sitting and sensed a rising swell in her chest that reminded her of the way she'd felt years ago when a toddler had pushed Chris at the playground, or when Chris's fifth-grade teacher had intimated at a parent conference that he was less than perfect. The tigress, James had called her, when Gus went on the warpath to protect her child. But what, this time, was she protecting him from?

'Chris,' the detective called softly. 'Chris . . . can I talk to you?'

Chris's eyes blinked open – bedroom eyes, Gus had always called them, so fathomlessly pale against his dark skin and hair. 'I'm Detective Marrone, from the Bainbridge police.'

'Detective,' James said, 'Chris has been through quite a trauma. I don't see what it is that can't wait.'

Chris's hands tensed on the edge of the blanket. He looked up at the detective. 'Do you know what happened to Emily?'

It took a moment for Anne-Marie to decide if the boy was

asking her for information, or offering his confession. 'Emily,' she said, 'was taken to the hospital, just like you.' She flicked the ballpoint of her pen. 'What were you doing at the carousel tonight, Chris?'

'We went to . . . uh, fool around.' He picked at the edge of his blanket. 'We took some Canadian Club with us.'

Gus's mouth dropped open. Chris, who had done volunteer work with her for MADD, had been drinking and driving?

'Was that all you had with you?'

'No,' Chris whispered. 'I sort of took my father's gun.'

'His what?' Gus exclaimed, stepping forward at the same time James began to object.

'Chris,' Detective Marrone said, not batting an eye. 'I just want to know what happened tonight.' She stared at him. 'I need to know your story.'

'Because Em can't give you hers, can she?' Chris said, curling forward. 'She's dead?'

Before Gus could approach the bed and put her arms around her son, Detective Marrone did it for her. 'Yes,' she said, as Chris broke into loud sobs. His back, the only part of him Gus could see in the policewoman's embrace, spasmed with coughs.

'Did the two of you have a fight?' she asked quietly, releasing Chris.

Gus recognized the exact moment that Chris realized what the detective was suggesting. *Get out*, she wanted to say, that feral defense spilling out of her, but she discovered that she could not speak at all. She found herself, like James, waiting for her son to object.

Wondering, for a flicker of a moment, if he would.

Chris shook his head forcefully, as if now that Marrone had planted the seed in his thoughts he needed to physically dislodge it. 'Jesus Christ, no. I love her. I love Em.' He brought his knees up beneath the blanket and buried his face against them. 'We were going to do it together,' he mumbled.

'Do what?'

Although Gus had not been the one to ask the question,

Chris glanced up at his mother, fear stamped on his face. 'Kill ourselves,' he said softly. ''Em was going to go first,' he explained, still speaking to Gus. 'She . . . she shot herself. And before I got a chance to do it, too, the police came.'

Don't think about it, Gus ordered herself silently. *Just act.* She ran to the bed and held Chris, her mind numbed by disbelief – Emily and Chris? Committing suicide? It simply was not possible – but that only left another, more sinister alternative. The one that Detective Marrone had posed. As unthinkable as it was that Emily would kill herself, it was even more ludicrous to believe that Chris could have killed her.

Gus raised her face above Chris's broad shoulder to see the detective. 'Leave,' she said. 'Now.'

Anne-Marie Marrone nodded. 'I'll be in touch,' she said. 'I'm sorry.'

Gus continued to rock Chris as the detective left, wondering whether she had been apologizing for what had taken place, or for what would happen when she returned.

Michael put Melanie into bed, drifting on the Valium a sensitive ER physician had prescribed. He sat on the opposite side, waiting until he heard her breathing level off into sleep, unwilling to leave until he knew for certain that she, too, would not be taken from him unawares.

Then he walked down the hall to Emily's room. The door was closed for privacy; when he opened it a rush of memories tumbled out, as if the essence of his daughter had simply been bottled up inside. Dizzy with the gift of it, Michael leaned against the doorjamb and breathed in the sweet nutty fragrance of Emily's Body Shop perfume, the waxy, ethylene odor of the drying canvas where a recent oil painting stood. He reached for a towel slung over the footboard, still damp.

She was coming back; she had to be coming back; there was too much left unfinished here.

At the hospital, he had spoken to the detective assigned to the case. Michael had assumed a masked assailant, a mugging, a drive-by shooting. He had been fantasizing about wrapping his hands around the throat of the stranger who'd taken his daughter's life.

He hadn't realized that person was Emily.

But Detective Marrone had spoken to Chris. She said that although any case like this – one survivor, one dead – would be treated as a homicide, Chris Harte had talked of a suicide pact.

Michael had tried to remember details, conversations, events. The last discussion he'd had with Emily had been over breakfast. 'Dad,' she had said, 'have you seen my backpack? I can't find it anywhere.'

Was that some kind of code?

Michael walked over to the mirror hanging over Emily's dresser and saw, in the reflection, a face that looked too much like his daughter's had. He flattened his hands on the dresser, knocking over a small tub of Blistex. Inside, pressed into the translucent yellow paraffin, was the imprint of a finger. Was it her pinky? Was it one of the ones Michael had kissed when she'd been tiny and had fallen off her bike or gotten it caught in a drawer?

He rushed out of the room, quietly left the house, and drove north.

The Simpsons, whose prize Thoroughbred had almost died giving birth to a pair of fillies last week, were surprised to see him in the barn at dawn when they went to feed the horses. They hadn't called him, they said, and everything really had been fine for the past few days. But Michael waved them away, assuring them that a free follow-up visit was always included for difficult labors. He stood in the stall with his back to Joe Simpson until the man shrugged and left, and then he stroked the slender flanks of the mare, touched the spiked, downy manes of her offspring, and tried to remind himself that he'd once had the power to heal.

When Chris woke up he felt like a lemon had wedged itself

right in the middle of his throat, and his eyes were so dry the lids might as well have been closing over splintered glass. He had a hell of a headache, too, but he knew that was from the fall, and the stitches.

His mother was curled at the foot of the bed; his father had fallen asleep in the only chair. There was nobody else there. No nurses, no doctors. No detective.

He tried to imagine Emily, where she was now. At some funeral home? In the morgue? Where was the morgue, anyway . . . it was never listed on the elevator stops. He shifted uncomfortably, wincing at the thunder in his head, trying to remember the last thing Emily had said to him.

His head hurt, but not nearly as much as his heart.

'Chris?' His mother's voice curled around him like smoke. She had sat up at the bottom of the bed; the blanket had etched a waffle print onto her cheek. 'Honey? Are you all right?'

He felt his mother's hand on his cheek, cool as a river. 'Does your head hurt?' she asked.

His father, at some point, had awakened. Now both his parents were flanking the bed, a pair of matched bookends, with pity and pain scribbled over their faces. Chris turned onto his side and pulled the pillow over his face. 'When you get home,' his mother said, 'you'll feel better.'

'I was going to rent a wood splitter this weekend,' his father added. 'If the doctors say you're up to it, there's no reason you can't lend a hand.'

A wood splitter? A frigging wood splitter?

'Honey.' His mother's hands fretted over his shoulders. 'It's all right to cry,' she said, repeating one of the zillion platitudes the ER psychiatrist had preached the night before.

Chris showed no sign of removing the pillow. His mother grabbed the edge of it, tugging gently. The pillow tumbled off the hospital bed to reveal Chris's face, scarlet, dry-eyed, furious. 'Go away,' he said, spitting each word carefully.

It was not until he heard the bell of the elevator at the end of the hall that he raised his shaking hands to his face, touching the span of his brows and the slope of his nose and the empty windows of his eyes, trying to discover who he had become.

James crumpled his paper napkin into a ball and stuffed it into the bottom of his coffee cup. 'Well,' he said, glancing at his watch. 'I ought to go.'

Gus looked up at him through the steam of her forgotten tea. 'You what?' she asked. 'Where?'

'I have an RK at nine this morning. And it's already eight-thirty.'

Gus's throat worked, choking on disbelief. 'You're going to operate today?'

James nodded. 'I can't very well cancel now.' He started to stack cups and paper plates on the cafeteria tray. 'If I had thought of it last night, that would have been one thing. But I didn't.'

The way he said it, Gus thought, made it sound like it was all her fault. 'For God's sake,' she hissed. 'Your son is suicidal, his girlfriend is dead, and the police still have possession of *your* gun, but you're going to pretend last night didn't happen? You can just go back to life-as-usual?'

James stood up, took the first step away. 'If I don't,' he said, 'how can we expect Chris to?'

Melanie sat in a room at the funeral home, waiting for one of the Saltzman sons to walk them through the practicalities of grief. Beside her, Michael fidgeted with a tie – one of the three he owned and insisted on wearing here. Melanie herself had refused to change the clothes she had worn from last night.

'Mr Gold,' a man said, hurrying into the room. 'Mrs Gold.' He clasped their hands in turn, holding them a moment longer than necessary. 'I'm so sorry for your loss.'

Michael murmured thanks; Melanie blinked at him. How could she trust this man, so imprecise with his words, to take care of the burial? To say there had been a loss was ludicrous; one lost a shoe or a set of keys. You did not suffer the death of a child and say there was a loss. There was a catastrophe. A devastation. A hell.

Jacob Saltzman slipped behind his wide desk. 'I assure you that we will do everything we can to make this transition a little more peaceful for you.'

Transition, Melanie thought. *Butterfly from cocoon. Not—*

'Can you tell me where Emily is now?' Saltzman asked.

'No,' Michael said, then cleared his throat. Melanie was embarrassed for him. He sounded so nervous, so sure of making a mistake in front of this man. But what did he have to prove to Jacob Saltzman? 'She was at Bainbridge Memorial, but the . . . circumstances of the death led to an autopsy.'

'Then she's been taken down to Concord,' Saltzman said smoothly, jotting down notes on a pad. 'I assume that you'll want the burial as quickly as possible, which would put us at . . . Monday.'

Melanie knew he was counting a day for the autopsy, a day to get the body back to Bainbridge. She made a small sound in the back of her throat before she could stop herself.

'There are some items that we're going to have to discuss,' Jacob Saltzman said. 'First, of course, is the coffin.' He stood up, gesturing to a connecting door in his office. 'Would you step inside for a moment, so that you can consider some of the options?'

'The best,' Michael said firmly. 'The top of the line.'

Melanie looked at Jacob Saltzman, nodding easily. She thought of how this would be something to laugh at with Gus – the funeral business, a natural moneymaker. What grieving relative would haggle over the price of a coffin, or ask for the bargain-basement model?

'And is there already a plot?' the funeral director asked.

Michael shook his head. 'Do you take care of that?'

'We take care of everything,' Saltzman said.

Melanie sat stone-faced through a discussion of announcements in the paper, of refrigeration, of acknowledgment cards, of headstones. Coming here was like being admitted to an inner sanctum that one silently questioned but did not really want the answers to. She had never realized, in fact, that there were so many details to death: if a casket would be open or closed, whether the funeral home's guest register would be leatherbound or paperback, how many roses to put in the breakaway spray.

Melanie watched the tally grow to a staggering amount: $2,000 for the casket, $2,000 for the cement case that would only postpone the inevitable, $300 for the rabbi, $500 to list the death in *The Times*, $1,500 to prepare the gravesite, $1,500 to use the chapel at the mortuary. Where would they get this money? And then it came to her: from Emily's college fund. Jacob Saltzman handed the total to Michael, who did not even blink. 'That's fine,' he said again, 'I want the best.'

Melanie turned to Saltzman very slowly. 'The roses,' she said. 'The mahogany casket. The cement around it. *The New York Times*.' She began to shake. 'The best,' she said flatly, 'is not going to make Emily any less dead.'

Michael blanched. He handed a grocery bag to the funeral director. 'I think we ought to get going,' he said quietly. 'Here are the clothes.'

Melanie, half out of her chair, stopped. 'The clothes?'

'To be buried in,' Jacob Saltzman said gently.

Melanie grabbed for the paper sack and unrolled the top. She pulled out a rainbow print summer dress far too thin for November; sandals that hadn't fit Em in two summers. She fished for a pair of panties that still smelled of fabric softener and a barrette that had a broken clasp. Michael hadn't brought a bra or slip. Were they even remembering the same daughter?

'Why these things?' she whispered. 'Where did you find them?' They were forgotten trends and fashions that Emily would not have wanted, clothes that she could not stand to be in for eternity. They had this one last chance to prove that they had known Emily, that they had listened. What if they got it all wrong?

She ran out of the room, trying hard not to see the real

problem. It was not that Michael was making all the wrong choices; it was that he was making choices at all.

Anne-Marie Marrone was waiting in the driveway when they got home.

Michael had met the detective briefly last night, but he hadn't been in much of a mood to listen. She had delivered the unwelcome news about Emily and Chris trying to kill themselves. Michael could not imagine what else she could possibly have to tell them, since Em was already gone.

'Dr Gold,' Detective Marrone called, stepping out of her Taurus. She walked up the gravel path to their car. If she noticed that Melanie was still sitting in the front seat, staring at nothing, she didn't comment. 'I didn't realize you were a doctor,' she said amiably. She pointed to his truck, parked to the left, stenciled with the name of his practice.

'Animals,' he said tersely. 'Not the same.' Then he sighed. However awful his own day was already going, Anne-Marie Marrone was not the cause of it. She was only doing her job. 'Look, Detective Marrone. We've had a difficult morning. I don't really have time to talk.'

'I understand,' Anne-Marie said quickly. 'This will only take a minute.'

Michael nodded and gestured toward the house. 'It's open,' he said. He watched the detective open her mouth to give him flak for that transgression, then think better of it. He walked to the passenger side of the car, unlatched the door, and pulled Melanie to her feet. 'Come on inside,' he said, gentling his voice to a sweet, slow croon, the same way he'd soothe a skittish horse. He led his wife up the stone steps and into the kitchen, where she sat down on a chair and made no motion to remove her coat.

Detective Marrone stood with her back to the counter. 'We spoke last night about the Harte boy's confession of a double suicide,' she said, cutting cleanly to the point. 'Your daughter might have killed herself. But you need to know that until proven otherwise, her death is being treated as a homicide.'

'Homicide,' Michael breathed. With that one awful, seductive word, he felt a sinkhole of vindication open up in his mind – a chance to blame someone, other than himself, for Emily's death. 'You're saying Chris killed her?'

The detective shook her head. 'I'm not saying anything,' she said. 'I'm explaining a point of law enforcement. It's standard procedure to closely consider the person found next to a smoking gun. The one who's still conveniently alive,' she added.

Michael shook his head. 'If you come back in a few days, when . . . things are more calm, I'd be happy to show you old photo albums, or Emily's school notebooks, or letters Chris wrote to her from camp. He didn't murder my daughter, Detective Marrone. If he says he didn't, believe him. I can vouch for Chris; I know him well.'

'As well as you knew your daughter, Dr Gold? So well that you didn't realize she was suicidal?' Detective Marrone crossed her arms. 'Because if Christopher Harte's story is true, it means that your daughter wanted to kill herself – that she did kill herself – without exhibiting any outward symptoms of depression.'

Detective Marrone rubbed the bridge of her nose. 'Look. I hope for your sake – for Emily's and Chris's sake – that this is a double suicide that got botched. Suicide isn't a crime in New Hampshire. But if there isn't evidence of suicide, the state attorney general will determine whether there's probable cause to charge the boy with murder.'

Michael didn't need it spelled out; he realized that the probable cause would come from what Emily told them postmortem, by means of an autopsy. 'Do we get a copy of the medical examiner's report?' he asked.

Anne-Marie nodded. 'If you'd like, I can show you one.'

'Yes,' Michael said. 'Please.' It would be the last statement, the note she hadn't left. 'But I'm sure it won't come to that.'

Anne-Marie nodded and started out the door. At the threshold, she turned. 'Have you spoken to Chris yet?'

Michael shook his head. 'I . . . it didn't seem like the right time.'

'Of course not,' the detective said. 'I was just wondering.' She offered her condolences once again and headed outside.

Michael walked to the basement door and opened it, releasing the two setters in a scramble of paws and frenzied movement. He shepherded the dogs to the driveway and stood in the open doorway for a moment. He did not notice Melanie, who pulled her coat closer in the sudden draft, her mouth rounded with the word homicide, her teeth sinking into it, unforgiving.

James was with Chris at the hospital, waiting for the attending physician to sign him out from the patient ward into the locked adolescent psychiatric unit. Gus had been relieved at the doctor's recommendation – she did not trust herself to see in Chris the signs of depression she'd apparently already missed. A trained hospital, an experienced staff, would keep him safe.

James had had a fit. Would it show up on his permanent medical record? Would he have the ability, as a seventeen-year-old, to sign himself out at any time? Would his school, his future employers, the government, ever have to know he'd spent three days in a psychiatric ward?

Gus looked out the picture window in the living room to the neat path that ran between their house and the Golds'. This time of year, it was gilded with pine needles and damp with frost. She saw a light on upstairs in Melanie's bedroom; then, she tiptoed up to check on Kate, who'd heard the news of Emily's death that afternoon. As she'd suspected, her daughter had fallen asleep crying.

Gus flung her coat over her shoulders and ran down the path, letting herself into the Golds' kitchen. There was no sound, except for the loud ticking of a cuckoo clock. 'Melanie?' she called. 'It's me.' She started upstairs, poking her head into the bedroom, the computer room. Emily's bedroom door was closed; Gus made the conscious decision not to check inside.

Instead she knocked on the other shut door, the bathroom, and she slowly swung it open.

Melanie was sitting on the closed lid of the toilet. At Gus's entrance she glanced up, but did not register surprise.

Now that she was there, Gus had no idea what to say. It seemed stupid, suddenly, to be the one to offer comfort when she was so closely tied to the pain. 'Hi,' Gus said softly. 'How are you holding up?'

Melanie shrugged. 'I don't know,' she said. 'The funeral's Monday. We went to the mortuary.'

'That must have been awful.'

'I didn't pay attention,' Melanie said. 'I can't stand Michael right now.'

Gus nodded. 'Yeah. James fought the doctor who wanted Chris signed into a psychiatric ward, because it's a blight on the family name.'

Melanie looked up at her. 'Did you see this coming?' she asked, and Gus did not pretend to misunderstand.

'No,' Gus said, her voice breaking. 'If I had, I would have told you. And I know you would have told me.' She sank down on the edge of the bathtub. 'What could have possibly been so awful?' she whispered. She was thinking the same things, she knew, that Melanie was: Chris and Emily had grown up with love, with wealth, with each other. What more could they have needed?

Melanie grabbed the edge of the toilet paper and fed it through her fingers like a seam. 'Michael brought this horrible outfit to have Em buried in,' she said. 'And I took it away. I wouldn't let him use it.'

Gus stood up, relieved by the thought of something to do. 'We have to find her something, then,' she said. She took Melanie's hand, tugging her upright, and led her to Emily's room. She turned the doorknob as if she wasn't scared to death of the memories that would come at her.

But it was still simply, wonderfully, Emily's room. A teenager's shrine to Gap clothing and perfume oils and snapshots of Gus's own son. Melanie stood uncertainly in the center of the room, ready to bolt, while Gus ferreted through the closet. 'How about that turquoise blouse she wore for the school picture?' Gus asked. 'Her eyes looked so beautiful in it.'

'It's sleeveless,' Melanie said absently. 'She'd freeze to death.' As Gus's hands stilled among the hangers, Melanie covered her mouth. 'No,' she moaned, her eyes brimming with tears.

'Oh, Mel.' Gus gathered her friend into her arms. 'I loved her, too. We all did.'

Melanie pulled away and turned her back. 'You know,' Gus said hesitantly. 'Maybe I could ask Chris. He would know better than either of us what she wore to make herself feel good.'

Melanie did not respond. What had the detective told the Golds? And more importantly, what did they believe? 'You do know Chris loved her,' Gus whispered. 'You know he would have done anything for Em.'

When Melanie swung around, she looked completely unfamiliar. 'What I know about Chris,' she said, 'is that he's still alive.'

Then

Summer 1984

This time, Gus dreamed she was driving down Route 6. In the back of the Volvo, Chris was ramming an action figurine against the buttress of his car seat. Beside him, face obscured by the angle of the rearview mirror, was the baby. 'Is she drinking her bottle?' Gus asked Chris, the big brother, the copilot.

But before he could answer, a man knocked on the window. She smiled and rolled it down, ready to give directions.

He waved a gun under her nose. 'Get out of the car,' he said.

Shaking, Gus turned off the ignition. She stepped out of the car – they always told you to get out of the car – and she threw the keys as far as she could, to the middle of the next lane.

'Bitch!' the man yelled, diving for the keys. Gus knew she had less than thirty seconds. Not enough time to unlatch both car seats, to drag both children out, to get them to safety.

He was coming at her again. She had to make a choice. She scrambled for the rear door latch, sobbing. 'Come on, come on,' she cried, jiggling the latch on the infant seat and pulling the baby into her arms. She raced to the other side of the car, Chris's side, but the man was already revving up the engine and she watched, hugging one child, while the other was spirited away.

'Gus. Gus!' She came awake sporadically, and tried to focus on her husband's face. 'You were whimpering again.'

'You know,' Gus said breathlessly, 'they say that if you whimper in your sleep, you're screaming in your dream.'

'Same nightmare?'

Gus nodded. 'This time it was Chris.'

James hugged his arm around Gus and rubbed the skin of her enormous belly, feeling the bumps and ridges that would be knees, would be elbows. 'This isn't good for you,' he murmured.

'I know.' She was soaked in sweat; her heart was going a mile a minute. 'Maybe I . . . maybe I should see someone.'

'A psychiatrist?' James scoffed. 'Come on, Gus. It's just a nightmare.' He gentled his tone, adding, 'Besides, we live in Bainbridge.' He pressed his lips against her neck. 'No one's going to carjack you. No one's going to steal our kids.'

Gus stared up at the ceiling. 'How do you know?' she asked quietly. 'How can you be so sure that your life is the one that's charmed?' Then she padded down the hall to her son's room. Chris slept sprawled across his bed, his body flung wide as a promise. He slept, Gus thought, with the conviction of someone who knows he is safe.

The summer had been unusually hot, something Gus attributed not to El Niño or to global warming but to Murphy's Law, since she happened to be in the middle of her second pregnancy. Every morning for the past two weeks, as the temperature had climbed to eighty-five degrees, Gus and Melanie had taken the children to Tally Pond, a town-run swimming hole.

Chris and Emily were at the water's edge, their heads bent together, their bare limbs tangled and brown as cider. Gus watched Emily muddy her hands and hold them tenderly to Chris's face. 'You're an Indian,' Emily said, the streaks of her fingers leaving war paint on his cheeks.

Chris bent down to the water and scooped up two palmfuls of mud. He slapped his hands onto Emily's bare chest, trailing dirt down over her belly. 'You too,' he said.

'Uh-oh,' Gus murmured. 'Guess I ought to break that habit early.'

Melanie laughed. 'Mauling girls, you mean? With any luck,

by the time it matters, his objects of attention will choose to wear their bikini tops.'

Emily bounced back from Chris, squealed, and took off at a run down the narrow beach. Melanie watched them disappear behind a promontory. 'I ought to go get them,' she said.

'Well, you'll certainly get there faster than I would,' Gus agreed. She tilted her head back and dozed off until the sand trembled with the pounding of feet, and she blinked up to find Emily and Chris standing in front of her, absolutely naked.

'We want to know why Emily has a giant,' Chris announced.

Behind them, Melanie came into view, holding the discarded bathing suits. 'A giant?'

Chris pointed to his penis. 'Yeah,' he said. 'I have a penis, and she has a giant.'

Melanie smiled benignly. 'I brought them back,' she said. 'You play wise woman.'

Gus cleared her throat. 'Emily has a vagina,' she said, 'because Emily's a girl. Girls have vaginas, boys have penises.' Emily and Chris looked at each other, speaking volumes.

'Can she buy a penis?' Chris asked.

'No,' Gus said. 'You get what you get. It's like Halloween candy.'

'But we want to be the same,' Emily whined.

'No, you don't,' Gus and Mel said simultaneously. Melanie held out the bottom of Emily's bikini. 'Now get dressed,' she said. 'You too, Chris.'

The children dutifully scrambled into their wet suits and wandered down to the sand city they'd built earlier that morning. Melanie looked at Gus. 'Halloween candy?'

Gus laughed. 'Like you could have done better.'

Melanie sat back down. 'At the wedding,' she said, 'we'll look back at this and laugh.'

Charlie, James's hunting dog, had been sick for some time. The previous year, Michael had diagnosed an ulcer, and prescribed medicines like Tagamet and Zantac – human medicines that cost a fortune. He had to be fed small amounts of very bland food, and God forbid he should get near a trash can with bacon grease. But the illness ran in cycles – for months at a time, Charlie was fine; then he'd have a flare-up, and Gus would take him over to see Michael. She hid the receipts from James for the veterinary visits, because she knew that James would never have condoned spending five hundred dollars per winter on a dying dog. But Gus refused to see any other option.

That summer, however, Charlie developed a new problem. He drank constantly – from the toilet, from Chris's bathwater, from mud puddles. He urinated on rugs and bed quilts, although he'd been house-trained for six years. Michael had told Gus that it was probably diabetes. It was not common in springer spaniels; it was not fatal. But it was tricky and difficult to control. And every morning, she'd have to give him a shot of insulin.

Saturday afternoons, Gus took Charlie next door to the Golds' and let Michael examine him. Every week they discussed the lack of improvement; the option of putting the dog to sleep. 'He's a sick dog,' Michael had told her. 'I'm not going to think badly of you if you make that decision.'

The third Saturday in August, Gus walked the path between her house and the Golds', Charlie circling about her heels. Chris was with her, and Emily – they'd been playing over at the Harte household that morning. They tumbled up the side steps in a tornado of paws and feet, the children rushing into the kitchen and Charlie bulleting between Melanie's legs as she held open the door. 'Still peeing?' Gus nodded. 'Charlie!' Melanie yelled, 'get back here!'

But before the dog could soil a carpet or sprint upstairs, Michael appeared with Charlie heeled at his side. 'How do you do that?' Gus laughed. 'I can't even get him to sit.'

'Years and years of practice,' Michael answered, grinning. 'You ready?'

Gus turned to Melanie. 'Keep an eye on Chris?'

'I think Em's doing that. What time are we supposed to be at your place tonight?'

'Seven,' Gus said. 'We can get the kids to sleep and then act like we don't have any.'

Michael patted Gus's stomach. 'Which should be exceptionally easy for you, with your girlish figure.'

'If you weren't my dog's vet,' Gus said, 'I'd sock you for that.'

They walked off toward the small office Michael had furnished over the garage, laughing and talking, oblivious to the fact that until they were out of sight Melanie watched them and the ease that fit over their shoulders like a weathered old flannel blanket.

James came up behind Gus in the mirror as she fastened her left earring. 'How old am I?' he asked, skimming his hand over his hair.

'Thirty-two,' she said.

James's eyes widened. 'I am not,' he insisted. 'I'm thirty-one.'

Gus smiled. 'You were born in 1952. Do the math.'

'Oh, my God. I thought I was thirty-one.' He watched his wife laugh. 'It's a big deal,' he said. 'You know how sometimes you wake up thinking it's Friday, and it's really only Tuesday? Well, I just lost a whole year.'

Downstairs, the doorbell rang. 'Daddy,' Chris said, bouncing into the bedroom in his Batman pajamas. 'Em's here. Em's here.'

'Go let her in,' Gus said. 'Tell Melanie we'll be right down.'

James's eyes met hers in the mirror. 'Did I tell you how nice you look tonight?' he murmured.

Gus grinned. 'That's only because I'm hidden from the waist down in this mirror.'

'Even so,' James whispered, and he kissed her neck.

'And did I tell you,' Gus said, 'that I love all thirty-one years of you?'

'Thirty-two.'

'Oh.' Gus frowned. 'In that case, forget it.' She smiled wide and pushed back, standing splendid in a pumpkin silk caftan. 'You coming?' she asked, and when James nodded, she turned off the bedroom light and started down the stairs.

In the middle of the dinner party, the dog got sick.

They had just finished eating. The men had gone upstairs to tuck Chris and Emily into the king-size bed in the master bedroom. James was coming down the stairs when he heard a cough, followed by an unmistakable hawking sound.

He walked down the hallway to find Charlie vomiting on the antique kilim carpet, standing in a spreading puddle of his own urine. 'Goddammit,' he muttered, hearing the others just footsteps behind him. He grabbed Charlie's collar to yank him outside.

'It's not his fault,' Gus said softly. Melanie was already on her hands and knees, cleaning up with a dishtowel.

'I know it's not,' James tersely responded. 'But that doesn't make it any easier.' He turned to Michael, who was watching from a distance, his hands in his pockets. 'You can't do anything?'

'No,' Michael said. 'Not without putting the dog into insulin shock.'

'Marvelous,' James said, scuffing his foot on the carpet. 'Great.'

Gus took the dishtowel from Melanie, who stood up slowly. 'Maybe we should go,' she said. Michael nodded, and as Gus and James tried to save their antique carpet, the Golds headed upstairs. They found their daughter lost in a sea of sheets with Chris, their hair crisscrossing the same pillow in streaks of gold and copper. Gently disentangling her, Michael lifted Emily into his arms and carried her down the stairs.

Gus was waiting by the front door. 'I'll call you,' she said.

'Do that,' Melanie answered, smiling sadly and holding open the door.

Michael stayed just a moment longer. He shifted the damp, warm weight of his child in his arms. 'It may be time, Gus,' he said.

She shook her head. 'I'm sorry about this.'

'No,' Michael said. '*I* am.'

This time the carjacker's face had a canine snout, and black receding gums. 'Get out of the car,' he said, and Gus scrambled, deliberately thinking as she threw the keys that this time they had to go farther, had to go faster.

She yanked the rear door wide, worked the sadist's latch on the infant seat, grabbed the baby from the car. 'Unhook yourself!' she shouted to Chris, who was trying, although his little fingers couldn't manage it. 'Unhook yourself!'

She ran to his side of the car. The carjacker slid into the driver's seat, pointing the gun right at her. There was a scratch at Gus's wrist. She looked down in her arms at the baby and realized that all along she'd been holding Charlie.

James got out of bed before the sun rose and pulled on jeans and a T-shirt. Amazing, how cool it could be up here before the fog lifted. He ate a bowl of cereal at the kitchen table, deliberately keeping his mind a wide, blank page, then walked down the basement stairs.

Charlie, who could always sense him before anyone else could, was leaping around in his wire cage. 'Hey, buddy,' James said, freeing the latch. 'You want to go out? You want to go hunting?' The dog's eyes rolled, his pink tongue lolling in delight. He squatted and peed on the cement floor.

James swallowed, then fished in his pocket for the key to the gun case. He took out the .22 he was saving for Chris, when he got old enough to hunt squirrels and rabbits. With a silicone cloth, James rubbed down the smooth wooden shaft, the bright barrel. He took a pair of bullets and buried them in the pocket of his jeans.

The dog sprinted out the front door ahead of James, in his

element. Charlie sniffed at the ground, pounced on a fat brown toad. He doubled back in circles, tracing his own scent.

'This way,' James said, whistling, leading the dog deeper into the wooded acreage at the rear of the property. He loaded the bullets into the gun and watched Charlie weaving through the thick underbrush, thinking to flush up a pheasant or partridge, as he'd been bred to do. He saw the dog stop, cock his head, look skyward.

Tears slowly running down his face, James stepped behind the dog, so quiet and so familiar that Charlie did not even turn around, and lifting the rifle, he shot the dog in the back of the head.

'Hi,' Gus said, coming into the kitchen. 'You're up early.'

James was washing his hands in the sink. He did not glance up. 'Look,' he said, 'the dog died.'

Gus paused, halfway across the kitchen. She leaned against the counter, tears immediately in her eyes. 'It must have been the insulin. Michael said—'

'It wasn't,' James said, still avoiding her gaze. 'I took him out this morning. Hunting.'

If Gus thought it odd that they would have gone hunting months before any major New England wildlife was in season, she did not say so. 'Was it a seizure?' she asked, frowning.

'It wasn't a seizure. It – Gus, I did it.'

She brought her hand up to her throat. 'You did what,' she whispered.

'I killed him, dammit,' James said. 'All right? I don't feel good about it. And I wasn't angry because of the rug. I wanted to just help him. To get rid of the pain for him.'

'So you shot him?'

'What would you have done?'

'I would have taken him to Michael,' Gus said, her voice hitching.

'So he could give Charlie a shot? And you could hold him and watch him die? This was more humane,' James said. 'He was my dog. I was the one who had to take care of it.' He crossed the room and looked down at his wife. 'What?' he challenged.

Gus shook her head. 'I don't know you,' she said, and she ran out of the house.

'What kind of person,' Gus asked, her hands shaking on her coffee mug, 'shoots his own dog?'

Melanie stared across her kitchen table. 'It wasn't malicious,' she said, but her heart wasn't in it. It was not until a few moments before, when her best friend had run through the side door sobbing, that Melanie realized how much she valued her husband's commitment to heal.

'He doesn't kill his patients, does he?' Gus sputtered, as if she had been reading Melanie's mind. 'And what am I supposed to say to Chris?'

'Tell him that Charlie died, and that he feels better now.'

Gus scrubbed her hands over her face. 'I'd be lying,' she said.

'You'd be making it hurt less,' Melanie answered, and without wanting to, both women thought of what James had done, and why.

Chris was waiting on the porch steps when Gus got home. 'Daddy says Charlie's dead,' he announced.

'I know,' Gus said. 'I'm sorry.'

'Are we going to put him in a lifeguard?'

'A graveyard?' Gus frowned. What had James done with the dog? 'I don't think so, honey. Daddy probably buried Charlie somewhere in the woods.'

'Is Charlie an angel now?'

Gus thought about the springer, who had always seemed to have wings on his feet. 'Yeah. I think he is.'

Chris rubbed his nose. 'So when will we see him again?'

'Not till we get to Heaven,' Gus said. 'Not for a long time.'

She looked up at Chris, his cheeks silver with tears.

Impulsively, she went into the house, Chris trailing her. There, Gus went into the bathroom and packed up her toothbrush and shampoo, her Bic razors and her apricot perfume. She wrapped these in her cotton nightgown and set them on the bed. Then she haphazardly pulled clothes from drawers and hangers. 'How would you like it,' she asked Chris, 'if we lived with Em for a while?'

Gus and Chris slept in the Gold guest room, a narrow space beside the veterinary examination quarters with a double bed, a rickety dresser, and a pervasive odor of alcohol. Aware of how awkward this was, and the imposition, Gus went to bed at eight o'clock when she settled Christopher in. She lay in the dark beside him, and she tried not to think about James.

Michael and Melanie had not said a thing. Not that they could have; anything mentioned would have come out wrong, anyway. To his credit, James had phoned four times. Twice, he'd walked all the way over, only to hear Gus shouting from a room within the Gold house that she didn't want to see him.

Gus waited until she could no longer hear water running through the pipes upstairs. She counted Chris's even breathing and then she gently eased herself up off the bed. She walked down the hall to the den, where the pushbuttons of the telephone were glowing in the dark.

James answered on the third ring. 'Hello,' he said groggily. 'It's me.'

'Gus.' She could hear him coming awake in starts, sitting up, huddling the phone closer. 'I wish you'd come home.'

'Where did you bury him?'

'In the woods. Back by the stone wall. I'll take you there if you want.'

'I just want to know,' Gus said, 'so I can tell Chris.' She had no intention of telling Chris, really. The reason she wanted to know was that she feared, in ways she could barely articulate to herself, walking in the woods several years from now after a rainstorm and finding a skeleton.

'I didn't do this to hurt him. I don't care about the goddamned carpet. If I could trade that in and get Charlie back healthy, you know I'd do it.'

'But you didn't,' she said. 'Did you?' She gently set the receiver back in its cradle and pressed her knuckles to her mouth. It was a moment before she realized Michael was standing in front of her.

He was wearing sweatpants with a hole in the knee, and a faded Tufts T-shirt. 'I heard noises,' he explained. 'I came down to make sure you were all right.'

'All right,' Gus said, turning the word over. She thought of Melanie's precision for words, and of what James had said that morning: The dog died. But the dog hadn't really, when you got right down to it. The dog was killed. There was a difference.

'I'm not all right,' she said. 'I'm not even fifty percent right.'

She felt Michael's hand on her arm. 'He did what he thought was best, Gus. He even took Charlie out hunting beforehand.' He knelt down beside Gus. 'When Charlie died, he was with the person he loved most. I could have given him a shot, but I couldn't have made him as happy before I did it.' He stood up, tugged at her hands. 'Got to sleep,' he said, and he led her back to the guest room, his hand riding light and warm on the small of her back.

The next day, Melanie and Gus took the children to the pond. Chris and Emily rushed toward the water while their mothers were still setting up the towels and beach chairs and coolers. Suddenly, a whistle sounded from the lifeguard's deck. A strong, tanned teenager in a red suit jumped into the pond, stroking quickly toward the rock. Melanie and Gus stilled in their beach chairs, paralyzed by the same sudden realization: They could not see their children.

Then Emily appeared, led by a woman they did not know. In the murky blue water was a slow-turning oval, trapped beneath the surface. The lifeguard dove under and reemerged, swiftly split the water before him and dragged his quarry onto the sand.

Chris lay perfectly still, his face white, his chest flat. Gus shoved her way through the crowd, unable to speak, unable to do anything but fall bonelessly to the ground a few feet away from her son. The teenager leaned down, sealed Chris's lips with his own, breathed life.

Chris's head turned to the side, and he vomited up water. Gasping, starting to cry, he reached past the lifeguard to the safety of Gus's arms. The teenager stood up. 'He should be all right, ma'am,' the boy said. 'The little girl? His friend? She slipped off the rocks and he jumped in to get her. Problem was, she landed in a spot where she could stand. Your son didn't.'

'Mom,' Chris said.

Gus turned to the lifeguard, shaking. 'I'm sorry. Thank you.'

'No problem,' the boy said, and walked back to the whitewashed stand.

'Mom,' Chris said, and then more insistently, 'Mom!' He framed his hands, fish-cold and trembling, on both sides of her face.

'What?' Gus said, her heart so full it was heavy on the baby inside. 'What is it?'

'I saw him,' Chris said, his eyes shining. 'I saw Charlie again.'

That afternoon Gus and Chris moved back to the Harte household. They carried their toiletries and clothes up the stairs. With some careful unpacking and casual rearranging, by nightfall – when James came home from the hospital and checked on his sleeping son and saw his wife waiting in bed – it seemed as though they had never left.

This time during the nightmare Gus managed to hurl the keys farther than she ever had before, under another vehicle that was parked all the way across the street. She unstrapped her seat belt and got to the baby's door, managed to unlatch her and drag her free as she heard the footsteps behind her again.

'You bastard!' Gus yelled, for the first time fighting back in this nightmare. She kicked the tire. She looked into the back seat, expecting to see Chris's face as they squealed away, but instead she saw her husband reach into the rear of the car to set him free. And she wondered why it had taken so long to notice that all this time, James had been sitting in the passenger seat.

Now

November 1997

'I'm hiring a lawyer for Chris,' James announced Saturday, over dinner. The words erupted from him, like a belch, and he belatedly covered his mouth with his napkin as if he could take them back and declare them more politely.

A *lawyer*. The serving platter dropped the last few inches from Gus's fingers, clattering on the table. 'You what?'

'I spoke confidentially to Gary Moorhouse about this. Remember him, from the Groton reunion? It was his suggestion.'

'But Chris didn't commit a crime. Being depressed is not a crime.'

Kate turned to her father, incredulous. 'You mean they think Chris killed Emily?'

'Absolutely not,' Gus said, crossing her arms, suddenly shivering. 'Chris doesn't need a lawyer. A psychiatrist, yes. But a lawyer . . .'

James nodded. 'Gary said that when Chris told Detective Marrone it was a double suicide, he implicated himself. Just by saying there wasn't a third person, that it was just Em and him, turns the suspicion onto him.'

'That's crazy,' Gus said.

'Gus, I'm not saying Chris did what they think,' James said softly. 'But I think we ought to be prepared.'

'You will not,' Gus said, her voice shaking, 'hire a defense lawyer for a crime that never happened.'

'Gus—'

'You will not, James. I won't let you.' Her arms went tighter around herself, almost meeting at the middle of her back. 'If

they find out we've gotten a lawyer, they'll think Chris has something to hide.'

'They already think that. They're doing an autopsy on Emily,
and sending the gun in for tests. Look. You and I know what
really happened. Chris knows what really happened. Shouldn't
we get someone trained to let the police know what really
happened?'

'Nothing happened!' Gus yelled. She spun around, facing
the kitchen. 'Nothing happened,' she repeated. *Tell that*, her
conscience murmured, *to Melanie*.

She suddenly remembered the day Chris woke up and wound
his arms around her neck, and she realized that he no longer
had the breath of a baby. It was stale and ordinary, not sweet
and milky, and she had instinctively reared back from him, as
if this had nothing to do with the transition to solid food but
instead with the fact that this small, toddling body was now
capable of holding in its sins.

Gus took several deep breaths, then turned back toward the
dining room table. Kate was bent like a willow stem over her
plate, her tears collecting in its pale reflection. The serving
platter remained untouched. And James's chair was empty.

Kate stood uneasily in the doorway of her brother's hospital
room, one hand resting on the knob in case he totally tripped
out and became some kind of head case, like that kid with the
greasy blond hair who'd been skulking behind a gurney when
she came down the hall with her mom. Actually, she hadn't
even wanted to come visit. Chris would be home on Tuesday.
Plus, the doctors had said something about surrounding him
with people who cared about him, but Kate didn't think that
included herself. Most of her interactions with her older brother
in the past year had been hostile: fighting over time in the bathroom, over entering a room without knocking first, over catching
him with his hands under Emily's sweater.

It freaked her out to think about Chris in a rubber room –
well, not rubber exactly, but *still*. He looked different, with

dark circles under his eyes and this hunted look, like everyone was out to get him. Certainly not like the swimming star who'd swum a two-minute butterfly last year. Kate felt a pang in her chest, and silently swore to let Chris have the bathroom first every morning. All those times she'd screamed at him to 'Drop dead,' and look at how close he had come.

'Hey,' Kate said, and she was embarrassed to see that her voice trembled. She glanced over her shoulder, but to her surprise her mother had disappeared. 'How are you feeling?'

Chris shrugged. 'Like shit,' he said.

Kate bit her lip, trying to remember what her mother had said. *Cheer him up. Don't discuss Emily. Make small talk.* 'We, uh, we won our soccer game.'

Chris lifted flat, dull eyes to her. He did not say a word but he did not have to. *Emily's dead, Kate,* he was sneering. *You think I care about your stupid game?*

'I scored three goals,' Kate stammered. Maybe if she didn't face him . . . She turned toward the window, which overlooked the incinerator, spitting out thick black smoke. 'God,' she breathed. 'I wouldn't give this view to someone who's suicidal.'

Chris made a sound; Kate whirled around and clapped her hand to her mouth. 'Oh. I wasn't supposed to say that . . .' she muttered, and then she realized Chris was smiling. She had made him smile.

'What'd they tell you to talk to me about?' Chris asked.

Kate sat down on the edge of the bed. 'Anything to make you happy,' she admitted.

'What would make me happy,' he said, 'is knowing when the funeral's going to be.'

'Monday,' Kate said, leaning back on her elbows, relaxing in this new, tentative trust. 'But I'm absolutely, positively not supposed to tell you that.'

Chris let a slow smile painfully stretch his face. 'Don't worry,' he said. 'I won't hold it against you.'

When Gus and James entered Chris's room on Monday

morning, he was sitting on the edge of the bed, dressed in an ill-fitting pair of blue chinos and the shirt he'd been wearing on Friday night. The bloodstains had been rinsed out, but lingered in the fabric like ghosts, shifting pink beneath the fluorescent lights. The gauze wrapping his head had been traded for a small butterfly bandage at his brow. His hair was damp, neatly combed. 'Good,' he said, coming to his feet. 'Let's go.'

Gus stopped. 'Go where?'

'To the funeral,' Chris said. 'You didn't plan to leave me here?'

Gus and James exchanged a look. That was exactly what they had been planning, at the recommendation of the adolescent psychiatric ward doctors, who had debated the pro of letting Chris grieve versus the con of touching a very raw nerve and reminding him that with Emily gone, he didn't want to be alive. Gus cleared her throat. 'Em's funeral isn't today.'

Chris looked at her dark dress, at his father's civilian clothes. 'I suppose you're going out dancing,' he said. He came toward them with jerky, uncoordinated movements. 'Kate told me,' he explained. 'And I'm going.'

'Honey,' Gus said, reaching for his arm, 'the doctors don't think this is a very good idea.'

'Fuck the doctors, Mom,' he said, his voice cracking. He threw off her touch. 'I want to see her. Before I can't see her ever again.'

'Chris,' James said, 'Emily's gone. Best put it behind you and get yourself healed.'

'Just like that?' Chris said, his words spinning higher, like threads of glass. 'So if Mom died and you were stuck in the hospital the day of her funeral and the doctors told you that you were too sick to leave, you'd just roll over and go back to sleep?'

'It's not the same,' James said. 'It's not like you have a broken leg.'

Chris rounded on them. 'Why don't you just say it?' he yelled.

'You think I'm going to watch Em get buried and throw myself off the nearest cliff!'

'The day you're released, we can go to the cemetery,' Gus promised.

'You can't keep me here,' Chris said, stalking to the door. James jumped up and grabbed his shoulders; he swatted his father away. 'Let go,' he panted.

'Chris,' James said, struggling. 'Don't.'

'I can sign myself out.'

'They won't let you,' Gus said. 'They know today's the funeral.'

'You can't do this!' Chris shouted, jerking away from James and cuffing him on the jaw with his arm. James staggered back, holding his hand to his mouth, and Chris ran out of the room.

Gus tore after him. 'Stop him,' she yelled to the nurses at the main desk. She heard a flurry of activity behind her, but she could not take her eyes off Chris. Not when the locked doors did not give way to his titan pulls; not when the orderlies twisted his arms behind his back and plunged a needle into his biceps; not when he slumped to the floor, with the glitter of accusations in his eyes and the taste of Emily's name on his lips.

It had been Michael's plan to sit *shiva* following the burial service. Because Melanie had refused to have anything to do with the preparations, it had fallen to Michael to order bagels and lox, salads, coffee and cookies. Some neighbor – not Gus – had arranged the food on the dining room table by the time they returned from the cemetery.

Melanie went straight upstairs with her bottle of Valium. Michael sat on the living room couch, accepting the condolences of his dentist, a veterinary colleague, some clients. Emily's friends.

They approached in a pack, a swelling, amorphous mass that looked as if it might part at any minute to reveal his daughter in its center. 'Mr Gold,' one girl said – Heather or Heidi, Michael thought – her sad eyes a faded liberty blue, 'we don't know how this could have happened.'

She touched his hand, her own palm milk-soft. Her hand was the same size as Emily's.

'I didn't see it either,' Michael replied, realizing for the first time how true that was. On the surface, Em had been busy and bright, a beautiful tempest of a teenager. He'd liked what he'd seen, so he never thought to dig deeper. Too frightening to unearth the specters of drugs, of sex, of adult choices that he didn't yet want her to be making.

He was still holding Heather's hand. Her fingernails were small ovals, pale seashells you might stash in a pocket. Michael raised the girl's hand to his face, and cradled it against his cheek.

The girl leaped backward, snatching away her hand, her fingers recoiling, her cheeks flushed. She turned away, swallowed immediately by a fold in the group of her friends.

Michael cleared his throat, wanting to say something. But what? *You reminded me of her. I was wishing you were my daughter.* Nothing seemed right. He stood and made his way past well-wishers and teary relatives to the foyer. 'Excuse me,' he said in a commanding voice. He waited until every eye was turned toward him. 'On behalf of Melanie and myself, I'd like to thank you for coming today. We, uh, appreciate your kind words and your support. Please stay as long as you like.'

And then, to the incredulous stares of fifty people who knew him well, Michael Gold left his own home.

There were two visiting sessions in the locked psychiatric ward; one at nine-thirty in the morning, and one at three. Chris's mother not only managed to be there for both of them, but also sweet-talked the nurses into letting her stay past the allotted time for a visit, so that when he came back from speaking with a psychiatrist or taking a shower in the communal bathroom, he'd often find her still there and waiting.

But when Chris woke up from his medically induced stupor

on the day of Emily's funeral, his mother was not there. He didn't know if this was because it was not yet three, if the doctors had prohibited her visit in light of the morning drama, or if she was just plain scared to show up after screwing him over like that. He inched up in bed and scrubbed his hand over his face. The inside of his mouth felt like sandpaper and his mind was wheeling, as if a fly were spirographing around inside his head.

A nurse carefully pushed open the door. 'Oh, good,' she said. 'You're up. You have a visitor.'

If his mother was here to tell him about the funeral, he didn't want to see her. He wanted to know everything – the design of the bevel on the coffin, the lyrics of the prayers they had said for Em, the texture of the earth where she was buried. His mother could not possibly have remembered these details, and having to fill in the holes in her story would be worse than never hearing it at all.

But as the nurse stepped out of the way, Emily's father came into the room. 'Chris,' he said, stopping awkwardly a foot away from the bed.

Chris felt his stomach muscles jerk.

'I probably shouldn't be here,' Michael said. He shrugged out of his coat and began to wring it in his hands. 'In fact, I know I shouldn't be here.' He laid the coat on the edge of a chair and stuffed his hands into his trouser pockets. 'You know, Em was buried today.'

'I heard that,' Chris said. He was pleased at how steady he sounded. 'I wanted to come.'

Michael nodded. 'She would have liked that.'

'They wouldn't let me,' Chris said, and his voice cracked. He tried to duck his head so that Michael wouldn't see the tears, instinctively assuming that Em's father, like his own, would see them as a weakness.

'I'm not sure it was so important to be there today,' Michael said slowly. 'I think you were with Em when it mattered the most.' He looked at Chris until the boy glanced up. 'Tell me,' Michael whispered. 'Tell me what happened Friday night.'

Chris stared at Michael, caught not by the power of his question but by the way Emily played over her father's face – her eyes the same marble blue; her chin as determined; her smile hiding just behind the lines of strain at his mouth. It was easy for him to picture Emily asking, not Michael. *Tell me*, she begged, her mouth still wet from his own, blood running down her temple. *Tell me what happened.*

His gaze slid away. 'I don't know.'

'You must know,' Michael said. He grasped Chris's chin, the remarkable radiant heat of adolescence burning his finger-tips so quickly he let go almost immediately. He spent five minutes trying to get Chris to speak to him again, to spit out a detail or a piece of information that he could carry with him in his breast pocket the way one might tuck the note of a lover or a lucky charm. But when Michael left the room, the only thing he knew for certain was that Chris had not been able to look him in the eye.

Anne-Marie Marrone closed the door to her office, kicked off her shoes, and sat down with the faxed autopsy report for Emily Gold. She curled her feet up beneath her on the chair and closed her eyes, intentionally clearing her mind so that she would not prejudge what she was about to read. Then she raked her fingers through her hair and stared until the words began to swim on the page.

The patient was a seventeen-year-old white female, admitted unconscious after a gunshot wound to the head. Within minutes of admission patient's blood pressure dropped to fifty-seventy/palpable. Patient was pronounced dead at 11:31 P.M.

Gross examination revealed powder burns surrounding the entrance wound at the right temple. The bullet had not cut a clean path across the head, but had crossed the temporal and the occipital lobes of the brain and nicked the cerebellum to exit somewhere right of center in the rear of the skull. A fragment matching a .45 caliber bullet had been found in the occipital lobe. Wounds were consistent with a .45 caliber bullet fired directly against the skull.

All in all, a death that suggested the suicide Christopher Harte had related.

Anne-Marie felt the hairs stand up on the back of her neck as she read through the second page of the autopsy report. The external examination had revealed bruising on the right wrist. The medical examiner had found flakes of skin beneath Emily's fingernails.

Signs of a struggle.

She stood up, thinking of Chris Harte. She had not yet received a report from Forensics on the Colt, but that didn't matter. It had been procured from his house, his fingerprints would be all over it. It remained to be seen whether Emily's would as well.

Something niggled at her mind, and she looked back at the first page of the report. The medical examiner had only roughly explained the entry and exit wounds, but they did not seem quite right to Anne-Marie. She took her right hand, pointed the finger like it was a gun, and held it to her temple. She cocked her thumb, pretended to shoot. The bullet should have come out near Emily's left ear. Instead, it exited in the back of her head, a few inches behind her right ear.

Anne-Marie twisted her wrist so that her imaginary gun would point in a similar path. It involved lifting her elbow and angling it in an odd fashion, so that the gun was almost parallel to the temple – a highly uncomfortable and unnatural position from which to shoot oneself in the head.

Yet the bullet trajectory made perfect sense if the person who shot the gun was standing in front of you.

But why?

She flipped to the last page of the autopsy to read about the gross examination of the gallbladder, the gastrointestinal tract, the reproductive system. Suddenly, she caught her breath. Slipping back into her shoes, Anne-Marie lifted the telephone, and dialed the attorney general's office.

*   *   *

'Mrs Gold,' the detective had said on the phone, 'I have the autopsy results on your daughter. I'd like to come over at your convenience and show them to you.'

Melanie had played the words over in her mind. Something about Detective Marrone's request had stuck in her craw, and she turned the sentences around, wondering what it was that seemed odd, studying them through different filters as if her mind were a kaleidoscope. Perhaps it was the detective's politeness, so diametrically opposed to the last few times she'd barreled into their grief. Perhaps it was simply hearing the words *autopsy* and *your daughter* in the same short breath.

Melanie and Michael sat on the couch, wide-eyed and clutching each other's hands like refugees. Detective Marrone sat across from them on a tufted chair. Spread out on the coffee table were the facts and statements of Emily's body, the last information she had to give.

'Let me get right to the point,' the detective said. 'I have reason to believe that your daughter's death was not a suicide.'

Melanie felt her whole body soften like butter left out in the sun. Wasn't this what she had been hoping for? This absolution by a law enforcement expert who was now saying, *It wasn't your fault; you didn't see signs of your daughter's impending suicide because there was nothing there to see.*

'The State of New Hampshire believes there is sufficient evidence to take this case to a grand jury and have them hand down an indictment for murder,' the detective was saying. 'Whether or not you, as Emily's parents, choose to be involved, the case will still proceed. But we hope that you'll comply with requests from the attorney general's office if need be.'

'I don't understand,' Michael said. 'You're suggesting . . .'

'That your daughter was killed,' Detective Marrone said, unblinking. 'Most likely by Christopher Harte.'

Michael shook his head. 'But he said that Emily shot herself. That they'd planned to kill themselves together.'

'I know what he said,' the detective replied more gently. 'But your daughter said something different.' She lifted the first page of the autopsy report, covered with foreign markings and measurements. 'In a nutshell, the medical examiner confirmed that Emily was killed by a gunshot wound to the head. However . . .' She gestured further down the page, outlining bodily evidence of violence, of Emily fighting back.

Melanie stopped listening. She folded her hands in her lap and pretended that Chris Harte was minuscule and hidden within them. She crushed her palms together, flattened them, until he would have no room to breathe.

'Wait,' Michael said, shaking his head. 'I don't believe this. Chris Harte wouldn't have killed Emily. There's not a malicious bone in his body. For Christ's sake, they grew up together.'

'Shut up, Michael,' Melanie gritted out.

He turned to her. 'You know I'm right,' he said.

'Shut up.'

Michael glanced at the detective again. 'Look, I watch the legal shows on TV. I know that mistakes can be made. And I know that every piece of evidence you've found in that autopsy probably has a perfectly logical explanation that has nothing to do with murder.' He exhaled slowly. 'I know Chris,' he said quietly. 'If he said that he and Em were going to kill themselves, well, then I don't understand why, and I'm shocked to find out, but I believe that that's what they were going to do. He wouldn't lie about something so painful.'

'He might,' Anne-Marie said, 'if his own life depended on it.'

'Detective Marrone,' Michael replied, 'I mean no disrespect. But you met these kids three days ago. I've known them all their lives.'

Michael had the distinct impression that Anne-Marie Marrone was sizing him up. What kind of father vouched for the boy who might have murdered his daughter? 'You're saying you know Chris Harte well,' she stated.

'As well as I knew my own daughter.'

The detective nodded. 'Then it should come as no surprise,' she said evenly, flipping to the final page of the autopsy, 'when I tell you that Emily was pregnant.'

*   *   *

'Eleven weeks,' Melanie said dully. 'She knew for two months. I should have known. Tampons never made it to the shopping list.' She twisted the sheets between her hands. 'I never even knew they were sleeping together.'

Neither had Michael. Since Detective Marrone had left, that was what he'd been imagining. Not that tiny peanut of life inside Emily's body, but what had brought it there: the strokes and caresses that peeled away the layers of girl to reveal a woman no one else had wanted to admit existed.

'That's probably what they were fighting about,' Melanie murmured.

Michael rolled over and faced his wife. Her profile, ribboned against the edge of the pillow, kept shifting and realigning, so that he could not see her clearly. 'Who?'

'Chris and Em,' Melanie said. 'He would have wanted her to get rid of it.'

Michael stared at her. 'And you wouldn't? A year before she was set to go off to college?'

Melanie sniffed. 'I would have wanted her to do whatever she felt she had to do.'

'You're lying,' Michael said. 'You're only saying that now because it doesn't matter.' He levered himself up on an elbow. 'You don't even know if she told Chris.'

Melanie sat up in bed. 'What is the matter with you?' she hissed. 'Your daughter is dead. The police believe that Chris killed her. And you're defending him at every turn.'

Michael glanced away. The bottom sheet was wrinkled, as if time took its toll on a marriage bed as surely as it would on a face. He tried in vain to smooth it. 'You told me at the funeral home that fancy trappings weren't going to bring Em back. Well, neither's crucifying Chris. The way I see it, he's all we have left of her. I don't want to see him buried too.'

Melanie stared at him. 'I don't understand you,' she said, and picking up her pillow, she fled from the bedroom.

*   *   *

On Tuesday morning, when the sun first slitted its eyes, James was already awake and dressed. He stood on the porch, his breath coming in small circles, clutching a stack of yellow posters in one hand. Rifle season for deer was almost over, but James had been determined. He'd finally located some signs that he'd purchased years ago and had forgotten in the attic. Slipping a hammer through the loop of his belt, he struck off toward the perimeter of his property, listening to the jangle of nails in his pocket.

At the first tree beside the driveway, he yanked loose the hammer and pounded a nail through the first sign. Then he moved to the second tree, just a few feet away, and he put up another. SAFETY ZONE, they read. More urgent than a traditional POSTED sign, they let hunters know they were within three hundred feet of a residence. That a stray bullet could have dire consequences.

James moved to the third tree, and the fourth. The last time he had done this, when Chris was just a child, he'd hung the signs every twenty feet or so. This time, he hung a sign on every single tree. They rustled in the light wind, a hundred yellow warnings, garish and obscenely festive against the dark trunks.

James stepped out on the road to look at his handiwork. He stared at his signs, thinking of amulets carried, of red worn to ward off the Evil Eye, of Hebrews painting lamb's blood on doorposts, and he wondered what, exactly, he was trying to keep away.

Then

1989

Chris huddled beside Emily, their hands twined together around the telephone receiver. 'You're chicken,' he murmured, as the dial tone swam in his ear.

'Am not,' Em whispered.

There was a pickup on the other end. Chris felt Emily's fingers flutter above his wrist. 'Hello?'

Em lowered her voice. 'I'm looking for Mr Longwanger.'

'I'm sorry,' the woman said. 'He's not available right now. Can I take a message?'

Em cleared her throat. 'Does he really have one?'

'Have what?' the woman asked.

'A long wanger?'

Then Em slammed down the receiver, rolling to her side in a fit of giggles and a flurry of phone book pages.

It took Chris a while to stop laughing. 'I didn't think you'd do it,' he said.

'That's because you're a dork.'

Chris grinned at her. 'At least my last name isn't Longwanger.' He skimmed his hand over the page where the phone book had fallen open. 'What should we do next?' he asked. 'Here's a Richard Ressler. We could ask if there's a Dick in the house.'

Emily flopped onto her belly. '*I* know,' she said. 'Call your mom and tell her you're Mr Chambers and Chris is in trouble.'

'Like she's going to believe I'm the principal.'

Em smiled slowly. 'Here, chicky chicky chicky,' she crooned.

'You do it,' Chris challenged. 'She won't recognize the school secretary.'

'What will you give me?' Emily asked.

Chris dug in his pockets. 'Five bucks.' Em held out her hand; he shook it, and handed her the telephone.

She dialed, pinched her nose. 'Yesss,' she drawled out. 'I'm looking for Mrs Harte? This is Phyllis Ray at the principal's office. Your son is in trouble.' Emily looked wildly at Chris. 'What kind of trouble? Uh, well, we'd like you to come down here and get him.' She quickly hung up the phone.

'What did you do that for?' Chris groaned. 'She's going to drive all the way down there and find out I left an hour ago! I'm going to be grounded for the rest of my life.' He ran his hands through his hair and then fell onto his side on Emily's bed.

She spooned behind him, her chin hooked over his shoulder. 'If you are,' she murmured, 'I'll stay with you.'

Chris sat with his head bowed, his parents standing over him like sequoias. He wondered if this was what marriage was all about: one of them picking up to yell when the other one's voice trailed off, as if they were really one giant with two separate heads. 'Well?' his mother huffed, finishing the tirade. 'Do you have anything to say for yourself?'

'I'm sorry,' Chris automatically returned.

'Sorry doesn't make up for stupidity,' his father said. 'Sorry doesn't bring back the appointment your mother had to cancel when she went to get you at school.'

Chris opened his mouth to say that if she'd reasoned logically, she would have realized no kids were at school that late in the afternoon – but thought better of it. He ducked his head again, staring at the weave of the carpet, wishing that while he and Em were making prank calls he hadn't forgotten that his mother was in the middle of starting up her own business. But it was so soon into it, how was he supposed to remember? And what kind of job was hanging around in lines nobody else wanted to waste time on?

'I had expected better of you and Emily,' his mother said.

Well, that wasn't a surprise. Everyone always expected better of him and Emily, as if they all knew some grand plan that Emily and Chris did not. Sometimes Chris wished he could sneak a peek at the back of the book, so to speak, and see how it was all going to turn out, so that he wouldn't have to bother going through the motions.

'Except for school, you are to stay in this room for three days,' his father said. 'Let's see if that gives you enough time to think about how many people you've inconvenienced with your little jokes.' Then, one giant monster, both of his parents stepped out of his bedroom.

Chris flopped back on the bed and threw his forearm over his eyes. God, they were such pills. So what if his mother had demanded to speak to Mr Chambers, who of course knew nothing about Chris getting into trouble? No one was going to remember a month from now.

He opened the curtains at one of his bedroom windows. Facing dead east, it stared directly at Em's bedroom. They couldn't really see each other from that distance, but they'd realized that at least the small square of light in the window was visible. Chris knew that Emily was being read the riot act, too; he wasn't sure if her parents disciplined in her bedroom or in the kitchen or whatever. He sat down beside the lamp near his bed and flicked off the switch, blackening the room. Then he flicked it back on. And off, and on. And off, and on.

Four long bleats of darkness, then three short ones.

He stood up and waited by the window. Emily's room, a small yellow square cut by the limbs of trees, went black. Then bright again.

They had learned Morse code at camp last summer. Emily's room kept flickering. *H . . . I.*

Chris flicked his thumb over the lamp's base again. *H . . . O . . . W . . . B . . . A . . . D.*

Emily's room darkened twice.

Chris signaled out three.

He smiled and leaned back on his bedspread, watching Emily's words to him light up the night.

Outside in the hallway, Gus and James collapsed against the wall and tried not to laugh. 'Can you believe,' Gus gasped, 'they called a man named Longwanger?'

James grinned. 'I don't know that I would have been able to restrain myself, either.'

'I feel like such an old fart shouting at him,' Gus said. 'I'm thirty-eight, and I might as well be Jesse Helms.'

'We had to ground him, Gus. Or else he'll be dialing around and asking for Prince Albert in a can.'

'What is Prince Albert in a can?'

James groaned and tugged her down the hall. 'You're never going to be the old fart, since I'll be holding that title.'

Gus walked into their bedroom. 'Fine. You can be the curmudgeon. I'll be the crazy lady who barges into the principal's office and insists that her son's done something wrong.'

James laughed. 'They did get you, didn't they?'

She threw a pillow at him.

James grabbed her ankle, making her squeal and roll away from him. 'You shouldn't have done that,' he said. 'I may be old, but I'm not dead.' He pressed her body beneath his, feeling her go soft, tracing the undercurves of her breasts and the cords of her throat. His mouth came over hers.

Gus let herself remember what it had been like over a decade ago when the house still smelled of planed wood and fresh paint, and time was a gift given from the hospital scheduler. She thought back to how she and James would make love on the kitchen table, in the mud room, after breakfast – as if the pressure of being a resident had knocked all those *Mayflower* sensibilities from his mind.

'You,' James said against her temple, 'are thinking too much.'

Gus smiled against his neck. She was rarely accused of that. 'Maybe I ought to just feel, then,' she said, slipping her hands up under James's shirt as the muscles in his back tightened in sequence, like a tide. She pushed him onto his side, slid down his zipper, and took the heat of him into her hands.

Then she looked up, eyes sparkling. 'Mr Longwanger, I presume?'

James grinned. 'At your service.'

He moved over her, into her. She drew in her breath, and then she was not thinking at all.

Dear Diary,

The class guinea pig Blizard is having babys.

Today in school Mona Ripling said she kissed Kenny Lawrence behind the wall mats during gym. Which is totaly crazy cause everyone knows Kenny is the grossest of all the other boys in 4th grade.

Except for Chris but Chris isnt like all the other boys.

Chris is reading an autobiography of Muhomad Alli for his book report. He asked what I was doing and I started to tell him about Lancelot and Guinevere and King Arthur but then I stopped. He'd probaly want to know about the knights and those are the parts I've been skipping.

The best chapters are where Guinevere spends time with Lancelot. He has dark hair and dark eyes. He does things like lift her off her horse and call her MY LADY. I bet he treats her like the kristle egg Mom has that she won't let anybody even BREATHE near. King Arthur is an old guy and a jerk. Guinevere should just run off with Lancelot because she loves him and because they were ment for each other.

I think its very romantic.

If Chris knew I was crazy over fairytales I'd just die.

Later that week, on a dare from Emily, Chris stole *The Joy of Sex* from the library stacks.

He hid it under his coat until they were home, and at their secret place. The boulder was shaped like an upside-down right triangle, the broad slab of rock at the top providing a ledge to perch on or cower beneath, depending on one's imagination. At different points in their childhood, it had been home base for hide-and-seek, a pirate's cave, an Indian's lean-to. Chris scuffed away some of the soft pine needles on the ground. He pulled the book out and sat down beside Emily.

For a moment neither said a word, tilting their heads to take in the drawings of twined limbs and grasping hands. Emily ran her finger over the pen-and-ink flanks of a man rearing over a woman. 'I don't know,' she whispered. 'I don't see anything joyous about that.'

'It must be different when you're really doing it,' Chris answered. He turned the page. 'Wow,' he said. 'That's like gymnastics.'

Emily flipped back to the beginning of the book. She stopped at a page that showed a woman on top of a man, stretched along the length of him, their hands clasped together over their heads.

'Big deal,' Chris said. 'You've pinned me a million times.'

But Emily didn't hear him. She was captivated by the facing page, which depicted a man and woman joined but sitting up, their legs splayed like two crabs, their hands holding on to each other's shoulders for purchase. Their bodies, together, looked like a big bowl, as if the whole reason for having sex was to create something that could hold all the feelings they had for each other. 'It must be different when you love somebody,' Emily reasoned.

Chris shrugged. 'It must be,' he said.

Gus was changing the sheets on Chris's bed when she found *The Joy of Sex* hidden between his mattress and box spring.

She picked up the book and leafed through the pages, finding positions she had long forgotten existed. Then she hugged it tightly to her chest and walked outside, heading toward the Golds'.

Melanie opened the door with a mug of coffee in one hand and took the book Gus held out wordlessly to her. 'Well,' she said, studying the cover. 'This certainly goes beyond the call of neighborly duty.'

'He is only nine,' Gus exploded, dropping her coat on the floor of the kitchen and sinking into a chair. 'Nine-year-olds are supposed to be thinking of baseball, not sex.'

'I think they're mentally linked,' Melanie suggested. 'You know, getting to first and second base and all that.'

'Who let him check this out at the library?' Gus demanded, turning to her friend. 'What kind of adult lets a child do something like that?'

Melanie scanned the rear of the book. 'No one,' she said. 'This was never checked out.'

Gus buried her face in her hands. 'Great. He's a pervert and a thief.'

The kitchen door swung open again, and Michael came through, carrying a large box of veterinary supplies. 'Ladies,' he greeted, dropping the box heavily to the floor. 'What's up?' He peeked over Melanie's shoulder and, grinning, took the book from her hands. 'Wow,' he said, flipping through the pages. 'I remember this.'

'But were you nine when you read it?' Gus asked.

Michael laughed. 'Can I take the fifth?'

Melanie turned to him, surprised. 'You were aware of girls that young?'

He kissed the top of her head. 'If I didn't start early,' he said, 'I wouldn't be the dynamo I am now.' He sat down in the chair across from Gus and slid the book toward her. 'Let me guess. You found it under his mattress. It's where I used to keep my *Penthouse*.'

Gus rubbed her temples. 'If we ground him again, Child Protective Services is going to show up at our door.' She glanced up miserably. 'Maybe we shouldn't even punish him,' she said. 'Maybe he's just looking for answers about girls.'

Michael raised his brows. 'When he finds them, will you tell him to come talk to me?'

Melanie sighed sympathetically. 'I don't know what I'd do, in your shoes.'

'Who says you're not?' Gus pointed out. 'How do you know

Em isn't in on this? Everything else those two do, they do together.' She looked at Michael. 'Maybe she's the master-mind.'

'Em's nine,' he said, appalled by the thought.

'Exactly,' Gus said.

Gus waited until she heard the sound of her son tearing his room apart. Then she knocked on the door, to be met by a whirlwind of clothing, mitts, hockey sticks, and anguish. 'Hi,' she said affably. 'Lose something?' She watched Chris turn several rich shades of red. Then she drew her hands out from behind her back. 'Lose this?' she asked.

'This isn't what it looks like,' Chris said immediately, and Gus was astounded. When had he learned to lie so easily?

'What do you think it looks like?'

'Like I've been reading something I shouldn't have?'

Gus sank down on his bed. 'Are you asking me, or telling me?' She gentled her voice, stroked her palm over the cover of the book. 'What makes you think you shouldn't be reading it?'

Chris shrugged. 'I don't know. The naked pictures and all.'

'Is that why you wanted to read it?'

'I guess,' Chris said, looking so miserable she almost – almost – felt sorry for him. 'It seemed like a good idea at the time.'

She stared at the crown of her son's head, and remembered how, when he was born, a labor nurse had held a mirror between her legs so that she could see it appear, dark and downy, for the first time.

'Can we just forget about it?' Chris begged.

She wanted to let him off, seduced by the way he was squirming beside her, a butterfly on a pin. But she chanced to look down at his hands, clenched over each bony knee. They were no longer toddler-soft, each digit puffy, like the hands on the balloons at Thanksgiving parades. At some point when Gus was too busy to notice, they had turned knuckled and blue-veined, larger even than hers, hands that already reminded her of James's.

Gus cleared her throat, aware that this boy sitting in front of her, whose face she could have identified by touch alone, whose voice said her name before any other word, was someone she did not recognize. He was someone who heard the word *woman* and no longer thought of Gus's features and a mother's embrace, but of a faceless girl with breasts and curved hips.

When had this happened?

'If you have questions, you know, about . . . this . . . you can always ask your father or me,' Gus managed, praying he'd hit up James. She wondered what had compelled her to confront Chris in the first place. At this point, it was a toss-up as to who was more embarrassed.

'I do.' Chris looked into his lap, twisting his hands together. 'Some of the stuff in that book . . . well, it's . . .' He lifted his gaze. 'Some of it doesn't look like it would work so well.'

Gus touched her hand to her son's hair. 'If it didn't work,' she said simply, 'we wouldn't have you.'

Emily and Chris sat under the tent of a blanket on her bed, a flashlight balanced between their bare feet. Chris's parents, off to some hospital charity ball, had asked the Golds to sit for him and his sister. Kate had gone to bed after her bath, but Chris and Em were planning to stay up past midnight. Melanie had tucked them in just before nine and called for lights out, but they knew if they were quiet, no one else would be the wiser.

'So?' Chris pressed. 'Truth or dare?'

'Truth,' Emily said. 'The worst thing I ever did . . . was call your mom and pretend to be the principal's secretary.'

'That's not true. You forgot the time you poured nail-polish remover on my mom's bureau and blamed it on Kate.'

'I only did it because you told me to,' Emily whispered fiercely. 'You said she wouldn't know any better.' Then she frowned. 'Anyway, if you knew the worst thing I ever did, why'd you even ask the question?'

'Okay. I'll ask another one,' Chris said. 'Read me what you wrote in your diary when I was brushing my teeth.'

Emily gasped. 'Dare.'

Chris's teeth gleamed white in the glow of the flashlight. 'Sneak into your parents' bathroom,' he said. 'And bring back their toothbrushes, so I know you did it.'

'Fine,' Emily said, throwing back the covers. Her parents had gone to sleep a half hour ago. Surely they wouldn't still be awake.

The minute she was gone, Chris stared at the tiny paisley-covered book into which Emily poured out her heart every single night. It had a lock, but he could jimmy it. He touched his hand to the back of the diary, and then snatched it back, his palm burning. Was he chicken because he knew Em wouldn't want him to read it? Or was he afraid of what he might see?

He shook the book and eased it open. His name was all over the place. His eyes widened, then he slapped the diary back down onto her desk and went back to the bed, certain that guilt was written right across his forehead.

'Here,' Em said, breathless, crawling back onto the bed. She held out two toothbrushes. 'Your turn.' She tucked her feet beneath her. 'Who's the prettiest girl in the fifth grade?'

Well, that was a no-brainer. Emily would expect him to say Molly Ettlesley, the only fifth-grader who really needed a bra. But if he did say Molly, he knew that Emily would get pissed off, because he was supposed to be her best friend.

His gaze cut to the diary. Did Em really think of him as some knight?

'Dare,' he muttered.

'Okay.' And before Emily could edit her thoughts, she told Chris he had to kiss her.

He threw the blanket off their heads. 'I what?'

'You heard me,' Em said, frowning. 'It's not as bad as sneaking into my parents' bathroom.'

His hands were sweaty all of a sudden, so he wiped them on the knees of his pajamas. 'Okay,' he said. He leaned forward and pushed his mouth up against hers. Then he drew back, just as flushed as Emily. 'Well,' he announced, wiping his lips with the back of his hand. 'That was pretty gross.'

Em gently touched her hand to her chin. 'Definitely,' she whispered.

The one McDonald's in Bainbridge, New Hampshire, sported a changing battalion of teenage workers who slaved over greasy grills and oil pits until they up and graduated. But for several years, one man had worked there consistently. In his late twenties, he had long black hair and a walleye. Adults politely said there was 'something wrong with him.' Kids called him The Creep and fashioned stories about him roasting infants in the french fryer and cleaning his fingernails with a Bowie knife. On the afternoon that Chris and Emily were eating lunch there, The Creep was on clean-up duty in the dining room.

Chris's parents had come over at lunchtime, his mother swooping down like a hawk to kiss his forehead. After gossiping with Emily's mom about who was wearing what to the party the night before, Gus offered to take Emily out to McDonald's with them for lunch – a thank-you for baby-sitting overnight. They had carried their trays to the dining area, but every time Emily turned around, The Creep was at the table beside her or behind her or just in front, rubbing down the slick Formica surface and staring at her with his one straight eye.

Chris sat beside her on the banquette. 'I think,' he whispered, 'he's your secret admirer.'

'Stop it,' Em shuddered. 'You're freaking me out.'

'Maybe he'll ask for your phone number,' Chris continued. 'Maybe he'll—'

'Chris,' Emily warned, punching him on the arm.

'What's going on?' Gus asked.

'Nothing,' they answered in unison.

Emily watched The Creep make his rounds, picking up ketchup packets people had dropped on the floor and mopping up a spilled Coke. He looked up at her, as if he could feel her eyes on him, and she immediately stared down at the seeded bun of her hamburger.

Suddenly Chris leaned over to whisper again. His breath was hot in the shell of her ear. 'Ultimate dare,' he said.

An ultimate dare was one that raised you in the other person's estimation by leaps and bounds, if completed. Not that they were keeping count, but if they were, it would definitely put Em in the lead. She wondered briefly if this was Chris's way of getting back at her for the kiss the night before.

The last ultimate dare challenge issued had been by Emily. Chris had mooned an entire residential street from the window of the school bus.

She nodded.

'Go pee,' Chris whispered. 'In the men's room.'

Emily smiled. It was, all in all, a pretty good dare. And it wasn't nearly as bad as sticking your rear end out a window. If anyone was in there, she'd just say it was a mistake and walk back out; Chris would never know whether or not she'd actually gone to the bathroom. She glanced around first for The Creep, because she didn't want to have to walk past him, as crazy as that sounded. He was out of the dining room by now, probably back on shift slinging burgers. As she scooted out of the banquette, James and Gus looked up. 'I have to go to the bathroom,' she said.

Gus wiped her mouth with her napkin. 'I'll take you,' she said.

'No!' Em cried. 'I mean, I can do it myself.'

'Melanie lets you go alone?' Gus asked dubiously.

Emily looked her in the eye and nodded. Gus turned to James, who shrugged. 'This is Bainbridge,' he said. 'What's going to happen?'

Gus watched Emily weave through the maze of bolted tables and chairs to the rest rooms in the rear of the McDonald's. Then she turned her attention to Kate, who was fingerpainting with ketchup on the table.

The men's room was to the left. The women's room was to

the right. Emily glanced back at Chris, to make sure he was looking, and then she went inside.

In less than five minutes, she slid back onto the seat beside Chris. 'Nice job,' he said, and touched her arm.

'It was no big deal,' Emily murmured.

'Oh, yeah?' he whispered. 'Then how come you're shaking?'

'It's nothing,' she said, shrugging, but she would not look at him. She methodically ate a burger she could no longer taste, and slowly convinced herself that she had told him the truth.

Now

November 1997

S. Barrett Delaney had spent most of her adult life trying to live down the fact that she was a lawyer named Sue. It had been years since she'd actually used her Christian name to sign for anything, but somehow word always managed to get out – some human resources joker looking for an easy laugh, some credit card company soliciting it from her birth certificate, someone picking up her high school yearbook. There were entire months that she had to convince herself the reason she became a prosecutor, and not a defense attorney, had to do with her love of justice and not self-doubt.

She glanced at her clock, realized she was running late, and scrambled down the hall to the cafeteria. Anne-Marie Marrone was already settled at a corner table with two Styrofoam cups. The detective glanced up as she slid into the opposite seat. 'Your coffee's getting cold.'

The best thing about Anne-Marie was that she'd known S. Barrett Delaney when S. Barrett Delaney was still Sue, yet she never called her that. They'd gone to school together at Our Lady of Perpetual Sorrow in Concord. Anne-Marie had decided to try law enforcement, Barrie settled for law.

'So,' Barrie said, simultaneously opening the lid on her coffee and the manila file that housed the police statements, the autopsy report on Emily Gold, and Anne-Marie's notes on Chris Harte. 'This is everything?'

'Everything so far,' Anne-Marie said. She took a sip of her own coffee. 'I think you've got a case.'

'We've always got a case,' Barrie muttered, engrossed in the evidence. 'The question is, do we have a good one?' She read the first few lines of the autopsy report, then hunched forward, her hands twisting the gold cross around her neck. 'Tell me what you know,' she said.

'Officers were called in at the sound of a gunshot. They found the girl unresponsive, three shades shy of dead. Boy was shocky and bleeding profusely from a head wound.'

'Where was the gun?'

'On the carousel where they were sitting. Some alcohol was found too, a bottle of Canadian Club. One bullet had been fired, one was still in the revolver; ballistics matched the bullet with the gun, and we don't have the fingerprints back yet.' She blotted her lips with a napkin. 'When I interviewed the boy—'

'Before which,' Barrie interrupted, 'you of course read him his rights . . .'

'Well, actually . . .' Anne-Marie grimaced. 'Not line for line. But I had to get in there, Barrie. He was fresh out of the ER and his parents didn't want me around at all.'

'Go on,' Barrie prompted. She listened as Anne-Marie finished her story, then sat silently for a moment. She picked up the remaining pages in the file and scanned them, occasionally murmuring. 'Okay,' she said. 'This is what I think.' She looked up at her friend. 'To make a murder-one charge stick, we've got to find premeditation, willfulness, and deliberation. Was this a deliberate act? Yes, or he wouldn't have taken the gun from his house – you don't carry an antique Colt around like a spare set of keys. Did he think about killing the girl, even for a minute? Obviously, since he'd carried the gun from his house hours before. Was it a willful act? Assuming his intent the whole time was to kill the girl, then yes, he carried through with his plan.'

Anne-Marie pursed her lips. 'His alibi is that it was a double suicide that got botched up before he had his turn.'

'Well, that tells us he's smart enough to think on his feet. Nice explanation; he just forgot what the forensic evidence would show.'

'What do you think about a charge of sexual assault?'

Barrie flipped through the detective's notes. 'I doubt it. Number one, she's pregnant, so they've had sex before. And if they've been having sex for a while, it'll be hard to make a rape charge stick. We can still use the evidence as signs of a struggle.' She glanced up. 'I need you to question him again.'

'Ten to one, he'll have a lawyer.'

'See what you can get,' Barrie urged. 'If he won't talk, try family and neighbors. I don't want to run off half cocked. We need to know if he realized the girl was pregnant. We need background on the relationship between the kids – is there a pattern of abuse between them? And we need to find out whether or not Emily Gold was suicidal.'

Anne-Marie, who had been scribbling in her own notepad, looked up. 'While I'm working my butt off, what are you going to do?'

Barrie grinned. 'Take this to a grand jury.'

The instant Melanie opened the door, Gus thrust her hand through it, holding the can of pitted black olives. 'I didn't have a branch,' she said, as Melanie tried to slam it shut again. Determined, Gus wedged her shoulder through the narrow space, then the rest of herself, so that she was standing opposite from Melanie in the kitchen. 'Please,' she said quietly. 'I know you're hurting. So am I. And it's killing me that we can't hurt together.'

Melanie's arms were crossed so tightly that Gus thought she looked in danger of squeezing herself in two. 'I have nothing to say to you,' she stiffly replied.

'Mel, my God, I'm sorry,' Gus said, her eyes shining with tears. 'I'm sorry that this happened, I'm sorry that you feel this way, I'm sorry that I don't know the right thing to say or do.'

'The right thing,' Melanie said, 'is to leave.'

'Mel,' Gus said, reaching out for her.

Melanie actually shuddered. 'Don't touch me,' she said, her voice vibrating.

Gus recoiled, shocked. 'I . . . I'm sorry. I'll come back tomorrow.'

'I don't want you to come back tomorrow. I don't want you ever to come back.' Melanie took a deep breath. 'Your son,' she said, crisply biting off each word, 'killed my daughter.'

Gus felt something small and hot spark beneath her ribs, fanning itself, spreading. 'Chris told you, and the police, that they were going to commit suicide. Now, granted, I didn't know they were . . . well, you know. But if Chris says it, I believe it.'

'You would,' Melanie said.

Gus narrowed her eyes. 'Listen,' she said. 'It isn't like Chris walked out of this fine and dandy. He had seventy stitches, and he spent three days in a psychiatric ward. He told the police what happened when he was still in shock. What reason could he possibly have had to lie?'

Melanie laughed outright. 'Do you hear yourself, Gus? What reason could he have to lie?'

'You just don't want to believe your daughter could have been suicidal without your knowing it,' Gus shot back. 'Not when you two had the perfect relationship.'

Melanie shook her head. 'As opposed to you? You can handle being the mother of a suicide risk. But you can't possibly accept being the mother of a murderer.'

Gus had so many comebacks, so many indignant responses, that they blistered the back of her throat. Convinced they would burn her alive, she pushed past Melanie and out the kitchen door. She ran home gulping cold draughts of air, and tried to push from her mind the knowledge that Melanie would consider her flight a surrender.

'I feel stupid,' Chris said. His knees were up to his chin in the tiny wheelchair, but it was the only way the hospital would let him off the grounds. In this dumb invalid contraption, and with a piece of paper printed with the name of the psychiatrist he would now be seeing twice a week.

'It's for liability reasons,' his mother said, as if he cared, and walked into the elevator beside the orderly who was pushing him. 'Besides, you'll be out in five minutes.'

'Five minutes too long,' Chris grumbled, and his mother rested her hand on his head.

'I think,' she said, 'you're already feeling better.'

His mother started chattering about what they were having for dinner, and who had called to ask about him, and did he think it was going to snow before Thanksgiving this year. He gritted his teeth, just trying to block her out. What he wanted to say was *Stop trying to act like nothing happened. Because something did, and you can't make it go back to being the same*.

Instead, he looked up when she touched his face, and he forced a smile.

She slipped an arm around his waist as the orderly dumped them out at the lobby. 'Thank you,' she said to the man, and headed for the sliding glass doors with Chris.

Outside, the air was wonderful. It snaked into his lungs, bigger and fresher than the air in the hospital. 'I'm going to get the car,' his mother said, while Chris leaned against the brick of the hospital. Past the highway he saw the gray knobs of the mountains, and he closed his eyes for a minute, memorizing them.

At the sound of his name he blinked. Detective Marrone was standing there, blocking that beautiful view. 'Chris,' she repeated, 'I wonder if you'd be willing to come down to the station.'

He wasn't under arrest, but his parents had been against it anyway. 'I'm only going to tell her the truth,' Chris had assured them, but his mother had just about fainted anyway and his father had run off to find a lawyer who would meet them at the station. Detective Marrone had pointed out that at seventeen, Chris could call his own shots in terms of legal representation, and he had to give her credit for that. He followed her down the narrow corridor of the police station to a small conference room with a tape recorder on the table.

She read him his Miranda rights, which he recognized from his Government course, and turned on the tape recorder. 'Chris,' she said, 'I'd like you to tell me in as much detail as possible what happened the night of November seventh.'

Chris folded his hands on the table and cleared his throat. 'Emily and I had talked at school, and we decided I'd pick her up at seven-thirty.'

'You have your own car?'

'Yeah. It was, you know, there when the cops came. A green Jeep.'

Detective Marrone nodded. 'Go on.'

'We had brought along something to drink—'

'Something?'

'Alcohol.'

'We?'

'*I* had brought it.'

'Why?'

Chris shifted. Maybe he shouldn't have been answering all these questions. As if Detective Marrone realized she was pushing too hard, she asked something else. 'Did you know then that Emily wanted to kill herself?'

'Yes,' Chris said. 'She had a plan worked out.'

'Tell me about this plan,' Detective Marrone pressed. 'Was it a Romeo and Juliet kind of thing?'

'No,' Chris said. 'It was just what Emily wanted.'

'She wanted to kill herself.'

'Yes,' Chris answered.

'And then what?'

'Then,' he said, 'I was going to kill myself.'

'What time did you pick her up?'

'Seven-thirty,' Chris replied. 'I already said that.'

'Right. And did Emily tell anyone else she was going to kill herself?'

Chris shrugged. 'I don't think so.'

'Did you?'

'No.'

The detective crossed her legs. 'Why not?'

Chris stared into his lap. 'Emily already knew. I didn't care if anyone else did.'

'And what did she tell you?'

He began to trace a pattern on the table with the nail of his thumb. 'She kept saying she wanted to keep things exactly the way they were, and that she wished she could stop everything from changing. She got really nervous, like, talking about the future. She once told me that she could see herself now, and she could also see the kind of life she wanted to have – kids, husband, suburbs, you know – but she couldn't figure out how to get from point A to point B.'

'Is that how you felt, too?'

'Sometimes,' Chris said softly. 'Especially when I thought about her dying.' He bit his bottom lip. 'Something was hurting Em,' he said. 'Something that she couldn't even tell me. Every now and then when we . . . when we . . .' His throat closed, and he looked away. 'Could I have a minute?'

The detective dispassionately shut off the recorder. When Chris nodded, red-eyed, she hit the button again. 'Did you try to talk her out of it?'

'Yeah,' Chris said. 'A million times.'

'That night?'

'And before.'

'Where did you go that night?'

'To the carousel. The one by the old fairground that's a kid's park now. I used to work there.'

'You chose the place?'

'Emily picked it.'

'What time did you arrive?'

'About eight,' Chris said.

'After you stopped for dinner?'

'We didn't have dinner together,' Chris said. 'We ate at home.'

'What did you do next?'

Chris exhaled slowly. 'I got out of the car and opened Em's

door. We carried the bottle of Canadian Club over to the carousel and sat down on one of the benches.'

'Did you have sexual intercourse with Emily that night?'

Chris's eyes narrowed. 'I don't think that's any of your business.'

'All of this,' Detective Marrone said, 'is my business. Did you?'

Chris nodded, and the detective gestured toward the tape recorder. 'We did,' he said quietly.

'And this was a consensual act?'

'Yes,' Chris ground out, his jaw tight.

'You're certain?'

Chris flattened his palms on the table. 'I was there,' he said.

'Did you show her the gun before or after having sex?'

'I don't remember. After, I guess.'

'But she knew you were bringing it?'

'It was her idea,' Chris said.

The detective nodded. 'And was there a specific reason you took Emily to the carousel to kill herself?'

Chris frowned. 'Emily wanted to go there,' he said.

'It was Emily's choice?'

'Yeah,' Chris answered. 'We talked in circles about it before finally agreeing.'

'Why the carousel?'

'Emily always liked it,' Chris said. 'I guess I did too.'

'So,' Anne-Marie said. 'You sat down on the carousel, had a drink, watched the sun go down, had sex . . .'

Chris hesitated, then reached over and shut off the tape recorder. 'The sun had already gone down. It was eight o'clock,' he said quietly. 'I told you that.' He looked the detective in the eye. 'Don't you believe what I'm telling you?'

Anne-Marie flipped open the recorder and ejected the tape without ever glancing away from Chris. 'Should I?' she asked.

On Tuesday afternoon, despite everyone's protestations, Melanie went back to work. It was a story-hour day, so the library was crowded with young mothers stuffing children into various stages of winter dress, but as Melanie walked in, they fell back in a hush, allowing her a clear path toward the staff room at the back. As she hung up her coat she wondered whether the news of Emily's death had truly traveled so fast, or whether instinct had somehow kicked in – some scent wafting from Melanie's skin or some disturbance of the electricity around her that warned other mothers: *Here is a parent who couldn't keep her child safe.*

'Melanie,' a voice gasped, and she turned around to find Rose, her second-in-command, standing behind her. 'No one expected you to come in.'

'I've been coming in for seventeen years,' Melanie said quietly. 'This is the place I felt most comfortable.'

'Well. Yes.' Rose didn't seem to know what to say. 'How are you holding up, honey?'

Melanie drew back. 'I'm here,' she said, 'aren't I?'

She walked to the front desk, settling into the head librarian's chair with some trepidation – what if this, too, had suddenly become unfamiliar? But no, it was just as it had always been, curved nearly to the conformation of her bottom, that annoying metal thing jamming up beneath her right thigh. She spread her hands on the counter and waited.

All it would take was one patron with a query, and she would be healed. She would be useful again.

She smiled benignly at two young student types, who nodded and passed her on the way to the periodical room. She slipped off her pumps, rubbed her stocking feet against the cold chrome legs of the swivel chair, and put her shoes on again. She typed in query words on her computer search screen, just to practice: *Salem Witch Trials. Malachite. Elizabeth Regina.*

'Pardon me.'

Melanie's head snapped forward to find a woman close to her own age on the other side of the reference desk. 'Yes. Can I help you?'

'God, I hope so,' the woman exhaled. 'I'm trying to find as

much as I can on Atalanta.' She hesitated. 'The Greek runner,' she clarified. 'Not the city in Georgia.'

Melanie smiled. 'I know.' Her fingers began flying over the keys, her body overrun with a giddiness not unlike a nicotine high. 'Atalanta would be with the Greek myths. The call number is—'

Melanie knew it firsthand: 292. But before she could say it the woman rolled her eyes, relieved. 'Thank God,' she said. 'My daughter is doing a social studies report, and we couldn't find information in the Orford Library. Atlas? Three books. But Atalanta . . .'

My daughter. Melanie looked at the list of books pulled up by her computer that were available right around the corner. She opened her mouth to give her the information, and heard instead a voice that surely could not have been her own. 'Check nonfiction,' Melanie said. 'Call number 641.5.'

It was the cookbook section.

The woman thanked her profusely, and set off to look in the wrong place.

Melanie felt something tussle and free inside of her, an embolism formed Friday night that – now dislodged – could slowly poison her system. She hugged her arms about herself, trying to keep close this mean-spiritedness. A man approached, asking her recommendation for a recent novel. He told her he liked Clancy, Cussler, Crichton, that he wanted to try someone new. 'By all means,' Melanie told him. 'The latest Robert James Waller.'

She sent college students off to the stacks of the children's room; historians to the self-help sections; videotape borrowers to the Fodor's travel guides. When one young man asked the way to the bathroom, she directed him to the closet where they stored books out of circulation. And all the while Melanie smiled, finding that doling out frustration and misery was far more gratifying than passing information had ever been.

Jordan McAfee, the defense attorney recommended by Gary

Moorhouse, sat at the Hartes' kitchen table, a sullen Chris to his right, Gus just behind. He had come directly from his health club and was wearing shorts and a rumpled henley shirt; his cheeks were flushed and a trickle of perspiration ran down his temple.

James was a big believer in first impressions. Granted, it was eight o'clock at night . . . but *still*. The lack of a suit; the spiky wet hair; the beads of sweat – Jordan McAfee might have merely been overheated, but to James he only seemed nervous. James was unable to imagine the man as anyone's white knight, much less his own son's.

'Now,' Jordan McAfee said, 'Chris already told me what he said to Detective Marrone. Because he went voluntarily, and because she did read him his rights, anything he said can be used against him. However, if it comes to this, I'll fight to have the hospital conversation made inadmissible.' He looked up at James. 'I'm sure you've got questions. Why don't we start there?'

How many cases, James wanted to ask, *have you won? How do I know you'll save my son*? But instead he swallowed his doubts. Moorhouse had said that McAfee was a legal star, Law Review at Harvard, sought after by every firm east of the Mississippi when he decided to join the New Hampshire attorney general's office instead. After ten years, he'd defected to the defense side. He was known for his charm, his quick mind, and his equally quick temper. James wondered if McAfee had any children of his own.

'What are the chances that there will be a trial?'

McAfee scratched his jaw. 'Chris hasn't formerly been named as a suspect, but he's been questioned twice. Any police case of this nature is going to be treated as a homicide. And Chris's alibi notwithstanding, if the AG's office feels there's enough to run with, they'll get an indictment handed down.' He looked James in the eye. 'I'd say there's a very good chance.'

Gus gasped. 'What happens then? He's seventeen.'

'Mom—'

'He'll be tried as an adult in the state of New Hampshire.'

'Which means?' James asked.

'If he's taken into custody, there'll be an arraignment within twenty-four hours, and we'll enter a plea and post bail, if necessary. Then a court date will be set.'

'You mean he'll be held in a jail overnight?'

'Most likely,' McAfee said.

'But that's not fair!' Gus exclaimed. 'Just because the attorney general says there was a murder, we have to play by his rules? There wasn't a murder. There was a suicide. That's not something you go to jail for.'

'There are whole books full of cases, Mrs Harte,' McAfee said, 'where the prosecution takes a running leap and finds out too late that the swimming hole was empty. Chris and Emily are the only two people who can say what truly happened. Bottom line? Emily can't give her version, and the State of New Hampshire has no reason to trust your son. All they see, right now, is a dead teenage girl and a bullet fired. They don't know the history behind these kids, the relationship they had, their states of mind. The case is going to be won, frankly, on its heart. I can tell you now that the AG is going to produce an autopsy report and read into it anything he can. I can tell you he'll make a production out of the fact that Chris's fingerprints were on the gun. As for what else he thinks he's got . . . well, I'm going to have to talk to Chris at length.'

Gus pulled up a chair.

'Alone,' McAfee added. He smiled tightly. 'You may be paying the retainer,' he said, 'but he's my client.'

'Congratulations, Dr Harte,' the receptionist said on Wednesday morning.

For a moment, James stared at her. What the hell could she be applauding him for? When he'd left the house this morning, Chris had still been sitting on the couch where James had left him the night before, staring blankly at the same Spanish-language television channel. Gus had been in the kitchen, making a breakfast that James could have told her Chris would not eat. There was not much in his life, right now, that could call for congratulations.

A colleague clapped him on the back as he made his way to his office. 'Always knew it would happen to one of us,' he said, grinning, and walked off.

James entered his small consultation room and closed the door behind him before anyone else could say something bizarre. Sitting on his desk was the mail he'd not had a chance to pore over since Friday. But open, on top of the stack, was the *New England Journal of Medicine*. Their annual report listing the best doctors, by field, was splayed over several pages. And under ophthalmological surgery, circled in red, was James's name.

'Holy cow,' he said, a smile starting somewhere in the region of his heart and spreading outward. He picked up the phone and dialed home, wanting to share the news with Gus, but there was no answer. He glanced up at his Harvard diplomas, considering how the award would look laminated.

Feeling much lighter in spirit, James hung up his coat and trekked through the corridors, in search of his first patient. If any of the staff knew about Chris's stay over the weekend, they did not mention it; or maybe the *NEJM* honor had supplanted the less savory rumor. He stopped at an examination room, pulling the file and flipping through the history of Mrs Edna Neely.

'Mrs Neely,' he said, swinging open the door. 'How are you doing?'

'No better, or I would have canceled the appointment,' the elderly woman said.

'Let's see if we can fix that,' he said. 'Now, you remember, what I said last week about macular degeneration?'

'Doctor,' she said, 'I'm here for eye problems. Not senility.'

'Of course,' James answered smoothly. 'Let's get this angiogram out of the way, then.' He directed Mrs Neely to a big camera and seated her in front of it. Then he took the hypodermic of fluorescein and injected it into Mrs Neely's arm. 'You might feel a burning sensation in your arm. The dye is what we're looking for,' he said. 'It will travel from your vein to your heart, and then around the body, eventually getting up to the eye. The dye stays in normal blood vessels, but will ooze out of the abnormal, hemorrhaging ones that caused your macular degeneration. We'll figure out where they are, exactly, and treat them.'

It took twelve seconds, James knew, for the dye to travel from the arm to the heart to the eye. The light, in the back of the eye, illuminated the fluorescent dye. Like the tributaries of a river, the normal blood vessels of Mrs Neely's retina branched out in fine, tentative lines. The abnormal vessels were sunbursts, minuscule fireworks, which softened into puddles of white dye.

After ten minutes, when all the dye was gone, James turned off the camera. 'All right, Mrs Neely,' he said, hunkering down to her level. 'Now we know where to guide the laser treatment.'

'What's that going to do to me?'

'Well, we hope it will stabilize the damaged retina. AMD is a serious problem, but there's a chance we can save some vision, although it might not be as good as it was before you noticed the disturbance.'

'I'm going to go blind?'

'No,' he promised. 'That won't happen. You may lose some central vision – the kind you use for reading, or driving – but you'll be able to walk around, shower, cook.'

He waited a moment, and then Mrs Neely gifted him with a lovely smile. 'I heard them talking in the waiting room, Dr Harte. They said you're one of the best.' She reached across the small space that separated them and patted his hand. 'You'll take care of me.'

James stared into her dilated, distorted eye. He nodded, suddenly drained of all his earlier enthusiasm. This accolade was not an honor, it was a mistake. Because James knew first-hand what it had been like for Mrs Neely to sit down one evening and realize the door was not the same shape it had been minutes ago, the newspaper was not printed as clearly, the world was not the way she remembered it. The panel at the *New England Journal of Medicine* would rescind the award when they learned about his suicidal son, on trial for murder. Surely you did not pay homage to a vision specialist who had not seen this coming.

'You promised,' Chris said heatedly. 'You said the day I got out. And it's already a whole day past that.'

Gus sighed. 'I know what I said, sweetheart. I just don't know if it's such a good idea.'

Chris jumped up from the kitchen chair. 'You already stopped me once from going to her,' he said. 'Have you got a sedative in the fridge, Mom? Because that's the only way you're going to do it again.' He came so close his words spat against her cheek. 'I'm bigger than you,' he said softly. 'And I'll get by you if I want to. I'll walk the whole way if I have to.'

Gus closed her eyes. 'No,' she said. 'All right.'

'All right?'

'I'll take you.'

They drove in silence to the cemetery. It was actually within walking distance of the high school; Gus remembered Chris telling her that some kids liked to come there during free periods to do their homework and their reading. Chris got out of the car. At first, Gus looked away, pretending to read a gum wrapper trapped in the fold of the passenger seat. But then she could not help herself. She watched Chris kneel down beside the rectangular mound, covered with its profusion of still-fresh flowers. She saw him run a finger over the chilled lips of roses, the hawked throat of an orchid.

He stood up far more quickly than she imagined he would and came back to the car. But he went to her window and knocked for her to roll it down. 'How come,' he asked, 'there's no gravestone?'

Gus looked at the freshly turned earth. 'It's too soon,' she said. 'But I think in the Jewish faith, it's different anyway. It doesn't go up for six months or so.'

Chris nodded and stuffed his hands in the pockets of his coat. 'Which way is the top?' he asked.

Gus looked at him dumbly. 'What do you mean?'

'The head,' he explained. 'Which end is Emily's head at?'

Shocked, Gus glanced wildly around the cemetery. The plots were not straight, but fairly haphazard. However, the predominant number of head-stones were facing a certain way. 'I guess the far end,' she said. 'I'm not sure.'

Chris walked away to kneel at the grave again, and Gus thought, *Ah, of course. He wants to talk to her.* But to her amazement Chris straddled the slight mound and lay down on top of it, his arms holding close the flower arrangements he was crushing, his head and shoes just spanning the six feet, his face pressed into the earth. Then he stood up, dry-eyed, and walked back to the Volvo. Gus put it in gear and continued along the cemetery road, shaking with the effort not to look at her son, whose mouth was ringed with a lipstick of soil as branding as any kiss.

Then

December 1993

Chris rode up to Sugarloaf in Emily's parents' car because they wanted to hook together their Game Boys and have a Tetris marathon. They were going skiing for Christmas, renting a condo with Em's family. Aerosmith blared from the tape deck, the speakers in the front turned down low. 'Jeez,' Chris laughed, his thumbs pounding the miniature computer. 'You are so cheating.'

Huddled against her side of the seat, Emily snorted. 'You are so lying.'

'Am not,' Chris said.

'Are too.'

'Oh, right.'

'Whatever.'

Driving, Michael glanced at his wife. 'This,' he said, 'is why we never had another kid.'

Melanie smiled and looked out the windshield at the tail-lights of the Hartes' car. 'Do you think they're listening to Dvorak and eating Brie?'

'No,' Chris said, glancing up. 'If Kate's getting her way, they're probably singing "One Hundred Bottles of Beer on the Wall."' He turned back to the small screen. 'Hey,' he said. 'That's not fair.'

'You shouldn't have answered my parents,' Emily said sweetly. 'I win.'

Chris flushed. 'What's the point of playing if you're going to do that?'

'It was a fair game!'

'Fair my butt,' Chris shouted.

'Hey,' Melanie and Michael said simultaneously.

'Sorry,' Chris sulked. Emily folded her arms across her chest, smiling faintly. Chris turned toward the window and scowled. So what if Emily could beat him at Tetris? It was a stupid game, anyway, for total geeks. He'd show her this weekend. He could ski circles around her.

That made him feel better. Charitably, he held out the Game Boy. 'Want to play another round?'

Emily stuck her nose up in the air and shifted so that she wouldn't have to see him.

'God,' Chris said. 'Now what.'

'You owe me an apology,' Emily said.

'What for?'

She turned hot, dark eyes on him. 'You said I cheat. I don't cheat.'

'Fine, you don't cheat. Let's play.'

'I don't think so,' Emily huffed. 'You have to say it like you mean it.'

Chris narrowed his eyes, and threw down the Game Boy like a gauntlet. Fuck the Tetris game, fuck the apology, fuck Emily. He didn't know why he'd let her talk him into riding in her car, anyway. She could be a lot of fun, sure. Then again, sometimes he wanted to kill her.

Chris's mom was so annoyed that his father had decided to go hunting with a man he'd met on the chair lift, of all places, that she did not speak to him all Christmas Eve morning, while he was getting ready to leave.

'But he brought his beagle,' his father tried to explain. What was the chance of meeting a guy on the chair lift who had carried along spare shotguns and his hunting dog, just for a foray through the Maine woods? And was it his father's fault that when Chris heard about it, he asked if he could go?

'What are we looking for?' Chris asked, all but bouncing in the passenger seat. 'Moose?'

'Not the right season,' his father said. 'Probably pheasant.'

But when they met Hank Myers at the end of an unmarked road in the middle of nowhere, the man said it was a good day for rabbit.

Hank was happy to meet Chris, and handed him a 12-gauge shotgun. The three men tramped into the heavy cover of the woods, with Hank's dog, Lucy, sniffing out the brush piles. They moved in the way of hunters, soft and alert, silence chaining their movements as if they were marionettes.

Chris kept his eyes trained on the snow, trying to see the strange five-footed pattern of a hare print, the final indentation made by a dragging tail. It was blinding, white on white. After an hour his feet were freezing; his nose was running; and he couldn't feel his earlobes where they stuck out from beneath his hat. Even skiing with Em wasn't as boring as this.

Who ever heard of eating hare stew on Christmas Eve, anyway?

Suddenly Lucy pounced. Beneath a tangle of branches Chris saw a flat-footed white hare with a black patch eye take off at a dead run.

Chris immediately raised his gun and sighted out the hare, which was moving so goddamned fast he didn't see how anyone ever shot one of the things. Lucy was still on its scent, but quite a ways behind. Chris suddenly felt a hand pushing down the barrel of the shotgun. Hank Myers smiled at him. 'Don't need to do that,' he said. 'Thing about hares is, they run in a circle. Lucy won't catch up, but that's okay. She'll run the hare back to where it started.'

Sure enough, as Chris waited, the dog's barks grew softer and more distant . . . then started coming toward them again. Out of nowhere the snowshoe hare burst back into the perimeter of his vision, scrambling for the pile of brush where it had been flushed out.

Chris raised his shotgun, sighted the flying hare, and pulled the trigger.

The recoil jerked him backward; he felt his father's hand steady his shoulder. 'You got him!' Hank Myers crowed, and

Lucy leaped over a stump to sniff at the catch, her tail wagging wide as a flag.

Hank stomped toward the kill, grinning. 'Hell of a shot,' he said. 'Blew it clean apart.' He lifted the animal by its ears and held it out to Chris. 'Not much left of him, but that's neither here nor there.'

Chris had killed deer; he would have enjoyed hunting moose or elk or bear. But he took one look at the hare and felt sick. He did not know if it was the contrast of the white snow with the bright blood, or the small stuffed-toy body of the hare itself, or the fact that this was the first time he'd preyed on something smaller and more defenseless than himself – but he turned to his side and threw up.

He heard his father swear under his breath. Chris wiped his mouth on his jacket and lifted his head. 'Sorry,' he said, tasting his own disgust.

Hank Myers spat in the snow and glanced at James. 'Thought you said he hunted with you regularly.'

James nodded, his mouth a tight line. 'He does.'

Chris did not look at his father. He knew he would see the veiled mix of anger and embarrassment that came when a situation turned out in any way differently from what James had expected it to be. 'I'll clean it,' he said, holding out his hands for the hare, trying to save face.

Hank started to give him the animal, and then realized Chris was wearing his ski parka. 'How about you and me trade coats?' he said, huffing in the cold as he shrugged out of his hunting jacket. Chris quickly slipped into the other man's coat, then lifted the hare and slid it into the rubber pouch in the back of the jacket. He could still feel the hare's body heat.

He walked beside his father in silence, afraid of saying anything and afraid of not saying anything at all, thinking of the hare that had circled home, expecting safety.

Gus slid her hand beneath the waist of her husband's boxers. 'Not a creature was stirring,' she whispered. 'Not even a mouse.'

She rolled on top of him, her hand working between his legs. 'Seems I found a creature after all.' James grinned, breaking apart her kiss. He did not understand his good fortune, but Gus had given up her anger by the time he and Chris had returned home from hunting. Which was a good thing, given how abysmal an experience it had been. He felt Gus's fingers squeeze his testicles. 'Now,' she murmured, 'is not a good time to laugh at me.'

'I wasn't laughing. I was just thinking.'

Gus raised a brow. 'About what?'

James laughed. 'Santa Claus coming,' he said.

Gus snickered and sat up, unbuttoning her nightgown in a slow, sweet striptease. 'What do you think,' she said, 'about unwrapping one of your presents tonight?'

'That depends,' James said. 'Is it a big one?'

'Say yes, buster, and it's the only present you're getting,' Gus warned, tossing her nightgown off the bed.

James pulled her on top of him, running his hands over her back and buttocks. 'How about that,' he murmured. 'It's just my size.'

'Good,' Gus gasped, as his fingers moved between her legs. 'Because I wouldn't know where to return it.'

James felt her legs clench around his hips and her body open for him. They rolled on the bed so that James was above her, locked their hands palm to palm. He eased inside her and pressed his mouth hard against her collarbone, afraid of what he might say or shout when he lost himself.

When it was over, Gus dissolved beneath him, her breath labored and her skin damp. James gathered her close, tucked her head beneath his. 'I think,' he said, 'I must have been very good this year.'

He felt Gus whisper a kiss on his chest. 'You were,' she murmured.

'You won't believe this,' Michael said, 'but I heard hoofbeats on the roof.'

Melanie paused in the act of setting her glasses on the night-stand. 'You've got to be kidding.'

'I'm not,' Michael insisted. 'While you were in the shower.'

'Hoofbeats?'

'As in reindeer.'

She laughed out loud. 'I suppose Santa's hiding in the closet.'

Michael scowled. 'I'm serious. Wait – listen to that. What does it sound like to you?'

Melanie tipped her head, hearing what indeed sounded like the scrape and pound of something on a solid surface. Her eye shot toward the ceiling, and then she frowned and turned toward the wall that the headboard rested against. She pressed her ear against the Sheetrock. 'You hear Gus and James,' she announced.

'Gus and—'

Melanie nodded, and smacked the headboard against the wall, so that Michael would understand. 'Reindeer, my foot.'

Michael grinned. 'Gus and James?' he said.

Melanie flipped back the covers and got into bed. 'Who else would be in there?'

'I know. But James?'

Melanie shut off the lamp beside the bed. She crossed her arms over her chest, her ears now straining for the next thump and cry on the other side of the wall. 'What's the matter with James?'

'Oh, I don't know. Isn't it easier for you to imagine Gus doing that, rather than James?'

Melanie frowned. 'I don't usually think about either of them doing it.' She raised her eyebrows. 'Do you?'

Michael blushed. 'Well, sure. It's crossed my mind once or twice.'

'Such lofty pursuits.'

'Oh, come on,' Michael laughed. 'I bet they've thought about us.' In one swift move, he rolled toward her. 'We could give them something to listen to,' he suggested.

Melanie was horrified. 'Absolutely not!'

They both settled back on their respective pillows. Through the thin wall came a low, sweet keen. Michael laughed and turned onto his side. Long after he'd fallen asleep, Melanie found herself still listening to her neighbors' lovemaking, trying to imagine those moans rolling from her own throat.

Chris could remember Christmas Eves when it was impossible to sleep, thinking of the race car under the tree, the train set, the new bike. It was a good feeling, insomnia fueled by excitement. Not at all what he was feeling now.

Every time he closed his eyes, he saw the dead hare.

Chris thought of what his father sometimes said when he was haunted by a really bad day at the hospital: What he needed was a good, stiff drink.

He waited until his parents finished playing Santa – pretty stupid, considering that Kate didn't even believe anymore – and then crept downstairs to the condo's kitchen. He knew there was a bottle of Sambuca in the freezer. His father and Emily's had done shots over a couple of good cigars the other night. It was still three quarters full.

Chris found a juice glass in the cabinet and filled it to the brim. He sniffed the alcohol – it reminded him of licorice – and took a sip. Fire ran down his throat, to his belly. *Hare*, he thought, grinning. *What hare?*

By the time he'd finished half the glass, he couldn't feel his toes or the tips of his fingers. The kitchen was pleasantly fuzzy. By now the bottle was less than half full, and Chris tipped it on its side to watch the alcohol shimmy and run. *Maybe they'll think Santa drank it*, he thought. *To hell with the cookies and milk.* He found this hilarious, suddenly, and started to laugh, and that was when he noticed Emily standing in the doorway of the kitchen.

She was wearing a flannel nightgown that had tiny penguins printed on it; at least he thought they were penguins. 'What are you doing?' she asked.

Chris smiled. 'What does it look like I'm doing?'

Emily didn't answer, just came closer and sniffed at the

bottle of Sambuca. 'Eww.' She wrinkled her nose, holding it away. 'This is disgusting.'

'This,' Chris corrected, 'is heaven.' He wondered if Emily had ever had hard liquor. As far as he knew, she hadn't. He entertained the thought of himself as purveyor of evil, and leaned forward, offering her the glass. 'Taste it. It's like the candy you get at the movie theatre.'

'Good and Plentys?'

Chris nodded. 'Just like.'

Emily hesitated, but her hand closed over the glass. 'I don't know,' she said.

'Chicken.'

Chris knew that was all it would take. Emily's eyes gleamed in the moonlight and her fingers flexed on the juice glass. She tipped it to her lips, upending it before Chris could warn her to taste just a little at a time.

She started coughing violently, her chest hitching and her mouthful of Sambuca sputtering across the kitchen table. Her eyes went wide, and her hands clutched at her throat. 'Jesus,' Chris said, whacking her on the back.

Finally Emily managed to draw a breath. 'Oh, my God,' she wheezed. 'That stuff . . .'

'. . . is not for your consumption.' Chris and Emily both jerked their heads up to find both sets of their parents crowded into the doorway of the kitchen, in various states of undress. James narrowed his eyes and stepped forward. 'Would you mind telling me what you're doing?'

Chris never did find out why Emily said what she did that night. In the past, when they'd been caught in various scrapes, they'd always stuck by each other – solidarity was the root of their friendship. But this time, beneath his father's furious glare, Emily buckled. 'It was Chris,' she said, pointing a shaking finger. 'He made me try it.'

Dumbfounded, Chris sat back in his chair. 'I made you?' he exclaimed. 'I made you? I held the glass up to your lips and poured it down?'

Emily's mouth silently opened and closed, like a fish's.

'More to the point,' his father said, 'why are you sitting here drinking alcohol, period?'

Chris started to explain. But when he looked into his father's eyes, he saw that hare again with its stomach blown apart, and the words he wanted to use could not push past the regret lodged in his throat. He shook his head, and that one movement brought him back to the woods with a smoking shotgun in his hand, staring down at the blood in the snow.

He covered his mouth and bolted toward the bathroom, but not before he saw Emily lower her eyes and turn away.

It was not a Merry Christmas.

Chris spent the morning alone in his room at the condo, sitting on the bed while he heard the strained voices of everyone else downstairs opening presents. The only person who actually seemed to be having a good time was Kate, who'd slept through the whole debacle the night before.

He wondered what they were going to do with his presents. Return them; give them to Goodwill? He doubted he'd ever see them, which truly sucked because he had a pretty good idea that he was getting a pair of new skis he could have used that very day. Chris flopped face down on his bed and tried to convince himself his old skis were fine just the same.

Just after three, his mother came into the room. She was wearing her ski bib and her goggles were looped around her neck. Seeing her, Chris felt a pang of envy. For all he'd been sick of skiing yesterday, he would have given anything to have stayed on the slopes, instead of hunting for that stupid hare.

Gus laid a hand on his arm. 'Hi,' she said. 'Merry Christmas.'

'Whatever,' Chris said, rolling away from her.

'Your father and I decided that if you want, you can go out skiing for the rest of the day.'

'The rest of the day' translated to, like, all of an hour. Chris noticed his mother hadn't mentioned any presents. 'Emily's here,' she said softly. 'She didn't want to ski without you.'

As *if I give a flying fuck*, Chris thought, but instead he only snorted. He watched his mother leave the room, and then he noticed Emily cowering in the doorway. 'Hi,' she said. 'How are you doing?'

'Peachy,' Chris grumbled.

'You, uh, want to come with me?'

He didn't; he wouldn't have crawled in a lifeboat with her if their ship was sinking. It didn't matter that she had been frightened last night, and sick probably from the one sip she'd taken; it didn't matter that Chris had never had a chance to tell her why he was drinking in the first place. Emily had become a traitor, and he couldn't forgive that so quickly.

'I went down Black Adder by myself,' she said.

At that, Chris looked up. Black Adder was one of the toughest runs Sugarloaf had, full of twists and dropoffs and curves that came out of nowhere. He'd gone down a few times but always slowly, since he had to wait for Emily to get over her fear and ski a little ways before she got terrified again. If Emily had gone down alone, it had probably taken her two hours.

Suddenly something unfurled in the center of Chris's chest. He could get back at Emily for last night, and so easily. She was feeling guilty – that was clear enough – she'd be willing to jump through whatever hoop he asked. He'd take her down a run tougher than Black Adder, one that would have her shaking in her boots by the time she reached the bottom.

Chris let a smile stripe his dark mood. 'Well,' he said, standing up. 'What are we waiting for?'

Emily shivered like an aspen leaf at the dropoff point of Sugarloaf's highest lift, holding her poles in front of her like a barrier between the steep ski run and herself. 'Em,' Chris yelled impatiently over the wind, 'come on.'

She bit her lip and pushed off, snowplowing to keep down her speed. But the curve was too sharp and she wound up in a tangle of arms and legs and skis just behind Chris. 'That sucked,' she breathed.

Chris smiled nastily. 'That's the easiest part,' he said.

She was seriously considering taking off her skis and walking down the mountain at this point, but she wanted to get back in Chris's good graces. After all, it was her fault that Chris had spent the morning in his room. If Chris was being charitable enough to let her ski with him, then she'd ski upside down, if that's what he wanted.

She watched Chris wind down the hill, his hips rolling from side to side with catlike grace, the tip of his tasseled hat catching in the wind. A natural athlete, he made it look easy. Taking a deep breath, Emily pushed off with her poles. *At the very least*, she thought, *he'll break my fall.*

She rounded the first turn with too much speed, so that she overshot Chris, parallel but a few feet below him on the hill, flying at an alarming speed to the edge of the groomed trail. 'Cut the corner!' she heard Chris yell, and she almost laughed: Did he really think she had that much control?

One ski, then the other, bumped over the ridge of the trail's edge. She felt thin branches score her cheeks, snow drop from the overhead boughs of pines. She tried to keep her knees together, her feet straight, praying as a cold sweat broke out beneath her arms and down her back. She sensed the air quiver as Chris called her name, and then her ski caught in a furrow of brush, and by the time Emily fell the only thing she felt was relief.

She's lucky she didn't break her neck.
  Could have been a lot worse.
  That's got to hurt like hell.
They didn't think Chris could hear them, but he'd managed to catch every word. The paramedics who'd come to the base lodge to transport Emily in an ambulance had no choice but to take Chris with them to the hospital, since he was attached to the stretcher like a leech and her parents had not yet responded to the page. He had remained beside Emily in the ambulance, and even in the ER, and after a while people stopped trying to remove him.

When she'd gone off the trail like that – Jesus, he couldn't even think about it without shaking. He hadn't wanted to leave her, but he'd needed to get help. He flagged someone over, told them to get the ski patrol, and ditched his skis so that he could run to where Emily was lying. Her hat had fallen off, and her hair was spread over the snow. He knew better than to move her, but he picked up her hand, and felt his stomach turn over.

It was his fault. If he hadn't brought Emily on this run, looking to make her miserable, she never would have skiied off the trail.

Emily regained consciousness while the ambulance was swaying toward the hospital. 'It hurts,' she said, swallowing hard. 'How come?' He would not tell her that her leg was broken, her ankle twisted in an impossible direction, like a silly cartoon character's. He would not tell her how far she'd rolled before she came to a stop; how scrapes and bruises changed her face. 'You fell,' he said simply. 'You're going to be okay.'

Emily's eyes filled with tears. 'I'm scared,' she whispered, and his throat tightened. 'Where's my mom?'

'Coming,' he said, 'but I'm here now.' He leaned closer, awkwardly slipping his arms around her. He let his eyes drift shut and decided in that instant that for the rest of Emily's life, he would be her guardian angel.

Emily's broken leg took priority over Chris's transgression with Sambuca. Melanie and Gus insisted that they ought to go back to Bainbridge, and Michael was leaning toward that too, but in the end Emily convinced them to finish out their vacation. Out of solidarity, everyone stayed in, forgoing skiing for marathon games of Scrabble and Monopoly. By the second day, Emily was tired of being treated like an invalid and she shooed everyone back to the slopes. After some deliberation, even Melanie agreed to go for an hour or so. But Chris refused to leave Emily's side.

'I don't feel like it,' he said, and nobody pushed him.

He sat with Em on the couch in front of the fireplace, her leg propped up on the coffee table. They watched the flames and talked, Chris telling her about the hare, Emily confessing her guilt about ratting on him. They joked about getting the Sambuca from the freezer, while their parents were out of the condo. He was reminded of what it had been like when they were little, how he could think his thoughts and they'd wind up in Emily's head.

It was not until the fire crackled loudly, water bursting within wood, that Chris realized he'd fallen asleep. He glanced down and saw that Emily had drifted off, too. She was still sleeping. And somehow she'd wound up tucked under his arm.

She was kind of heavy, and uncomfortable. He felt the damp heat of her cheek through the cotton of his shirt; measured the amazing length of her eyelashes. Her breath smelled like berries.

Just like that, he was hard as a rock. Flushing bright red, he tried to adjust the fly of his jeans without waking Em. But that only made his arm brush against her chest. Her breast.

For God's sake. This was Emily. The same Emily who'd used his high chair when he'd outgrown it; who had helped him dry up slugs with salt; who camped out with him for the first time in his own backyard.

How could a girl he'd known his whole life suddenly be someone he didn't recognize at all?

She stirred, blinking a little and pushing off him when she realized she was draped across his chest.

'Sorry,' she said, still close enough for her word to fall onto his lips; so that even as Chris shrugged, he could taste her.

Chris didn't think he'd ever get her alone.

For three days he'd tried to finagle ways for Emily to lean on him, brush against him, touch him.

He wanted to kiss her. And his golden opportunity was vanishing before his eyes.

Their parents were supposed to be going to a New Year's party thrown by Sugarloaf. But Melanie and Michael were reluctant to go, afraid that if Emily needed them they'd be unreachable. The four of them stood in their snazzy black evening clothes, trying to come to a decision.

'I'm thirteen,' Emily said. 'I don't need a baby-sitter.'

'If anything happened,' Chris added, 'I know how to drive. I could always just take the other car to the base lodge.'

Gus and James whirled around. 'That,' James said dryly, 'is something we didn't need to know.' He turned to Michael. 'Take your keys,' he said.

Melanie, sitting beside Emily on the couch, felt her forehead. 'I broke my leg,' Emily groaned. 'I don't have the flu.'

Gus touched Melanie's shoulder. 'What do you think?'

Melanie shrugged. 'What would you do?'

'Go, I guess. There's nothing else you can do to make her comfortable.'

Melanie stood up, smoothing Emily's hair back from her forehead. Emily scowled and fussed it back into position. 'All right. But I may come back before midnight.' Melanie smirked at Gus. 'And you're a liar, you know. If that was Kate you wouldn't go farther than three feet away.'

'You're right,' Gus said amiably. 'But didn't I sound convincing?' She turned to Chris. 'You'll get Kate to bed on time?'

Kate, upstairs, wailed. 'Mo-o-om,' she cried. 'Can't I stay up till midnight?'

'Sure,' Gus yelled back. She glanced at Chris, speaking more softly. 'When she conks out on the couch in a half hour, carry her upstairs.' Then she kissed her son and waved to Emily. 'Be good,' she said, and with the others, left Chris and Emily to their own devices.

Chris's hands twitched in his lap. They ached, waiting to touch Emily, who was all of ten inches away. He curled his fingers into fists, hoping they wouldn't betray him by crawling over toward Emily's thigh, skimming her hip.

'Chris,' Emily whispered. 'I think Kate's out.' She nodded

to her left, where Kate was curled asleep. 'Maybe you should carry her up.'

Was she trying to say she wanted to be alone with him, too? Chris tried to catch Em's eye, to see what she really meant, but she was scratching the itchy skin around the top of her cast. He scooped his sister into his arms and hauled her to her bedroom. He tucked her in, then closed the bedroom door.

He made sure to sit closer to Emily this time, stretching his arm along the back of the couch. 'Can I get you something? A drink? Popcorn?'

Emily shook her head. 'I'm okay,' she said. She took the remote control and flipped through the channels.

Chris let his thumb graze the edge of Emily's sleeve. When she didn't jump, he added another finger. And another. Until his whole hand was brushing her shoulder.

He couldn't look, just couldn't. But he felt Emily go absolutely still, felt the temperature of her skin increase by faint degrees; and for the first time that night he began to relax.

In the flurry of the quandary whether or not to leave Emily alone, everyone had neglected to notice that the party invitation said 'Bring Your Own Booze.' James volunteered to run out and get a bottle of champagne, Gus reminding him to return before midnight.

He did not bother to check his watch until after pulling into the parking lot of the third closed supermarket. *It's 11:26*, he thought, unaware that the Timex's batteries had died just moments before. *I'll run back to the condo and get a bottle of wine.*

But it was actually two minutes before midnight.

Chris remembered once when he'd gotten a butterfly to land in his palm. He'd kept absolutely still, certain that if he even thought a weird thought the beautiful creature would flutter away. It was like that, now, with Emily. She hadn't said a thing and neither had he, but for the past forty-two minutes he'd had his arm around her as if it was a perfectly normal thing for him to do.

On the television, people in Times Square were going nuts. There were men with purple hair and women dressed like Marie Antoinette, guys his age bouncing tiny babies who should have been asleep. The ball began to slip down, tugged by the crowd's chants, and Chris felt Emily shift the tiniest bit toward him.

And then it was 1994. Emily rubbed her thumb over the mute button on the remote. There was no shouting in the living room of the condo, no fanfare. Chris was certain he could hear his own pulse. 'Happy New Year,' he whispered, and he bent his head toward hers.

She turned in the same direction, and they bumped noses hard, but then she laughed and it was all right because this was Em. Her mouth was the softest thing he'd ever felt, and he pulled on her jaw to make it open a little, and his tongue ran over the neat line of her teeth.

Immediately she pulled back, and so did Chris. From the corner of his eye, he could see a million people in Times Square, jumping up and down and laughing. 'What are you thinking?' he whispered.

Emily turned bright red. 'I'm thinking . . . *wow*,' she said.

Chris smiled against her neck. 'Me too,' he said, searching for her again.

When James entered the condo, the television was blaring with celebration. Then suddenly, it fell quiet. He stopped in the kitchen, wrapping his hand about the throat of a champagne bottle. Setting it on the kitchen table, he continued toward the living room.

The first thing he saw was the television, which mutely and definitively announced that it was already 1994. The second thing he saw was Chris and Emily on the couch, kissing.

Stunned at first, James couldn't move, couldn't speak. They were kids, for God's sake. The incident with the Sambuca was still raw in his mind, and he could not believe that his son would be stupid enough to do, in quick succession, two things he shouldn't.

Then he realized Chris and Emily were doing exactly what everyone had always hoped they would.

He backed away without disturbing them, leaving the condo and getting into the car. By the time he reached the base lodge he was still smiling. Gus spotted him, her anger riding bright on her cheeks, confetti graying her hair. 'You're late,' she said.

Grinning, James told her and the Golds what he'd stumbled across. Melanie and Gus laughed, delighted; Michael shook his head. 'You're sure,' he said, 'they were just kissing?' The four lifted their water glasses, toasting 1994. And none of them noticed that James had forgotten the champagne.

Now

Mid to Late November 1997

In the days after Emily's death, Melanie found herself riveted by the most ordinary things: the whorl of the wood of the dining room table; the mechanism of a Ziploc baggie; the pamphlet on toxic shock syndrome in the tampon box. For hours at a time she could stare at these things as if she had not seen them a million times before, as if she had never known what she was missing. She felt a call to detail that was obsessive, but necessary. What if, tomorrow morning, one of these things turned up missing? What if her only knowledge of these items came from memory? She knew now that, at any time, she might be tested.

Melanie had spent the morning tearing off the pages of a small notepad and throwing them into the trash can. She watched the white pages pile up, a tiny blizzard. When the trash bag was half full, she yanked it from the can to carry it outside. It had started to snow, the first snow of the season. Mesmerized, she dropped the trash bag, oblivious to the cold or the fact that she was shivering without her coat, and held out her hand. As a snow-flake landed on her palm, she brought it close to examine, and watched it melt before she'd had the chance.

The telephone startled her, its harsh jangle wrangling through the open kitchen door. Melanie turned and ran inside, breathlessly reaching for the receiver on the wall. 'Hello?'

'Yes,' a floating voice said. 'I'd like to speak with Emily Gold.'

Me, too, Melanie thought, and she silently hung up the phone.

Chris stood uncomfortably in the office of Dr Emanuel

Feinstein, pretending to look at the photographs of covered bridges decorating the walls and glancing surreptitiously instead at the secretary who was typing so fast her fingers were a blue blur. Suddenly there was a buzz on the intercom. The secretary smiled at Chris. 'You can go in now,' she said.

Chris nodded and walked through the adjoining door, wondering why he'd been cooling his heels for the past half hour if there wasn't another patient in there. The psychiatrist stood up, walked around his desk. 'Come on in, Chris. I'm Dr Feinstein. It's nice to meet you.'

He nodded to a chair – not a couch, Chris noticed – and Chris sank into it. Dr Emanuel Feinstein was not the old geezer he'd conjured up in his head based on that name, but a guy who would have looked just as comfortable hauling wood as a lumberjack or manning an oil rig. He had thick blond hair that brushed his shoulders, and he stood a good half foot taller than Chris. His office was decorated much like Chris's dad's study – dark wood and tartan plaids and leather books.

'So,' the psychiatrist said, taking the wing chair across from Chris, 'how are you feeling?'

Chris shrugged, and the doctor leaned forward to pick up the tape recorder on the coffee table between them. He played back the snippet, hearing his own question, and then shook the device. 'Funny thing about these,' Dr Feinstein said. 'They don't pick up nonverbal clues. There's only one rule in here, Chris. Your answers have to actually emit a sound frequency.'

Chris cleared his throat. Any begrudged liking he'd started to have for this shrink vanished again. 'Okay,' he said gruffly.

'Okay what?'

'I'm feeling okay,' Chris muttered.

'Are you sleeping all right? Eating?'

Chris nodded, then stared at the tape recorder. 'Yes,' he said pointedly. 'I've been eating okay. But sometimes I can't sleep.'

'Was this something you had a problem with before?'

Before, like with a capital B. Chris shook his head, and then his eyes filled with tears. It was an emotion he was getting used to; it happened whenever he thought about Emily.

'How are things at home?'

'Weird,' Chris admitted. 'My father acts like nothing ever happened, my mom talks to me like I'm a six-year-old.'

'Why do you think your parents are treating you the way they are?'

'I guess it's because they're scared,' Chris answered. 'I would be.'

What could it be like to find out, in a matter of minutes, that the kid you believed the sun rose and set on was not the person you'd thought? Suddenly, he frowned at the psychiatrist. 'Do you tell my parents what I say here?'

Dr Feinstein shook his head. 'I'm here for you. I'm your advocate. What you say here, stays here.'

Chris eyed him warily. Like that was supposed to make him feel better. He didn't know Feinstein from a hole in the wall.

'Do you still think about killing yourself?' the psychiatrist asked.

Chris picked at a hole in his jeans. 'Sometimes,' he murmured.

'Do you have a plan?'

'No.'

'Do you think Friday night might have changed your mind?'

Chris looked up sharply. 'I don't understand you,' he said.

'Well, why don't you tell me what it was like for you. Seeing your friend shoot herself.'

'She wasn't my friend,' Chris corrected. 'She was the girl I loved.'

'That must have made it even more difficult,' Dr Feinstein said.

'Yes,' Chris said, watching it all over again, Emily's head snapping to the left as if an invisible hand had slapped her, the blood that ran through his fingers. He glanced at the psychiatrist, wondering what the man expected him to say.

After prolonged silence, the doctor tried again. 'You must be very upset.'

'I pretty much cry at the drop of a hat.'

'Well,' the psychiatrist said, 'that's perfectly normal.'

'Oh, right.' Chris snorted. 'Perfectly normal. I spent Friday night getting seventy stitches. My girlfriend is dead. I've been locked up in a psycho ward for three days and now I'm here, where I'm supposed to tell someone I don't even know everything that's on my mind. Yeah, I'm a perfectly normal seventeen-year-old.'

'You know,' Dr Feinstein said evenly, 'the mind is a remarkable thing. Just because you can't see the wound doesn't mean it isn't hurting. It scars all the time, but it heals.' He leaned forward. 'You don't want to be here,' he said. 'So where would you like to be?'

'With Emily,' Chris said unhesitatingly.

'Dead.'

'No. Yes.' Chris averted his gaze. He found himself looking at a second door, one he hadn't noticed, one that did not lead back to the waiting room through which he'd entered. It would be, Chris realized, the door through which he'd exit. A way out so that no one would ever have to know he'd been inside.

He looked at Dr Feinstein and decided that someone who protected your privacy could not be all that bad. 'Where I'd like to be,' Chris said softly, 'is a few months back.'

The moment the elevator doors opened, Gus was fluttering all over her son, slipping her arm about his waist and falling into step and chattering as she whisked him out of the medical building where Dr Feinstein's office was located. 'So,' Gus said, the moment they settled into the car. 'How did it go?'

There was no answer. Chris's head was turned away from her. 'For starters,' she said, 'did you like him?'

'Was this a blind date?' Chris muttered.

Gus pulled the car out of the lot, silently making excuses for him. 'Is he a good psychiatrist?' she pressed.

Chris stared out the window. 'As opposed to what?' he asked.

'Well . . . do you feel better?'

He turned to her slowly, pinned her with his eyes. 'As opposed,' he repeated, 'to what?'

James had been raised by a set of Boston Brahmin parents who had elevated New England stoicism to an art form. In the eighteen years he'd lived in their household, he'd seen them kiss publicly only once, and that was so fleeting that he came to believe he'd surely imagined it. Admitting to pain, to grief, or to ecstasy was frowned upon: The one time James, as a teenager, had cried over the death of a pet dog, his parents acted as if he'd committed hara-kiri on the marble tiles of the foyer. Their strategy for dealing with things unpleasant or emotional was to push past the mortifying situation and get on with their life as if it had never happened.

By the time James had met Gus, he'd fully mastered the technique – and had rejected it out of hand. But that night, alone in the basement, he tried desperately to recapture that blessed, intentional blindness once again.

He was standing in front of the gun cabinet. The keys were still in the lock; he'd mistakenly believed his children were old enough to dispense with the excessive caution he'd used years ago. He twisted the keys and let the door swing open, revealing the rifles and shotguns lined up like matchsticks. Conspicuously absent was the Colt pistol, still impounded by the police.

James touched the barrel of the .22, the first gun he'd ever given Chris to shoot.

Was this his fault?

If James hadn't been a hunter, if the guns were not accessible, would any of this have happened? Would there have been pills or carbon monoxide poisoning, would the results have been less catastrophic?

He shook off the thought. This sort of obsessing would get

him nowhere. He needed to move on, to get going, to look forward.

As if he'd suddenly discovered the secret of the universe, James pounded up the cellar stairs. He found Gus and Chris sitting in the living room together. They both looked up when he burst into the doorway. 'I think,' he announced breathlessly, 'that Chris should go back to school on Monday.'

'What?' Gus said, coming to her feet. 'Are you crazy?'

'No,' James said. 'But neither is Chris.'

Chris stared at him. 'You think,' he said slowly, 'that going back to school, where everyone's going to look at me like I'm some kind of head case, is going to make me feel better?'

'This is ludicrous,' Gus said. 'I'll call Dr Feinstein. It's too soon.'

'What does Feinstein know? He's met Chris once. We've known him forever, Gus.' James crossed the room and stood in front of his son. 'You'll see. You'll get back in with your own crowd, and you'll be yourself in no time.'

Chris snorted, and turned away.

'He's not going to school,' Gus insisted.

'You're being selfish.'

'I'm being selfish?' Gus laughed and folded her arms over her chest. 'James, he isn't even sleeping at night. And he—'

'I'll go,' Chris interrupted softly.

James beamed, clapped Chris hard on the shoulder. 'Excellent,' he said triumphantly. 'You'll get swimming again, and excited about college. Once you're busy, things are going to look a hell of a lot better.' He turned to his wife. 'He just needs to get out, Gus. You coddle him, and he's got nothing better to do than think.'

James rocked back on his heels, certain that the air in the house was circulating lighter and more freely with this small shift of focus. Disgusted, Gus pivoted and walked out the room. He frowned at her retreating back. 'Chris is fine,' he called out, for good measure. 'There's nothing wrong with him.'

It was a few moments before he felt the heavy burden of his son's gaze. Chris's head was tipped to the side, as if he was not angry at James, but truly confounded. 'Do you really think that?' he whispered, and left his father standing alone.

The telephone woke Melanie with a start, causing her to sit up disoriented in her own bed. When she'd lay down for a nap, the sun had been shining. Now, she could not even see her hand in front of her.

She fumbled along the nightstand. 'Yes,' she said. 'Hello.'

'Is Emily there?'

'Stop,' Melanie whispered, and let the receiver drop while she buried herself once again beneath the covers.

Melanie went grocery shopping every Sunday morning at eight-thirty, when the rest of the world was still relaxing in bed with the paper and a cup of coffee. Last Sunday, of course, she hadn't. And with the exception of food left over from sitting *shiva*, there was nothing in the house to eat. As she tugged on her coat and struggled with the zipper, Michael watched her. 'You know,' he said awkwardly, 'I can do this for you.'

'Do what?' Melanie said, stuffing her hands into mittens.

'Go shopping. Run errands. Whatever.' Seeing Melanie's pinched face made Michael think he was going about grieving all wrong. He was dying on the inside because of Emily, but not on the outside, and somehow it didn't seem as potent a sorrow as his wife's. He cleared his throat, forcing himself to look at her. 'I can go if you don't feel up to it yet.'

Melanie laughed. Even to her own ears, it sounded wrong, like a melody for a flute being played on a honky-tonk piano. 'Of course I'm up to it,' she said. 'What else do I have to do today?'

'Well,' Michael said, making a spur-of-the-moment decision, 'why don't we go together?'

For the slightest moment, Melanie's brows drew together. Then she shrugged. 'Suit yourself,' she said, already leaving.

Michael grabbed his coat and ran outside, where Melanie was in the car. The engine was running, the exhaust creating a cloud around the vehicle. 'So. Where are we going?'

'Market Basket,' Melanie said, turning the car around. 'We need milk.'

'We're going all the way there for milk? We could get that at—'

'Are you going to be pleasant company,' Melanie said, her lips twitching, 'or are you going to be a backseat driver?'

Michael laughed. For a moment, it had been easy. In the past week he could count on one hand the number of moments like that.

Melanie pulled out of the driveway and turned onto Wood Hollow Road, accelerating. Although he tried to keep his eye from straying there, Michael instinctively glanced toward the Hartes' house. A figure was walking along the edge of the driveway, setting out the trash can at the lip of the road. As the car drew closer Michael made out Chris's face.

He was wearing a hat and gloves, but no coat. His eyes lifted at the sound of the approaching car, and – as Michael had experienced – instinct kicked in when he realized it was the Golds. Probably before he even realized what he was doing, Chris had lifted his hand in greeting.

Michael felt the car pull toward the right, toward Chris, as if the boy had magnetized not only the direction of their thoughts but also the vehicle's tracks. He shifted in his seat and waited for Melanie to realign the car.

Instead, it swerved so far to the right that she went off the blacktop. Michael felt the car jolt forward as she pressed down on the gas pedal, barreling toward Chris. Chris's mouth rounded into an O; his hands twitched on the handle of the garbage can as his feet remained rooted to the driveway. Melanie's hands shifted, cutting the car even closer; and just as Michael snapped out of his stupefied paralysis to wrench the steering wheel from her grasp, she turned it herself, nicking the trash can. Chris safely bolted several feet back down the driveway as the barrel bounced into the street and spilled garbage across Wood Hollow Road.

Michael's heart was pounding so heavily in his chest that he could not even gain the composure to look at his wife until they were all the way down Wood Hollow, waiting at the stop sign to take a left toward town. He put his hand on Melanie's wrist, still speechless.

She turned to him, unruffled, guileless. 'What?' she said.

Chris remembered being a little kid, pretending along with Em that he had the power to make himself invisible. They'd put on some goofy baseball hats or cheap dime-store rings and, *bam*, just like that, no one would be able to see them sneak into the pantry for an Oreo or empty the bottle of bubble bath into the toilet. It was a handy thing, the suspension of disbelief. And it was apparently something you outgrew pretty fast, because no matter what Chris did to imagine that no one could see him as he walked down the dull, narrow halls of the high school, he could not convince himself that this was truly the case.

He kept his eyes trained straight ahead as he maneuvered around the salmon flow of kids between classes, couples making out against the lockers, and surly underclassmen spoiling for a fight. In class, he could just sit with his head ducked and zone out like he usually did. In the hallways, though, it was brutal. Was everyone in the whole school staring at him? Because it sure as hell felt that way. Nobody had tried to talk to him about what happened; instead they all whispered behind their hands. One or two guys he knew said it was good that he was back at school and all that, but they made sure not to come too close while they talked, in case unhappiness was contagious.

You always knew, after shitty things happened, who your friends really were. It was perfectly clear to Chris that his one real friend had been Emily.

Fifth period he had AP English with Bertrand. He liked the class; he'd always done all right in it. Mrs Bertrand was after him to major in English in college. When the bell rang, Chris didn't hear it at first. He was still sitting slumped in his chair when Mrs Bertrand touched his arm. 'Chris?' she said softly. 'Are you all right?'

He blinked up at her. 'Yeah,' he said, clearing his throat. 'Yeah, sure.' He made a big production of gathering his books into his backpack.

'I just wanted you to know that if you want someone to talk to, I'm here.' She sat down at the desk in front of his. 'You may want to write about your feelings,' she suggested. 'Sometimes it's easier than speaking them out loud.'

Chris nodded, wanting nothing more than to get away from Mrs Bertrand.

'Well,' she said, clasping her hands. 'I'm glad you're all right.' She stood up and walked back to her desk. 'The faculty is planning a memorial assembly for Emily,' she said, and she looked at Chris, waiting for a response.

'She'd like that,' Chris murmured, and he dashed from the frying pan into the fire, where a hundred pairs of curious eyes stood their distance.

The irony of the relief that swept over Chris as he entered Dr Feinstein's office did not escape him. This had been the last place in the world he'd wanted to be, but that trophy now belonged to Bainbridge High School. He sat with his elbows resting on his knees, his feet anxiously tapping.

Dr Feinstein himself opened the door to the waiting room. 'Chris,' he said. 'It's good to see you again.' When Chris chose to pace in front of the bookshelves, he shrugged and came to stand beside him. 'You seem a little restless today,' Dr Feinstein said.

'I went back to school,' Chris answered. 'It sucked.'

'Why?'

'Because I was a freak. No one came up to me and God forbid they should touch me . . .' He exhaled, disgusted. 'It's like I have AIDS. No, scratch that. They'd probably be more accepting.'

'What do you think sets you apart from them?'

'I don't know. I have no idea how much they know about what happened. And I couldn't get close enough to people to hear the rumors.' He rubbed his temples. 'Everyone knows Em died. Everyone knows I was there. They're filling in the blanks.' He leaned against the back of the wing chair, skimming his thumb over the row of leatherbound books closest to him. 'Half of them probably think I'm gonna slit my wrists in the cafeteria.'

'What do the other half think?'

Chris turned slowly. He knew perfectly well what the other half of kids believed – anything that could be escalated into a juicy story would be, in the rumor mill. 'I don't know,' he said as off-handedly as he could manage. 'Probably that I killed her.'

'Why would they think that?'

'Because I was there,' he blurted out. 'Because I'm still alive. Christ, I don't know. Ask the cops; they've thought that since day one.'

Chris did not realize until he'd spoken how bitter he was about the accusation, veiled as it had been.

'Does that bother you?'

'Hell, yes,' Chris said. 'Wouldn't it bother you?'

Dr Feinstein shrugged. 'I can't say. I guess if I knew I was being true to myself, I'd want to believe that everyone would come around sooner or later to my way of thinking.'

Chris snorted. 'I bet all the witches in Salem were thinking that, too, when they smelled the smoke.'

'What is it that bothers you the most?'

Chris fell silent. It wasn't that he was not being taken at his word; if the situation had been reversed, he too might have his doubts. It wasn't even that everyone in the whole goddamned school was treating him like he'd grown six heads overnight. It was that, having seen him with Emily, they could believe he would ever willingly hurt her.

'I loved her,' he said, his voice breaking. 'I can't forget that. So I don't see why everyone else can.'

Dr Feinstein motioned again toward the wing chair; Chris sank into it. He watched the tiny cogs inside the tape recorder chug in slow circles. 'Would you tell me about Emily?' the psychiatrist asked.

Chris closed his eyes. How could he convey to someone who'd never even met her the way she always smelled like rain, or how his stomach knotted up every time he saw her shake loose her hair from its braid? How could he describe how it felt when she finished his sentences, turned the mug they were sharing so that her mouth landed where his had been? How did he explain the way they could be in a locker room, or underwater, or in the piney woods of Maine, but as long as Em was with him, he was at home?

'She belonged to me,' Chris said simply.

Dr Feinstein's eyebrows lifted. 'What do you mean by that?'

'She was, you know, all the things I wasn't. And I was all the things she wasn't. She could paint circles around anyone; I can't even draw a straight line. She was never into sports; I've always been.' Chris lifted his outstretched palm and curled his fingers. 'Her hand,' he said. 'It fit mine.'

'Go on,' Dr Feinstein said encouraging.

'Well, I mean, we weren't always going out. That was pretty recent, a couple of years. But I've known her forever.' He laughed suddenly. 'She said my name before anything else. She used to call me Kiss. And then, when she learned the word *kiss* for real, she'd get it all confused and look at me and smack her lips.' He looked up. 'I don't remember that, exactly. My mom told me.'

'How old were you when you met Emily?'

'Six months, I guess,' Chris said. 'The day she was born.' He leaned forward, considering. 'We used to play together every afternoon. I mean, she lived right next door and our moms would hang all the time, so it was a natural.'

'When did you start going out?'

Chris frowned. 'I don't know the day, exactly. Em would. It just sort of evolved. Everyone figured it was going to happen, so it wasn't much of a surprise. One day I kind of looked at her and I didn't just see Em, I saw this really beautiful girl. And, well . . . you know.'

'Were you intimate?'

Chris felt heat crawling up from the collar of his shirt. This was an area he did not want to discuss. 'Do I have to tell you if I don't want to?' he asked.

'You don't have to tell me anything at all,' Dr Feinstein said.

'Well,' Chris said. 'I don't want to.'

'But you loved her.'

'Yes,' Chris answered.

'And she was your first girlfriend.'

'Well, pretty much, yeah.'

'So how do you know?' Dr Feinstein asked. 'How do you know that it was love?'

The way he asked was not mean or confrontational. He was just sort of wondering. If Feinstein had been bitter, or direct, like that bitch detective, Chris would have clammed up immediately. But as it stood, it was a good and valid question. 'There was an attraction,' he said carefully, 'but it was more than that.' He chewed on his lower lip for a second. 'Once, we broke up for a while. I started hanging around with this girl who I'd always thought was really hot, this cheerleader named Donna. I was, like, totally infatuated with Donna, maybe even when I was still together with Em. Anyway, we started going out places and fooling around a little and every time I was with Donna I realized I didn't know her too well. I'd hyped her up in my head to be so much more than what she really was.' Chris took a deep breath. 'When Em and I got back together, I could see that she had never been less than what I'd figured her to be. If anything, she was always better than I remembered. And that's what I think love is,' Chris said quietly. 'When your hindsight's twenty-twenty, and you still wouldn't change a thing.'

As he fell silent, the psychiatrist looked up. 'Chris,' he asked, 'what's your earliest memory?'

The question took Chris by surprise; he laughed aloud. 'Memory? I don't know. Oh – wait – there was this toy I had, a little train that had a button on it which honked. I remember holding onto it and Emily trying to grab it away.'

'Anything else?'

Chris steepled his hands and thought back. 'Christmas,' he said. 'We came downstairs and there was an electric train running around the tree.'

'We?'

'Yeah,' Chris said. 'Emily was Jewish, so she'd come over to our place to celebrate Christmas. When we were really little she'd sleep over Christmas Eve.'

Dr Feinstein nodded thoughtfully. 'Tell me,' he said, 'do you have any early childhood memories that don't include Emily?'

Chris tried to run backward in his mind, replaying his life like a loop of film. He saw himself standing in a bathtub with Emily, peeing in the water while she giggled and his mother yelled bloody murder. He saw himself making a snow angel, swinging wide his arms and legs and hitting Emily, who was doing the same thing beside him. He caught glimpses and snippets of his parents' faces, but Emily was off to the side.

Chris shook his head. 'Actually,' he said, 'I don't.'

That night while Chris was in the shower, Gus ventured into his bedroom to clean up. To her surprise, the mess was contained – basically a pile of dirty dishes covered with meals that remained uneaten. She smoothed Chris's covers and then fell to her knees, instinctively checking under the bed for mismatched socks to place in the wash, for food that had unobtrusively rolled beneath.

Her thumb pricked the hard edges of the shoebox before her mind could consciously register what she'd stumbled across. She reached inside; her fingers ruffled over pages of secret codes, filmy 3-D glasses, invisible lemon juice ink messages that had been decoded over a bare lightbulb. God, how old had they been? Nine? Ten?

Gus picked up the secret message on the top. In Emily's daisy-chain handwriting, it emphatically announced that 'Mr Polaski is a dork.' She traced her finger over the word *is*, the 'i' punctuated by a fat circle, as if it were a balloon that might light off the page at any moment. She scrabbled beneath the loose pages and found a flashlight, batteries dead, and a mirror. Smiling, heartsick, Gus sat down on the bed and wiggled the mirror in her hand. She watched the reflection bounce off, skittering over the woods.

In the window of Emily's bedroom, there was a mated flash of light.

With a gasp Gus came to her feet, walking toward the sill. She saw the silhouette of Michael Gold at Emily's bedroom window, holding in his hand a small silver square of mirror.

'Michael,' she whispered, raising her hand in greeting, but even as she did she could see Emily's father drawing down the bedroom shade.

On Wednesday Bainbridge High School staged a memorial for Emily Gold.

Her artwork – a legacy – dotted the auditorium. Her school picture from the previous fall had been blown up to an almost obscene size and hung from the rear curtain on the auditorium stage, a trick of the light making her gaze spookily follow students in the audience when they shifted seats or got up to go to the bathroom. On bridge chairs in front of the picture were the principal and assistant principal, the senior guidance couselor and a Dr Pinneo, an expert on teenage depression.

Chris sat in the front row with a bunch of teachers. It wasn't as if someone had saved him a seat there, but it was implicitly assumed he had the right to the space. In a way, it was kind of nice. He was able to stare at that photo of Em and not see other kids doing what everyone did during an assembly: whisper, or finish their homework, or feel each other up in the dark. Mrs Kenly, who was sitting next to him, rose as the principal introduced her. As the art teacher she probably knew Em better than anyone else. She talked for a while about how much creativity Emily had in her soul and other bullshit, but it was nice bullshit, Chris thought. Emily would have liked it.

Then the doctor got up and did this weird little song and dance on teen suicide. Warning signs, as if everyone in the audience had as much chance of coming down with it as they did the flu. Chris picked at the leg of his jeans while the guy was speaking, aware of the man's heavy stare on his own fore-head.

Before Chris realized what was happening, the whole first third of the auditorium – the 363 seniors – were on their feet and being herded toward the rear of the room. Teachers in the back thinned the milling bunch into a single file, which snaked up the stairs of the stage. By the time each senior reached Emily's photo, he or she had been handed a carnation to toss at the foot of the portrait.

It was a good idea, in theory. But Chris – who was last not by association to Em but simply because no one had realized there was a senior in the front row with all the teachers – found it ridiculous. The flowers were being tossed into a kiddie pool that was used for a fishing game at the spring carnival; little yellow ducks peeked through the pink flowers. *Tacky*, Emily would have said. When Chris reached the pool, he was standing alone on the stage. He threw the carnation on top of the heap that had accumulated already and glanced up at the monstrous face of Emily. It was her, but it was not her. Her teeth had been airbrushed supermodel-white. Her nostril was the size of his whole head.

He turned to walk off the stage and saw the principal motioning him nearer. 'As one of her closest friends,' Mr Lawrence was saying, 'Chris Harte may have something to share with us.'

He felt the principal's hand clench on his shoulder, drawing him toward a podium and a microphone that looked like the head of a rattlesnake poised to strike. His hands started to shake.

Chris found himself staring at a rippling field of faces. He cleared his throat; the microphone screeched. 'Oh,' he said, leaning back. 'I'm sorry. This . . . um . . . is a really special thing you've all done for Emily. I'm sure she's watching, some- where.' He turned a little, blinking into the floodlights. 'And she'd want to say . . .' Chris glanced at the pile of wilting flowers, at the shrine they'd made to Em. He could too easily see her in the back row next to him, snorting over the cheesy display, checking her watch to see how much time was left before the bell rang.

'And she'd want to say . . .' Chris repeated.

Later, he would never know where it came from. But suddenly the surfeit of emotion he'd been concealing since he'd returned to school at his father's command began to leak out of the hollow in his heart where he'd bottled it up. Overwhelmed by the smell of the flowers rotting under the lights and the garish photo and the hundreds of faces waiting for him, of all people, to give them answers, Chris began to laugh.

He laughed softly at first, and then a guffaw burst out, impolite and rancid as a belch. He laughed and he laughed in counterpoint to the utter silence of the auditorium. He laughed so hard, he started to cry.

His nose running, his eyes so blurry that he could not see the podium in front of him, Chris pushed away and headed toward the stairs at the edge of the stage. He ran down the long aisle of the auditorium until he exploded through its double doors into the empty corridors of the high school, and he sped toward the locker rooms of the gym.

They were empty – everyone had been watching him – and he changed into his Speedo in record time. He left his clothes in a puddled heap on the cement floor, and exited through the door that led directly to the pool. Its soothing blue surface was glass, he thought, and he imagined it shattering and slicing through him as he dove into the deep end.

The healing wound on his scalp stung; the stitches had been removed only the day before. But the water was as familiar as a lover, and in its ample embrace Chris heard nothing but his own heartbeat and the intermittent pump of the heater. He let himself float motionless underwater, glancing up occasionally at the rippling bleachers and fluorescent lights. Then, carefully, deliberately, he blew bubbles from his mouth and nose, depleting his supply of oxygen and feeling himself sink inch by excruciating inch.

'Listen,' the voice said, more hostile now. 'Does Emily live there or not?'

Melanie's fingers clenched the phone receiver so hard her knuckles went white. 'No,' she said. 'She does not.'

'And is this 656-4309?'

'Yes.'

'You're sure, now.'

Melanie rested her head against the cold door of the pantry. 'Don't call back,' she said. 'Leave me alone.'

'Look,' the voice said. 'I have something of Emily's. Can you just tell her that, when you see her?'

Melanie raised her face. 'What do you have?' she asked.

'Just tell her,' the voice said, and hung up.

Dr Feinstein opened the adjoining door with a frown on his face. 'Chris,' he admonished, 'you can't just run in here, you know. If you have a problem, call. But the only reason I'm free is because another patient is ill.'

Chris didn't bother to listen. He shoved past the psychiatrist into the office. 'I wasn't going to do it,' he muttered.

'Excuse me?'

Chris lifted his face, contorted with pain. 'I wasn't going to do it.'

Dr Feinstein closed the office door and sat down across from Chris. 'You're upset,' he said. 'Take a minute to calm down.' He waited patiently for Chris to take several deep breaths, then sit up in his chair. 'Now,' the psychiatrist said, satisfied. 'Tell me what happened.'

'They had a memorial for Emily at school today.' Chris scrubbed the heels of his hands against his eyes, the combination of his sorrow and residual chlorine creating a powerful sting. 'It was totally lame, with these flowers and . . . whatever.'

'Is that what upset you?'

'No,' Chris said. 'They had me go up to the stage and, you know, speak. And everyone was looking at me like I was supposed to know exactly how to make it better, what to say. 'Cause I was there, and I wanted to do what Emily did, so I should have been able to explain what happened to make us want to commit suicide.' He snorted. 'Like a frigging Alcoholics Anonymous meeting. *Hi, my name is Chris, and I wanted to kill myself.*'

'Maybe this was their way of telling you that you're important to them.'

'Oh, right,' Chris sneered. 'Most of the kids spent the assembly throwing spitballs.'

'What else happened?'

Chris bowed his head. 'They wanted me to talk about Emily, a eulogy kind of thing. And I opened my mouth and . . .' He glanced up and lifted his palms. 'I cracked up.'

'Cracked up?'

'I laughed. I fucking laughed.'

'Chris, you've been under an extraordinary amount of stress,' Dr Feinstein said. 'I'm sure that when people—'

'Don't you get it?' Chris exploded. 'I laughed. It was this little mock funeral and I laughed.'

Dr Feinstein leaned forward. 'Sometimes very strong emotions cross over with each other. You've been—'

'Depressed. Upset. Grieving.' Chris stood, began to pace. 'Take your pick. Am I upset that Emily died? Every damn minute, every damn breath I take. But everyone thinks I'm a basket case, one turn away from slicing open my own wrists. Everyone thinks I'm waiting for the right opportunity to try and kill myself again. The whole school thinks it – they expected me to have a breakdown, probably, right at the podium – and my mother thinks it and even you think it, don't you?' Chris glared heatedly at the doctor and took a step foward. 'I'm not going to kill myself. I'm not suicidal. I was never suicidal.'

'Not even that night?'

'No,' Chris said softly. 'Not even that night.'

Dr Feinstein nodded slowly. 'Why did you say you were, at the hospital?'

Chris blanched. 'Because I fainted, and then I woke up and the cops were standing over me, holding the gun.' He closed his eyes. 'I got scared, so I said the first thing that made sense.'

'If you weren't going to kill yourself, why did you have a gun?'

Chris sank down onto the floor, his muscles giving out. 'I got it for Emily. Because she did want to kill herself. And I thought—' He dropped his head, and spat the words out again. 'I thought that I could stop her. I figured that I'd be able to talk her out of it long before we got to that point.' He lifted shining eyes to Dr Feinstein. 'I'm tired of pretending,' he whispered. 'I wasn't going there to kill myself. I was going there to save her.' Tears ran unchecked over his cheeks, soaking the front of his shirt. 'Except,' Chris sobbed, 'I didn't.'

The grand jury which currently sat in the Grafton County Superior Court spent one day hearing assistant attorney general S. Barrett Delaney recount the mounting evidence against Christopher Harte in conjunction with the murder of Emily Gold. They listened to the medical examiner discuss the time and nature of the victim's death, the path of the bullet through her brain. They heard a duty officer from the Bainbridge Police Department describe the scene of the crime as he'd found it. They watched Detective-Sergeant Anne-Marie Marrone explain the ballistic evidence. They heard the A. A. G. ask the detective what percentage of murders were perpetrated by criminals who knew their victims; they heard the detective answer ninety percent.

As in most grand jury hearings, the defendant was not only

absent, but blissfully unaware that a court was convening in his name.

At 3:46 P.M., S. Barrett Delaney was handed a sealed envelope, inside which was a paper indicting Christopher Harte on the count of murder in the first degree.

'Hello. Can I speak to Emily?'

Melanie stilled. 'Who is this?'

There was a hesitation. 'A friend.'

'She's not here.' Melanie clawed at the receiver, swallowing convulsively. 'She's dead.'

'Oh.' The voice on the other end seemed stupefied. 'Oh.'

'Who is this?' Melanie repeated.

'Donna. Over at The Gold Rush. The jewelry store on the corner of Main and Carter?' The woman cleared her throat. 'Emily bought something from us. We have it ready.'

Melanie grabbed her car keys. 'I'm on my way,' she said.

The drive took less than ten minutes. Melanie parked in a spot directly in front of the jewelry store and went inside. Diamonds winked at her from within their cases; parabolic ropes of gold rested on blue velvet. A woman, her back to Melanie, was fiddling at the cash register.

She turned around with a brilliant smile, which withered and died as she took in Melanie's wild hair, her lack of a winter coat. 'I'm Emily's mother,' Melanie said.

'Of course.' Donna stared at Melanie for a full five seconds before her body shocked itself into response. 'I'm so sorry,' she said. She went to the cash register and retrieved a long, narrow box. 'Your daughter ordered this some time ago. It was engraved, too,' she said, lifting the lid to reveal a man's watch. *To Chris*, Melanie read. *Forever. Love, Em.* She laid the watch back on its satin cushion and picked up the sales receipt. Boldly printed at the bottom was a note to the store personnel: 'Gift is a secret. When calling, just ask to speak to Emily. Leave no information.' Which explained the cloak and dagger routine, she thought. But why keep it a secret?

Then Melanie saw the price. 'Five hundred dollars?' she exclaimed.

'It's fourteen-karat gold,' the woman hastened to point out.

'She was seventeen!' Melanie said. 'Of course she wanted to keep this secret. If her father or I found out she'd spent that much money we would have forced her to take it back!'

Clearly uncomfortable, Donna shifted. 'The watch is paid for in full,' she offered as a concession. 'Perhaps you'd still like to give the gift to the person your daughter was thinking of.'

Then it struck Melanie. This would have been a birthday gift for Chris, something special to mark his turning eighteen. That, in Emily's mind, would justify spending a full summer's wages.

Melanie picked up the box and carried it back to her car. She sat down and stared at the windshield, still seeing that incredibly ironic message. *Forever.*

And she wondered why Emily would have ordered a watch for Chris's birthday, if – as he said – they were going to kill themselves before then.

Melanie had her hand on the doorknob when the telephone began to ring. She pushed inside, hurrying, some small part of her certain that this was Donna the jeweler calling to tell her this had all been a mistake; there was another Chris and another Emily and—

'Hello?'

'Mrs Gold? It's Barrie Delaney of the attorney general's office. I spoke to you last week?'

'Yes,' Melanie said, dropping the watch on the counter. 'I remember.'

'I thought you'd want to know,' Barrie said, 'that a grand jury indicted Christopher Harte today on the charge of first-degree murder.'

Melanie felt her knees give out. She slid to the floor, her legs awkwardly splayed. 'I see,' she said. 'Is he – is there a hearing?'

'Tomorrow,' Barrie Delaney said. 'At the Grafton County Courthouse.'

Melanie scribbled down the name on a pad she used as a grocery list. She heard the prosecutor talking, but she was incapable of understanding another word. Softly, she replaced the receiver in its cradle.

Her gaze fell on the jewelry box. Very carefully she lifted the watch from its satin bed and rubbed her thumb over the wide face. Chris's birthday was tonight. She knew the date as well as she knew Emily's.

She pictured Gus and James and even Kate sitting at their wide cherry table, their conversations tangling in knots the size of fists. She pictured Chris standing up and bending over the cake, the flicker of candles softening his features. Under different circumstances, Melanie and Michael and Emily would have been invited, too.

Melanie clutched the watch so tight its edges cut into her palm. She felt the rage grow inside, uncontainable. It pushed past her heart, broke through her skin, sprouting thick as an extra limb on which she gingerly, doggedly, tested her weight.

Everything had to be perfect.

Gus stepped back from the table, then moved closer to fuss with a napkin again. The crystal goblets stood at attention, the spiral ham curled introspectively on its serving platter. The fancy china that hibernated in the hutch with the exception of Thanksgiving and Christmas had been arrayed in full regalia, gravy boat and all. As Gus left the dining room to call everyone in, she tried to tell herself they were not celebrating another year of life for someone who'd wanted to prevent just that.

'Okay,' she yelled. 'Dinner's ready!'

James, Chris, and Kate came in from the family room, where they'd been watching the early news. Kate was gesturing with her hands, talking about a helium balloon the size of a Chevy that had been released with a message attached as part of a school science project. 'It'll maybe get to China,' she exuberantly proclaimed. 'Australia.'

'It won't get around the block,' Chris muttered.

'It will too!' Kate shouted, then closed her mouth and looked into her lap. Chris glanced from his sister to his parents and slammed himself into his chair with more force than necessary.

'Now,' Gus said. 'Isn't this nice?'

'Look at that cake,' James said. 'Coconut frosting?'

Gus nodded. 'With strawberry filling.'

'Really?' Chris asked, seduced in spite of himself. 'You made that for me?'

Gus nodded. 'It's not every day,' she said, 'that someone turns eighteen.' She glanced at the ham and the carrots, the sweet potato pie. 'In fact,' she added, 'in honor of the event I think we should start with the cake.'

Chris's eyes gleamed. 'You're all right, Mom,' he pronounced.

Gus took the pack of matches from beside the cake platter and lit the nineteen candles – one for good luck. She had to strike three matches in all, the shafts burning down to her fingertips before she'd finished. 'Happy Birthday to you,' she sang, and when nobody joined in, she stood, hands on her hips, and scowled. 'You want to eat,' she said, 'you've got to sing.'

At that, James and Kate joined in. Chris picked up his fork, ready even before Gus managed to cut him the first slice.

'Does it feel different being eighteen?' Kate asked.

'Oh, yeah,' Chris joked. 'Arthritis is setting in.'

'Very funny. I meant, do you feel, like, smarter? Mature?'

Chris shrugged. 'I could be drafted now,' he said. 'That's the only difference.'

Gus opened her mouth, about to say that, thank God, there weren't any current wars, but realized this was untrue. A war was what you made of it. Just because U.S. troops were not involved did not mean Chris was not fighting.

'Well,' James said, reaching for a second slice of cake. 'I think Chris should turn eighteen every day.'

'Here, here,' Gus said, and Chris ducked his head, smiling.

The doorbell rang. 'I'll get it,' Gus said, tossing her napkin onto the table.

It rang again just before she reached the door. She swung it open, the porch light falling on two uniformed police officers. 'Good evening,' the taller officer said. 'Is Christopher Harte at home?'

'Well, yes,' Gus said, 'but we've just sat down—'

The officer held out a sheet of paper. 'We have a warrant for his arrest.'

Gus gasped, the air knocked from her lungs. 'James,' she managed, and her husband appeared. He took the warrant from the policeman's hand and scanned it. 'On what grounds?' he asked tersely.

'He's been charged with murder in the first degree, sir.' The policeman pushed past Gus, toward the lighted dining room.

'James,' Gus said, 'do something.'

James grasped her shoulders. 'Call McAfee,' he said. He rushed toward the dining room. 'Chris!' he shouted. 'Don't say anything. Don't say a word.'

Gus nodded, but did not turn to the phone. She followed James toward the commotion in the dining room. Kate was sitting at the table, crying. Chris had been pulled out of his chair. One officer was cuffing his hands behind him, the other was reading him his rights. His eyes were huge; his face chalk white. Coconut frosting trembled on his lower lip.

The policemen each took one of Chris's elbows to escort him out of the house. He stumbled between them blindly, his brows drawn together in confusion, his eyes unable to light on any of the familiar furnishings of the house. At the threshhold of the dining room, where Gus stood, the officers hesitated, waiting for her to step aside. In that brief pause, Chris looked directly at her. 'Mommy?' he whispered, and then he was yanked away.

She tried to touch him, but they'd moved too quickly. Her hand, hovering in midair, clenched into a fist which she pressed against her mouth. She could hear James racing around the house, calling McAfee himself. She could hear Kate hiccupping in the other room. But over all this Gus could hear Chris, eighteen years old, and calling her by an endearment he had not used in a decade.

2

The Girl Next Door

And, after all, what is a lie? 'Tis but
The truth in masquerade.
— LORD BYRON
Don Juan

There is no refuge from confession but suicide; and suicide
is confession.
— DANIEL WEBSTER

Now

Late November 1997

In the back of the police car, Chris shivered. They had the heat turned up full blast but he had to sit sideways so that his handcuffs didn't cut into his back and no matter what he did to get his bearings, he found himself shaking. 'You all right back there?' the officer who wasn't driving asked, and Chris said yes, his voice cracking like a melon on that single syllable.

He was not all right. He was not even marginally okay. He had never been so scared in his life.

The car was redolent with the scent of coffee. The radio chattered in a dialect Chris did not understand, and for a moment that made perfect sense – if his whole world went to pieces, didn't it stand to reason that he'd no longer be able to speak the language? He bounced a little on the seat, concentrating on not peeing his pants. This was a mistake. His father and that lawyer would meet him wherever they were taking him, and Jordan McAfee would do a Perry Mason speech and everyone would realize they'd made a mistake. Tomorrow he would wake up and laugh this off.

Suddenly the car lurched to the left and he saw light flash by the window. He'd completely lost track of time and direction, but he figured they were at the Bainbridge police station. 'Let's go,' the taller policeman said, opening one of the rear doors. Chris scooted to the edge of the seat, trying to keep his balance with his hands all houdinied behind his back. With one foot on an embankment, Chris levered himself from the cruiser and landed flat on his face.

The policeman hauled him up by his handcuffs and unceremoniously dragged him toward the station. He was carted in a back door he'd never noticed. The officer locked his gun in a box and radioed on an intercom, then a connecting door buzzed open. Chris found himself at the booking desk, where a sleepy-eyed sergeant sat. He was allowed to sit while they asked him questions about his name and age and address that he answered as politely as possible, just in case he got brownie points for good behavior. Then the policeman who'd taken him in stood him against a wall and had him hold a card up, just like in TV movies, with a number on it and the date. He turned right and left while a camera flashed.

On command, Chris emptied his pockets and held out his hands for fingerprinting – twenty-one separate prints; a set for the local police, the state police, and the FBI. Then the officer cleaned his hands with a diaper wipe, took his shoes, his coat, his belt, and called on the intercom to have cell three opened. 'Sheriff's on his way,' he told Chris.

'The sheriff?' Chris asked, shuddering all over again. 'How come?'

'You can't stay here overnight,' the policeman explained. 'He'll transport you to the Grafton County jail.'

'Jail?' Chris whispered. He was going to jail? Just like that?

He stopped walking, effectively halting the cop who was beside him. 'I can't go anywhere,' he said. 'My lawyer's coming here.'

The policeman laughed. 'Really,' he said, and tugged him forward again.

The holding cell was six feet by five feet, in the basement of the police station. Chris had actually seen it before, when he was in Cub Scouts and they'd taken a field trip to the Bainbridge public safety building. It had a stainless steel sink and toilet combination, and a bunk. Its door was made of actual bars, and there was a video camera trained on the inside. The policeman checked beneath the mattress – for bugs? weapons? – then unlocked the handcuffs and ducked Chris inside.

'You hungry?' he asked. 'Thirsty?'

Shocked that the policeman would care about his creature comforts, Chris blinked up at him. He was not hungry, but sick to his stomach from everything else. He shook his head, trying to block out the sound of the cell clanking shut. He waited for the policeman to move down the hall, then stood up and urinated. He wanted to tell the policeman who had booked him, and the one who'd led him to this cell, that he had not murdered Emily Gold. But his father had told him to keep quiet, and the warning cut through even the thick swath of fear that blanketed Chris.

He thought about the birthday cake his mother had made; the candles burning down to the frosting, the untouched half that was still on his plate, with its strawberry filling as bright as a line of blood.

He ran his fingers along the pitted cinderblock, and he waited.

To Jordan McAfee, there was nothing better than sliding one's way down the terrain of a woman.

He rustled beneath the covers of his own bed, his lips and his hands measuring their way, as if he were going to map this information. 'Oh, yes,' she murmured, fisting her hands in his thick, black hair. 'Oh, God.'

Her voice was getting loud. Uncomfortably loud. He smoothed his hand over her belly. 'Quiet,' he murmured against her thigh. 'Remember?'

'How,' she said, '. . . could I . . . ever . . . forget!'

She grabbed his head and held it against her at the same moment he reared back to clap a hand over her mouth. Thinking it was a game, she bit him.

'Shit,' he said, rolling off her. He slanted a glance at the woman, lush and cross. Jordan shook his head, not even aroused anymore. He was usually better at judging these things. He rubbed his sore palm, thinking that he'd never go out with a friend of his paralegal's again, and that if he did, he sure as hell wouldn't drink enough at dinner to invite her home. 'Look,' he said, trying to smile amiably. 'I told you why—'

The woman – Sandra, that was it – rolled on top of him, fusing her mouth to his. She pulled back and traced her lower lip with her finger. 'I like a guy who tastes like me,' she said.

Jordan felt his erection swell again. Maybe he wouldn't end the evening just yet.

The telephone rang, and Sandra batted it off the nightstand. As Jordan cursed and went to grab for the receiver, she wrapped her hand around his wrist. 'Leave it,' she whispered.

'I can't,' Jordan said, rolling away from her to fumble along the floor. 'McAfee,' he said into the phone. He listened quietly, coming alert instantly, his body performing by rote to pull a pen and pad from the night-stand and write down what the caller had said. 'Don't worry,' he said calmly. 'We'll take care of this. Yes. I'll meet you there.'

He hung up the phone and came to his feet with leonine grace, smoothly stepping into the trousers that had been discarded near the bathroom door. 'I'm sorry to do this,' Jordan said, zipping the fly, 'but I've got to go.'

Sandra's mouth dropped open. 'Just like that?'

Jordan shrugged. 'It's a job, but someone's got to do it,' he said.

He glanced at the reclining woman in his bed. 'You, uh, don't have to wait for me,' he added.

'What if I want to?' Sandra asked.

Jordan turned his back on her. 'It could be a long time,' he said. He stuffed his hands into his pockets, offering her a last look. 'I'll call you,' he said.

'You won't,' Sandra cheerfully disagreed. Swinging her naked body off the bed, she disappeared into the bathroom and locked the door.

Jordan shook his head and walked quietly into the kitchen. He fumbled around, looking for something to write on. Suddenly, the room flooded with light, and Jordan found himself staring at his thirteen-year-old son. 'What are you doing up?'

Thomas shrugged. 'Listening to things I shouldn't be,' he said.

Jordan scowled at him. 'You ought to be fast asleep. It's a school night.'

'It's only eight-thirty,' Thomas protested. Jordan's brows shot up. Was it really? How much had he had to drink at dinner? 'So,' Thomas said, grinning. 'Did you come up for air?'

Jordan smirked. 'I liked it better when you were little.'

'Back then I used to pee on the bathroom wall if I wasn't careful. I think this age is a hell of a lot better.'

Jordan wasn't so sure. He'd been raising his son alone since Thomas was four, when Deborah had decided that motherhood and marriage to a career-driven lawyer did not suit her. She had walked into his office with their son, divorce papers, and a one-way ticket to Naples. The last Jordan had heard, she was living with a painter twice her age on the Left Bank in Paris.

Thomas watched his father swill straight from the carafe of day-old, cold coffee. 'That's gross,' he said. 'Although maybe not quite as gross as bringing home a—'

'Enough,' Jordan said. 'I shouldn't have. Okay? You're right, and I'm wrong.'

Thomas smiled radiantly. 'Yeah? Can we get this historic moment on video?'

Jordan set the carafe back in the Mr Coffee machine and tightened the noose of his tie. 'That was a client on the phone. I've got to go.' He whirled into his jacket, still draped over a chair, and turned back to his son. 'Don't call the beeper number if you need me. Apparently it's on the blitz. Ring the office; I'll check my voice mail.'

'I won't need you,' Thomas said. He gestured toward his father's bedroom. 'Maybe I should go say hi.'

'Maybe you should get your butt back into your own room,' Jordan said, smiling at Thomas, and then he whisked out the door with the feel of his son's admiration lightly riding on his shoulders.

Gus leaned into the rear of the car, buttoning Kate's jacket up to the throat. 'You're warm enough?' she asked.

Kate nodded, still too shocked by the thought of her brother being dragged off by the police to function fully. She would wait in the car while Gus and James and the lawyer sorted out this mess – not the best solution, but the only available one. At twelve, Kate was too young to be left alone at night, and who was Gus supposed to call? Her parents lived in Florida, James's would have had heart failure even hearing about this scandal. Melanie – the only close friend Gus would have felt comfortable phoning as a last-minute baby-sitter – thought that Chris had killed her child.

But as much as Gus wished she could have spared her daughter all this, there was a niggling voice in her head that urged her to have Kate as close as possible. *You have one child left*, it said. *Keep her in sight*.

Gus reached across the foot of space between them and smoothed Kate's hair. 'We'll be back in a little while,' she said. 'Lock the doors when I leave.'

'I know,' Kate said.

'And be good.'

Like Chris wasn't. The thought leapt between Gus and Kate, a hideous, traitorous current, and they broke apart before either of them could say it aloud, or admit that they'd even thought it.

Gus and James Harte hovered in the small cone of light produced by the outside lamp at the police station, as if crossing the threshold without a legal knight in tow was unthinkable and surely risky. Jordan raised a hand in greeting as he crossed the street, reminded of that old adage about people who live together for a long time coming to look like each other. The Hartes' features were not so similar, but the singular, burning purpose in their eyes twinned them in an instant.

'James,' Jordan said, shaking the doctor's hand. 'Gus.' He glanced toward the door of the station. 'Have you been inside?'

'No,' Gus said. 'We were waiting for you.' Jordan thought about hustling them into the lobby, but then decided against it. The conversation they were going to have was better done in privacy, and as a former prosecutor he knew that the walls of cop shops had ears. He pulled his coat a little closer and asked the Hartes to tell them what had happened.

Gus recounted the arrest during dinner. Through the recitation, James stood off to one side, as if he'd come to admire the architecture rather than protect his son. Jordan listened to Gus, but watched her husband thoughtfully. 'So,' Gus finished, rubbing her hands together for warmth. 'You can talk to someone and get him out, right?'

'Actually, I can't. Chris has to be held overnight until his arraignment, which will most likely be in the morning at the Grafton County Courthouse.'

'He has to stay in a cell here overnight?'

'Well, no,' Jordan said. 'The Bainbridge police aren't equipped to keep him in their holding cell. He'll be moved to the Grafton County jail.'

James turned away. 'What can we do?' Gus whispered.

'Very little,' Jordan admitted. 'I'm going to go in and speak to Chris now. I'll be there first thing in the morning when he's called in for the arraignment.'

'And what happens there?'

'Basically, the attorney general will enter the charge against Chris. We'll enter a plea of not guilty. I'll try to get him released on bail, but that may be difficult, given the fact that he's up against a very serious charge.'

'You're saying,' Gus replied, her voice shaking with rage, 'that my son, who did nothing wrong, has to sit overnight in jail, probably even longer than that, and there's nothing you can do to stop this from happening?'

'Your son may have done nothing wrong,' Jordan said gently, 'but the police didn't buy his story about the suicide pact.'

James cleared his throat, breaking his silence. 'Do *you*?' he asked.

Jordan looked at Chris's parents – his mother on the verge of puddling to the sidewalk; his father distinctly embarrassed and uncomfortable – and decided to tell them the truth. 'It sounds . . . convenient,' he said.

As Jordan had expected, James looked away and Gus flew off into a rage. 'Well,' she huffed. 'If your heart's not in it, we'll just find someone else.'

'It's not my job to believe your son,' Jordan said. 'It's my job to get him off.' He looked directly into Gus's eyes. 'I can do that,' he said softly.

She stared at him for a long moment, long enough for Jordan to feel like she was picking through his mind, sifting the wheat from the chaff. 'I want to see Chris now,' she said.

'You can't. Only during shift changes – that's several hours away. I'll tell him whatever you want.' Jordan held the door of the station open for her, the perfume of her indignation following in her wake. He was about to move inside himself when James Harte stopped him. 'Can I ask you something?' Jordan nodded. 'In confidence?' Jordan nodded again, a bit more slowly.

'The thing is,' James said carefully, 'it was my gun.' He took a deep breath. 'I'm not saying what did or didn't happen. I'm just saying that the police know the Colt came out of my gun cabinet.' Jordan's brows drew together. 'So,' James said, 'does that make me an accessory?'

'To murder?' Jordan asked. He shook his head. 'You didn't deliberately put that gun there with the intention that Chris use it to shoot someone.'

James exhaled slowly. 'I'm not saying Chris did use it to shoot someone,' he clarified.

'Yes,' Jordan said. 'I know.' And he followed the man into the Bain-bridge police station.

When he heard footsteps, Chris came to his feet and pressed his face to the small plastic window of the cell. 'Lawyer's here,' the policeman said, and suddenly Jordan McAfee was standing on the other side of the bars.

He sat down on a chair the officer brought and took a legal

pad out of his briefcase. 'Have you said anything?' Jordan asked abruptly.

'About what?' Chris answered.

'Anything to the cops, to the desk sergeant. Anything at all.'

Chris shook his head. 'Just that you were coming,' he said.

Jordan visibly relaxed. 'All right. That's good,' he said. He followed Chris's glance toward the video camera trained on the cell. 'They won't tape this,' he said. 'They won't listen to the monitor. That's basic prisoner rights.'

'Prisoner,' Chris repeated. He tried to sound like he didn't care, like he wasn't whining, but his voice was trembling. 'Can I go home yet?'

'No. First off, you don't say anything to anybody. In a little while, the sheriff's going to come take you to the Grafton County jail. You'll be brought in and booked there. Do what they tell you to; it's only a few hours. By the time you get up in the morning I'll be there, and we'll go over to the courthouse for your arraignment.'

'I don't want to go to jail,' Chris said, paling.

'You don't have a choice. You have to be held pending your arraignment, and the prosecutor arranged it so that you'd have to wait overnight. Which means Grafton.' He looked directly at Chris. 'She did it this way to scare the shit out of you. She wants you shaking when you see her face tomorrow in the courthouse.'

Chris nodded and swallowed hard. 'You've been charged with first-degree murder,' Jordan continued.

'I didn't do it,' Chris interrupted.

'I don't want to know if you did or didn't,' Jordan said smoothly. 'It doesn't matter one way or the other. I'm still going to defend you.'

'I didn't do it,' Chris repeated.

'Fine,' Jordan said dispassionately. 'Tomorrow the prosecutor will move that you be held without bail, which is likely given the severity of the charge.'

'You mean, like, in jail?' Jordan nodded. 'For how long?'

Something in Chris's voice struck a chord. Jordan tilted his head and suddenly the panicked features of his client reconfigured, and he was staring at Thomas, much younger, asking when he was going to see his mother again. There was a universal tone of voice for a boy who had just realized he was not invincible, who understood how slowly time could pass. 'For as long as it takes,' he said.

In the middle of the night, James awakened with a start. Disoriented, his mind took him back years, and he sat up abruptly to listen for the thick wail of Kate with an infant's earache, or the sound of Chris's padding feet as he untangled himself from a nightmare and crept into his parents' bed for comfort. But there was only silence, and as his eyes adjusted to the darkness he realized that Gus's half of the bed was completely empty.

He shook off sleep and started down the hall. Kate was snoring peacefully, and Chris – well, Chris's bed was neatly made. The fresh realization hit James just below the breastbone, a physical ache that made him stumble. He wandered downstairs, drawn by a humming sound. A small rosy glow emerged from the mud room. James walked softly across the kitchen, his back to the wall, stopping a few feet shy of the mud-room door.

Gus sat on the cold tile floor, her back pressed to the spinning dryer, which she'd turned on to muffle the sounds of her cries. Her face was red and splotched, her nose running, her shoulders as bent and weary as an old woman's.

She had never been a pretty crier. She sobbed the way she did everything else – with passion and excess. That she had managed to keep it inside her this long was astounding to James.

He thought of pushing open the half-closed door and kneeling before his wife, wrapping his arms around her shoulders and helping her upstairs. He raised his hand, stroking the wood of the door, planning to say something to calm her. But what wisdom could he offer Gus, when he could not even heed it himself?

James walked upstairs again, got into bed, covered his head with a pillow. And hours later, when Gus crept beneath the sheets, he tried to pretend that he did not feel the weight of her grief, lying between them like a fitful child, so solid that he could not reach past it to touch her.

There were high metal fences around the jail, capped off with curls of barbed wire. Chris closed his eyes, wondering with a child's tenacity if maybe he could block the whole ordeal out, so that it wouldn't really be happening.

The sheriff helped him out of the car and walked him to the door of the jail. A correctional officer unlocked the heavy steel door to admit them; Chris watched it being secured into place again. 'You got another one, Joe?'

'Like fleas,' the sheriff said. 'They just keep on coming.'

They all seemed to think this was hilarious, and laughed for a while. The sheriff handed over a plastic bag, inside which were items Chris recognized – his wallet, his car keys, his loose change. A second officer took it. 'You gonna do the paperwork? We've got it from here.'

The sheriff left without even making eye contact with Chris. Alone with two men he knew even less well than he'd known the sheriff, Chris started to shiver again. 'Hands out to your sides,' one of the officers said. He stood in front of Chris, patting his hands from Chris's neck down to his waist and then up each of his legs. The second officer began to catalog Chris's personal possessions.

'Come on.' The first guard caught Chris by the elbow and led him toward the booking room. He fussed with a placard, handed it to Chris, then stood him up against a wall. 'Smile,' he grunted, and there was a flash as a picture was taken.

He sat Chris down at the single table, rolled his fingertips in ink again for prints. Then he handed Chris a cloth to wipe his hands off, and slid a piece of paper across the table. Chris glanced down at the questionnaire as the officer scrounged for a pencil. 'Fill this in,' he said.

The very first question stumped Chris. '*Are you suicidal?*' His psychiatrist knew he wasn't. His attorney thought he was. Hesitantly, he checked off 'Yes,' then erased it and answered 'No.'

'*Do you have AIDS?*'

'*Do you have any ongoing medical problems?*'

'*Do you wish to see a doctor while here?*'

Chris chewed at the end of the pencil. 'Yes,' he checked off. Then wrote in the margin, 'Dr Feinstein.'

He finished the questionnaire and looked over his answers with the same attention to detail he'd given the SAT exam. What if someone lied? What if they were really suicidal, or dying of AIDS, and said they weren't?

Who would care enough to check?

The officer led him upstairs, to a control area filled with tiny TV monitors. He exchanged some information with the officer on duty, which made no sense to Chris, then guided him toward another small room. As the gate locked behind him, Chris shivered. 'You cold?' the officer said dispassionately. 'Lucky for you this room comes with free clothes.' He waited until Chris stood up and then handed him a blue jumpsuit. 'Go on,' he said. 'You put that on.'

'Here?' Chris asked, embarrassed. 'Now?'

'No,' the officer said. 'Aruba.' He folded his arms.

It's no big deal, Chris told himself. He'd stripped naked a million times in the locker room in front of a bunch of guys. One prison guard, and only down to his shorts – that was nothing at all. But by the time he pulled the zipper of the coveralls up to his throat, his hands were trembling so badly he hid them behind his back.

'All right,' the officer said. 'Let's go.'

He escorted Chris down a hallway, into the maximum security division. With every breath, Chris's lungs had to work harder. Was it his imagination, or was the air inside a jail thinner than it was outside? The officer unlocked a heavy door and led Chris onto a narrow, gray catwalk. There were individual cells, two side by side along the catwalk, but the barred doors were open. At the end of the pod, outside the bars, was a TV. The nightly news was on.

Suddenly there was a call through the air, which rippled through the open bars and hollow catwalks. 'Lockdown,' the voice yelled, and Chris heard the pounding of feet as prisoners slowly returned to their cells.

'Here you go,' the officer said, leading Chris to an unoccupied cell. 'Bottom bunk.'

There were three other people in the pod. A small man with tiny, deepset black eyes and a goatee walked into the cell beside Chris's and sat down on the bunk. At the end of the catwalk, the TV blinked black.

The officer slid home the door of Chris's cell. The lights dimmed, but did not go out. Gradually the entire jail hushed, save for the collective breaths of the prisoners.

Chris crawled onto the bottom bunk. As his eyes adjusted to the dimness he could make out the form of an officer walking by on the other side of those bars, the flash of the man's smile.

Chris rolled over so that all he could see was the cinderblock wall that confined him. He pressed a wad of jumpsuit into his mouth to muffle the sound, and he let himself cry.

When Michael came down to the kitchen the next morning, he could barely believe his eyes. Melanie stood at the stove, a spatula in one hand and a potholder gracing the other. He watched her flip a pancake and tuck a strand of hair behind her ear and he thought, *Ah, yes. This is who I married.*

He intentionally made a noise, so that she would think he was just entering. Turning, Melanie flashed a bright smile. 'Oh, good,' she said. 'I was just going to get you up.'

'To eat, I hope.'

Melanie laughed. It was so unfamiliar a sound that both she and Michael stopped for a moment. Then, Melanie briskly turned away and picked up a platter of pancakes. She waited until Michael slid into his customary spot at the table, then set them down in front of him while never taking her eyes off his. 'Buckwheat,' she said softly.

'Actually,' he said, 'the name's Michael.' Melanie smiled at him, and without thinking it through Michael looped an arm around her thighs and drew her closer, pressing his head to her stomach. He felt her hand stroke his hair. 'I've missed you,' he murmured.

'I know,' Melanie said. She let her hand linger a moment longer, then pushed back. 'You need syrup,' she said.

She carried a saucepan from the stove, maple syrup bubbling, and drizzled it over Michael's pancakes. 'I thought we might take a ride this morning.'

Michael closed his mouth around a succulent bite of breakfast. He had to worm a litter of puppies next town over, check a colicky horse, and pay a house call on an sick llama. But he hadn't seen Melanie this . . . well, this together in days. 'Sure,' he said. 'I just have to call some people to reschedule.'

Melanie slid into the chair across from him. When Michael stretched out his hand, she slipped hers into it. 'That would be nice,' she said.

He finished eating and went to his office to make the phone calls. When he returned, Melanie was standing in front of the mirror in the foyer, running a thin coat of lipstick over her mouth. She smacked her lips together and saw Michael's reflection. 'Ready?' she asked.

'Sure,' he said. 'Where are we going?'

Melanie linked her arm through his. 'If I told you,' she said, 'it wouldn't be a surprise.'

Michael silently guessed where she was taking him. Not to Emily's grave; Mel wouldn't be chipper about that. Not out to eat, certainly, although they passed the main strip with all of Bainbridge's restaurants. Not shopping; it was too early. Not to the library, which was in the opposite direction.

But then Melanie turned the car out of town. They passed

barren fields and dairy farms, long stretches of road with nothing at all. A small green road sign announced that the town of Woodsville was ten miles away.

What the hell was in Woodsville?

He'd been there once, to put down a horse that had broken its leg. If he'd driven through the main part of town, he no longer remembered it.

Melanie drove past a brick building, from behind which a tuft of barbed wire peeked. And Michael remembered that the county jail was in Woodsville. Conveniently down the street from the county courthouse.

His wife turned into the parking lot of that courthouse. 'There's something here,' she said evenly, 'that I think you should see.'

Chris was already awake when the door to his cell screeched open at 5:45 A.M. His eyes felt like they had sand under the lids, no matter how much he rubbed them. The zipper of the jumpsuit was cutting into his skin, and he was starving. 'Chow,' an officer said, slinging a tray into the cell.

Chris looked from the unappetizing lumps on the plate to the catwalk. The man with the black eyes was staring at him from the other cell. The man stalked away and disappeared behind a shower curtain.

Chris ate, brushed his teeth with the toothbrush he'd gotten in the booking room the night before, and picked up the disposable razor an officer had put in his cell. Unsure of himself, he walked out of the cell and down the catwalk to the shower stall and sink.

Chris shaved while he waited for the other man to finish showering, squinting into a mirror that offered as clear a reflection as tinfoil. When the other man stepped out, Chris nodded and went inside.

He drew closed the curtain but just past the edge he could see the black-eyed man soaping his face in front of the sink, towel slung around his waist while he shaved around his goatee.

Chris undressed and hung his clothes over the curtain rod. Then he turned on the water and lathered himself with the soap, closing his eyes and trying to make believe he'd just swum an in-fucking-credible four-hundred-meter butterfly, and was getting ready to go home after the meet.

'What are you in for?'

Chris blinked water out of his eyes. 'Excuse me?' he said.

Through the crack between the shower curtain and the wall, Chris saw the man leaning against the sink. 'How come you're here?'

Wet, his hair reached almost to his shoulders. That was the way Chris could tell the prisoners from the detainees awaiting arraignment – those serving sentences had their hair cut military-short. Like his already was. 'I shouldn't be here,' Chris said. 'It's a mistake.'

The man laughed. 'Says you and everyone else. For a prison, there are a heck of a lot of people in here who didn't do jack-shit.'

Chris turned away and soaped up his chest.

'Just 'cause you can't see me don't mean I gone away,' the man said.

Shaking water out of his hair, Chris turned off the shower faucet. 'What did you do?'

'Cut off my old lady's head,' the man said dispassionately.

Suddenly Chris felt his knees give out. He did not think he could stay upright, so he leaned against the plastic wall of the shower. He was not standing beside a felon in a county jail. He was not going to be charged with murder. He blindly wrapped his towel around his waist, grabbed his clothes, and stumbled back to his cell, where he sat down on the bunk and tucked his head between his knees so he wouldn't throw up.

He wanted to go home.

An officer walked to his cell to retrieve the razor he had been given. 'Your lawyer's here,' he said. 'He's brought clothes for you. Get dressed and we'll bring you upstairs to change.'

Chris nodded, expecting him to stand by and watch him

change again, but the officer left. The doors of the cells were open. The man who'd decapitated his wife was watching the *Today* show at the end of the catwalk.

'I'm, um. . .ready,' he said to a different officer, who escorted him to the door that led out of the pod.

'Good luck,' the black-eyed man called out, eyes still on the TV show.

Chris paused, looked over his shoulder. 'Thanks,' he said softly.

The clothes were waiting for him in the booking room. Chris recognized the Brooks Brothers blazer he'd bought with his mother down in Boston. They had gone shopping specifically for an outfit he could wear on college interviews.

Instead, he was wearing it to his arraignment.

He dressed in the white button-down shirt and gray flannel trousers, the buttery loafers. He slid the tie through the collar of the shirt and tried to knot it, but couldn't get it right. He was used to watching himself do it in front of a mirror, and there wasn't one in the booking room.

He settled for the back tail of the tie hanging a fraction lower than the front.

Then he shrugged into his blazer and walked toward the officer who was waiting, doing some paperwork. They walked in silence to a room Chris hadn't seen before, and the officer opened the door.

Jordan McAfee was waiting in the interview room. 'Thanks,' he said to the officer, motioning for Chris to sit across from him at the table. He waited until the door closed behind the officer. 'Morning,' he said. 'How was your night?'

He knew damn well how it had been; any idiot could look at the circles beneath Chris's eyes and realize he hadn't slept at all. But Jordan waited to see what his client would say. It would go a long way toward indicating how much fortitude he could expect from Chris for the remainder of the long haul.

'It was okay,' Chris said, unblinking.

Jordan stifled a smile. 'You remember what I told you about today?'

Chris nodded. 'Where are my mom and dad?'

'Over at the courthouse, waiting.'

'My mom brought you the clothes?'

'Yes,' Jordan said. 'Nice outfit. Very preppy, very classy. It will help set your image for the judge.'

'I have an image?' Chris asked.

Jordan waved his hand. 'Yeah. White, upper middle class, student athlete, rah-rah good ol' boy.' He locked his gaze on Chris. 'As opposed to lowlife scum murderer.' He tapped his pencil on the legal pad in front of him, on which he'd written nonsense. The thing about arraignments was that as a defense attorney you went in cold, like a cat ready to land on the balls of its feet no matter how it was thrown. You had the charge that had been leveled against a client, but you had no idea what the prosecutor was thinking until you got your hands on the files after the arraignment. 'Follow my lead today. If I need you to do something, I'll write it on the pad. But this is going to be pretty straightforward.'

'Okay,' Chris said. He stood up, shaking his legs as if he were getting ready to step up to the block before a race. 'So let's go,' he said.

Jordan glanced up, surprised that he hadn't expected this. 'You can't walk over to the courthouse with me,' he said. 'The sheriff will bring you over.'

'Oh,' Chris said, sinking back into his chair.

'I'll be there, waiting,' Jordan hastened to add. 'So will your parents.'

'Right,' Chris said.

Jordan slid the legal pad back into his briefcase. He looked at Chris, frowned at his tie. 'Come here,' he said, and when Chris stood he snugged the tie so that it lay correctly.

'I couldn't do it right,' Chris said. 'No mirror.'

Jordan did not say anything. He clapped Chris on the shoulder and nodded at his overall appearance. Then he walked out of the room, leaving Chris to stare at the open door, the hall that led outside the jail, and the guard who stood between the two.

It was felony day at the Grafton County Courthouse.

In a state as rural as New Hampshire, serious crimes were committed fairly infrequently, so the felony arraignments were gathered into bunches every few weeks. More interesting than petty infractions, the proceedings were attended by local reporters, court groupies, law students.

Even so, the Hartes were sitting in the front row, behind the defense table. They'd arrived at the courthouse shortly after six in the morning, *just in case*, Gus had said. Gus's hands were clenched so tightly in her lap that she did not know if she'd ever be able to untangle them. James sat beside her, staring at the judge. She was a grandmotherly, middle-aged woman with a bad perm. Surely, Gus thought, someone who looked like that would take one look at a child like Chris and would stop this debacle from going any further.

Gus leaned toward Jordan McAfee, who was arranging documents on his lap. 'When is he going to be brought in?' she asked.

'Any minute,' Jordan said.

James turned to the man beside him. 'Is that the *Times*?' he asked. When the man offered the discarded paper, James grinned and thanked him.

Gus stared at her husband, stunned. 'You can read?' she said. 'At a time like this?'

James meticulously creased the first section. He ran over the crease with his thumbnail, then did it again. 'If I don't,' he said evenly, 'I will go crazy.' He began to scan the front page.

There were other women in here like her, Gus knew; women who might not have been wearing a designer suit or diamond studs like hers but who had a son who was going to be brought to that table like Chris was, accused of something too horrible to imagine. Some of those children had actually committed the crimes. In this, she supposed, she was lucky.

She could not imagine what it was like for those mothers, whose sons had intentionally set fire to houses or stabbed enemies or raped young women. She could not fathom what it was like to know that you'd grown someone within your body capable of these atrocities; to know that if you hadn't given birth, this small measure of evil in the world might not have come to pass.

At the sound of heels clicking down the aisle, Gus turned her head. Melanie and Michael Gold slid into the seats across from Gus. Melanie glanced at Gus blankly and Gus felt her chest constrict. She had expected disdain; she had not realized that indifference could cut more deeply.

A bailiff opened a door at the right rear of the courtroom and led in Chris. His hands were cuffed in front of him, attached to a waist chain. He kept his eyes lowered. Jordan immediately rose and stepped up to the defense table, helping Chris into the chair beside him.

The assistant attorney general was a young woman with short black hair and a nervous walk. Her voice irritated Gus. It was low and gravelly; it reminded her of the rasp a cinnamon stick made when you drew it over a grater. Judge Hawkins pushed her glasses up the bridge of her nose. 'What's next?' she asked.

The clerk read: '*The State of New Hampshire v. Christopher Harte.* Grand Jury 5327 handed down an indictment on November seventeenth, 1997, on a count of murder in the first degree. Christopher Harte is charged with willfully, knowingly, and deliberately shooting Emily Gold in the head and intentionally causing her death.'

The handcuffs rattled as Chris swayed. Hearing the words out loud, and his name linked to them, he felt a horrible, bubbling urge to laugh again, like he had at Em's memorial service. He thought of Dr Feinstein telling him how close together certain strong emotions were, and he wondered what might be the flip side of panic.

There was a harsh laugh from the gallery, and for a moment

Chris thought he'd actually done it – let it fly loose past his clenched teeth. But when his head whipped around, like everyone else's, he saw Emily's mother still snickering.

The judge was staring at Chris. 'Mr Harte, how do you plead?'

Chris looked at Jordan, who nodded. 'Not guilty,' he said, his voice thin.

Behind him, Melanie Gold snorted. 'Not guilty of what?'

The judge narrowed her eyes at Melanie. 'Ma'am,' she said, 'I must ask you to remain quiet.'

During the reprimand, Gus did not look at Melanie. Her head had bowed farther and farther toward her lap during the reading of the indictment. Murder in the first degree was the stuff of courtroom novels, of TV movies. It did not happen in real life. It did not happen in her life.

'Does the state wish to be heard on bail?'

The assistant attorney general stood. 'Your Honor,' Barrie Delaney said, 'given the severity of the charge we request that the defendant be held without bail.'

Jordan McAfee was arguing before she even finished. 'Your Honor, that's ludicrous. My client's a good student, a respected athlete. His family is well-established in the community. He has few resources of his own; he poses no flight risk.'

'How come,' Melanie called, 'he should get to go free? My daughter can't.'

The judge rapped her gavel. 'Bailiff, escort this woman from the court.'

Gus listened to the click of Melanie's heels the entire way out.

'Your Honor,' said the prosecutor, as if the interruption had never occurred, 'given the sentence accompanying a charge of murder in the first degree, there is certainly a flight risk.'

'Your Honor,' Jordan retorted, 'the prosecution is wrongly assuming there will be a conviction.'

'All right, all right.' The judge pressed her hands to her temples and closed her eyes. 'Counsel, save it for the trial.

We're talking about murder in the first degree; the defendant will be held without bail.' Gus drew in a breath, but could not get enough air. She felt James's hand steal into her lap and grasp hers tightly.

A bailiff walked toward Chris to lead him from the courtroom. 'Wait,' Chris said, looking back over his shoulder. He looked at his mother, at his lawyer. 'Where am I going now?'

Chris began shaking all over. The handcuffs were cutting into his wrists and the waist chain sang with every step he took. He found himself back in the holding cell at the sheriff's office in the county court, a deputy locking the door behind him. 'Excuse me,' Chris said, summoning all his strength to call back the man who was already retreating. 'Where do I go now?'

'Back,' the deputy said.

'To court?'

The man shook his head. 'To jail.'

In a small cafeteria at the county courthouse, Gus rounded on Jordan McAfee. 'You didn't even say anything,' she hotly accused. 'You didn't even try to keep him out of jail!'

Jordan held his hands out in front of him, placating. 'That was a standard arraignment for a charge of that nature; there was very little I could do. A conviction of first-degree murder carries with it a sentence of life imprisonment. The AG figured that's enough reason for Chris to skip town. Or for you to help him do that.' He hesitated for a second. 'It has nothing to do with Chris. It's just that judges don't grant bail to accused murderers.'

Gus, white-faced, fell silent. James sat forward, hands clasped. 'There must be someone we can call,' he said. 'Strings we can pull. Surely this isn't fair – to be innocent, but kept in jail until the trial.'

'First of all,' Jordan said, 'it's the way the legal system works. Second of all, it's in Chris's best interests to have several months pending trial.'

'Months?' Gus whispered.

'Yes, months,' Jordan answered, unblinking. 'I'm not about to motion for a faster trial – the time he waits to come up on the docket is the same amount of time I have to come up with a defense.'

'My son,' Gus said, 'is going to live for months with criminals?'

'He'll be housed in general population at the jail, and I'm sure with his conduct he'll be promoted to medium security. He's not mixed in with convicts serving out sentences, just with other people awaiting their own trials.'

'Oh,' Gus spat. 'You mean like the man who raped the twelve-year-old, or the guy who shot the gas station owner during the robbery, or any of the other good citizens who were arraigned this morning.'

'Gus,' Jordan said calmly, 'any of those men could be just as wrongly accused as you believe your son to be.'

'Come off it!' Gus said, standing up so abruptly she knocked over her chair. 'Look at them. Just look at them compared to Chris.'

Jordan had defended his share of well-to-do clients, all shelled in a clean-cut persona and guilty as sin inside. He thought of the Preppy Murderer, of the Menendez brothers, of John Du Pont – all rich, all presentably charming. But he said, 'The time will go by more quickly than you think.'

'For you,' Gus said. 'Not for Chris. What's this going to do to him? If he wanted to kill himself a week ago . . .'

'We can move to have his psychiatrist visit him at Grafton,' Jordan said.

'And what's he supposed to do about school?'

'We'll have something arranged.'

He looked at James, who watched his wife from a distance, stuck behind his own wall of terror. Jordan had seen that expression before; it was not so much disinterest as apprehension, stemming from the belief that any smidgen of emotion revealed would crack the careful mask of control and leave the person in pieces. 'Excuse me,' James said thickly, walking out of the cafeteria.

Gus jackknifed, hugging her knees. 'I've got to see him. I've got to get in to see him.'

'You can do that,' Jordan said. 'They have weekly visiting hours.' He sat back and sighed. 'Look, Gus,' he said, 'I'm going to jump through every possible hoop to figure out what I can do to get Chris out permanently. I want you to believe that.'

Gus nodded. 'Okay.'

'Okay,' Jordan said quietly. 'Why don't I walk you out?'

Gus shook her head stiffly. 'I'm just going to stay here for a while,' she said, rocking back and forth on the perch of her chair.

'Well. All right.' Jordan stood up. 'I'll give you a call the second I have some information.'

Gus nodded absently, staring at the table. Her voice, when it came, was so soft that at first Jordan thought he'd imagined it. He turned anyway to find her staring at him. 'Does Chris know?'

She was asking, he realized, whether her son understood that he'd be in jail for several months. But Jordan heard the question at its simplest level: *Does Chris know?* And he thought that, perhaps, Chris was the only one who did.

The bailiff had escorted Melanie to a point several feet down the hall from the courtroom door. It did not bother her that she'd been kicked out of court after making a fool of herself. She had never intended to call out; the words just burst out of her like an odd, vengeful bout of Tourette's syndrome. The first time she'd spoken, she felt something give in her chest, like the spring on an old watch that had been wound too tight. The second time, a righteousness coursed through her that felt like the few dizzy moments after childbirth, when she had felt simultaneously exhausted and powerful enough to move mountains. It had not even hurt to see Chris sitting in the courtroom. Melanie had stared at the handcuffs on his wrists, at the red spots where they'd rubbed raw his skin. *Good*, she had thought.

She leaned against the brick wall now, waiting for the arraignment to be over so that Michael could come out and tell her what had happened. Her eyes were closed and her head tipped back when the door to the courtroom swung open. A young man wearing a suede driving jacket approached her and stopped a few feet away. From inside his coat he withdrew a pack of Camels and held it out to her.

Melanie had not smoked since 1973. She reached for one. 'Thanks,' she said, smiling.

'You looked like you needed a fix.'

A fix. She did. But in the more elemental sense of the word.

'I saw you in there,' the man said, holding out his hand. 'I'm Lou Ballard.'

'Melanie Gold.'

'Gold,' Lou said, whistling. 'You must be the victim's mother.'

Melanie nodded. 'Which explains why I was there.'

'I'm a stringer for the *Grafton County Gazette*.'

Melanie raised her eyebrows, inhaling deeply. 'Court beat?'

'None other.' He laughed. 'I'm sure you've seen my stuff buried on page eighteen behind the weather map.'

Melanie crushed the cigarette beneath her heel. 'Did the judge rule yet?'

'Bail was denied.'

Melanie exhaled. 'Wow,' she said softly. She felt as if she were floating an inch above the ground. 'I think I need another cigarette,' she said.

Lou dug into his coat again. 'How about an even trade? You get the cigarettes.' He handed her the whole pack. 'And I get a front-page story.'

Chris changed back into a jumpsuit in the booking room of the jail. An officer led him to the pod where he'd spent the night. The TV was still on, and there were two new men in the area. One, who looked to be violently drunk, was throwing up in the toilet in Chris's cell.

Heedless of the sound and the smell, Chris crawled onto the mattress where he'd slept the night before. He stayed there for a few minutes, curled into himself. 'I want to go home,' he said. The drunk stared blearily at Chris. 'I want to go home.'

He stood up, walking out of the cell toward the end of the pod where the officer stood behind a locked metal door. Like the door of a fucking cage. He was an animal now. Chris grabbed at the bars and rattled them hard.

The officer stared at him. The other inmates ignored him; a few snickered. Chris rattled the bars again, and then more, until his hands hurt from clenching them. He fell to his knees and stayed that way for a long while.

Then Chris stood up. Dry-eyed, he walked past his cell toward the TV at the end of the catwalk. He sat down in a chair behind the black-eyed man with the goatee. No one spoke to him; no one even indicated they'd heard his tantrum. *Sally Jessy Raphaël* was on. Chris let his eyes go wide and he stared at the screen until he was seeing absolutely nothing.

Then

April 1996

'*Swimmers, take your marks.*'

Emily leaned forward at the edge of her seat in the middle of the high school bleachers. She watched Chris snap the band of his goggles twice, for luck, and shake out the muscles of his arms and legs. Then he hooked his toes over the edge of the starting block. As he bent down, he turned his head and unerringly found Emily's face in a sea of others. He winked.

There was a buzz, then Chris bulleted into the water, streaking beneath the surface of the water to emerge halfway across the pool. His shoulders rose like a great whale, and his arms windmilled in a powerful butterfly stroke. He reached the fifty-meter mark before any of the other swimmers.

Then he turned, the soles of his feet flashing silver as he raced home.

The gymnasium swelled with the yells of the crowd, and Emily found herself smiling. Chris reached the wall in an eruption of sound. Over the cheers, the student announcing the meet warbled Chris's time. 'A personal best,' he crowed, 'and a new school record for the hundred-meter butterfly!'

Panting, Chris hauled himself out of the pool. He was grinning from ear to ear. Emily stood up and pushed past the other people sitting on that row of the bleachers. Walking down the aisle, she made her way to the floor, where the next race was about to start.

Chris hugged her and buried his face in her neck. Emily could feel the exertion of his heart and his lungs. She imagined the crowd watching as they embraced. The fact that everyone knew someone like him had picked someone like her was one of the things she loved about being Chris's girlfriend.

Unfortunately, there were also things she hated.

Carlos Creighton, who was nearly as legendary a breastroker as Chris was a butterflyer, had the locker beside his. 'Nice race,' Carlos said as Chris emerged from beneath a towel, his hair sticking up in spikes.

'Thanks. You too.'

Carlos shrugged. ''Course, I could have probably gone faster if I had a hot little piece waiting for me at the finish line, too.'

Chris smiled tightly. It was no secret that he and Em were going out – they had been for almost three years – but that led to assumptions that were not necessarily true. Like the fact that Emily put out, or why else would Chris have stuck around so long?

The thing was, if he chose to set Carlos straight, it made Chris look like a fool.

'Bet you get some tonight,' Carlos said.

Chris shrugged into his shirt. 'Who knows,' he said, just off-handed enough to sound modest.

'Well, when she gets sick of you give her my phone number,' Carlos said.

Chris buttoned his fly and swung his knapsack over his shoulder. 'Don't hold your breath,' he said.

Emily knew that her relationship with Chris was very different from most of the other teenage relationships she saw at school. First, it was not a fleeting thing – she had known Chris her entire life. Second, it was truly love, and not infatuation: Chris was practically a member of her family.

That was why Emily could not understand what was the matter with her.

When she and Chris had first started going out, two whole years back, it had been an amazing exploration. There was no safer way to stumble through intimacy than with a good friend.

But then something had changed. Chris's hands moved; Emily found herself fighting him off. At first it was fear, which gave way to curiosity. The problem was, curiosity gave way to something else.

Em did not know what sex was supposed to feel like, but she guessed it wasn't having your skin shrink back from his, your stomach roll, your head pound out that this was wrong. Every time her body betrayed her like that, she was embarrassed. It was clear that Chris loved her; of course he'd want to make love to her. And certainly it was right – for God's sake, she'd been hearing her name linked to Chris's since before she could speak. She could not imagine exposing herself so vulnerably to anyone but Chris. Unfortunately, she could not see exposing herself so vulnerably to Chris, either.

He'd yelled at her when she pulled away; once he had even called her a cocktease. But Emily didn't mind, because the alternative was having Chris ask what was the matter. When that happened, she went silent, unwilling and unable to hurt him with the truth.

With a vicious yank of the brush through her hair, Emily turned away from her bedroom mirror. Dinner had been a quiet affair, her father off on house calls and her mother absorbed in the nightly news. She dropped her brush on her bed and gathered up her math books.

'Where do you think you're going on a school night?' her mother asked, as soon as Emily came into the kitchen wearing her coat.

'To Chris's,' she said. 'To study.'

'Oh. All right.' Melanie poked at several buttons on the dishwasher; it hummed to life. 'Call when you're ready to come home. I don't want you walking through the woods when it's dark.'

Emily nodded and zipped up her jacket. It was still cool for April. She felt her mother's hand on her shoulder. 'Are you feeling okay?'

'Yeah. I guess.' She lifted her eyes, staring into her mother's, willing Melanie to put together pieces that Emily could not fit into place by herself. 'If it was someone else – not Chris – would you let me go?'

Melanie smoothed her daughter's hair. 'Probably not,' she said, smiling. 'But why talk about something that isn't going to happen?'

For a moment they both stood at the threshold to Chris's bedroom, afraid to enter.

Chris swallowed. How come he'd never noticed how little furniture was in here? The dresser, the tiny desk, and that bed. 'Why don't we sit on the floor?' he suggested.

Relieved, Emily sank down and immediately began spreading out her notes. 'I think that McCarthy's going to try to get us on the proofs. So I thought we could go over some of the—' She broke off as Chris leaned down and kissed her. 'We're supposed to be studying,' she whispered.

'I know. I just had to do that.'

Emily's mouth twitched. 'You had to.'

'Like you can't imagine,' Chris said. He settled behind her, curved into the shape of her body, one big hand protectively slung over her ribs.

This she liked. Being close to Chris, and being held, and well, just being. It was the other that upset her.

She stared at a carefully printed page of graphs, wiggling because of what Chris was doing to her. She could feel his teeth scraping the tendons of her neck. Emily thought of the wavy sine curve on her homework: one half leaning in, one half pulling away.

The floor; that had seemed like a good idea. Monkish. But with Emily on her side, the slides and curves of her body were more apparent. It never failed to amaze Chris how one moment, Em could be as familiar as his own sister, and the next, a mystery.

He kept thinking of what Carlos had said. Everyone on the

planet probably thought he and Em were having sex. It was practically a given that they'd get married one day, so what was the big deal? It wasn't like that was the only reason he wanted to be with Emily. She certainly knew that.

She let him kiss her. Sometimes, she let him slide a hand under her shirt. He'd never tried anything below the waist. For that matter, neither had she.

Chris curled closer behind her and began to kiss her neck. She twisted in his embrace. 'We're not going to get any studying done, are we?'

He shook his head. 'I studied last night,' he admitted.

'Well, that's just great,' Emily grumbled, turning to face him. 'What am I supposed to do?'

He was going to say, 'Study tomorrow.' But the words came out wrong, and before he knew it he had grasped Emily's wrist and pressed it between his legs. 'You're supposed to touch me,' he said.

For a moment, her fingers curled around the length of him. Chris closed his eyes, drifting. Then her hand jumped up, trembling. Emily jerked into a sitting position. 'I . . . I . . . *can't*,' she whispered, her face turned away.

Stunned – was she crying? – Chris got up on his knees. 'Em,' he said softly. 'I'm sorry.' Afraid to touch her, he held out his arms. She looked up at him, her eyes wide and wet. It took a moment, and then she came to him.

'I like this time of year best,' Gus announced. She was sitting on Melanie's porch, drinking lemonade, the unseasonably warm temperatures melting away the last of the winter's snow. 'No black flies, no mosquitoes, no snow.'

'Mud,' Melanie said, her eyes fixed on something beyond the tree line. 'Lots of it.'

'I always rather liked mud,' Gus said. 'Do you remember how we used to let Em and Chris roll around in it like piglets?'

Melanie laughed. 'I remember scrubbing dirt out of the bathtub,' she said.

Both women stared down the length of the driveway. 'Those were the good old days,' Melanie sighed.

'Oh, I don't know. They still roll around . . . just not for the same reasons.'

Gus took a sip of her drink. 'I caught them in Chris's room the other night.'

'Doing what?'

'Well, they weren't actually doing anything.'

'And how do you know?'

'I just do.' Gus drew her brows together. 'Don't you think?'

'Not with the same level of certitude that you do,' Melanie said.

'Well, if they do, so what? They're going to have sex one day anyway.'

'Yes,' Melanie said slowly, 'but it doesn't have to be at fifteen.'

'Sixteen.'

'Wrong. Chris is sixteen. Emily is fifteen.'

'A mature fifteen.'

'A female fifteen.'

Gus set down her lemonade. 'What does that have to do with it?'

'Everything.' Melanie shook her head. 'You wait till it's Kate's turn.'

'I'll assume, as I do now with Chris, that Kate is old enough and bright enough to be making the right decisions.'

'No, you won't. You'll want to keep her your little girl for as long as you can.'

Gus laughed. 'Emily's always going to be your little girl,' she said.

Melanie turned in her chair. 'Think of yourself, after your first time,' she urged. 'Emily is mine now. But afterward, well, she'll belong to Chris.'

Gus was silent for a moment. 'You're wrong,' she said softly. 'Even now, Emily belongs to Chris.'

The previous spring, Chris had begun working at Shady Acres –

a small playground that was neither shady nor on a full acre. It sported an octopuslike plastic climbing structure, a sandbox, and an antique carousel, which could be ridden for twenty-five cents.

Chris ran the carousel. It was mindless, dizzying work – collecting the quarters, settling the kids on the horses, checking safety belts, pushing the button that activated the motor, then waiting for the calliope tape to finish one entire round of song before shutting the power and letting the carousel spin slowly to a stop. He liked the candied smell of the toddlers he hefted into the saddles. He liked swinging up on a support pole as the carousel slowed, to help the children unlatch their belts and slide down. He liked taking a damp cloth at the end of the day to wipe down the manes of the horses and to stare into their frozen, rolling eyes.

This year, the owners had given him his own key.

It was Friday, and exceptionally warm for a night in April. Chris and Emily had gone to see a movie, but it was early and Chris wasn't ready to go home. Driving aimlessly, he wound up in the parking lot of the playground. 'Hey,' Emily said, her face lighting up. 'Let's go on the swings.'

She got out of the car and raced across the mud. By the time Chris made his way there, she was already in the air, her face tipped up to the night sky. He walked in the other direction, hearing Em call out, then used his carousel key to open the control panel.

In the moonlight, the horses began to run.

Delighted, Emily got off her swing and came closer. 'When did they give you the key?' she asked.

Chris shrugged. 'Last weekend.'

'Oh, it's wonderful. Can I get on?'

He grabbed her around the waist and swung her up by the white horse she loved best. 'Be my guest,' he said.

Emily climbed onto the wooden horse and, after the carousel made one full revolution, held out her hand to Chris. 'You come too,' she urged.

He chose the horse beside hers, and as soon as he was seated he realized his mistake: When Emily was up, he was down, and vice versa. He leaned into her as their horses came level and kissed her cheek. Emily laughed, then leaned back to kiss him.

He slid off his horse and held out his arms for Emily. And then they were lying on the thick painted planks beneath the horses, the churning wooden hooves just clearing their arms and legs. Emily leaned back, her eyes closed, her mind full of the music. Chris slipped his hands up her shirt.

Her bra unhooked in the front. And oh, God, she felt good. Soft and full all at the same time, and she smelled of peaches. Chris leaned his head toward the curve of her neck and licked her, certain she would taste of them too. He heard Emily make a noise at the back of her throat, and he took it to mean that she liked this as much as he did.

He slid his hand down the front of her jeans, slipping beneath the waist-band of her panties as well, so that his fingers brushed against silky hair. Holding his breath, he inched his fingers downward.

'Stop,' she whimpered. 'Chris, stop.'

And when he didn't, she took her fist and clubbed him in the ear.

He reared back, his head ringing like a sonofabitch. But before he could yell at Em he saw the white oval of her face shake in denial, then she was standing. She leaped off the moving carousel, falling once before she gained her footing, leaving Chris spinning in circles.

In the movies, when things like that happened, the heroine somehow found her way home. But all Emily could think was that in real life the ultimate indignity was having to shove your boyfriend away, then still need him to drive you home.

She felt Chris slide into the seat beside her, and kept her face averted until the overhead light in the Jeep went off. But she did not have to look to know that his jaw would be tight, his lips pressed into a line.

For a moment she wanted to mold herself against him, in

hopes that that would make him soften. She remembered being a toddler, screaming to her mother that she wanted to be put down, but clinging all the harder. 'Maybe,' she whispered, 'we shouldn't see each other for a while.'

Chris put the car into drive. And nodded.

Everything about Donna DeFelice was legendary – from her spun-sugar hair to her grapefruit-size breasts to her cheerleader split, the fastest anyone could ever remember seeing at the high school. For two years she had made it clear to Chris that if he was willing, she was available. And finally, pushed over the edge by Emily, he'd decided to reciprocate.

He could not see in the Jeep, and moisture that had fogged the insides of the windows seeped through the shoulder of his shirt when he brushed up against it. Beneath him, Donna writhed on the backseat.

Chris hadn't even taken her out to dinner. She'd put her hand on his leg during the drive to the restaurant and asked what he was really hungry for.

And now she was, remarkably, totally naked, and her hand was wrapped around him, and Chris didn't think she even realized he'd never done this before.

In the thin light from the dashboard, Donna's chest was tinted a luminous green, but magnificent for all that. Her eyes were slitted and her mouth rounded on his own name. The only thing wrong with her was that she wasn't Em.

'Oh, God,' Donna moaned. 'Give it to me now.' She pulled him onto her.

One thrust, he thought, *and I'm gonna lose it.* But to his surprise, he wasn't nearly as carried away as he'd expected to be. He felt almost as if he was watching himself from a corner of the car; seeing Donna buck beneath him like an animal he couldn't put a name to.

When it was over she pushed him off her and wriggled into her underwear. Then she curled up under his arm, feeling all wrong there. 'That was something,' she breathed, 'wasn't it?'

'Something,' Chris agreed. He stared out the windshield, wondering how he could have been stupid enough to think that it was sex he had wanted all along, when in fact he had only wanted Emily.

All day long Emily had hidden in school corridors and ducked into bathrooms so that no one would see her cry. Everywhere she went, though, she heard people talking about the way Chris Harte had been walking with his arm around Donna DeFelice. At sixth period, when Emily had walked toward the trig class she had with Chris and found him leaning over Donna on a bank of lockers just outside the door, she finally broke down. She asked Mrs McCarthy for a pass to the nurse and had no problem getting the woman to believe she was ill. It wasn't her throat, and it wasn't a fever, but it hurt all the same to be heartbroken.

When her mother came to pick her up, Emily slouched down in the passenger seat and turned her head away. Then she went up to her room and crawled under the covers. She stayed there until it was dark.

Chris's Jeep left at six-fifteen. Emily watched the headlights disappear down Wood Hollow Road until she could not see them anymore. She imagined where Chris would be taking Donna DeFelice on a Friday night. She did not have to imagine what they would be doing.

Disgusted with herself, she sat down at her desk and tried to concentrate on the English paper she had to write by Monday. But she only got as far as sliding the paper clip from the pages she'd drafted. She stared down at the words, reading none of them, and bent the clip back and forth, letting friction work up a heat until it broke apart.

At eleven, when Chris was still not home, Emily's mother knocked on the door and let herself in. 'How are you feeling, honey?' she asked, sitting down beside Emily on the bed.

Emily turned toward the wall. 'Not good,' she said thickly.

'We can go to the doctor in the morning,' Melanie offered.

'No . . . it's not that. I'm all right. I just . . . I just want to stay up here for a while.'

'And does this have to do with Chris?'

Amazed, Emily whipped around to face her mother. 'Who told you?'

Melanie laughed. 'It doesn't take a graduate degree to figure out that you two haven't called each other all week.'

Emily ran a hand through her hair. 'We had a fight,' she admitted.

'And?'

And what? She certainly wasn't going to tell her mother what they'd been fighting about. 'And I think I made him mad enough for him to stay away.' She took a deep breath. 'Mom,' she said, 'what do I do to bring him back?'

Melanie looked stunned. 'You don't have to do anything. He'll come around.'

'How do you know that?'

'Because you're two halves of a whole,' Melanie said, then kissed her daughter's forehead and left the room.

Emily glanced down at a sharp pain in her forearm to find that she was still holding the jagged edge of the paper clip. Curiously she drew it over her skin, scratching the surface. The red line grew brighter when she traced a second time, and a third. She dug deeper and deeper until she was bleeding, until Chris's initials were carved hard enough into her arm to leave a scar.

Chris's Jeep got home shortly after one in the morning. Emily watched him from her bedroom window; he turned on light after light as he worked his way through the kitchen and up the stairs. By the time he entered his own room and started to get ready for bed, Emily had thrown a sweatshirt over her nightgown and stuffed her bare feet into sneakers.

The ground, considerably softened by the recent weather, was damp and soft, and pine needles that had been sleeping beneath snow squelched under her feet. Chris's window was directly over the kitchen. It had been years since she'd done it, but Emily picked up a thin twig and tossed it at the panes of glass. It landed with a light snap, and bounced back toward her. She picked it up from between her feet and threw it again.

This time, a table lamp flared on and Chris's face appeared at the window. Seeing Emily, he opened the sash and stuck his head out. 'What are you doing?' he hissed. 'Stay there.'

Seconds later, he eased open the kitchen door. 'What?' he demanded.

There was much she had imagined in this reunion, but anger had never been part of it. Remorse, maybe. Joy, acceptance. Certainly not the look that was on Chris's face right now. 'I came to ask,' she said, her voice trembling, 'if you had a nice time on your date.'

Chris swore and rubbed a hand down his face. 'I don't need this. I can't do this right now.' He turned on his heel and started back into the house.

'Wait!' Emily cried. Her words were thick with tears, but she lifted her chin and crossed her arms tight over her chest to keep from shaking. 'I, um, I have this problem. I broke up with my boyfriend, you see. And I'm pretty upset about it, so I wanted to talk to my best friend.' She swallowed and looked at the black ground. 'The thing is, they're both you.'

'Emily,' Chris whispered, and pulled her close.

She tried not to think of the unfamiliar scent of him, something perfumed mixed with something else lush and ripe. Instead Emily concentrated on the way it felt to be next to Chris again. Two halves of a whole.

He kissed her forehead, her eyelids. She buried her face against his shirt. 'I can't stand it,' she said, and she was not certain what she was talking about.

Suddenly Chris grasped her wrist. 'Jesus,' he said. 'You're bleeding.'

'I know. I cut myself.'

'On what?'

Emily shook her head. 'It's nothing,' she said. But she let

Chris lead her into the kitchen and sit her down while he retrieved a Band-Aid. If he noticed that his own initials were on her arm, he was wise enough to keep silent. She closed her eyes while he touched her with all the care in the world, and she started to heal.

Now

December 1997

Chris had thirty-five square feet to himself.

His cell was painted a strange shade of gray that sucked up all the light. The bottom bunk had a pillow and plastic mattress, and the blanket he'd been given. Beside it was a toilet and sink. His cell was sandwiched between two others, like a tight row of teeth. When the barred doors of the cell were open – most of the day, except for mealtimes – Chris could stand on the narrow walk that ran the length of the pod. At one end was a shower and a phone, where he could make collect calls. At the other end was a television, strategically placed on the free side of the bars.

Chris learned a great deal his first day, without ever asking for information. He discovered that from the moment you entered jail, your slate was wiped clean. Where you wound up – from the security level to the position of your bunk – was not determined by your charged offense or behavior prior to incarceration, but by the way you acted once you got there. The good news was that the classification board met every Tuesday, and you could petition for a change of locale. The bad news was that today was Thursday.

Chris decided that he would simply go for a week without speaking to anyone. Then, next Tuesday, he'd surely be moved out of the maximum security section, into medium security.

He'd heard that upstairs, the walls were yellow.

He'd just finished a meal, served in his locked cell on an insulated plastic tray, when two inmates came to the door. 'Hey,' one said, the man he'd spoken to yesterday. 'What's your name?'

'Chris,' he said. 'You?'

'Hector. And that's Damon.' The unfamiliar man with long greasy hair nodded at Chris. 'You never did tell me what you're in here for,' Hector said.

'They think I murdered my girlfriend,' Chris muttered.

Hector and Damon exchanged a look. 'No shit?' Damon said. 'I had you pegged for a narc.'

Hector scratched his back against the bars. He was wearing boxer shorts and a T-shirt, with rubber thongs. 'What'd you use?' Chris stared at him blankly. 'Knife, gun, you know.'

Chris tried to push past them. 'I don't want to talk about it,' he said. He broad-shouldered Damon, only to feel the larger man's hand on his shoulder. He glanced down to find a makeshift knife in Hector's hand, a razor blade pressed against Chris's ribs. 'Maybe I do,' Hector said.

Chris swallowed and backed off. Hector slipped the knife inside his shirt. 'Look,' Chris said carefully. 'Why don't we try acting rationally?'

'*Rationally*,' Damon said. 'There's a five-dollar word.'

Hector snorted. 'You sound like a fancy-ass college boy,' he said. 'You from the college?'

'I'm in high school,' Chris said.

At that, Hector crowed. 'Actually, college boy, you're in jail.' He rapped his hand against the bars. 'Hey,' he yelled out. 'We got us a genius down here.' He cocked one foot up against the lower bunk. 'Tell me this, college boy. If you're so smart, how come you got caught?'

Chris was saved from answering by an officer walking down the length of the barred catwalk. 'Anyone want to go to the exercise room?'

He stood up. Hector and Damon also started toward the door at the end of the pod. Damon turned around and whispered, 'We're not done, man.'

They filed through a corridor dotted with cameras. A few men called out to each other; this was the only time each day they had contact. As they went around the corner, Chris noticed Damon slipping behind, person by person, until he could jab a well-aimed elbow into the back of another inmate at a certain turn of the hall. It was, Chris realized, the blind spot between two cameras.

Just before the exercise room were two isolation cells. You could wind up in isolation two ways – by force, because you were acting out; or by request, because you were scared of the other inmates. Only one was occupied now. The prisoners started to holler, pounding on the door, one even leaning down to spit in the slotted opening.

The exercise room was small and sparsely furnished, with only a handful of equipment. But it filled like everything else in jail, by prearrangement. There was no waiting and no fight as two large black men claimed the stationary bicycles; as Hector and Damon picked up the table tennis paddles; as a tall guy with a swastika tattoo on his cheek began to bench press. There was a pecking order, Chris realized, that he was not privy to. But then again, why should he be? He did not fit in.

Frowning, he walked out to the exercise courtyard, a muddy square heavily ringed with barbed wire. Men were talking in small groups, gesturing with their hands. Others moved aimlessly, counterclockwise. Chris found someone leaning against the chain-link fence, staring at the mountains in the distance. 'That guy in the isolation room,' he said without preamble. 'What did he do?'

The man shrugged. 'Shook his baby to death. Frigging animal.'

Chris looked over the barbed wire, and thought of honor among thieves.

He called home collect.

'Chris?'

'Mom,' he said, just that word, over and over, with his head leaning against the blue pay phone.

'Oh, honey. I tried to come to see you, did they tell you?'

Chris closed his eyes. 'No,' he said tightly.

'Well, I did. But they said visiting hours aren't until Saturday.

So I'll be there first thing.' She took a deep breath. 'This is a horrible mistake, you know. Jordan's already got the prosecution's files. He's going to find a way to get you out as quickly as possible.'

'When is he coming to see me?'

'I'll call him and ask,' his mother said. 'Are you eating all right? Can I bring you anything?'

He thought about that, unsure what was allowed in. 'Money,' he said.

'Hang on, Chris. Your father wants to talk to you.'

'I . . . no. I've got to go. Someone needs the phone,' he lied.

'Oh . . . all right. You call here whenever you want, do you understand? We don't care about your reversing the charges.'

'Okay, Mom.'

Suddenly there was a tinny, recorded voice: 'This call,' it announced, 'is being made from the county correctional facility.' Both Chris and his mother were silent for a moment. 'I love you, sweetheart,' Gus finally said.

Chris swallowed, and slipped the receiver back into the cradle. He stayed there for a moment, leaning his head against the pay phone, until he felt the hard press of a body behind him.

Damon was rubbing his spine, his breath on Chris's neck. 'You miss your mama, professor?' He pushed his hips forward, his groin coming in contact with Chris's behind.

Wasn't this what he had been expecting? Wasn't this what he had been afraid of? Chris whirled around, catching the bigger man by surprise. 'Get away from me,' he said, his eyes glittering, and he backed into his cell.

Even with the covers over his head, he heard Damon laughing.

Chris thanked God for his lack of a cellmate. He lived in fear of suddenly having Damon thrown into his bunk, because although the officers were fairly good about keeping control during the day, who knew what they bothered to hear at night? He picked up the story lines on *Days of Our Lives*. He went to an AA meeting on Wednesday night, just to get out of the pod.

He filled out a commissary order, which reminded him of the room service breakfast sheet at the hotel in Canada his family had visited last summer. An eight-ounce jar of coffee was $5.25; a Three Musketeers bar was sixty cents. Thongs were $2. His items were delivered to him that afternoon by an officer, and the total amount was deducted from his prison account.

He slept a lot, pretending even when he wasn't tired so that people would leave him alone. And when clusters of men gathered in the exercise yard, Chris was always standing by himself.

A long time ago, Jordan had stopped believing in the truth.

There was no truth, at least not in his profession. There were versions. And a trial was not based on truth, anyway, but on what the police had, and how you could respond to it. A good criminal defense lawyer did not think about the truth, and focused instead on what a jury was going to hear.

Years earlier, Jordan had stopped asking his clients for the real story. Now he went in with a blank face, and simply said, 'What happened?'

He was standing at the control area of the maximum security unit, waiting for the officer in charge to slide the clipboard out so that he could sign in as a visitor. For his first post-arraignment interview with Chris, he'd brought along Selena Damascus, a six-foot-one black female private investigator who seemed better suited to fashion runways than doing Jordan's legwork, but who had been doing a damn good job all the same for several years.

'Where are they keeping him?' Selena asked.

'Maximum,' Jordan answered. 'He's only been here two days.'

A heavy barred door closed somewhere upstairs, and a uniformed prison officer came down. 'Hey, Bill,' the officer at the control station said. 'Tell Harte his lawyer's here.'

Another gated door snapped open – no matter how many times Jordan heard it, he just couldn't get used to the sound, which was rather like a gunshot – and he walked in, getting only the slightest glimpse of the inmates before he turned left toward the conference room used for client visitation.

Selena moved behind him, a shadow, and took a seat beside him at the conference table. She tipped her chair back and stared at the ceiling. 'Damn ugly jail,' she said. 'I think that every time I'm here.'

'Mmm,' Jordan agreed. 'The decor certainly isn't the reason it's so popular.'

The door swung open and Chris entered the room, his eyes moving from Jordan to Selena. 'Chris,' Jordan said, standing up. 'This is Selena Damascus. She's a private investigator who'll be helping with your case.'

'Look,' Chris said without preamble, 'I have to get out of here.'

Jordan took out a stack of papers from his briefcase. 'In the best-case scenario, Chris, that's exactly what's going to happen.'

'No, you don't understand. I need to get out of here *now*.'

Something in the boy's tone made Jordan look up. Gone was the frightened boy who'd been on the verge of tears in the Bainbridge police lockup, and in its place was someone harder, stronger, and capable of hiding his terrors.

'What, exactly, is the problem?'

At that, Chris exploded. 'What's the problem? What's the problem? I'm sitting on my ass in a jail cell, that's all. I'm supposed to graduate this year. I'm supposed to go to college. But instead I'm locked in a cage with a bunch of . . . of criminals!'

Jordan did not blink an eye. 'It's unfortunate that the judge didn't grant you bail. And you're right – it means you're stuck in jail until the trial, which could be six to nine months. But it's not wasted time. Every minute you're sitting in that cell, I'm coming up with a stronger case to get you free.'

He leaned forward, hardening his voice. 'Let's get something straight,' Jordan said. 'I'm not the enemy here. I'm not the reason you wound up in jail. I'm the lawyer, and you're the client. Period. And you've been indicted on a charge of first-degree murder, which carries a life sentence of imprisonment. What that means, Chris, is that your life is literally in my hands. Whether you spend it in prison or at Harvard comes down to whether or not I can get you off.' He stood up and walked behind Selena. 'And that depends on the amount of cooperation I get from you.

'Whatever you tell me and Selena does not leave this room. I'm in control of what you say, and who you say it to. And I need to know what I need to know when I need to know it. Understood?'

'Understood,' Chris said, meeting his gaze.

'All right. Let me explain where we stand. I'm going to make a lot of the decisions in this case, after I consult with you – but there are three things that only you can decide. The first is whether or not to accept a plea bargain or go to trial. The second is, if you do go to trial, whether you want that trial held in front of a judge only, or a jury as well. Finally, if there is a trial, whether or not you want to take the stand. I'll give you as much information as possible to make informed decisions, but you'll have to make your choices as we prepare. You following me?'

Chris nodded.

'Okay. Next. I'm going to be getting the discovery from the attorney general's office fairly soon. After I do, I'll come back here and we'll review it together in detail.'

'When is that going to be?'

'In about two weeks,' Jordan said. 'Then in five weeks or so, there'll be a preliminary pretrial conference.' He raised his brows. 'Before we start, do you have any other questions?'

'Yeah. Can I see Dr Feinstein?'

Jordan narrowed his eyes slightly. 'I don't think it's a good idea.'

Chris's mouth dropped open. 'He's a psychiatrist.'

'He's also someone who could be subpoenaed. The doctor-patient confidentiality relationship isn't always inviolable, especially when you throw in a charge of murder. Having you speak to anyone about the crime could come back to haunt us. Which reminds me – don't say a thing to anyone in the jail.'

Chris snorted. 'Like I've made so many friends here.'

Jordan pretended not to hear him. 'There are guys in here for drug cases, up for seven-year sentences. But if they can get any information on you and plead it up, they will. The cops might even put a narc in with you for that very purpose.'

'What if Dr Feinstein and I don't talk about what . . . happened?'

'What are you going to talk about, then?'

'Stuff,' Chris said softly.

Jordan leaned against the table, next to Chris. 'If you need someone to confide in,' he said, 'that person will be me.' He began walking back to his seat. 'Any other questions?'

'Yeah,' Chris said. 'Do you have any kids?'

Jordan stopped dead. 'Do I what?'

'You heard me.'

'I don't see why that has anything to do with your case.'

'It doesn't,' Chris admitted. 'It's just that if you're going to know me inside out by the time this is all over, I thought I ought to know something about you.'

Jordan heard Selena snicker. 'I have a son,' he said. 'He's thirteen. Now, if we're finished with the introductions, I want to get down to business. Today's agenda involves getting as much information as possible. We need you to sign release forms so that we can get your medical records. Are there any hospitalizations we should know about? Physical or mental disabilities that would make you incapable of physically pulling a trigger?'

'The only time I've been hospitalized was after that night. For my head, and I cut that when I passed out.' Chris bit his lip. 'I've been hunting since I was eight.'

'Where did you get the gun that night?' Selena asked.

'It was my father's. It was in the gun cabinet with all the hunting rifles and shotguns.'

'So you're accustomed to firearms.'

'Sure,' Chris said.

'Who loaded the revolver?'

'I did.'

'Before you left your house?'

'No,' Chris stared at his hands.

Jordan raked his hand through his hair. 'Can you give me the names of people who would be able to describe your relationship with Emily?'

'My parents,' Chris said. 'Her parents. I guess just about anyone at school.'

Selena looked up from her notepad. 'What should I expect these people to tell us?'

Chris shrugged. 'That Emily and I were, you know, together.'

'Might these people also have noticed that Emily was suicidal?' Selena asked.

'I don't know,' Chris said. 'She kept it pretty close to her chest.'

'We'll also need to show a jury that you were planning to kill yourself that night. Any counselors you spoke to? Mental health people you'd seen?'

'I wanted to talk to you about that,' Chris said, licking his dry lips. 'There isn't anyone who's going to tell you I was planning on killing myself.'

'Maybe you mentioned it in a journal?' Selena suggested. 'A note you wrote to Emily?'

Chris shook his head. 'The thing is, I wasn't.' He cleared his throat. 'Suicidal.'

Jordan briskly pushed the admission aside. 'We'll talk about that later,' he said, silently groaning. It was better, in Jordan's opinion, not to know any more than you needed to about a client's crime. That way you could proceed with your defense without violating any ethics. But once a client told you his story, that was the story. And if he took the stand he had to stick to it.

Confused, Chris looked from Jordan to Selena. 'Wait,' he said, 'don't you want me to tell you what really happened?'

Jordan flipped his pad to a new, blank page. 'Actually,' he said, 'I don't.'

That afternoon, Chris got a cellmate.

Shortly before dinner, he'd been curled up on his bunk, his thoughts pulled close around him, when an officer brought the man in. He was wearing a jumpsuit and sneakers, like everyone else, but there was something different about him. Something removed and standoffish. He nodded at Chris and climbed into the top bunk.

Hector came to the cell door. 'Get tired of seeing your own face, man?'

'Get lost, Hector,' the man sighed, without turning over.

'Don't you be telling me to get lost, you—'

'Chow,' an officer called.

As Hector left to get into his cell for lockdown, the man unfolded himself from the bunk and came down to accept his tray. Chris, on the bottom bunk, realized there was nowhere for the other guy to sit. If he crawled back into the top bunk, he'd have to eat lying down. 'You, uh, can sit here,' he said, glancing at the far end of his bunk.

'Thanks.' The man uncovered his tray. An unappetizing tricolored lump sat in the center. 'Name's Steve Vernon.'

'Chris Harte.'

Steve nodded and began to eat. Chris noticed that Steve was not much older than he was. And seemed just as inclined to stay uninvolved.

'Hey, Harte,' Hector called from his own cell. 'You better sleep with your eyes open tonight. Youngsters ain't safe around him.'

Chris's gaze flew to Steve, who was still methodically eating. This was the guy who'd killed a baby?

Chris forced his attention back to his plate, trying to remember that a man was innocent until proven guilty. He was proof of that.

All the same, Chris remembered the things Hector had said when they passed the isolation cell: *Picked up his kid in the middle of the night, and went crazy, man. Shook him so hard to stop crying his neck snapped.* Who knew what set someone like that off?

Chris's insides went to jelly. He set his plate down and started for the door of the cell, intending to head for the bathroom at the end of the hall. But it was lockdown for another half hour at least, and for the first time since his arrival, he did not have the cell to himself. He stared at the gray toilet, just inches from Steve Vernon's knee, and reddened with embarrassment. Dropping his pants, Chris sat down and tried not to think about what he was doing. He kept his arms crossed over his middle, his gaze on the floor.

He finished and stood to find Steve in the upper bunk again, his half-cleaned plate on the lower bed. Vernon's face was turned away from the toilet, toward the bare wall, offering Chris as much dignity as possible.

The telephone rang just as Michael was getting ready to leave for a house call. 'Hello?' he asked impatiently, his body already beginning to sweat beneath the weight of his winter jacket.

'Oh, Mikey,' said his cousin Phoebe, from California – the only person who ever called him Mikey. 'I just wanted to call and tell you how very, very sorry I am.'

He had never liked Phoebe. She was his aunt's child; she must have been alerted by his own mother after the funeral, since Michael had done no calling around of his own to let relatives know of Emily's death. She wore her hair in Haight-Ashbury braids and had made a career out of throwing pots that were intentionally lopsided. When Michael spoke to her, which was infrequently at family gatherings, he was reminded of the time they'd been four, and she'd snickered when he wet his pants.

'Phoebe,' he said. 'Thanks for calling.'

'Your mother told me,' she added, which Michael found

interesting: how could his mother pass along information that Michael could not yet accept? 'I thought you might want to talk.'

To you? Michael almost asked, before he remembered himself. And then he recalled that Phoebe's common-law husband had hanged himself from a closet rod two years ago. 'I know what it's like,' Phoebe continued. 'Suddenly discovering something you should have noticed a long time ago. They go on to this better place, you know, which is what they wanted all along. But you and me, we're still left behind with all the questions they couldn't answer.'

Michael remained silent. Was she still grieving, then, after two years? Was she suggesting that he had anything at all in common with her? He closed his eyes and felt himself shiver, in spite of his heavy coat. It wasn't true; it simply wasn't true. He had not known Phoebe's husband, but she couldn't have known him as well as he had known Emily.

So well, Michael thought, *that this would come out of the blue?*

He felt a stab of pain in his chest and realized that guilt came from all angles: from not being able to see his daughter's distress in the first place; from being so selfish that even now he focused on what Emily's suicide said about his parenting skills, and not about Emily herself.

'What do I do?' he murmured, unaware he'd spoken aloud until he heard Phoebe's answer.

'You survive,' she said. 'You do what they couldn't.' On the other end of the telephone line, Phoebe sighed. 'You know, Michael, I used to sit around looking for a way to make sense of what had happened, like there was some kind of answer I could find if I just looked hard enough. Then one day I realized that if there had been one, Dave would still be here. And I wondered if this . . . this feeling that I couldn't figure it all out . . . was what Dave had been feeling, too.' She cleared her throat. 'I still don't get why he did it; and I don't like that he did it; but at least I understand a little better what was going through his head.'

Michael imagined Emily's stomach tied up in the same Gordian knots as his own, Emily's thoughts equally tangled. And he wished, for the millionth time, that he'd been vigilant enough to have spared her such pain.

He murmured his thanks to Phoebe again and hung up the phone. Then, still wearing his shearling coat, he trudged upstairs in the empty house. He entered Emily's room and stretched out on the bed, staring in turn at the mirror, the schoolbooks, the discarded clothing, as he tried to see the world through his daughter's eyes.

Francis Cassavetes had been sentenced to six months in jail, but he was serving it on weekends. It was a common punishment for those who were employed and contributing to society – a judge would have them come into the jail on Friday and leave on Sunday, allowing them to work the rest of the days in between. Weekenders were visiting royalty in the jail, and spent most of their serving time taking bribes from inmates less fortunate in their sentencing. They smuggled in cigarettes, needles, Tylenol – anything – for a price.

When Francis entered the maximum security pod, he cupped Hector's face in his hands. 'Am I your man?' he said. He pushed past Hector, heading toward the john.

Francis returned, his hand fisted around something. 'You owe me double for this, Hector. Fucking things made me bleed.'

Chris watched as Hector's hand brushed Francis's and a small, white tube winked in the transfer. He turned and walked back into his cell.

Steve folded down a corner of the magazine he was reading. 'Francis brought him cigarettes again?'

'I guess,' Chris said.

Steve shook his head. 'Hector ought to ask for a nicotine patch, instead,' he muttered. 'Probably easier for Francis to smuggle in, too.'

'How does he?' Chris asked, curious. 'Smuggle them in?'

'Used to hide them in his mouth, I hear. But he got caught,

so now he's using a different opening.' When Chris continued to stare at him blankly, Steve shook his head. 'How many holes have you got?' he asked pointedly.

Chris turned bright red. Steve rolled away and opened his magazine again. 'Jesus fucking Christ,' he muttered. 'How the hell did you get in here?'

As soon as Chris entered the room with its long, scarred tables and collection of inmates and relatives, he saw his mother. She threw her arms around him as he reached her. 'Chris,' she sighed, smoothing his hair the way she had when he was a little boy. 'You're okay?'

The officer gently tapped his mother on the shoulder. 'Ma'am,' he said, 'you'll have to let go now.' Startled, Gus released her son and sat down. Chris settled across from her. There was no Plexiglas window between them, but that did not mean there wasn't a barrier.

He could have told his mother that in the superintendent's rule book – a binder big as a dictionary – it was decreed that a visit could begin with a brief embrace or kiss (not open-mouthed) and end the same way. In this same binder were the rules against possession of cigarettes, against use of profanity, against pushing another inmate. Such slight infractions in the real world were, in jail, a felony. The punishment was time added to one's sentence.

Gus reached across the table and took Chris's hand. For the first time, he noticed that his father was there too. James sat with his chair back a bit, as if he was afraid to come in contact with the table. It brought him nearly up against an inmate with a tattoo of a spiderweb on his left cheek.

'It is so good to see you,' his mother said.

Chris nodded, ducked his head. If he said what he wanted to – that he needed to go home, that he'd never seen anything more beautiful than her, right now, all his life – he would burst into tears and he could not afford to do that. God only knew who was listening, how it would be held against him.

'We brought you some money,' Gus said, holding out an envelope stuffed with bills. 'If you need more you can call us.' She handed the envelope to Chris, who immediately signaled an officer, and asked him to put it in his prison account.

'So,' his mother said.

'So.'

She looked into her lap, and he almost felt pity. There was nothing to talk about, really. He had spent all week sitting in a maximum security pod at the county jail, and his parents would not consider that sanctioned conversation.

'You'll get a chance next week to be moved to the medium level, no?'

James's voice startled him. 'Yeah,' Chris said. 'I have to petition the classification board.'

A silence fell. 'The swim team won its meet against Littleton yesterday,' Gus said.

'Oh?' Chris tried to sound like he gave a damn. 'Who swam my race?'

'I'm not sure. Robert Ric – Rich – something.'

'Richardson.' Chris scuffed his sneaker against the floor. 'Probably had a crappy time.'

He listened to his mother tell him about the history assignment Kate had received, for which she'd be dressing up as a colonial woman. He listened to her talk of the movies that were playing at the local theater and of her trip to the AAA to find the quickest route between Bainbridge and Grafton. And he realized that this was how they would fill these visiting hours for the next nine months – not with Chris discussing horrors he did not even want his parents to know of, but with his mother painting for him the world he had left behind.

His attention was captured as his mother cleared her throat. 'So,' she said. 'Have you met anyone?'

Chris snorted. 'This isn't the Christmas social,' he said, and immediately realized his mistake when his mother, red-faced, looked into her lap. He was amazed for an instant at how alone he really was: unable to blend in with the inmates because of who he had been; unable to blend in with his parents because of who he currently was.

James glared at his son. 'Apologize,' he said tersely. 'Your mother is having a very difficult time with this.'

'And if I don't?' Chris shot back. 'What are you going to do to me? Throw me in prison?'

'Christopher,' James warned, but Gus cut him off by placing her hand on his arm. 'It's all right,' she soothed. 'He's upset.' She reached across the table and took Chris's hand.

He remembered, just like that, being a toddler: how she would tell him that they were in a parking lot, or a busy street, then reach down to grasp his fingers. He remembered the smell of rubber on asphalt and the lumbering tug of machinery rolling past, and how safe he had felt in spite of it, as long as he could feel her hand covering his. 'Mom,' Chris said, his voice breaking, 'don't do this to me.' Before he could cry he stood, summoning an officer.

'Wait!' Gus exclaimed. 'We still have twenty minutes left!'

'To do what?' Chris said softly. 'Sit here, and wish we weren't?' He leaned across the table and awkwardly embraced her.

'You call us, Chris,' Gus whispered. 'And I'll see you Tuesday night.'

Those were the next visiting hours scheduled for the maximum security division. 'Tuesday,' Chris confirmed. Then he turned to his father. 'But . . . I don't want you to come.'

That afternoon the temperature dropped to zero. The exercise courtyard was empty, the weather having driven everyone else away. Chris stepped outside, his breath fogging a path before him. He walked around the courtyard once and noticed Steve Vernon leaning against the brick wall.

'Two guys went over that last year,' Steve said, nodding toward the high corner where the razor wire met the brick building. 'Officer went to close the door to the exercise room, and bam, they were gone.'

'Did they get away?'

Steve shook his head. 'Caught them two hours later, right on Route Ten.'

Chris smiled. Anyone dumb enough to stay on the main thoroughfare after skipping out of jail deserved to be caught. 'Do you ever think of doing that?' Chris asked. 'Jumping the fence?'

Steve exhaled through his nose, a white cloud. 'No.'

'No?'

'Nothing out there for me to run back to,' he said.

Chris swung his head around. 'How come you were in isolation?'

'I didn't want to be around the other guys.'

'Are you really in here because you shook your kid to death?'

Steve's eyes narrowed the slightest bit, but held Chris's. 'Are you really in here,' he said evenly, 'because you killed your girlfriend?'

Chris immediately thought of Jordan McAfee's warning: that the jail was full of snitches. He looked away, stamped his feet, and blew on his hands to warm them up. 'Cold,' he stated.

'Yeah.'

'You want to go in?' Steve shook his head. Chris leaned back against the brick wall, aware of the body heat of the man beside him. 'I'm not ready yet either,' he said.

Just after dinner, there was a shakedown.

It happened once a month, at the decree of the superintendent: the officers would canvass the cells, tossing mattresses and pillows, sticking their hands into spare clothing and discarded shoes in hopes of finding something incriminating. Chris and Steve stood outside the bars, watching their small square of privacy being violated.

The officer, a fat man, suddenly stood up, clutching something in his hand. He pointed to the sneakers on the floor – Chris had been sleeping, barefoot, when they entered. 'Whose are these?'

'Mine,' Chris said. 'Why?'

The officer unrolled his sausage fingers, one by one. In the middle of his palm was a fat, white cigarette.

'That's not mine,' Chris said, clearly stunned.

The officer looked from Chris to Steve. 'Save it for the DR,' he said.

As the guard left, Chris righted his bed and crawled back into the bunk. 'Hey,' Steve said, shaking his shoulder. 'I didn't plant it.'

'Go away.'

'I'm just telling you.'

Chris buried his head beneath his pillow, but not before seeing the flash of Hector's grin as he passed by the cell.

In the eighteen hours that passed between the finding of the cigarette and Chris's official disciplinary review, he fit together all the pieces of the puzzle. Hector had parted with one of his precious bootleg prizes because he could kill two birds with one stone: test Chris, the newcomer, for his loyalties; and fuck over Steve, the baby killer. If Chris ratted out Hector, he'd regret it for some time. If he pinned the blame instead on Steve – who, as his cellmate, would have the best opportunity to plant a cigarette in Chris's sneaker – Chris would align himself with Hector's crowd.

An officer led Chris to the small room where the assistant superintendent worked. Inside was the officer who'd wrecked the cell, and the assistant superintendent himself, a beefy man more suited to coaching football than pushing paper at a jail. Chris stood very straight while the assistant superintendent read a formal charge and advised him of his rights. 'So, Mr Harte,' the man said. 'Do you have anything to say in your defense?'

'Yes. Ask me to smoke it.'

The assistant superintendent raised his brows. 'I can't imagine you'd like anything better.'

'I don't smoke,' Chris said. 'This'll prove it.'

'It will prove that you can fake a cough,' the man said. 'I don't think so. Now: do you have anything to say in your defense?'

Chris thought of Hector, and his razor-bladed pen. He thought of Steve, with whom he'd reached a tentative truce. And he remembered what he had been told about minor transgressions in jail – this cigarette could add three to seven years to his sentence, if he was convicted.

Then again, that was a big if. 'No,' Chris said quietly.

'No?'

He looked the assistant superintendent in the eye. 'No,' Chris repeated.

The officers looked at each other and shrugged. 'You're aware,' the assistant superintendent said, 'that if you feel we're missing part of the story, you can suggest we speak to another inmate.'

'I know,' Chris said. 'But you don't have to.'

The man pursed his lips. 'All right, Mr Harte. Based on the evidence, you've been found guilty of possession of an illegal substance in your cell, and you're sentenced to a five-day lockdown. You'll remain in a cell for twenty-three hours of the day, with one hour free to shower.'

The superintendent nodded at the officers, who escorted Chris from the room. He walked silently through the maximum security pod, collecting his things without speaking a word to anyone. It was not until he was being led to his new cell that Chris realized he would sit there until Thursday, two days too late for his mother to visit; two days too late for the Classification Board to transfer him to medium security.

Chris slept during those days. He dreamed often. Of Emily, the touch and taste of her. Of kissing her, tongue deep, and having her push something into his mouth, something small and hard like a peppermint candy. But when he spit it into his hand, he saw it for what it really was: the truth.

He did sit-ups, endless numbers of them, because it was the only exercise he had room for in the narrow cell. During showers, he scrubbed until his skin went pink and raw, just so that he'd get his full hour out. He relived swim races, nights with Em, class lectures, until his cell became uncomfortably full of memories and he started to understand why inmates did not bother thinking of what they had left behind.

He did not call his mother, of course, and on Tuesday he wondered whether she had come all the way to Woodsville just to be told her son was in a disciplinary lockdown. He also wondered who had been moved to medium security. Steve would have petitioned the Classification Board that day.

On Thursday morning he banged on the bars as soon as breakfast was finished and told an officer he wanted to be moved. 'You will be,' the officer said. 'Soon as we get a chance.'

They didn't get a chance until four o'clock that afternoon. An officer swung open the door of the cell and led the way to the other maximum security pod, the one he'd been in the previous week.

'Welcome home, Harte,' he said.

Chris dumped his few belongings on the lower bunk. To his surprise, a figure curled out of the upper one. 'Hey,' Steve said.

'What are you doing here?'

Steve laughed. 'I was going to head out to a bar, but I couldn't find my car keys.'

'I meant that I thought you'd be upstairs by now.'

They both looked at the ceiling of the cell, as if it was possible to see medium security, with its yellow cinder-block walls, its horseshoe day room, its spacious showers. Steve shrugged, not saying what Chris knew he was thinking: that following the discovery of the cigarette, anyone in the jail would have pointed a finger at Steve, although Chris had chosen not to. 'Changed my mind,' he said. 'You get more room upstairs, but three more guys in your cell.'

'Three more?'

Steve nodded. 'I figured I'd wait until I knew someone else up there.'

Chris lay back on his bunk and closed his eyes. After all this time, he liked hearing the sound of another person's voice, another person's thoughts. 'Tuesday's coming around soon again,' he said.

He heard Steve's sigh. 'That it is,' he answered. 'Maybe we'll go.'

The funny thing was, Chris had become a hero. By not ragging on Hector about the cigarette, when he perfectly well could have, he'd been elevated to the level of a worthy inmate, one who was willing to take the punches for someone else. No matter how undeserving that someone else was.

'My man,' Hector now called him. Chris was allowed to decide, from four P.M. to five P.M., what channel the TV stayed on. In the exercise room, he was given time on the weight bench.

It was on the way back from the exercise room one day that Hector cornered him in the dark curve of the stairwell, the place that the cameras couldn't see. 'Shower,' he hissed, 'ten-fifteen.'

And what the hell was that supposed to mean? Chris spent the rest of the day wondering if he had been issued an appointment to get the shit kicked out of himself, or if Hector had some other agenda for needing to meet him in private. He waited until ten, then grabbed his towel and walked down the small cubicle at the end of the pod.

There was no one else there. Shrugging, Chris stripped and turned on the water. He stepped into the stall and had just begun to lather up with the soap when Hector peered over the edge. 'What the fuck is up with you?'

Chris blinked water from his eyes. 'You told me to be here,' he said.

'I didn't tell you to shower,' he said.

Actually, he had. But Chris wasn't about to point that out. He shut off the water, only to have Hector snake an arm inside the stall and turn it on again. 'Leave it,' he said. 'It hides the smoke.' Then he drew from his jumpsuit a Bic pen that had been burned down into a curve and stretched at one end to make a small tobacco bowl. He unfolded a small square of paper and shook something precious into the makeshift pipe, then quickly flared a forbidden lighter. 'Here,' he said, drawing deeply.

Chris wasn't stupid enough to turn down hospitality from Hector. He bent his head away from the thin trickle of water and inhaled, exploding in a fit of coughing. It was not a cigarette, that much was true, but it didn't have the sweet taste of pot, either. 'What is this?' he asked.

'Banana peels,' Hector said. 'Damon and me burn them down.' He took the pipe and tamped it down. 'For a jar of coffee I'll make you a packet.'

Chris felt the water run cold down the back of his neck. 'We'll see,' he said, taking the pipe again when Hector offered it.

'You know, college boy,' Hector said, 'I had you figured all wrong.'

Chris didn't respond. He fit his lips over the edge of the pipe, inhaled, and was not altogether surprised to find that this time, it came naturally.

On Saturday morning Chris was one of the first inmates taken down to meet their visitors. Unlike the last time his mother had come to the jail, she was standing painfully erect, fury and fear crackling around her like electric currents that Chris could see even this far off. She folded Chris into her arms and for the briefest moment he had the sense that years had fallen away; that he was once again smaller and weaker than she was.

'What happened?' she said tightly. 'I come here on Tuesday to find out that I can't see you because you're serving some kind of disciplinary sentence, and when I ask what that is they tell me it means you're locked inside some . . . some cage for twenty-four hours a day.'

'Twenty-three,' Chris said. 'You get an hour to shower.'

Gus leaned closer, her lips white. 'What did you do?' she whispered.

'I was set up,' Chris murmured. 'One of the other prisoners was trying to get me in trouble.'

'He was – he was what?' Shocked, Gus sat back heavily. 'And you just . . . went along with it?'

Chris felt two flags of color rise in his cheeks. 'He planted a cigarette in my sneaker; one that the officers found when they tossed the cell. And yeah, I went along with it, because sitting by myself for five days was better than having this guy come at me with the knife he made out of razor blades.'

Gus pressed her fist against her mouth, and Chris wondered what words she was trying to hold inside. 'There has to be someone I can talk to,' she said finally. 'I'll go to the super-intendent when I leave here today. This isn't the way a jail is supposed to be run and—'

'How would you know?' Chris shook his head. 'Don't go fighting my battles for me,' he said wearily.

'You're not like all these criminals,' Gus said. 'You're just a child.'

At that, Chris's head snapped up. 'No, Mom. I'm not a child. I'm old enough to be tried as an adult; old enough to serve time in an adult jail.' He looked past her. 'Don't make me into someone I'm not,' he said, his words laid like a frank hand of cards on the table between them.

On Saturday night there was a terrible windstorm, and even the solid cement walls of the jail seemed to creak and threaten. Lockdown was late on weekends – two A.M. – with most of the inmates rowdier than usual. Chris had not yet cultivated the art of sleeping like a log when the rest of the pod was animated and noisy, but he lay in his bunk with a pillow over his head, wondering if it was truly possible to hear the sound of the rain soaking into the bricks and whipping the ceiling.

There had been a fight earlier – an argument about whether to watch *Saturday Night Live* or *Mad TV*, which had resulted in two cells being locked down for an hour, the inmates screaming at each other through the bars. Steve had watched TV for a while, then come into the cell and crawled into the upper bunk. Chris had been feigning sleep, but he listened to Steve rip open the wrapper of the NutRageous bar he'd purchased from the commissary that week.

He'd gotten Chris some stuff, too. M&M's, and coffee, and Twinkies. Because of the disciplinary sentence, Chris had missed the commissary order day, and he supposed this was Steve's way of thanking him for not being a snitch.

After a while there was no more rustling in the upper bunk, and Chris realized Steve had fallen asleep. He waited until the officers called for lock-down, and then listened to the slap of rubber thongs on the floor; the soft sound of someone pissing in a urinal; the gradual slouch toward quiet.

Lights out.

The lights, actually, never went out. They dimmed considerably, but then again it was so dreary in the maximum security section that it took just as much time to get adjusted to seeing during the daytime as it did to sleeping in shadows. Chris listened for that wind, imagining that he was outside in the middle of a field so big that he couldn't see any of its boundaries. The rain would run over him, and he'd lift his face into it and all he would see was sky.

There was a whimper, and then another.

Chris smacked the flat of his hand against the upper bunk; he'd done that once or twice before when Steve was snoring. But instead of hearing the other man roll over and settle into sleep, there was a sharp, keening cry.

He got out of bed and stood up as Steve began thrashing back and forth on his bunk, chest convulsing with sobs. Stunned into immobility for a moment, Chris watched him. Steve's eyes were closed, his breathing labored. He was clearly upset, and he was just as clearly still asleep.

At the second cry, Chris clamped his hand on Steve's shoulder. He shook a little harder, and in the dim night light of the jail he saw the silver slits of Steve's eyes. Steve shrugged off Chris's hand, and he felt himself flush with embarrassment. The cardinal rule of jail was that you did not touch someone unless you were expressly asked to do so.

'Sorry,' he mumbled. 'You were having a nightmare.'

At that, Steve blinked. 'I was?'

'You were crying out and everything,' Chris said, hesitating. 'I didn't think you wanted to wake up the whole place.'

Steve slipped out of the upper bunk. He walked around Chris and sat down on the closed toilet, cradling his head in his hands. 'Shit,' he said.

Chris sank onto his bunk. In the distance, he could still hear the whistle of the wind. 'You should go back to sleep.'

Steve lifted his gaze. 'Did you know that sometimes you yell out at night, too?'

'I do not,' Chris automatically countered.

'You do,' Steve said. 'I hear you.'

Chris shrugged. 'Whatever,' he said, picking at a cuticle.

'Do you see her? Em?'

'How the hell do you know about Em?' Chris asked.

'That's the name you say. At night.' Steve stood up, his back against the metal bars of the cell. 'I just wondered if you see her, like I see . . . him.'

Chris thought about Jordan McAfee's warning, about rats that the cops put in your cell just to feel out your confessions. If he questioned, he would be questioned, and he was not sure that he wanted that sort of connection forged. But all the same, Chris heard himself whisper, 'What happened?'

'I was home alone with him,' Steve whispered. 'Me and Liza had a big fight, and she stormed off to the hairdresser's where she worked. She wasn't even speaking to me by the time she left, but she told me to take care of the baby. I got pissed off, and I started drinking whatever was left in the fridge. And then he woke up, crying so loud that it was giving me a headache.' Steve turned around, his forehead pressed against the bars. 'I tried to give him his bottle and I changed his diaper, but he kept screaming. So I carried him, with him yelling all the time in my ear, and my head about to split. Before I know it I'm shaking him, telling him to just stop crying already.' He took a deep, wet breath. 'And then I was shaking him, trying to get him to start crying.'

Steve spun around, his eyes gray and glazed. 'Do you know what it's like, to hold this . . . this little person in your arms . . . afterward . . . and to know that you were supposed to be the one to protect it?'

Chris swallowed past the constriction of his throat. 'What was his name?'

'Benjamin,' Steve said. 'Benjamin Tyler Vernon.'

'Em,' Chris answered softly, a perfectly appropriate response. 'Emily Gold.'

Then

May 1996

*H*is breath is so close I can taste him. His hands come to my waist, then slide up and up and pinch at me. I want to tell him it hurts, but I can't speak. I want to tell him I don't like this anymore.

He pushes me back and then his hand is down there and I start to scream.

The scream of the alarm clock made Emily bolt upright in her bed. The sheets were tangled around her feet; she had sweated through her night-gown. Swinging her legs over the edge, she stretched. She walked to the bathroom and turned on the shower, waiting until steam clouded about her head before stepping into the stall. As she passed the mirror, she turned away. There was something about seeing herself naked that didn't seem quite right.

She leaned back her head and let the water soothe her scalp. Then she picked up the soap and scrubbed at her skin until some spots were bleeding, but she still could not make herself feel clean.

For once, History was interesting. Gross, but completely riveting. Mr Waterstone had taken a break from the dry unit on taxation without representation and was detailing life in colonial America. They'd spent the past week learning the going prices for a bolt of calico, a crop of cotton, a healthy slave. Today, they were studying the Indians.

Oops. Native Americans. The whole point of this diversion from the standard textbook was to give students an appreciation for what the life of a colonist was like. Which included not only interference from the English crown, but also studious lack of contact with the natives.

Emily's eyes were glued to the screen at the front of the class. As far as she could see, not even the biggest skanks in the class – total druggies – were passing notes now. Everyone was watching the remarkable, reenacted footage of a Mohawk warrior cutting open the chest of a captured French-Canadian Jesuit priest, and eating his heart before his eyes.

There was a thump in the rear of the class, and Emily tore her eyes away long enough to notice Adrienne Whalley, a cheerleader, sprawled in a dead faint on the floor. 'Oh, shit,' Mr Waterstone said under his breath, but a curse all the same. He stopped the movie, flipped on the lights, and dispatched a student to run down to the nurse's office. Mr Waterstone himself crouched over Adrienne, rubbing her hand, and Em wondered if that wasn't Adrienne's intention to begin with. Young Mr Waterstone, with his shoulder-length jet hair and bright green eyes, was the most attractive male teacher in the school.

The bell rang just as the nurse waddled into the classroom with a bottle of ammonia that Adrienne, now awake, didn't need. Emily gathered up her books and headed for the classroom door, where Chris was already waiting. Her hand slid neatly into his as they began moving in tandem. 'How's Waterstone's class?' he asked; Chris had History seventh period.

Emily squeezed closer to him as a crowd passed by, and then stayed at his side. 'Oh,' she said. 'You'll like it.'

She liked the kissing.

In fact, if she could have gone back to just that, she would have. She liked opening her mouth against Chris's and having him fill it with his tongue, as if he was slipping her secrets. She liked feeling his moan roll, candy-round and warm, into her own mouth. She especially liked the way his big hands cradled her head, as if he could hold her thoughts together even when they started running off in directions she didn't want to explore.

But lately, it seemed like they kissed less and spent more time fighting over where Chris's hands should stay.

They were in the back of the Jeep now – how many times had Emily wondered if Chris had picked this car because of the way the seats folded down? – with the windows all steamed up. On one, Emily had drawn a heart with their initials. She watched now as Chris's back rubbed against it, erasing.

'I want you so bad, Em,' Chris whispered against her neck, and she nodded. She wanted Chris too. Just not quite in the same way.

In the abstract, the idea of making love with Chris was intriguing. Why wouldn't she, when she loved him more than anyone else in the world? It was just that the actual physical part of it – the way that he touched her body – made her feel sick. She was afraid that by the time she got up the nerve to have sex, she'd be too busy throwing up to actually finish what she'd started. The problem was that she'd look down at Chris's hand on her breast and she'd picture that same hand, albeit smaller, stealing a half dozen cookies from a fresh baked bunch before Chris's mom could see. Or she'd imagine the long fingers crossed in a game of Scissors, Paper, Stone while they sat side-by-side in the backseat on the way to some family vacation.

Sometimes she felt like she was rolling around in the back of the Jeep with this incredibly gorgeous, sexy guy. And sometimes she felt like she was wrestling with her own brother. Try as she might, she couldn't untangle one from the other.

She gently pushed on Chris's chest, trying to get him to sit up. When he lifted his head with a frown on his face, she smiled at him. His lips were still shiny and wet, and she felt a cooling ring around her nipple. She twisted her fingers with his. 'Do you feel, you know, close to me?'

Chris's eyes burned. 'God, yeah.'

Emily faltered. 'I don't mean it . . . like that,' she corrected. 'I guess, well, it's just that you know me better than my own brother.'

'You don't have a brother.'

'I know,' Emily said. 'But if I did, you'd be it.'

Chris grinned wickedly. 'Well, let's all thank God I'm not,' he said, bending his head again.

She tugged at his hair. 'Do you ever think about me like that?' she asked shyly. 'Like a sister?'

'Not right now,' he said in a strangled voice, and he touched his lips to hers. 'I can promise you that I never,' he kissed her again, 'ever,' and again, 'have wanted to do this with Kate.' He rolled away of his own volition, the thick ridge beneath his jeans going soft. 'God,' he said, shuddering. 'Now you've got me all freaked out.'

Emily placed a hand on his chest. She loved his chest, with its light dusting of hair and long muscles. 'I'm sorry. I didn't mean to.' She moved into Chris's arms and felt them close around her. 'Let's not talk,' she suggested, and buried her face in the heat of his skin.

His breath falls into my mouth, the only air I have. His hands start at my ankles and slide up my shins, pulling them apart like a vise, and I know what is coming as his fingers stab into me.

He won't let me close my legs, he won't let me curl away. There is blood on his hand. He pushes against my shoulders and draws a red line down the middle of my chest. It cracks open and I feel him reaching deep inside me, tight and uncomfortable; then something snakes out like jelly and when I lift my eyes I see Chris's teeth sinking into my heart.

'No.'

Emily tugged at the collar of Chris's shirt. 'No,' she repeated, and when his hands held her tighter, she pinched his neck. 'No!' she yelled, rolling him off her with an unholy shove. 'I said no,' she panted.

Chris swallowed hard, his erection pink over the edge of his unzipped jeans. 'I didn't think you meant it,' he said.

'Jesus, Chris,' she said. She rubbed her arms, covered with

goosebumps, and turned away. The problem was, in a Jeep, there was not all that far to go.

She waited for his hands to close over her shoulders, like they always did once they came to this point. It was like a play, coming to the same end of the act, every night. The curtain would come down, and they'd do it all over again tomorrow. But Emily didn't feel Chris coming toward her this time. She heard the rasp of his zipper as he dressed himself, the creak of the Jeep's flatbed as he came to his knees, maneuvering around her. 'Move,' he ordered tersely, and when she did he snapped the rear seat back up into place.

It was not until the overhead light went on as Chris opened the front door to slide into the driver's seat that Emily realized he meant to leave. Scrambling over the steering console, she managed to lock herself into her seat belt as Chris roared out of the empty parking lot.

He was driving fast and frenzied, very unlike Chris's natural caution. When he took a turn in the road on two wheels, Emily put her hand on his arm. 'What is the matter with you?'

He stared at her, his face so tight in the glare of the street-lights that for a moment Em did not recognize him at all. 'What's the matter with me?' he parroted. 'What's the matter with me?'

Without warning, he swung the car down a dead-end street off to the right and slammed the stick shift into Park. 'You want to know what's the matter with me, Em?' He grabbed her hand and shoved it hard against his groin. 'That's what's the matter with me.' He released her wrist, letting her hand crawl beneath her thigh in hiding. 'It's the only thing I can think of, the only thing that keeps me going. And night after night you say no, and I'm supposed to sit back and deal with it my own way, but the thing is I can't deal with it. Not anymore.' Emily's face reddened and she stared at her lap, hearing Chris sigh after a moment. He rubbed his hand through his hair, making it stand on end. 'Do you have any idea,' he said, his voice soft, 'any idea at all, how much I want you?'

She bit her lip. 'Wanting isn't the same as loving.'

He laughed, startled. 'Are you joking? I've loved you for – well, Christ, for my whole life. It's the wanting part that's new to me.' He stroked Emily's temple with his thumb. 'Wanting isn't the same thing as loving,' he agreed. 'But they might as well be, at least for me.'

'Why?' Emily managed.

Chris smiled at her, melting her strongest defenses. 'Because wanting you, Em,' he said, 'has only made me love you that much more.'

Everything was sharper. She could smell his black breath, feel the coarse hairs on the back of his hand, see her own face staring back at her. She was wearing something with elastic at the waist; it snapped back against her hips. There were the familiar sensations of his fingernails scratching at her, his palms grinding up against her nipples, the burning between her legs.

But this time there was more. The droning whirr of – what? – bees? The tang of disinfectant. And the unmistakable scent of a kitchen, of something being fried in grease.

Rattled, Emily woke up, unable to remember what it was that had left her so alert and tense that going back to sleep was an impossibility. Probably, she'd been dreaming of what would happen the next night. The night she and Chris had reserved to have sex for the first time.

Make love, she reminded herself, as if the euphemism might change it into something easier to accept.

She squinted in the dark, trying to locate her sneakers. She dragged them out from beneath the desk and slipped her feet inside, leaving them untied. Then she pulled Chris's swimming sweatshirt over her nightgown and tiptoed downstairs and out of the house.

It was warm for May and the moon was high and swollen, ribboning the path between the Hartes' and the Golds' like a silver stream. Emily hurried, her arms flashing white as the thin limbs of the birches she passed.

To her surprise, when she reached Chris's house, his bedroom light was still on. At three in the morning? On a Thursday night? She picked up a small stone and whipped it at his window, seeing his face appear almost instantly. The light winked black and suddenly Chris was standing a few feet away, in a T-shirt and boxers, his fingers flexing on the frame of the side door.

'I couldn't sleep,' Emily said.

'Me neither,' Chris admitted, with a smile. 'Kept thinking about tomorrow and getting all worked up.'

Emily didn't say anything. Let him think that was what had kept her awake, too.

He came off the porch, barefoot, wincing at the gravel and twigs that cut into the soles of his feet as he approached Emily. 'Come on,' he said. 'Might as well have insomnia together.'

He pulled her along the edge of the Hartes' lawn, to the point where it ran into forest. The ground there was softer – pine needles still wet with winter, moss that grew in a ratty green fringe. Chris's step grew more sure as they headed into the woods, toward a massive granite slab.

It had been years since they'd come there to play, with sticks for muskets and small cannonball boulders. Chris climbed onto the high, flat rock and helped Emily up. He curled his arm over her shoulders and looked back toward his house. 'You remember when you pushed me off here and I had to get stitches?'

Emily's hand went blindly to the spot on Chris's jaw. 'Seventeen,' she said dryly. 'You still haven't forgiven me.'

'Oh, I've forgiven you,' Chris assured her. 'I just haven't forgotten.'

'Okay,' she said, spreading her arms. 'Push me off, so we'll be even.'

Chris lunged, rolling Em onto her back as she laughed and kicked her heels against his shins. They tickled and squirmed the same way Emily remembered them doing as children, like puppies intent on catching each other's tails. And then all of a sudden Chris's hands stilled over her breasts and his mouth hung over hers in the space of a breath. 'Say Uncle,' he whispered, and gently squeezed.

'Unc—' Emily said, and then his tongue filled her mouth and his hands swept her from collarbone to hip, a completely different kind of game. She closed her eyes, listening to Chris's breathing and the throaty call of that owl.

Just as quickly as it had begun, Chris levered himself off her. He hauled Emily to a sitting position and chastely settled his arm around her. 'I think,' he said, 'that's enough of that.'

Emily turned to him, mouth agape. 'All of a sudden you can wait?'

In the dark, his teeth were very bright. 'Now that there's a light at the end of the tunnel, I can,' he said.

He slid his arm down to her waist. Emily shivered, and tried to convince herself that it was from the cold.

They lay on the wooden plank floor of the carousel, watching the stars spin through the tangle of carved tails and hooves. They were touching at the shoulders, the elbows, the hips, all spots that seemed to burn. Chris covered her hand with his own, and she nearly jumped out of her skin.

He leaned up on an elbow. 'What?'

She shook her head, her throat painfully tight. 'I can't just sit here and wait for it to happen,' she said. 'I want to get it over with.'

Chris's eyes widened. 'It's not an execution, you know,' he said.

'Says you,' Emily muttered.

Chris laughed and sat up. 'Well,' he said. 'What if we just talk for a little while, and see what happens?'

'Talk,' Emily snorted, as if the very concept of that leading straight to sex was unthinkable. 'What are we supposed to talk about?'

'I don't know. How about the time we watched the dogs going at it?'

Emily giggled. 'I forgot about that,' she said. 'Mrs Morton's poodle and the springer spaniel from Fieldcrest Lane.' She felt Chris's fingers slip between her own, and speaking suddenly became a little easier. 'I didn't think the poodle would be able to get on top of her.'

Chris smiled. 'Looked funny, didn't it?' Then he laughed.

'What?'

'I was thinking fair's fair – we should find those dogs,' he said, 'and let them watch us.'

She thought of the long, stringy penis of the poodle, sliding out of the bigger spaniel and slapping between its prancing legs. Whatever she and Chris were about to do couldn't be any more awkward than that. Chris's arm snaked over her shoulders. 'Better?'

'Yeah,' she admitted, turning her face into the hollow beneath his arm. He smelled of sweet deodorant, sweat, and excitement.

'How about,' he said, tipping up her face, 'I just kiss you?'

'Just kiss,' she said.

'For now. Don't think about the other.'

Emily smiled against his lips. 'Oh, right.'

Chris's mouth curved with hers. 'Humor me.' He traced the line of her lips with his tongue, then trailed his kisses down her neck. She felt his hands shake as they came up beneath her shirt, and this made her feel better than anything else: the knowledge that Chris, too, was nervous.

Then, in that way time has during adolescence of going both far too quickly and entirely too slow, Emily realized her clothes were off, her skin prickled with tiny goosebumps. She watched Chris roll a condom onto himself, and was surprised that she found him beautiful, not strange or ugly. She let Chris come down on top of her, his chest burning against hers, his body neatly set between her legs. 'Do you think,' she whispered, panicked, 'it will hurt?'

That stopped him. 'I don't know,' he said. 'I think it's supposed to, a little.' He rolled to Emily's side and stroked his hand over her hip, preoccupied. 'What's the matter?' Emily asked.

'Nothing,' he said, meeting her eyes. 'It's just that I forgot that part.'

'I'm sure it's not too bad,' Emily said. 'I don't think anyone's ever died of it.' *What am I doing?* she thought wildly. *Why am I urging him on?*

Chris smiled and brushed the hair off her forehead. 'If I could keep it from hurting you, I would,' he said. 'I wish I was the one who'd feel it.'

Emily touched his forearm. 'That's very sweet,' she said.

'It's not sweet,' Chris said, 'it's selfish. I know that *I* can stand a little bit of pain. But I don't think I'll be able to watch yours.'

Emily reached between his legs and wrapped her fingers around Chris, making him gasp. He rolled onto her and shifted his weight to his elbows. 'If it hurts,' he said, 'pinch me. So we're in it together.'

She felt him touching her, felt something wet that she realized came from herself, and then he was stretching her and stopping. She had a fleeting vision of the thousand-piece puzzles they'd done as children, how Chris had a tendency to try to jam pieces in where they would never comfortably fit.

'Em,' he said, sweat standing out on his brow. 'Do you want to do this?'

He would stop, she realized, if she shook her head. But she considered that what she wanted and what Chris wanted were inextricably tangled, and knew that he wanted this more than anything.

At her slight nod, Chris pushed himself gently inside her.

It hurt for a moment, and she dug her fingernails into his back. Then it wasn't so bad anymore. It felt odd, stretched from the inside out, but not painful. She felt her hips wobble as Chris began to push and moan, faster and faster, scooting her back a few inches on the planks of the carousel floor.

When he cried out, she was staring wide-eyed at the bare underbelly of a horse, aware for the first time that it had not been painted all over.

Chris rolled off her, chest heaving. 'Oh, God,' he said, sprawled on his back. 'I think I'm dead.' A moment later he gathered her close. 'I love you,' he whispered, touching his finger to her temples. 'But I made you cry.'

She shook her head, only realizing now that tears were still streaming. 'You made me . . .' Her voice trailed off, and she left it like that.

It's just a dare, she had told herself that day, and she'd pushed open the door of the men's bathroom in McDonald's. To her surprise it was exactly like the ladies' room, except for the two urinals on the wall, and the fact that it was more smelly. There was someone in the other stall; Emily could see his legs. Paralyzed by embarrassment – what if he noticed that her shoes were those of a nineyear-old girl? – she stayed rooted in front of the sink. There was a flush, and then the door to the stall opened. The Creep stood there, his clothes smelling of grease and disinfectant.

'Well,' he said. 'What have we here?'

Emily felt her legs trembling. 'I – I must have gone in the wrong one,' she stuttered. She whirled, heading for the door, but he grabbed her wrist.

'Oh, yeah?' he said, his voice curling like smoke about her, pulling her closer. 'How do you know it's the wrong one?'

He pushed her up against the door, barring anyone else's entrance. Holding her hands over her head, he slid his hand up her shirt. 'No titties,' he said. 'Might be a man.' Then he slipped his hand under the elastic of her shorts and rubbed his fingers between her clamped legs. 'Don't feel no prick either, though,' he said. He leaned forward, so close that she could smell his breath. 'Gotta make sure,' he said, and he jammed his finger inside her.

Panic was a shroud around her, stiffening her body and filling her mouth so that even though she screamed in her mind, no sound came from her throat. Just as quickly as the man had grabbed her, he let her go. Emily fell to the brown tile floor as he left, feeling the burn of disinfectant from his hands inside her. She was sick on the floor, then stood and rinsed her mouth. She straightened her clothing and walked back to the table, where Chris was waiting for her.

'Ssh,' Chris said, holding her against his chest. 'You were screaming.'

She was still naked, and so was Chris, his erection stirring again against her hip. She shoved away from him, huddling into a ball. 'I fell asleep,' she said, her voice unsteady.

'Oh,' Chris said, smiling softly. 'Sorry things got so boring.'

'It's not that,' Emily explained.

'I know. Just come here and sit with me.' He held out his hand, unthreatening, and Emily crawled onto his lap, trying to believe it was perfectly okay to do this although neither of them was wearing a stitch of clothing.

She felt Chris's hands on her, laying her down against the cool wooden planks again. When she tried to roll away, he held her, and she whimpered. 'I know you're sore,' he said. 'I just want to look at you. I was in a hurry before.'

He touched her breasts with his eyes, and then his fingers. He ran circles around her nipples, bit her collarbone. He let his hands pray their way down her belly, her hips, and then he parted her and stroked one finger over the folds. Trembling, she tried to kick him away, but he held her ankles. 'No,' he said. 'Just let me look at you.'

She felt his mouth make a damp mark on her navel, then slip downward. 'You're perfect,' he pronounced, and she blanched, knowing now that nothing could be farther from the truth. 'Don't move,' he said, his words vibrating between her legs, and by then she was sobbing.

He immediately reared up, alarmed. 'What's the matter? Did I hurt you?'

She shook her head, sending tears flying. 'I don't want to stay still. I don't want to stay still.' She wrapped her arms around

Chris, and her legs, and without intending it felt him slip into her again, a tight and startling fit.

'I love you,' Chris mouthed, already past coherence.

Emily turned her face away. 'Don't,' she answered.

Now

December 1997

G us wondered if Chris missed making decisions.
Staring down at the bright feast of fruits at the supermarket, sitting shoulder to shoulder like a rainbow of soldiers,
she couldn't help comparing the serviceable russets and grays
of the Grafton County Correctional Facility to the unintended
beauty of the grocery store. The options were staggering –
should she pick the tangerines, the green Granny Smith apples,
the smooth-cheeked tomatoes? A choice at every turn – the
complete antithesis of being told to eat this, to walk here, to
shower now.

She reached toward the clementines. They were Chris's
favorite, and she would have loved to bring him some the
following Tuesday . . . but was that even allowed? She imagined one of those burly blue-suited men splitting the fruit into
sections to check for razor blades, much as Gus herself had
mashed Chris's Halloween candy when he was a child, looking
for pins. Except she had been searching out of love. The officers would be searching out of duty.

Gus opened the bag and spilled the clementines back onto
their pile.

Can you believe it?

In that household?

Gus turned around, pushing her cart toward the array of
lettuce, but all she saw were several Bainbridge biddies doing
their weekly shopping.

Well, I believe it. I saw the boy once, and he was . . .

Did you know the father won some medical honor?

Gus clenched her hands on the grip of the shopping cart.

Steeling herself, she wheeled toward the women who'd busied themselves sniffing melons. 'Pardon me,' Gus said, baring her teeth in a tight smile. 'Did you have something you wanted to say to me, directly?'

'Oh, no,' one of the women said, shaking her head.

'Well, I would,' her companion announced. 'I think when a child that young commits a crime as horrible as this one, you have to lay the blame at the feet of the parents. After all, he'd have to learn that behavior somewhere.'

'Unless he's just a bad seed,' the first woman murmured.

Gus gaped at them. 'Do you mind telling me,' she said softly, 'why this is any concern of yours?'

'When it happens in our town, it becomes our problem. Come along, Anne,' the second woman said, and they sailed into an adjoining aisle.

With high color spotting her cheeks, Gus left her partially filled shopping cart and headed out of the store. It was only because she had to jostle past a mother with twins at the checkout that she even noticed the newspapers on the stand. Folded to reveal its headline banner, the *Grafton County Gazette* screamed MURDER IN A SMALL TOWN, PART II. And in much smaller print: 'Evidence Mounts Against High School Scholar-Athlete Jailed for Killing Girlfriend.'

Gus focused on the headline again. PART II, it said. What had happened to PART I?

The Hartes received the *Grafton County Gazette*, most people in the area did. As hokey as it was, with its lead stories about dairy farm silos that burned down and school budget impasses, it also was the one paper that covered the town of Bainbridge. A good number of households got the *Boston Globe*, too, but only to compare the crime statistics and political posturing and basically remind them how idyllic their lives were in New Hampshire. On nights they were too busy to crack open the *Globe*, the *Gazette* – a maximum of thirty-two pages – was something they had the time to read.

The only time Gus could remember not reading the paper,

in fact, were those days surrounding the arraignment, when she had been so sick at heart that she could barely function in her own world, much less read about the one around her.

Gus took several deep breaths and read the article. Then she flipped to the masthead, found what she was looking for, and rolled the newspaper up beneath her arm. So what if they found proof that Chris had been at the carousel? There had never been any question that he was at the scene of the crime. She did not realize until she had reached her car that she'd taken the paper without paying. For a moment she considered going back in to leave thirty-five cents, then she decided against it. *Fuck* it, she thought. *Let them think the whole family's full of felons.*

The offices of the *Grafton County Gazette* were almost as somber as the jail, a pleasant thought which gave Gus the impetus to march up to the receptionist with two-toned hair and demand to see Simon Favre, editor in chief. 'I'm sorry,' the receptionist predictably said. 'Mr Favre is in—'

'Trouble,' Gus finished for her, and pushed through the double doors that led to the editorial offices.

Green computer screens scrolled and beeped; in the background was the sound of a printer. 'Excuse me,' Gus said, addressing a woman who was sitting at one of the desks, bent over a string of negatives with a loupe. 'Could you tell me where Mr Favre is?'

'That way,' the woman said, pointing to a door at the far end of the room. Gus nodded and crossed toward it, knocking once and then swinging open the door to find a smallish man with a telephone tucked to his ear. 'I don't care,' he said. 'I told you that already. All right. Good-bye.'

He looked up at Gus and narrowed his eyes. 'Can I help you?'

'I doubt it,' Gus said crisply. She slapped her copy of the *Gazette* down on his desk so that the offensive headline was clear. 'I want to know when newspapers started printing fiction.'

Favre made a sound at the back of his throat and twisted the paper so that he could read it right side up. 'And you are?'

'Gus Harte,' she said. 'The mother of the boy who is accused of an alleged murder.'

Favre pointed to a word. 'We say it's an alleged crime right here,' he said. 'I don't understand—'

'No, you couldn't,' Gus cut in. 'You couldn't, because you don't have a son who's innocent, but who has to sit in jail for nine months until he has a chance to prove it. You couldn't, because you let a reporter take a piece of information from the police for the shock value. My son never hid the fact that he was with Emily Gold when she died, so why make it seem like that's the turning point of the case?'

'Because, Mrs Harte,' Favre said, 'it's a good hook. And there aren't a hell of a lot of those in our neck of the woods.'

'That's exploitation,' she said. 'I could sue you.'

'You could,' the editor in chief said. 'But I'd think you're paying enough for legal bills right now.' He stared at her until she looked away. 'Of course, we'd be willing to hear your side of the story. As you're probably aware, the girl's mother gave Lou an exclusive; he'd be happy to interview you as well.'

'Absolutely not,' Gus said. 'Why should I have to make explanations for what happened, when Chris did nothing wrong?'

Favre blinked once. 'You tell me,' he said.

'Look,' Gus said, 'my son is innocent. He loved that girl. I loved that girl. There's your truth.' She smacked her palm down on the newspaper. 'I want a retraction printed.'

Favre laughed. 'Of the story?'

'Of the tone. Something which says more clearly than this garbage that Christopher Harte is not guilty until he's convicted in a court of law.'

'Fine,' Favre agreed.

He'd given in too easily. 'Fine?'

'Fine,' Favre repeated. 'But it won't make any difference.'

Gus crossed her arms over her chest. 'Why not?'

'Because the public's already got wind of this,' the editor

said. 'It might even have been picked up on the AP.' He crumpled up the newspaper into a ball and tossed it into the trash. 'I could say your boy sprouted angel wings and flew to heaven, Mrs Harte. That could even be the truth. But if people have already sunk their teeth into the story, they're not going to let it go.'

Selena walked into Jordan's house, slipped off her coat, and stretched out on the couch. Thomas, who'd heard the door, came running out of his bedroom. 'Oh, hey,' he said. 'What's up?'

'Look at you,' Selena said, yawning. 'You get more handsome every day.'

'You gonna go out on a date with me yet?'

Selena laughed. 'I told you. Your senior prom, or when you hit six feet two, whichever comes first.' She picked up a half-finished can of Pepsi, sniffed it, and drank, eyes scanning the mess of paperwork on the living room floor. 'Where's your father?'

'Here,' Jordan announced, stomping out of the bedroom in baggy pair of sweats and a Nike T-shirt. 'Who the hell gave you the key to my house?'

'I did,' Selena said, unruffled. 'Made a copy months ago.'

'Well, by all means,' Jordan said. 'Don't ask my permission first.'

'Lighten up.' Selena turned to Thomas. 'What's gotten into him?'

'He got the discovery from the AG's office today.' Thomas shook his head dolefully. 'He needs a soft shoulder to cry on.'

'I don't have soft shoulders, and I don't make a habit of getting it on with people who pay me,' Selena said.

'*I'm* not paying you,' Thomas pointed out.

'Good-bye, Thomas,' Selena and Jordan chorused. With a laugh, Thomas went back to his room and closed the door.

Selena rolled to a sitting position on the couch as Jordan sank into the piles of paper littering the floor. 'That bad?'

Jordan tapped his finger against his lips. 'I wouldn't necessarily say it was all bad. It just isn't categorically good. A lot of the evidence could go both ways, depending on the point of view.'

'You're going to keep him off the stand.'

Selena said it as a statement, knowing full well that would be Jordan's intention.

'Yeah.' Jordan's eyes swept over Selena, reclining against the pillows with the Pepsi in her hand. 'I think we've got a stronger case that way.' Now that Chris had volunteered the information that he had not planned to kill himself, that was his story. Period. If he got up on the stand, that was what Jordan ethically would have to coach him to say. On the other hand, if he kept Chris off the stand, Jordan could say whatever the hell he wanted to get his client free. As long as Chris didn't perjure himself, Jordan could use any damn defense he liked.

'Say you're a juror,' Jordan hypothesized. 'Which of these two versions are you more likely to believe: Chris, who outweighed Emily by fifty pounds, was really along for the ride that night to try to stop her from killing herself, but couldn't manage to yank the gun away from her? Or: they were both going to kill themselves in this beautiful testimony to their love . . . except then Emily blew her brains out and they were all over Chris's shirt and it wasn't so beautiful anymore, and he passed out before he could use the gun on himself.'

'I see your point,' Selena said. She gestured toward the loose piles. 'Where should I start?'

Jordan rubbed his hands over his face. 'I don't know. It's going to take me days to get through this. I guess, first off, try his parents. We need a flawless character witness or two.'

Selena reached for a piece of paper, flipped it over – laundry ticket – and began to make a list. As Jordan buried his nose in a forensics report, Selena picked up the nearest file. The police interview with the Golds, postmortem. Nothing unexpected from Emily Gold's mother – a lot of hysteria, a healthy dose of grief, a strict refusal that her darling girl was suicidal.

'Oh, that?' Jordan said, glancing over. 'I skimmed it this afternoon. You're not going to get squat out of the woman. She gave an exclusive to the *Gazette*.' He grimaced. 'Nothing like a little unbiased reporting to help speed justice along.'

Selena didn't answer. She had turned the page and was riveted by the second interview. 'Melanie Gold's a lost cause,' she agreed. Then she smiled at Jordan. 'But Michael Gold might be your saving grace.'

Being a mother gives you a singular sort of vision, a prism through which you can see your child with many different faces all at once. It is the reason you can watch him shatter a ceramic lamp, and still remember him as an angel. Or hold him as he cries, but imagine his smile. Or watch him walk toward you, the size of a man, and see the dimpled skin of an infant.

Gus cleared her throat, although there was no way Chris would be able to hear her across the din of other visitors and the sizable distance. She crossed her arms and gripped her elbows, trying to pretend that the sight of her firstborn in regulation prisonwear did not affect her; that the dull wash of fluorescent lights on his hair did not seem unnatural. As he came closer, she fixed a wide smile across her face, certain the strain would split her in two.

'Hi,' she said brightly, hugging Chris as soon as the officer stepped back. 'How are you doing?'

Chris shrugged. 'All right,' he said. 'Considering.' He began to pick at the snaps on his overwashed shirt – not the faded jumpsuit he'd been wearing before, Gus noticed. The matching shirt and elastic-waist pants looked like surgical scrubs, and were short-sleeved, even in December. 'Aren't you cold?'

'Not really. They keep the thermostat at seventy-eight degrees,' Chris told her. 'Most of the time I'm too hot.'

'You should ask the officers to turn it down,' Gus suggested, and Chris rolled his eyes.

'Now why,' he said, 'didn't I think of that?'

A tight silence noosed them. 'I saw Jordan McAfee,' Chris said, finally. 'And some lady who helps him with his cases.'

'Selena,' Gus said. 'I've met her. Striking, isn't she?'

Chris nodded. 'We didn't really talk that much,' he said. He looked into his lap. 'He told me not to tell anyone about what happened.'

'Your case, you mean,' Gus said slowly. 'That's not surprising.'

'Mmm,' Chris agreed. 'But I was wondering if that included you.'

Well, there it was. All the normalcy Gus had worked so hard to create – the smile, the embrace, the idle conversation – dissolved against the simple fact that no matter how hard she pretended, the relationship of mother to son was irrevocably altered when one of the parties was in jail. 'I don't know,' she said, trying to keep the dialogue light. 'I guess it depends on what you're going to tell me.' She leaned forward, whispering. 'Professor Plum, in the Library, with the Wrench?'

Startled, Chris laughed, and it was the best moment Gus had had since this whole nightmare had begun. 'I wasn't going to be that obvious,' he said, his eyes still smiling. 'But I think it might hurt you all the same.'

She tried to ignore the chill fluting over her skin. 'I'm made of fairly hearty stock.'

'You must be,' Chris said, 'or else where would I have gotten it from?' The thought of James, with his *Mayflower* antecedents, fell between them like a stone. 'The thing is,' Chris continued, 'I told Jordan something that I already told Dr Feinstein. Something I didn't tell you.'

Gus sat back, trying not to assume the worst. She smiled, encouraging him.

'I wasn't suicidal,' Chris whispered. 'Not that night, and not now.'

The bald fact that this confession had not been 'I'm guilty' had Gus grinning like an idiot. 'Well, that's wonderful,' she said, before she had a chance to reason it through.

Chris stared at her patiently, waiting for the other shoe to drop. When her eyes widened and her palm covered her mouth, he nodded. 'I was scared,' he admitted. 'That's why I said what I did. And Em, well, she *was* going to kill herself. I was playing along to try and keep her from doing it.'

Gus reeled from the implications of the admission. It meant that her son was not a hair away from killing himself, certainly that was news for celebration. And it meant that the reason she and James had not seen suicidal tendencies in their son prior to that night was not due to their own negligence, but because there were no suicidal tendencies.

It also meant that Chris, unjustly accused to begin with, was being condemned for being a hero. And that, had he turned to someone else to help him save Emily, this entire horrible outcome might never have come to pass.

Suddenly aware of all the other ears around them, Gus shook her head imperceptibly. 'Maybe you should write all this down,' she suggested, 'and just mail it to me.' She cocked her head at the inmate beside Chris.

Turning slightly, he reddened. 'You're right,' he said.

'I'm glad you told me,' Gus hastened to add. 'I can even understand why you said what you did to the . . . authorities. But you didn't have to lie to us.'

Chris was silent for a moment. 'I didn't see it so much as lying,' he said finally. 'It was more like not telling all of the truth.'

'Well,' Gus said. She wiped at her eyes, feeling silly for having to do it. 'Your father will be thrilled. He didn't understand how someone with so much going for him would want to kill himself.'

Chris pinned her with his gaze. 'It can happen,' he assured her.

'Maybe you'd like to tell your father yourself,' Gus said softly. 'He's in the car. He wanted to come in—'

'No,' Chris interrupted. 'I don't want to see him. You tell him, if you want. I don't care one way or the other.'

'You do care,' Gus insisted. 'He's your father.' When Chris shrugged, she felt her anger rise on James's behalf. 'He's just as much a part of you as I am,' she reminded Chris. 'Why won't you see him, when you let me visit?'

Chris traced a scar in the table. 'Because,' he said quietly. 'You never expected me to be perfect.'

On Wednesday afternoon, one of the officers stopped on the catwalk in front of Chris and Steve's cell. 'Get your stuff together, guys,' he said. 'You're getting a room with a view.'

Steve, who'd been reading in the upper bunk, leaned down and looked at Chris. Bounding to the floor, he gathered his belongings. 'Do we get to stay together upstairs?' Steve asked.

'Far as I know,' the officer said, 'that's the plan.'

They had both petitioned the Classification Board for a transfer to medium security, although the likelihood of actually being granted permission seemed slim after the debacle with Hector still fresh in everyone's minds. But neither Chris nor Steve was about to look a gift horse in the mouth. Chris jumped up from his own bunk and collected his toothbrush, his spare jumpsuit, a pair of shorts, and his stash of commissary food. He glanced at the pillow and blanket on his bunk, then turned to the officer. 'Do I need to take those?' he asked.

The officer shook his head, then directed them out of the catwalk, past the other maximum security cells. Some of the inmates hooted as they passed, or called out questions. By the time they reached the stairwell near the control room, it was quiet again.

'You two have the top bunks,' the officer said as they made their way upstairs. This did not come as a surprise to Chris; the less seniority you had, the worse position you got – and upper bunks were considered less desirable than lower ones. It also meant that there would be two people already in the cell he and Steve were about to enter, and like any combination of elements, it remained to be seen how they all would mix.

The walls upstairs were cinder block, but painted a pale, sunny yellow. The catwalks were twice as wide; the cells a foot and a half bigger in all directions. There were four bunks in each cell, but there was also a large common room that connected the two pods, with tables and chairs and so much space that Chris felt his spine stretch and was only then aware that he'd been stunting himself.

'What did I tell you?' Steve said, tossing his things onto the left upper bunk. 'Nirvana.'

Chris nodded. Their other cellmates were not in, but their belongings were neatly arranged in boxes set squarely on the two lower bunks, a clear attempt to let the newcomers know their place.

About fifteen men were sitting in the common room, some watching the television mounted high on the wall, others fitting together pieces of the jigsaw puzzles that were stacked on top of the lockers.

Chris sank down onto a plastic chair – plenty of room for it here, unlike the narrow catwalk in maximum security. Steve sat across from him and propped his feet on the table. 'What do you think?'

Chris grinned. 'That I'd sell my own grandmother to keep from being sent down to maximum again.'

Steve laughed. 'Yeah, well. Everything's relative.' He reached on top of some lockers and pulled down two Milton Bradley boxes. 'This is all they've got,' he complained. 'Someone set the Monopoly board on fire last month.'

Chris laughed out loud. A room full of felons, and the only games were Sorry! and Risk.

'What's funny?' Steve asked.

Chris reached for the box in Steve's left hand, Sorry! 'Nothing,' Chris said. 'Nothing at all.'

James stood up and walked toward the podium to the

thunderous applause of his colleagues. Gus thought he was strikingly handsome against the burgundy walls of the dining room, holding up his plaque. 'This,' he said, brandishing the award, 'is a tremendous honor.'

Bainbridge Memorial Hospital toasted one of its own every year in conjunction with the teaching staff of the nearby medical school. Ostensibly, the dinner was supposed to make the young men and women entering the medical field realize what sort of demigods they'd be joining. This year, Dr James Harte had been chosen as the honoree for his continuing contribution to Bainbridge Memorial Hospital, although everyone present knew that James was being feted because of his inclusion in the 'Best Doctors' listing. Unfortunately for the nominating committee, the event had already been planned when the small glitch regarding Dr Harte's son had come to pass.

'The good thing about this particular award,' James said, 'is that I've had some time to figure out what I'm supposed to say to you all. I was told: *something inspirational.* So before I begin perhaps I should apologize for choosing to become a surgeon, instead of a minister.'

He waited for the polite laughter to die down. 'When I was much younger, I believed that studying hard and passing a battery of exams was all I needed to become a doctor. But there is a great difference between being a practicing physician, and a practiced physician. I used to think that the study of ophthalmology was all about getting to the malady. I was looking people, literally, right in the eye, and I wasn't necessarily seeing them. In hindsight – no pun intended – I realized how much I was missing. I urge those of you at the start of your careers to remember that you aren't being trained to treat afflictions, but patients.'

He gestured to the director of surgery. 'Of course, I never would have gotten this wise without a brace of bright colleagues to spur me on, and a fabulous institution like Bainbridge in which to do it. And I'd have to thank my parents, who gave me my toy doctor's kit at age two; my mentor, Dr Ari Gregaran, who blessed me with everything I know; and of course, Augusta and Kate, for teaching me that if there are patients at a hospital, there has to be patience at home.' He lifted his plaque again, and the room dissolved into applause.

Gus clapped woodenly, a smile pasted to her face. He had forgotten to mention Chris.

Intentionally?

Her head was spinning. She stood up before James could even make his way back to the table and pushed her way blindly toward the ladies' room. Inside, she leaned against the sink and ran cool water over her wrists, James's words circling inside her head: *I was looking people right in the eye, and I wasn't necessarily seeing them.*

She straightened her dress and took her handbag, intending to walk out of the bathroom and head into the lobby where she'd ask the concierge to call her a cab. James would figure it out, and maybe by the time he got home she'd have spit enough anger out of her mouth to be able to speak to him.

She yanked open the wooden door of the bathroom and almost fell on top of James. 'What's the matter?' he asked. 'Are you sick?'

Gus tilted her head. 'As a matter of fact,' she said. 'I am.' She crossed her arms. 'Do you realize you didn't mention Chris in your acceptance speech?'

James had the grace to blush. 'Yeah. I realized it just as I was coming off the podium, when I saw you leaving the room. I always said it was a damn good thing I wasn't an actor, because I'd forget someone important when I went up to get my Oscar.'

'It's not funny, James,' Gus said tightly. 'There you were, preaching acceptance to all these . . . fawning medical students, and you can't even practice that in your own backyard. You left Chris's name out on purpose. You didn't want anyone associating the little scandal with your Big Night.'

'I didn't do it intentionally, Gus,' James said. 'Sub-consciously? Well, that's a different story. Yes, if I'm going to be truthful, I didn't want anything to ruin tonight. I'd much rather have the audience pointing at me and saying "Oh, that's the Best Ophthalmalogical Surgeon in the Northeast" than "His son's on trial for murder."'

Gus felt her face heating. 'Just get away from me,' she said, trying to push past him. 'No wonder you feel so comfortable here. These people are all like you. Not one of them mentioned Chris to me. Not one of them asked if he's all right, if we know when the trial is going to be, nothing.'

'That's not my fault,' James pointed out. 'It hits too close to home. Don't you see, Gus? I *am* too similar to these people. If this sort of thing can happen to me, who's to say that one day, it couldn't happen to them?'

Gus snorted. 'Well, it has happened, James. It is happening. And no matter what you say – or don't say – you can't just wish it away.'

She was halfway down the hall when she heard her husband's voice, so soft that she might have imagined the pain striped through it. 'No,' he said. 'But you can't stop me from trying.'

One of the things that Selena Damascus had learned in her ten years as a private investigator was that accidents did not just happen. From time to time they were carefully plotted, calculated, and arranged to one's advantage – all, of course, under the cloak of happenstance.

She would tell anyone who asked that there was no magic to being an investigator; it required only common sense and an ability to get people to talk. To that end, however, she had developed a repertoire of skills, designed to get her as much information as quickly as possible. She was not above using her looks, her body, or her brain to get her behind a closed door; and once she weaseled her way inside she'd be damned if she left before she had something worthy to take home.

The day she intended to meet Michael Gold, Selena woke up at four in the morning. She dressed in jeans and a white Gap T-shirt, and was waiting in her car on a Class IV road that veered off Wood Hollow when Michael Gold's truck rambled out of his driveway shortly after five. Of course, by that point, she already knew that Michael owned his own veterinary practice, mostly large animals. She knew that he drove a Toyota 4X4. She knew that when he stopped for coffee en route to his first call, he added milk but no sugar.

Selena followed Michael's truck discreetly, an act made all the more challenging by the lack of cars on the road at this hour. When he pulled into a long driveway marked 'Seven Acre Farm,' she drove by without glancing back. She parked a half mile down the road and doubled back, following the sweet scent of hay and horses to a field in the distance.

Having studied Michael for a few days, Selena knew that he started in the barn, greeting all the animals and getting the lay of the land no matter what the call was for. That morning, the farrier was working as well, which was a wonderful boon since the burly man pounding horseshoes would assume she was the vet's assistant, and the vet would assume that she was the farrier's. She smiled at everyone she passed – bloody busy here, for so early in the morning – and found Michael bent over the foreleg of a sorrel mare in one of the stalls.

Hearing her approach, he let the horse's leg fall to the straw. 'I don't see any signs of abcess, Henry,' he said, twisting to see over his shoulder. 'Oh.' He came to his feet, brushing off his hands and leaning against the horse. 'Sorry. Thought you were somebody else.'

Selena shook her head. 'No problem. Can I help you in there?'

'Everything's under control. You haven't seen Henry around, have you?'

'No,' she answered honestly. 'If I do, though, I'll send him your way.' Before he could ask any questions, she disappeared down the aisle of the barn.

She studiously avoided Michael for an hour, until he shook hands with a man leading a big bay out of the barn and walked toward the driveway. Then she positioned herself at the fence post closest to his truck, smiling when he greeted her as he began to store away the tools of his trade.

'You're Dr Gold?' Selena asked.

'Yeah,' Michael said, 'but only on my letterhead. My clients call me Michael.'

'I'd imagine your clients don't call you much of anything at all,' Selena teased.

Michael laughed. 'Okay, then. Their owners.'

'I wonder if you've got a minute to talk,' Selena said.

'Sure. Is it about one of the horses at the farm?'

'To be honest,' Selena said, 'it's about Christopher Harte.'

She watched the shock leap into his expression, carefully smoothed by a creditable blankness. 'Are you a reporter?' he asked finally.

'I'm an investigator,' Selena admitted. 'Working for the defense.'

Michael laughed. 'And you actually thought I'd want to talk to you?' He pushed past her and opened the door of his truck, swinging himself inside.

'I didn't think you'd want to,' Selena called out. 'But I thought you might need to.'

He unrolled the window of the door he'd already closed. 'What do you mean by that?'

Selena shrugged. 'I've seen how you go about your work. And I can't imagine why someone who goes to such great lengths to save animal lives would intentionally ruin a human one.' She paused, watching the play of emotions on his face. 'That's what it would be, you know,' she added softly.

Michael Gold looked at her, his throat working. Selena placed a hand on his forearm. 'What happened to your daughter was horrible, and terribly sad. No one on our side is discounting that.'

'I don't think I'm the person you ought to be talking to,' Michael said.

'You're wrong,' Selena countered. 'You're exactly who I ought to be talking to. I want to ask you – Emily's father – a question: would she have wanted Chris caught up in this circus? Would she have believed he could kill her?'

Michael ran his thumbnail along the lip of the steering wheel. 'Ms, um . . .'

'Damascus. Selena Damascus.'

'Selena, then,' he said. 'How would you like a cup of coffee?'

The diner that Michael drove to was more of a truck stop than anything else, peopled with burly men in red flannel and grimy baseball caps, whose rigs were lined up in the parking lot like the long keys of a xylophone. 'Not much in the way of cuisine around here,' he said, by way of apology, and slid into the booth in the rear of the restaurant. He played with the salt and pepper shakers – nervous, Selena thought – while waiting for the waitress to bring over two white ceramic mugs filled with steaming coffee.

'Careful,' he warned, as Selena brought the rim to her lips. 'It can be pretty hot here.'

Selena took a more tentative sip, and grimaced. 'And as corrosive as battery acid,' she added. She set her cup down on the table and spread her palms flat on the table, on either side of a small notebook and pen. 'So,' she said casually.

Michael exhaled. 'I need to know,' he said. 'Is this off the record?'

'I already told you, Dr Gold. I'm not a reporter. There is no record.'

He seemed surprised by this. 'Then why do you need to speak to me?'

'Because there is going to be a trial,' Selena said softly. 'It's important for us to know what you might have to say.'

'Oh,' Michael said. Clearly the thought had not yet occurred to him that he'd be dragged onto the stand to replay his grief in front of a jury. 'Is anyone going to know that you and I talked?'

Selena nodded. 'The defense attorney will know,' she said. 'Chris will know.'

'Well, that's all right,' Michael said. 'It's just – how can I explain this to you? I don't want it to look like I've switched to the other side.'

'I don't see how it could,' Selena said. 'I only want to ask you some questions about your daughter, and her relationship with Chris. You don't have to answer if you feel uncomfortable.'

'Okay,' Michael said after a moment. 'Shoot.'

'Did you know that your daughter was suicidal?'

Michael sighed. 'Wow. Don't start off soft, do you?' He shook his head. 'That's a catch-22, you know. If I tell you that she was suicidal, I'm admitting to something I don't really want to. The thing is, I don't know if I can't believe it because of what it is – you know, suicide with a capital S – or because I'm still in denial.' He bit his lower lip. 'But if I tell you that Emily wasn't suicidal, then how do I explain the fact that she's dead?'

Selena waited patiently, fully aware that he hadn't really answered – and that he hadn't blamed Chris. Michael exhaled slowly. 'I didn't know she was suicidal,' he said finally. 'But I'm not sure if that's because I didn't know what I was supposed to be looking for, or because she wasn't suicidal at all.'

'Did she come freely to you to discuss problems?'

'She could have,' Michael said, leaving Selena to think that she didn't.

'Who else,' she pressed, 'would Emily have turned to for support?'

'Melanie, I suppose, more than me.' He smiled ruefully. 'It's a girl thing, I guess. Sometimes when she was angry she'd lock herself in a room and paint three or four canvases until she got it all out of her system.' He hesitated, then shook his head.

'What?' Selena urged.

'I was going to say: And of course she'd talk to Chris. But then I decided I shouldn't.'

'It's no secret that your daughter and Chris were involved,' Selena pointed out.

'Involved,' Michael said, turning the word over on his tongue. 'You could say that.'

'What would you say?'

He smiled. 'They were flip sides of the same coin. There were actually times when the kids were growing up that I forgot Chris wasn't my own son.'

'Sounds like they spent a lot of time together.'

'Inseparable, I think you'd call it.'

'Pretty intense for a high school romance,' Selena observed.

'It wasn't a high school romance,' Michael said. 'At least, nobody saw it like that. Nobody would have been surprised to find them getting married after college.'

'You think that's what Emily wanted?'

'Yeah. And Chris. Hell, to be honest, all four of us parents.'

Selena wrote down: *Together out of love? Or to live up to their parents' expectations?* 'It would be very helpful to the defense if you'd grant me access to Emily's bedroom.' A total longshot, but inside, she knew, would be a multitude of clues that might help the defense – photos tucked into a mirror, love notes stored in a jewelry box, pads still imprinted with the curl of Chris's practiced name.

'I couldn't,' Michael said. 'Even if I – well, my wife wouldn't understand.' He ran a finger around the rim of the coffee cup. 'Melanie, you know, she's seized on this . . . trial. I look at her sometimes, and I wish it was that easy for me, too. I wish I could forget that, oh, six months ago we all were joking about where we'd hold the wedding. I've tried, you know, because of Emily, but I can't seem to throw the past away.'

Selena held her tongue, the time-honored interrogator's trick for getting a subject to keep talking. 'See, I identified Emily's body at the hospital. But the morning before that I had seen Emily at breakfast, running outside when Chris honked in his car to take her to school. I watched him kiss her as she got into the car. And I can't hold the two things together in my head.'

Selena studied his face. 'Do you think Chris Harte killed your daughter?'

'I can't answer that,' Michael said, staring at the table. 'If I do, I wouldn't be putting my daughter first. And nobody loved Emily more than me.' He lifted his eyes. 'Except, maybe, for Chris.'

Selena inclined her head. 'Will you speak to me again, Dr Gold?'

Michael smiled, feeling a weight burst free. 'I'd like that,' he said.

For a moment Melanie stood at the doorway of her daughter's bedroom, staring at the thick layer of paint on the six-panel door, which could not completely obliterate the deeply carved warning KEEP OUT.

Emily had been, oh, maybe nine, when she'd scraped the message into the wood with an X-Acto knife, earning her a grounding for defacing the door and another one for taking a dangerous tool from her father's desk drawer. And if Melanie recalled correctly, she'd made Emily paint the door again by herself. But even if the words had been erased, the idea behind it hadn't, and from that day on neither Michael nor Melanie entered the bedroom without knocking first.

Feeling only slightly stupid, Melanie raised her fist to the door and pounded twice, then turned the knob. As far as she knew, Michael had not been coming in here, either. The last people through had been the police, searching for God knew what. Melanie didn't think they'd taken anything, at any rate. The pictures of Chris were still tacked around the dresser mirror, the arms of his swim team sweatshirt still wrapped around the pillow on the bed – Em had said it smelled of him. The book Emily had been reading for English class was cracked open, face down, on the nightstand. A pile of clothing that Melanie had washed and given to Em to put away remained on the edge of the bureau.

Sighing, Melanie took the first items of clothing and began

to put them back in their respective drawers. Then she stood in the center of the room, turning around, trying to decide what she should do next.

She was not ready to take down all the evidence that Emily had lived here, slept here, breathed here only weeks before. But there were some things in this room that she could no longer stand seeing.

Melanie began by plucking the photos of Chris from the edge of the mirror. *He loves me, he loves me not*, she thought. She collected the pictures into a pile and put them on the bed, then unwrapped Chris's sweatshirt from the pillow and rolled it into a ball. She peeled the tape carefully from a caricature of Emily and Chris that had been stuck to the closet door and added it to the cache on the bed. Then, satisfied, she looked around for something in which to put it all.

If Melanie hadn't been reaching for one of the empty shoe-boxes in the back of Emily's closet, she never would have noticed that there was a hole in the plaster. But she was down on her hands and knees, groping, when she felt her hand go through the wall.

Thinking of rats and bugs and bats, she was relieved when the only object her fingers closed around was solid and immobile. She withdrew a cloth-bound book which fell open to reveal the familiar, neat loops of Emily's handwriting.

'I didn't know she still kept one,' Melanie murmured. When Em had been younger, she'd had a diary, but it had been years since Melanie had seen her writing in it. Flipping to the last page and then back to the first, she realized that this journal was recent. It went back almost a year and a half. And as far forward as the day before Emily's death.

Feeling decidedly uncomfortable, Melanie began to read. Many of the entries were mundane, but certain sentences leaped out at her:

Sometimes it's like I'm kissing my brother, but how do I tell him *that?*

I have to look at Chris's face to figure out what I'm supposed to be feeling, and then I spend the rest of the night wondering why I don't.

I had that dream again, the one that makes me feel dirty.

What dream? Melanie skipped back a few pages, and then forward. And before she could find another reference to that dream, she found herself reading about the night her daughter had lost her virginity.

Emily had made love for the first time at the same spot where she was murdered.

Melanie read the whole book through, losing track of time. Her hands relaxed, and the journal fluttered to the last page; to the entry made the day Emily had died.

If I tell him, he will marry me. It's that simple.

She was talking about the baby. It was clear, even without the specific word on the page. As of the time she'd written this, on November 7, Emily hadn't told Chris she was pregnant. Just as she hadn't told her parents.

Barrie Delaney's whole case against Chris was based on this baby, on the premise that he planned to kill Emily to get rid of it. But how could he get rid of a child he knew nothing about?

Melanie closed the journal, feeling ill. Her mind still trembled with revenge, so full with justice that she did not even notice that in her journal, Emily had not said good-bye.

She gathered the photos of Chris that she'd pulled from the mirror and knotted them in the belly of his sweatshirt. Then she walked downstairs, the book tucked beneath her arm, the sweatshirt clutched in her hand. She went to the formal living room, the one nobody really lived in, which held the house's only fireplace.

They'd used it maybe four times in their whole history of owning the house. With a wood stove in the kitchen, the fireplace seemed extraneous, especially in a room filled with uncomfortable Queen Anne furniture bequeathed from some forgotten relative. Melanie knelt down and scattered the photos across the iron grate, then bunched the sweatshirt on top of it. She retrieved a pack of matches from the kitchen and lit the fire, watching the flames lick at the pictures of Chris before burrowing into the weave of the sweatshirt and erupting in a high blue peak. Then she threw the journal onto the grate, her arms crossed tightly as the binding began to curl and the pages became ash.

'Melanie?'

Coming home from work, Michael's footsteps circuited the house, finally stopping at the small, unused living room. He stared at the fireplace, still smoldering, and then at his wife. 'What are you doing?'

Melanie shrugged. 'I was cold,' she said.

Then

September 1997

In his right hand, Coach Krull held a banana. In his left hand was a condom.

'Ladies and gentlemen,' he said dispassionately, 'take your marks.'

There was a general wave of ripping as the class, grouped in twos, opened their own individual Trojans. Emily had to use her teeth to get the wrapper open. From the next desk over, a boy watched her bite at foil. 'Ouch,' he winced.

Heather Burns, a friend of Emily's and her partner for this ridiculous Health Education class, giggled. 'He's right,' she whispered. 'You're not supposed to use your teeth.'

Emily blushed furiously, thanking God for the millionth time that Heather, and not Chris, was her partner. It was bad enough doing this, but doing it with him would be that much more embarrassing.

Health Education was mandatory for seniors, although most of them had been rolling their own condoms down actual penises for several years by the time they entered the class. The fact that high school coaches – like Coach Krull of the swim team – served as teachers made it even less palatable. To a letter, all the coaches were fat and male, pushing fifty. Whatever wisdom they could offer to teens regarding sex could only be taken with a grain of salt. In fact the only saving grace of the class was seeing Coach Krull stammer over the word *menstruation*.

The coach lifted a whistle to his lips and blew, and there was a flurry of caressing hands as thirty condoms were rolled down thirty bananas. Furrowing her brow, trying very hard not to think of Chris, Emily stroked her hand down the yellow skin of the banana and worked out the wrinkles on the condom.

'Hey! My banana broke!' a boy shouted.

Someone else snickered. 'That happen to you a lot, McMurray?'

Emily snapped the condom into place at the base of the banana. 'Done,' she sighed.

Heather leaped to her feet. 'We won!' she shrieked.

Everyone else's eyes turned to them. Coach Krull ambled down the aisle and stopped in front of their desks. 'Let's see, now. We've got a nice space at the top, like we ought to. And the condom isn't bunched up on one side . . . and it fits snugly at the bottom. Ladies,' he said, 'my congratulations.'

'Well,' said McMurray, eating his banana, 'now we know why Heather Burns.'

The class snickered at his joke. 'Keep wishing, Joey,' Heather said, tossing her hair. Coach Krull presented Emily and Heather with SKOR candy bars. Emily wondered if that was supposed to be a joke.

'In real life,' Coach Krull said, 'putting on a condom isn't a race.' He grinned, adding, 'Although it probably feels like one.' He picked up a banana peel from the floor and looped it into the trash can. 'If used correctly – correctly – we know it's the best way barring abstinence to prevent an STD or AIDS,' he said, 'but seventy-five-percent effectiveness isn't a great form of birth control. At least not for those twenty-five women out of a hundred who wind up pregnant. So if that's your method of choice, consider a backup plan.'

As Coach Krull talked, Heather unwrapped her candy bar and took a bite. Emily caught her friend's eye and smiled faintly. 'Ouch,' she mouthed.

With her heart pounding, Emily locked the door to the bathroom and drew the cardboard box out from beneath her shirt. She rubbed at the spots on her stomach where the sharp edges had dug in and then set the box on the sink counter and stared at it.

Remove test stick from kit. Make sure you read all directions before beginning test.

With trembling hands Emily extracted the foil packet. The test kit was a long, narrow piece of plastic with a squared-off swab at the end and two small windows cut out higher up.

Hold swab end of stick in urine stream for ten seconds.

Who could pee for ten seconds?

Place test stick in holder and wait for three minutes. You will know the test is working when you see the blue 'control' line appear in the first window. If you see a blue line appear in the second window, no matter how faint, you are pregnant. If there is no blue line in the second window, you are not pregnant.

Emily wiggled down her jeans and sat on the toilet, positioning the stick between her legs. She closed her eyes and tried to go slowly, but counted only to four before her bladder ran dry. Then she took the stick, beads of urine still beaded on the plastic, and set it in the provided plastic spoon rest.

Three minutes was a very long time.

She watched the control line appear in the first window, and thought, *We were always careful.*

Then she heard Coach Krull's voice: *Seventy-five-percent effectiveness isn't a great form of birth control, at least not for those twenty-five women out of a hundred who wind up pregnant.*

The second line came thin as a hairline fracture, and carried just as much pain. Emily doubled over, her hand unconsciously curled over her stomach, as she stared up at the packaging of the only test she'd ever wanted to fail.

The muscles of Chris's back gleamed with exertion, and his shoulders blocked Emily's view of the moon as he reared over her. She raised her hips to him, with the uncharitable thought that maybe he could drive the thing out of her, but Chris interpreted this gesture as passion and began to stroke, slow and deep inside her. Her head turned to the side, she could feel him, a battering ram. She felt his hand slip between them – he hated it when she didn't come, too – and she clamped her legs together before she could remember to relax. 'Sssh,' he said, so far in her now she could feel an unbearable pressure, as if this person inside her was pushing Chris out of its space.

Suddenly Chris convulsed, and – as she always did when he came apart – she laced her arms and legs tight and held him close. He lay heavily, a stone on her heart, squeezing the air from her lungs, and almost, with it, her secret.

The Planned Parenthood office was conveniently on a bus line that linked Bainbridge with several less affluent communities to the south and east. The waiting room boasted a mix of ethnicities, some single women and some with partners, some with swollen bellies and some crying into their hands, but no one had the look of Emily herself: a rich girl from a bedroom community where things like this did not happen.

'Emily?' The counselor, a nurse practitioner named Stephanie Newell, was calling her back inside. Gathering her coat, Emily followed the nurse into a small, homey room. 'Well,' Stephanie said, sitting across from Emily. 'You are pregnant. Approximately six weeks, from the looks of things.' She paused, searching Emily's face. 'I take it this isn't welcome news.'

'Not exactly,' Emily whispered.

It had not been real, until now. There was always the margin for error with the home pregnancy test, or the possibility that it had all been nothing more than a bad dream. But this – a stranger telling her it was true – was incontrovertible proof.

'Have you told the father?'

Emily noticed, in a hazy, detached way, that no one was using the word *baby*. 'Pregnant,' sure. 'Father,' yes. But just in case, she assumed, there was no need to put a face to something you might not keep. 'No,' she said tightly.

'It's your choice,' Stephanie said gently, 'but it's easier to go through something like this – no matter which option – with someone beside you.'

'I won't be telling him,' Emily said, her voice firm, realizing as the words came that they were true. 'He's not in the picture.'

'He isn't,' Stephanie pressed, 'or you don't want him to be?'

Emily turned to the nurse. 'I can't have this baby,' she said flatly. 'I'm going to college next year.'

Stephanie nodded, nonjudgmental. 'We offer abortion as one option,' she said. 'It costs three hundred twenty-five dollars and you have to pay up front.'

Emily blanched. She figured there would be a cost, but that was an awful lot. She'd have to ask her parents . . . or Chris . . . and that was impossible.

She rucked the edge of her shirt up and twisted it between her hands. She had spent her entire life being what everyone wanted her to be. The perfect daughter, the budding artist, the best friend, the first love. She had been so busy meeting everyone's expectations, in fact, that it had taken her years to remember exactly why it was all one big farce. She was not perfect, far from it, and what you saw on the outside was not what you really were getting. Deep down, she was dirty, and this was the kind of thing that happened to girls like her.

'Three hundred twenty-five dollars,' she repeated. 'All right.'

In the end, it was easy. She initially thought of going to Chris and asking him to help her get the money, but he would ask what it was for, and even if she told him it wasn't something she could talk about, he'd figure it out. There were not many things a seventeen-year-old would need so much cash for, and quick.

So Emily set her clock radio to go off in the middle of the night. She crept downstairs and fumbled in her mother's purse for the checkbook. Ripping off number 688, she made the check out to cash for the total amount, easily forging Melanie's signature. Her mother used her checks only to pay bills, and that was just once a month. By the time Melanie was going crazy trying to remember what check number 688 had been for, the entire procedure would probably be over.

The next day after school, Emily asked Chris to drive her to the bank. She had to cash a check for her mother, she said. The teller knew her; in Bainbridge, everyone knew everyone. And Emily had gone home $325 richer.

The night before Emily was scheduled to have the abortion, she and Chris went to the beach at the edge of the lake. For September, it was balmy – Indian summer, the night flung across the sky like sheer gauze, bringing darkness but no weight. Emily could not settle or concentrate; her skin felt too small for her body, and she was convinced she could feel the thing growing inside her. Desperate to push it out of her mind, she threw herself at Chris, kissing him with a fury, so that at one point he leaned back and looked at her quizzically. 'What?' she demanded, but he just shook his head. 'Nothing,' he murmured. 'You just don't seem like you.'

'Who do I seem like?' she asked.

Chris smiled. 'My wildest dream,' he said, and buried his hands in her hair. And then all of a sudden he had pulled Emily on top of him, her legs falling open on either side of his hips. 'Sit up,' Chris urged, and she did, only to feel him slipping inside her with the change of position.

It was too soon. Emily immediately braced her hands on Chris's shoulders, leaning back in an effort to rear away. 'Oh, that's good,' Chris murmured, his head turned to the side. Emily froze, and then urged by Chris's palms on her hips, moved tentatively. 'You look like a centaur,' he said, and – surprised – she laughed.

The movement drove Chris even deeper inside her, making the whole thing worse. They were joking around, just like they used to. They might as well have been wrestling, as they had when they were children, practically siblings. But they weren't wrestling, and they weren't siblings, so it was all right to have sex. Wasn't it?

Emily squeezed her eyes shut, scattering her thoughts. 'That would make you the horse,' she said, slightly queasy.

Chris flexed his buttocks. 'Giddyap,' he said, and bucked beneath her so that the moon rippled over her shoulder, lying light on her breast.

Afterward, she lay on her side, her head pillowed by Chris's arm and his hand resting on her hip, spooning. This was the part she waited to get to, the part worth suffering through the sex. She had curled up against Chris a million times in her life. Afterward, it was like it had always been, with nothing embarrassing between them.

'Sand,' he suddenly whispered, 'is greatly overrated.'

She smiled faintly. 'Oh?'

'My ass is rubbed raw,' he admitted.

Emily grinned. 'Serves you right,' she said.

'Serves me right? I was doing the chivalrous thing, letting you be on top.' He splayed his palm over her stomach.

Abruptly, Emily sat up, grabbed the nearest piece of clothing – Chris's shirt – and wrapped herself in it to walk along the edge of the lake.

Did Chris have a right to know? Would she be lying, if she did not say anything at all?

If she did tell him, they'd get married. The problem was, she wasn't sure she wanted that.

She told herself that it wasn't fair to Chris, who thought he'd be getting a girl who'd never been touched by another man.

But a small, nagging throb at the back of her thoughts said that it wasn't fair to her, either. If she sometimes went home after making love with Chris and vomited for hours; if she sometimes couldn't bear his hands roaming under her bra and panties because it felt more like incest than excitement – could she really spend her whole life married to him?

Emily tossed a pebble into the lake, breaking the smooth surface. It was a strange feeling, knowing that her life would always be intertwined with Chris's – God, it had been since the day she was born – and yet realizing that she was still secretly hoping for an out. Everyone expected Chris and Emily to be together forever, but forever had always seemed a long way off.

She pressed her hand to her stomach. Forever had a real time line, now.

Emily supposed then, that the answer was yes. She could marry Chris. The alternative would be explaining that she cared about him like a sister, like a friend, not necessarily like a wife. And she would see his face whiten, feel his heart crumble in her hands.

She did not love Chris enough to marry him, but she loved him too much to tell him that.

Emily blinked at the surface of the lake, rippling deep and ringed with the sounds of crickets. She imagined how easy it would be to walk into that lake, her feet slipping along the silty bottom, until the black water covered her head and weighted down her lungs, sinking her like a stone.

She felt Chris walk up behind her and gently slip his arm around her shoulders. 'What are you thinking about?'

'Drowning,' she said softly. 'Walking in there until it was over my head. Very peaceful.'

'Jesus,' Chris said, clearly startled. 'I don't think it would be peaceful at all. I think you'd start thrashing around and try to get to the surface—'

'You would,' Emily said. 'Because you're a swimmer.'

'And you?'

She turned in his arms, and laid her head on his chest. 'I would just let go,' she said.

Perhaps it would have gone well, but the physician scheduled the day of Emily's abortion was a man. She lay on the gurney, her legs bent up and revealing, Stephanie beside her. She watched the doctor enter and turn to the sink to wash. The soap slipped between his fingers, greasy and white, exaggerating the size and shape of him. He turned around and smiled at Emily. 'Well,' he said, 'what have we got here?'

Well. What have we got here?

Then he reached under the gown, just like the other had, after saying that same awful thing, and slid his fingers into her. Emily began to kick, her ankles knocking aside the stirrups, her foot striking the doctor on the side of the head as he cautiously backed away.

'Don't touch me,' she yelled, trying to sit up, curling her hands between her legs and tucking the gown beneath her thighs. She felt Stephanie's hand on her shoulder and turned her face into the counselor's arm. 'Don't let him touch me,' she whispered, even after the physician left the room.

Stephanie waited until Emily stopped crying, then sat down on the doctor's stool. 'Maybe,' she suggested, 'it's time to tell the father.'

She would not tell Chris, especially not now. Because as soon as she did, she would have to tell him about this horrible abortion and the doctor and why she couldn't stand to have the man touching her. And why she couldn't stand to have Chris touch her. And why she was not the girl Chris thought she was. As soon as she told him, she'd have made her own bed, and she would have to lie in it – with him.

Eventually, too, she would have to tell her parents. And they'd stare at her in shock – their little girl? Her fault, because she was having sex now, when she shouldn't. Her fault, because she attracted that disgusting man's attention when she was still so young.

Everyone would find out soon enough, anyway. She was well and neatly trapped, with only one small and hidden exit, so dark and buried that most people never even considered breaching its hatch.

Emily listened to Stephanie, her options counselor, talking and talking for over an hour. Amazing, considering there really were no options at all.

'Can you pass the butter?' Melanie asked, and Michael handed it to her.

'This is good,' Michael said, pointing to his dinner. 'Em, honey, you ought to try the chicken.'

Emily pressed her fingers to her temples. 'I'm not that hungry,' she said.

Melanie and Michael exchanged a glance. 'You haven't eaten anything all day,' Melanie said.

'How do you know?' Emily shot back. 'I could have polished off a whole banquet at school. You weren't there.' She bowed her head. 'I need Tylenol,' she murmured.

'Did you see the application from the Sorbonne?' Melanie said. 'It came with today's mail.'

Emily's fork clattered against her plate. 'I'm not going.'

'What's the harm in applying?' Melanie said. She smiled at Emily across the table, clearly misreading her reluctance. 'Chris will be just where you left him, when you get home,' she teased.

Emily shook her head, her hair flying. 'Is that what you think this is? That I can't live without him?' She tamped down the question that burned at the base of her throat: *Could she?* Throwing her napkin on top of her plate, she stood. 'Just leave me alone!' she cried, running out of the room.

Melanie and Michael stared at each other. Then Michael cut a slice of chicken and placed it in his mouth, chewed it. 'Well,' he said.

'It's the age,' Melanie agreed, and reached for her knife.

There was a clearing down the Class IV road that ran behind the Harte and Gold properties where people left off old stoves and refrigerators, bags of thick glass bottles and rusted tin cans. For lack of a better word, it was known in Bainbridge as the Dump, and had served for years as a field for target practice. Chris four-wheeled into the clearing and left Emily sitting on the hood of the Jeep while he set up a gallery of bottles and cans thirty yards away. He loaded the Colt revolver, batting away the flies that buzzed in the sweet, tall grass around the Jeep's tires. Chris snapped the chamber back into place as Emily leaned down to pluck one green stalk and threaded it between her front teeth. He took a Kleenex from his pocket and wadded small balls of it into his ears, then handed it to Emily. 'Plugs,' he said, pointing, urging her to do the same.

He had just lifted the revolver, braced in both his hands, when he heard Emily's shout. 'Wait! You can't just shoot,' she said. 'You have to tell me what you're aiming for.'

Chris grinned. 'Oh, right. So that I can look bad when I miss.' He squinted, shutting one eye, and raised the Colt again. 'Blue label, I think it's an apple juice jug.'

The first shot was deafeningly loud, and in spite of the tissue Emily clapped her hands over her ears. She didn't see where it went, exactly, but the trees behind the targets rustled. The second shot hit the blue-labeled bottle dead on, the glass exploding against the rough bark of the trees.

Emily hopped off the hood of the car. 'I want to try,' she said.

Chris pulled the Kleenex from his ear. 'What?'

'I want to try.'

'You what?' He shook his head. 'You hate guns. You tell me all the time you don't want me to hunt.'

'You use a rifle, and they're too big,' Emily pointed out, staring at the revolver curiously, her eyes slightly narrowed. 'This looks different.' She sidled closer and touched her hand to Chris's. 'So can I?'

Chris nodded, wrapping her hands around the gun. She was surprised at how heavy it was, for such a little thing, and how unnatural her palms felt molded to its sleek, cool curves. 'Like this,' Chris said, coming up behind her. He showed her the bead on the barrel, explained sighting a target.

She would not let him know she was sweating. Her hands slipped a bit on the metal as Chris raised them, still covered by his, to the level at which she should brace herself to shoot.

'Wait,' Emily cried, pivoting out of Chris's embrace so that she faced him with the gun. 'How do I—'

His face had gone white. Gingerly he raised a finger and pushed aside the short barrel. 'You don't ever wave a pistol at someone like that,' he said in a strangled voice. 'It could have just gone off.'

Emily flushed. 'But I didn't cock it yet.'

'Did I know that?' He sank down on the ground, his head on his knees, a puddle of limbs and muscle. 'Holy Christ,' he breathed.

Chagrined, Emily lifted the revolver again, braced her legs, pulled back the hammer, and fired.

A tin can sang and spun, lifting into the air and hanging there for a moment before tumbling to the ground.

Emily herself had jerked backward with the recoil, and would have fallen if Chris hadn't scrambled to his feet to steady her.

'Wow,' he said, genuinely impressed. 'I'm in love with Annie Oakley.'

'Beginner's luck,' she said, but she was smiling, and her cheeks were red with pleasure. Emily looked down at her fingers, still clasped around the gun, now as comfortably warm as the hand of an old friend.

It was damp in the Jeep, the heater fogging the windows and creating a sticky, tropical humidity. 'What would you do,' Emily said softly, sitting back against Chris, 'if things didn't work out the way you planned?'

She felt him frown. 'You mean like if I didn't get into a good college?'

'Like if you didn't even go to college. If your parents died in a car accident, and you had to take care of Kate all of a sudden.'

He exhaled softly, stirring her hair. 'I don't know. I guess I'd try to make the best of it. Maybe go to college later on. Why?'

'You think your parents would be disappointed in you, for not becoming what they thought you'd be?'

Chris smiled. 'My parents would be dead,' he reminded her. 'So the shock of it couldn't hurt them too badly.' He shifted, so that he faced her, propped on an elbow. 'And I don't really care what anyone else thinks. Except you, of course. Would you be disappointed?'

She took a deep breath. 'What if I was? What if I didn't want to be . . . to be with you anymore?'

'Well, then,' Chris said lightly, 'I'd probably kill myself.' He kissed her forehead, smoothing a crease. 'Why are we talking about this, anyway?' He curled forward, unlatching the rear door of the Jeep so that it flew open, exposing a night spread with stars.

Indian summer was gone, and the air smelled crisp and thin, full of the tang of wild crab apples and the hint of an early frost. Emily drew it into her lungs and held it there, the sharpness itching at her nostrils, before her breath burst out in a small white cloud. 'It's cold,' she said, burrowing closer.

'It's beautiful,' Chris whispered. 'Like you.' He touched her face and kissed her deeply, as if he meant to drain away her sorrow. Their lips separated with a faint ripping sound.

'I'm not beautiful,' Emily said.

'You are to me.' Chris drew her between his bent legs, her back to his chest, and wrapped his arms around her ribs. The sky seemed rich and heavy, and the moment was suddenly full of a thousand tiny things which Emily knew she would always remember – the tickle of Chris's hair against the back of her neck, the seal-smooth callus on the inside of his middle finger, the parking lights of the Jeep, casting a blood-red shadow over the grass.

Chris nuzzled her shoulder. 'Did you read the science chapter yet?'

'How romantic,' Emily laughed.

Chris grinned. 'It is, kind of. It says how a star is just an explosion that happened billions of years ago. And the light's just reaching us now.'

Emily squinted at the sky, considering. 'And here I thought it was something to wish on.'

Chris smiled. 'I think you can do that, too.'

'You first,' Emily said.

He tightened his arms around her shoulders, and she felt the familiar sensation of wearing Chris's own skin, like a cloak of heat or a barrier for protection, maybe even a second self. 'I wish that things could stay like this . . . like now . . . forever,' he said softly.

Emily turned in his arms, afraid to hope, even more afraid to let this opportunity slip by. Her head was canted at an angle, so that she could not quite look Chris in the eye but could make her words fall onto his lips. 'Maybe,' she said, 'they can.'

Now

Christmas 1997

'Harte to Control.'

Chris looked up from the book he was reading and rolled out of his bunk, studiously ignoring one of his cellmates, Bernard, who was sitting on his own bunk cracking ice between his teeth. The officers brought ice once a day and set it in a cooler in the common room, where it was supposed to last well into the night. Unfortunately, Bernard managed to siphon most of it away before other inmates even noticed it had arrived.

He walked down the catwalk to the locked door at the end of the medium security unit, where he waited until one of the officers hovering at the control booth noticed his face. 'Visitor,' the officer told him, unlocking the door and waiting for Chris to take a step forward.

His mother had tearfully informed Chris the last time she'd come that she'd be unable to make it on Saturday, since Kate's dance recital fell at the same exact time. Chris had told her, of course, that he understood, although he was jealous as hell. Kate had their mother seven days a week. Couldn't she give up one lousy hour?

At the door of the basement, an officer was waiting. 'There you go,' he said, pointing Chris in the direction of the table farthest away.

For a moment, Chris stood motionless. The visitor was not his mother. It was not even his father, which would have been enough of a shock.

It was Michael Gold.

Chris took one wooden step, and then another, mechanically bringing himself toward Emily's father. He took some courage from the fact that the same officers who kept him from escaping were also there to protect him. 'Chris,' Michael said, nodding toward a chair.

Chris knew that he had the right to refuse a visitor. Before he could speak, however, Michael sighed. 'I don't blame you,' he said. 'If I were you, I would have hightailed it upstairs the minute you saw my face.'

Chris sat down slowly. 'The lesser of two evils,' he said.

A shadow passed across Michael's features. 'Is it that bad here, then?'

'It's a fucking party,' Chris said bitterly. 'What did you expect?'

Michael blushed. 'I just meant, well . . . compared to the alternative.' He looked into his lap for a second, and then raised his head. 'If things had gone the way you planned, you wouldn't be here. You'd be dead.'

Chris's hands, drumming on the tabletop, stilled. He was wise enough to know an olive branch when he saw one, and unless he was mistaken, Michael Gold had just admitted that, in spite of whatever garbage the prosecution was dishing up, he believed Chris's story.

Even though it wasn't the truth.

'How come you're here?' Chris asked.

Michael rolled his shoulders, one at a time. 'I've been asking myself that question. The whole drive out here, I've been wondering.' He turned his frank gaze onto Chris. 'I don't really know,' he said. 'What do you think?'

'I think you're spying for the AG,' Chris said, not so much because he believed it but because he wanted to see the reaction on Michael's face.

'God, no,' Michael said, stunned. 'Do they have spies?'

Chris scuffed his sneaker on the floor. 'I wouldn't put it past them,' he said. 'The whole point is to lock me away, right? To keep me from killing a whole string of girls, like I did to Em?'

Michael shook his head. 'I don't believe that.'

'Don't believe what?' Chris asked, his voice growing louder.

'That the attorney general doesn't plan to throw away the key? Or that I didn't kill her?'

'You didn't,' Michael said, his eyes tearing. 'You didn't kill her.'

Chris found his throat too tight to speak. He scraped his chair along the floor, wondering what the hell had ever made him sit down in the first place, what had made him think that he had anything to discuss with Emily's father.

Michael stared at the table, running his thumb along the battered edge. 'I came ... the reason I came,' he began, 'is because I wanted to ask you something. It's just that we didn't see it. Melanie and I, we didn't know Emily was upset. But you did; you must have. And what I was wondering is . . .' He paused, glanced up. 'How did I miss it?' he whispered. 'What did she say when I wasn't listening?'

Chris swore softly and rose, intending to escape, but Michael gripped his arm. Chris swung toward him, eyes burning. 'What?' he said roughly. 'What do you want me to say to you?'

Michael swallowed. 'That you loved her,' he said thickly. 'That you miss her.' He pinched his fingers into the corners of his eyes, fighting for composure. 'Melanie's not – well, I can't speak about Emily to her. But I thought . . . I thought . . .' He looked away. 'I don't know what I thought.'

Chris rested his elbows on the table and buried his face in his hands. He couldn't promise Michael Gold anything. Then again, if the man wanted to talk about Emily, you couldn't get better than Chris for a captive audience. 'Someone will find out you came,' he warned. 'You shouldn't be here, you know.'

Michael hesitated. 'No,' he said finally. 'But neither should you.'

Gus pushed her shopping cart absently through the aisles of Caldor, amazed that her family, which was no longer by any means ordinary, would still cling to the trappings of the mundane, needing shampoo and toothpaste and toilet paper just like any other. Driven to shopping out of desperation, she wandered through the big store, sometimes so engrossed in her thoughts that she passed the Kleenex without putting any in her cart, that she stared blankly at cat food for minutes although they had never owned a cat.

She wound up in the sporting goods section, idly passing shiny bicycles and Rollerblades until she stopped short, arrested by the display of the hunting/fishing area. Buffeted by huge camouflage-print raincoats and blaze orange vests, she examined the small items hanging on the pegboard – Hoppes Solvent #9, and gauze cleaning patches, and bluing. Fox urine, doe estrus. Things she could not believe were sold to the public, but that never failed to make her husband smile when he found them in his Christmas stocking or Easter basket.

She stared at a picture of a hunter taking aim and realized that she didn't want James ever to pick up a gun again.

If he had never purchased the antique Colt, would this have happened?

Gus sank down on the metal shelf that edged the floor of the pegboard. She took deep breaths, her head between her knees. And with her ears ringing, she did not hear the approaching cart until it nicked the edge of her shoe.

'Oh,' she said, her head snapping up at the same moment another voice said, 'I'm so sorry.'

Melanie's voice.

Gus stared at the tight lines of her face, the dulled skin, the anger that made her seem several inches taller than she actually was. Melanie drew the cart across the aisle. 'You know,' she said softly, 'I'm not sorry, after all.' She pushed her wagon away. Leaving her own cart in the middle of the aisle, Gus ran after her. She touched Melanie's arm only to have the woman swing around, her eyes filled with a cold, banked rage. 'Go away,' she bit out.

Gus remembered what it had been like when she first met Melanie; how they would sit and hold their hands over their bellies, knowing that the other understood the ripple and hum of a stretching child; the quiver at the fingertips and nape and nipples that came late in the pregnancy, when you had given your body up to someone else.

What she wanted to say to Melanie was: *You aren't the only one who was hurt. You aren't the only one who lost a person you love.* In fact, when it came down to it, Melanie grieved for one person, whereas Gus grieved for two. She had lost Emily – and she'd also lost her best friend.

'Please,' Gus finally managed, her throat working. 'Just talk to me.'

Melanie abandoned her cart and headed out of the store.

All of a sudden, Jordan stood up from the cramped table in the small conference room and yanked hard on the window sash, gritting it open. It was lined on the outside with bars, of course, but a cooling breeze threaded into the room. Chris leaned into it, smiled. 'You trying to help me break out of here?'

'No,' Jordan said, 'I'm trying to keep us from suffocating.' He wiped his sleeve across his forehead. 'I'd love to see the heating bills for this place.'

Chris laced his hands over his stomach. 'You get used to it.'

Jordan looked up briefly. 'I imagine you have to,' he said, and then spread his hands on a stack of papers.

They had been going over the discovery from the attorney general's office for three hours. It was the longest continuous stretch that Chris had ever spent away from his cell. He waited for Jordan to ask him another question, absently reading the names on the spines of the New Hampshire statute books arranged on a metal cart for the convenience of the visiting counselors.

Jordan had told him, almost immediately after arriving this morning, that his defense strategy would be based on a double suicide that had not been carried through to its end. He had also told Chris that he would not be taking the stand in his own defense. It was the only way, Jordan insisted, to win the case. 'How come,' Chris said for the second time, 'on TV, the defendant always takes the stand?'

'Oh, holy Christ,' Jordan muttered. 'Are we back to that again? Because on TV the jury says whatever the hell the script tells it to. Real life is considerably less certain.'

Chris's lips thinned. 'I told you that I wasn't suicidal.'

'Exactly. That's why you won't be on the stand. I can say whatever I want to at the trial to get you acquitted, but you can't. If I put you on the stand, you have to tell the jury that you were never going to kill yourself, and that weakens the defense.'

'But it's the truth,' Chris said.

Jordan pinched the bridge of his nose. 'It's not the truth, Chris. There is no one truth. There's only what happened, based on how you perceive it. If I don't put you on the stand, all I'm doing is giving my idea of how I perceive what happened. I'm just not asking for yours.'

'It's a lie of omission,' Chris pointed out.

Jordan snorted. 'Since when did you become a good Catholic?' he asked. He leaned back in his chair. 'I'm not going to go around and around on this,' he said. 'You want to go on the stand and do it your way? Fine. First thing the prosecutor's going to do is hold up the police interviews and show the jury how you've already changed your story once. Then she'll ask you how come, if you were going to save Emily, you brought a gun with bullets in it, instead of an empty revolver for show. And then the jury will hand back a guilty verdict and I'll be the first one to wish you well at the State Pen.'

Chris muttered something under his breath and stood up, facing the rear wall of the conference room. 'According to the ballistics report,' Jordan said, ignoring him, 'the shell of the one bullet that was fired was still in the revolver chamber, along with that second bullet. Your fingerprints were on both, which is a good piece of evidence for us: Why put two bullets in the chamber unless you were planning on one for yourself?

I also like the fact that her fingerprints are on the gun, along with yours.'

'Yeah. But they only found her fingerprints on the barrel,' Chris said, reading over Jordan's shoulder.

'Doesn't matter. All we have to do is cast a reasonable doubt. Emily's fingerprints are somewhere on that gun. Therefore, she held it at some point.' He spread his hands.

'You sound confident,' Chris said.

'Would you rather I wasn't?'

Chris sank down in his chair. 'It's just that there's an awful lot of evidence there to explain away.'

'There is,' Jordan briskly agreed. 'And all it does is place you at the scene of the crime – something you've never denied. It does not, however, prove what you were doing there.' He smiled at Chris. 'Relax. I've won cases with far less to go on than this one.'

Jordan opened up the medical examiner's report with the details of Emily's autopsy. Entranced, Chris reached out and twisted the folder, reading the distinguishing marks of her body that he could have cataloged himself, the measure of her lungs, the color of her brain. He did not have to read the careful number to know the weight of Emily's heart; he'd held it for years.

'Are you left-handed or right-handed?' Jordan asked.

'Left,' Chris said. 'Why?'

Jordan shook his head. 'Trajectory of the bullet,' he said. 'What about Emily?'

'Right-handed.'

Jordan sighed. 'Well, that's consistent with the evidence,' he said. He continued to leaf through the records that had been sent by the prosecutor's office. 'You had sex before she killed herself,' Jordan stated.

Chris reddened. 'Um, yes,' he said.

'Once?'

He felt his cheeks burning even hotter. 'Yeah.'

'Straight intercourse? Or did she go down on you?'

Chris ducked his head. 'Do you really need to know this?'

'Yes,' Jordan said evenly. 'I do.'

Chris picked at a nick in the table. 'Just straight,' he murmured. He watched his attorney flip through the autopsy report. 'What else does it say?'

Jordan exhaled through his nose. 'Not enough of what we need.' He stared at Chris. 'Is there any physical condition you know of that could have accounted for Emily's depression?'

'Like what?'

'Like some kind of hormonal imbalance? Cancer?' Chris shook his head twice. 'What about the pregnancy?'

For a moment, all the air in the room thickened. 'The *what*?' Chris said.

He was aware of Jordan watching his face carefully. 'Pregnancy,' Jordan said, turning the autopsy report toward Chris again. 'Eleven weeks.'

Chris's mouth opened and closed. 'She was . . . oh, God. Oh, God. I didn't know.' He thought of Emily as he had last seen her: lying on her side, her blood spreading beneath her hair, her hand draped over her abdomen. And then the room went black, and he imagined that he was falling into place beside her.

Usually a visit to the jail's nurse cost three dollars, but apparently fainting in the middle of a meeting with one's attorney won an inmate high triage status and a free trip to the small room used for medical treatment. Chris awakened to the feeling of cool hands on his brow. 'Are you all right?' a voice said, high-pitched and muted, as if through a tunnel. He tried to sit up, but the hands were surprisingly strong. After a moment, he took deep breaths and tried to focus, and his eyes seized upon the face of an angel.

The nurses rotated, on loan from the old folks' home next door. Chris knew of certain inmates who'd fill out the request for a medical visit and pay the three bucks just to see whether they'd get Nurse Carlisle, hands down the hottest of the three women. 'You passed out,' Nurse Carlisle said to him now. 'Just keep your feet up, yes, like that, and you'll be fine in a few minutes.'

He kept his feet up, but turned his head on the scratchy pillow so that he could watch Nurse Carlisle move with economical grace around the small closet that passed for a sickroom. She returned with a glass of water – filled with, oh, God, precious ice. 'Drink this slowly,' she said, and he did, slipping the small cubes into his mouth the moment she turned away.

'Have you fainted before?' Nurse Carlisle asked, her back to him, and he almost said *no*, until he remembered the night that Emily had died.

'Once,' he said.

'Well, I've been in those little conference rooms,' the nurse confided. 'I'm surprised anyone makes it through without fainting, given the heat.'

'Yeah,' Chris said. 'That must have been it.' But now that she had mentioned the conference room, it was all coming back. The discovery he'd been going over with Jordan. The small black letters that made up Emily's autopsy report. The baby.

He felt himself sinking back down on the table, and almost immediately the nurse was at his side. 'Are you feeling sick again?' she asked, propping his feet up again and covering him with a blanket.

'Do you have kids?' Chris asked thickly.

'No,' the nurse laughed. 'Why? Am I acting like a mother?' She tucked the blanket in at his sides. 'Do you?'

'No,' Chris answered. 'No, I don't.' His hands fisted on the fabric.

'You stay here as long as you want,' Nurse Carlisle said. 'Don't worry about the officers; I'll let them know what's happened.'

What had happened? Chris wasn't even certain he knew anymore. Emily . . . pregnant? He had no doubt that the baby was his; he knew this in the way he knew that the sun would go down that night and that the sky would be blue the next morning – a fact that had always been that way and would always continue to be. He squinched shut his eyes and tried to remember whether her stomach had been any less flat; whether her features had seemed different; whether the truth had always been there for the taking. But all he could seem to recall was Emily, drawing away from him every time he touched her.

Maybe Jordan had been right; the pregnancy had been the thing that made her so depressed. But why? They could have gotten married and had the baby; they could have gone together for an abortion. Surely she would have known that they'd figure it out together.

Unless that was exactly what she was afraid of.

All of a sudden a powerful rage shuddered through Chris. How dare she depend on him for the one thing, but not the other?

With great precision, Chris rolled to his side and put his fist through the plasterboard wall.

Selena sat on a high stool, waiting for Kim Kenly to finish rinsing her hands. She let her eyes roam about the classroom, taking in the wide, black tables and the wall of shelving that held a rainbow of construction paper, a brace of easels, a festival of paints. The art teacher wiped her palms on the front of her denim apron and turned toward Selena with smile on her face. 'Now,' she said, briskly pulling up a stool. 'What can I do for you?'

Selena opened her notebook. 'I'd like you to tell me about Emily Gold,' she said. 'I understand she was one of your students?'

Kim smiled wistfully. 'She was. A particular favorite.'

'I've heard that she was very artistic,' Selena prodded.

'Oh, yes. She designed the Thespian Club's stage sets, you know. And she won a statewide high school art contest last year. With her grades, we had discussed her going to a college of fine arts, or even off to the Sorbonne.'

Now that was interesting. Pressure could come from many angles, not only parental, to make a kid feel overwhelmed. 'Did you ever sense that Emily was worried about living up to everyone's expectations?'

The art teacher frowned. 'I don't know if anyone was harder on Emily than herself,' she said. 'Many artistic personalities have a wide streak of perfectionism.'

Selena sat back, patiently waiting for Kim to explain.

'Well, maybe a case in point would be best,' she said. She stood up and rummaged in the back of the room, emerging with a medium-size canvas painted with the spitting image of Chris.

Emily Gold had been better than good; she was an accomplished painter. 'Oh,' Kim said, 'that's right. You'd know Chris.'

'Do you?'

She shrugged. 'A bit. I have every high school student, for some small block of time in ninth grade. The interested ones sign up for continuing art classes, the others beat a path to the door.' She smiled ruefully. 'Chris would have been among the first ones out, if not for Emily.'

'He took art classes, too, then?'

'Oh, God, no. But he came here quite a lot during his free periods to pose for Emily.' She lifted a hand toward the canvas. 'This was one of many.'

'Were you always here with them?'

'Most of the time. I was impressed by the maturity of their relationship. In my line of work, you see a lot of giggling and necking in the halls, but rarely the connection those two had.'

'Can you explain that?'

She tapped her finger against her lips. 'I guess the best example would be Chris himself. He's an athlete, always in motion. Yet he thought nothing of sitting perfectly still for hours just because it was something Emily asked of him.' She lifted the canvas, preparing to put it away, and then remembered why she'd brought it out in the first place. 'Oh – the perfectionism. See here?' She peered closer to the canvas, and

Selena did too, but only made out the layered shadings of paint. 'Emily must have reworked the hands six or seven times, over a period of months. Said she couldn't get them exact. I remember that Chris, who was getting awfully sick of modeling at that point, told her that it wasn't supposed to be a photograph. But, you see, it was, to Emily. If she couldn't capture a portrait the way it was in her own mind's eye, it wasn't acceptable.' Kim slid the canvas behind some others. 'That's why I have it,' she said. 'Emily wouldn't take it home. In fact, I'd seen her destroy some others that didn't work out precisely the way she wanted, slashing the canvases or painting over them entirely. And I couldn't let that happen to this one, so I hid it and told her one of the custodians had misplaced it.'

Selena penciled a note in her little book, then looked up at the art teacher again. 'Emily was suicidal,' she said. 'I wonder if she seemed depressed to you over the past few months, if there was any change in behavior at all.'

'She never said anything to me,' Kim admitted. 'She really never said much of anything at all. She'd come right in and get down to business. But her style had changed,' she said. 'I thought it was just experimentation.'

'Can you show me?'

Emily's most recent work was propped beside an easel near the big windows of the art room. 'You saw her painting of Chris,' Kim said, by way of explanation. This last canvas was washed with a red and black background. A floating skull grinned out from the picture, bone white and gleaming, a painfully blue sky streaked with clouds showing through the holes of the eye sockets. A realistic red tongue snaked out from between yellowed teeth.

At the bottom, Emily had signed her name. And titled it *Self-Portrait*.

Jordan's cleaning woman, like the six before her, finally got sick of dusting and vacuuming around heaps of papers that were 'absolutely, positively not to be disturbed,' and quit. Well, actually, she'd quit a month ago, but that was just when Chris's case arrived on his doorstep and he'd put it out of his mind entirely. Until that evening, when he'd been leafing through his notes while reclining on the bed and realized that the smell which wouldn't go away came from his own sheets.

Sighing, Jordan hiked himself off the bed and carefully set his notes on the dresser. Then he stripped the sheets from the mattress, wadding them into a ball and heading toward the washing machine. It was only when he passed Thomas, doing his homework in front of *Wheel of Fortune*, that he realized he probably ought to get his son's sheets, too.

All in all, if Maria hadn't quit, Jordan might never have found the *Penthouse*. As it was, when it tumbled into the tangle of sheets, all he could do was stare at it, stunned.

Finally, he shook himself into motion and picked up the magazine. Emblazoned on the front was a woman whose breasts defied gravity, her privates shielded by a low-hanging pair of binoculars. Jordan rubbed his hand along his jaw and sighed. He was completely at a loss when it came to this part of fatherhood. How could he tell his son to get rid of a porno magazine, when he himself paraded in bimbo after bimbo?

If you're going to have this conversation, he told himself, *you might as well have Thomas listen.* Tucking the magazine beneath his arm, Jordan walked into the family room.

'Hi,' he said, sinking down on the couch. Thomas crouched over the coffee table, a textbook spread in front of him. 'What are you working on?'

'Social studies,' Thomas said, and before Jordan could stop himself, he thought, *A little too social.*

He watched his son write in his three-ring binder, his left hand carefully printing so that the pencil wouldn't smudge. Left-handedness; Thomas had gotten that from Deborah. And also the thick black hair, and the shape of the eyes. But the promised breadth of his shoulders, and the long line of spine, all that was straight from Jordan himself.

Apparently he'd also bequeathed his son a healthy lust.

Sighing, he pulled the magazine out and threw it over the looseleaf paper. 'Want to tell me about this?' he asked.

Thomas flicked a glance at the cover. 'Not really,' he said. 'Is it yours?'

Thomas rocked back on his heels. 'Seeing as how only you and I live here, and you know it's not yours, then I guess that's pretty obvious.'

Jordan laughed. 'You've been hanging around lawyers too long,' he said. Then he sobered, capturing Thomas's gaze. 'How come?' he asked simply.

Thomas shrugged. 'I wanted to see it, is all. I wanted to know what it was like.'

Jordan glanced at the Binocular Babe on the magazine cover. 'Well, I can tell you, it's not really like that.' He bit his lip. 'In fact, I can tell you anything you feel like asking me.'

Thomas blushed, the color of a peony. 'Okay, then,' he said. 'How come you don't have a girlfriend?'

Jordan's mouth gaped. 'A what?'

'You know, Dad. A steady girlfriend. A woman who actually sleeps with you and then comes back.'

'This is not about me,' Jordan said tightly, wondering why it was so much easier to keep control in front of strangers at a trial. 'We're talking about how you came to have a *Penthouse* in your possession.'

'Maybe that's what you're talking about,' Thomas shrugged. 'I'm not. You said I could ask you anything, but you won't answer me.'

'I didn't mean about my private life.'

'Why the hell not?' Thomas exclaimed. 'You're asking about my private life!'

'What I do with my free time is my own business,' Jordan said. 'If it bothers you when I bring women home, you may voice your opinion, and we'll discuss it. Otherwise, I expect you to respect my privacy.'

'Well, what I do with my free time is my own business, too,'

Thomas responded, and he slid the *Penthouse* beneath his stack of schoolbooks.

'Thomas,' Jordan said, his voice terrifyingly soft, 'give it back.'

Thomas stood up. 'Make me,' he said.

They squared off, tension thickening the air, their differences punctuated by the applause of the studio audience on the television. Suddenly Thomas grabbed the magazine from beneath his books and dashed toward his bedroom.

'Get back here!' Jordan roared, striding in the direction of Thomas's room only to hear the door slam and the lock twist home. He was standing in the hall, considering breaking down the door on principle, when the doorbell rang.

Selena. She would be coming over to discuss the Harte case. Which actually might be the best thing for all concerned parties, right now.

Jordan walked to the front door and opened it, surprised to find an unfamiliar man in a uniform. 'Telegram,' he said.

Taking the envelope, Jordan walked back inside. GETTING MARRIED DEC 25 STOP WOULD LIKE THOMAS TO BE THERE STOP PLANE TICKET TO PARIS BEING SENT TO YOUR OFFICE STOP THANKS JORDAN STOP DEBORAH.

He glanced in the direction of Thomas's closed bedroom door, and thought, as he had a thousand times before, that timing was everything.

'Let me guess,' Selena said a few minutes later when she came into the house and found Jordan sprawled miserably on the couch. 'Emily came back to life and pointed a finger at your client.'

'Hmm?' Jordan levered himself on an elbow and swung his feet off the edge so that Selena could sit down. 'No, nothing like that.' He passed the telegram to Selena and waited for her to read it.

'I didn't even know your wife was alive, much less dating someone.'

'Ex-wife. I knew she was alive. Or, rather, my accountant did. Got to send that alimony somewhere.' He sighed and sat up. 'The hell of it is, Thomas and I just had a fight.'

'You two never fight.'

'Well, there's a first time for everything.' Jordan scowled. 'And now he gets to run off with the other parent.'

'In Paris,' Selena added, glancing around. 'I've got to tell you, Jordan. You can't compete with the Left Bank.'

'Thanks a lot,' he grumbled.

Selena patted his knee. 'It will all work out,' she predicted.

'What makes you so sure?'

She glanced at him, surprised. 'Why, because that's your forte.' She unloaded a stack of small notebooks and set them on the coffee table beside Thomas's school binders. 'Are we going to brood tonight? Or talk about the case? Not that I mind either one,' she hastily added.

'No, no, the case,' Jordan said. 'Get my mind off Thomas.' He walked into the dining room, returning with a high stack of papers. 'What are you doing for Christmas?'

'Going to my sister's,' Selena said, looking up. 'Sorry.' She waited for Jordan to sit down next to her again. 'Okay,' she said. 'I'll show you mine if you show me yours.'

Jordan laughed. 'What did you get from Michael Gold?'

Selena flipped through her notebook. 'I think he's going to help us. Reluctantly. You can use him to bring up how little time Emily spent with her parents, cast doubt on how well he knew his own daughter . . .'

Jordan's mind flashed back to Thomas, hiding his *Penthouse*. How long had it been here, with Jordan away and working and lacking the time to find it?

Selena was still talking about Michael Gold. '. . . while he won't tell a jury that Chris didn't do it, I think you can get him to admit that Chris loved Emily.'

'Mmm,' Jordan said, looking over her notes. 'And we can mention that Michael's been to visit Chris in jail.'

'He has?'

Jordan smiled. 'You must have triggered something in him.'

'The only other thing I've got is Emily's art teacher, who has no verbal mention of suicide but a whopper of a convincing painting.' She told Jordan about Emily's self-portrait.

'I'll have to think about that. Who could we get to interpret the difference in styles? It's not like we're talking about a real artist.'

'You'd be surprised,' Selena said. She shucked off her shoes. 'What have you got?'

'Well,' Jordan said, 'Emily was eleven weeks pregnant.'

'What?'

'That's exactly what Chris said,' Jordan murmured, 'before he passed out.' He looked at Selena. 'You know, I've seen a lot of liars over the years. Hell, I've made a career out of consorting with them. But either this kid is the best one I've ever met, or he really didn't know about that baby.'

Selena's mind was racing. 'That's the prosecution's motive,' she calculated aloud. 'He knew and was trying to eliminate the whole problem.'

'Add college into the mix, and you too can be S. Barrett Delaney,' Jordan mocked.

'Well, then, it's simple. All we have to offer is a two-pronged defense. We get proof that Emily was suicidal, and we get proof that Chris didn't know about the baby.'

'Easier said than done,' Jordan reminded her. 'Just because he didn't tell someone doesn't mean he didn't know.'

'I'll go back and talk to Michael Gold,' Selena said. 'And there was something the art teacher said – about Emily wanting to go study abroad, or attend a school of fine arts. Maybe she was the one who didn't want the baby.'

'Suicide seems a bit extreme as a method of abortion,' Jordan said.

'No, it's the pressure, don't you see? Emily's this perfectionist, and all of a sudden her plans had a wrench thrown into them. She wasn't going to live up to what everyone expected her to be, so she killed herself. End of story.'

'Very nice. Too bad you're not the jury foreman.'

'Can it,' Selena said pleasantly. 'Did her regular doctor know about the pregnancy?'

'Apparently not,' Jordan said. 'It's not in the medical files the prosecution handed over.'

Selena began writing in her notepad. 'We can try Wellspring and Planned Parenthood,' she said. 'May have to subpoena the records, but I'll see if I can find someone willing to talk. The other thing I want to do is try to plant doubt about who brought the gun. Maybe put James Harte on the stand and ask if Emily ever had access to the gun cabinet, if she knew where the key was, you know. Get the jury off on another tangent. Oh, and I'm meeting with Chris's English teacher. Scuttlebutt has it that she thinks he's the Second Coming.'

She paused for breath and looked up to find Jordan staring at her, a faint smile dancing at the edge of his mouth. 'What?' she demanded.

'Nothing,' Jordan said, looking away. He clapped his hand over his collar, as if he could tamp down the blush creeping up his neck. 'Nothing at all.'

It was highly unlikely that any medical professional would be willing to talk to the defense team's investigator without being formally subpoenaed. Still, the rules at the clinics set up for free prenatal testing and care were slightly different. Although the records were sealed, the walls had ears. People talked in clinics, and cried, and other people heard them.

Selena had tried Wellspring first, without making a dent in the hatchet-faced receptionist. Then she'd gathered up her reserve at a nearby coffee bar and optimistically headed toward Planned Parenthood. Located two towns over from Bainbridge, it was on the bus line. Emily, who did not have her own vehicle, would have been able to get there without much difficulty.

The office was small and lemon yellow, located inside a converted Colonial. The receptionist here had high, teased hair the same color as the walls, and eyebrows that were painted on. 'May I help you?' she asked.

'Yes,' Selena said, handing her a card. 'I wonder if I might be able to speak with the director.'

'I'm sorry, she's not here now. May I ask what this is in reference to?'

'I'm working with the defense in a case involving the alleged murder of Emily Gold. It's possible that she was a patient here recently. And I'd like to speak to someone who examined her.'

The receptionist looked at the card. 'I'll give this to the director,' she said, 'but I can save you some trouble. She'll tell you you have to subpoena a request for the records, if they're here.'

'Marvelous,' Selena said, baring her teeth. 'Thanks for your help.'

She watched the receptionist turn toward a ringing phone, and walked back to the waiting room. A counselor holding a chart looked at her as she shrugged on her coat. As she walked out the door, the woman was escorting a heavily pregnant woman into the inner sanctum.

Selena slid into her car and turned over the ignition. 'Goddamn,' she said, slamming her hand on the steering wheel so hard it honked. The last thing she really wanted was to subpoena the records, because that meant the State would be present too, and God only knew what Planned Parenthood would have to say. For all Selena knew, Emily Gold had come in crying that the baby was some other guy's, and that Chris had threatened to kill her.

She jolted as there was a sharp rap on the window. Rolling it down, Selena found herself face-to-face with the counselor from inside. 'Hi,' she said. 'I heard you in there.' Selena nodded. 'I – could I come in? It's cold.'

Selena noticed that the woman was still wearing her short, smocked nurse's uniform. 'Be my guest,' she said, sliding over to open the passenger door.

'My name is Stephanie Newell,' the counselor said. 'I was

working the day Emily Gold came in here.' She took a deep breath, and Selena began to pray very, very hard. 'The only reason I even remember that name is because I've been reading about her in the papers so much. She came a few times. At first she was talking abortion, but then she got scared and kept putting it off. There are counselors here – you know that the women all have to talk to counselors?' Selena nodded. 'Well, I was the one who talked to Emily. And when I asked about the father of the baby, she said that he was out of the picture.'

'Out of the picture? Those were the words she used?'

Stephanie nodded. 'I tried to get her to elaborate, but she wouldn't. Every time I asked if he lived out of state, or if he even knew about the baby, she just said she hadn't told him yet. As counselors, we're trained to help clients see all the options, but not to force them to change their minds. Emily cried a lot, and mostly I just listened.' She fidgeted in the seat. 'Then I started reading in the papers about this boy, who'd killed Emily because of the baby, and I thought that didn't seem right, because he didn't even know she was pregnant.'

'Is it possible that you convinced Emily to tell him? Maybe after one of your visits?'

'It's possible,' Stephanie said. 'But every time I saw Emily she said the same thing – she hadn't told the father; she didn't want to. And the last time I saw her was the day she died.'

At the sound of the heavy barred door slamming shut, Dr Feinstein jumped, leading Jordan to believe that it would not be all that difficult to convince the man not to come back. 'This way, Doctor,' Jordan said solicitiously, directing the man toward the narrow staircase that led up to the attorneys' conference room at the jail. The officer who unlocked the door smiled grimly, hitched his hands into his belt, and told them Chris was on his way.

'Interesting fellow,' Jordan said, taking a seat in the small, stifling room.

'You mean Chris?'

'No, the officer. He's the one who was held hostage here last year.'

'Oh,' Dr Feinstein said, peering out the door. 'I remember seeing that on the news.'

'Yeah. Messy thing. Ax murderer who was waiting for trial led the uprising, and they locked the guy in one of the cells after they cut up his face with a razor blade.' He leaned back, linking his hands on his belly and enjoying the way Dr Feinstein's face leached of color. 'You remember, now, the conditions for this interview?'

Dr Feinstein turned his head away from the door with effort. 'Conditions? Oh, yes. Although I will tell you again that my primary interest is healing Chris's mind, and there's a certain benefit associated with exploring the moment it was damaged in a now-safe environment.'

'Well, you'll have to go about your "healing" in another way,' Jordan said flatly. 'No discussing the crime, or the case.'

Dr Feinstein rallied once more. 'Whatever Chris says is protected by patient confidentiality,' he said. 'You really don't have to be present.'

'Number one,' Jordan said, 'patient confidentiality has been violated before in extreme circumstances, and Murder One certainly qualifies as one of those. Number two, the dynamics of your relationship with my client come second to my relationship with him. And if he's going to be putting his trust in anyone these days, it's me, Doctor. Because you might be able to save his mind, but I'm the only one who can save his life.'

Before the psychiatrist could answer, Chris appeared at the doorway. A smile broke over his face at the sight of Dr Feinstein. 'Hi,' he said. 'I've, uh, had a change of address.'

'I can see that,' Dr Feinstein chuckled, settling back in his chair with such ease that Jordan found it difficult to believe this same man had been shaking at the control booth only minutes before. 'Your attorney graciously arranged for me to have a private meeting with you. Provided he's allowed to chaperone.'

Chris cut a glance toward his lawyer and shrugged. Jordan took that as a very good sign. He sat down at the last empty chair and flattened his palms on the table.

'Why don't we start with how you're feeling?' Dr Feinstein began.

Chris turned toward Jordan. 'Well . . . I feel weird with him here,' he said.

'Pretend I'm not,' Jordan suggested, closing his eyes. 'Pretend I'm taking a nap.'

Chris scraped his chair along the floor, turning it sideways so that he wouldn't see Jordan's face. 'At first I was pretty scared,' he told the psychiatrist. 'But then I figured out that if you keep to yourself it's okay. I just try to ignore most everybody.' He picked at the cuticle on his thumb.

'You must have a lot you want to say.'

Chris shrugged. 'Maybe. I talk a little to one of my cellmates, Steve. He's all right. But there are things I don't tell anyone at all.'

Atta boy, Jordan thought silently.

'Do you want to talk about these things?'

'No. I don't,' Chris said. 'But I think I need to.' He looked up at the psychiatrist. 'Sometimes it feels like my head's going to crack apart.' Dr Feinstein nodded. 'I found out that Emily was . . . we were going to have a baby.'

He paused, as if waiting for Jordan to swoop in, avenging legal angel, to say that this was too closely related to the case to discuss. In the silence, Chris knotted his hands together, squeezing the knuckles tight against each other so that the pain would keep him focused. 'When did you find out?' Dr Feinstein asked, his face carefully blank.

'Two days ago,' Chris said softly. 'When it was too late.' He looked up. 'Do you want to hear the dream I had? Don't psychiatrists like dreams?'

Dr Feinstein laughed. 'Freudians do. I'm not a psychoanalyst, but go right ahead.'

'Well, I don't dream much in this place. You've got to understand, the doors are slamming shut all night, and every few minutes one of the more obnoxious officers comes around on the catwalk and shines his flashlight in your face. So the fact that I slept deep enough to dream anything is pretty amazing. Anyway, I dreamed she was sitting next to me – Emily, I mean – and she was crying. I put my arms around her, and I could feel her shrinking away, into only skin and bones, so I hugged her a little tighter. But that just made her cry more, and curl up closer, and all of a sudden she hardly weighed anything at all and I looked down and saw that I was holding this baby.'

Jordan shifted uncomfortably. When he'd included himself in this private session, he had not thought beyond the point of protecting Chris legally. Now, he was beginning to realize that the relationship between a psychiatrist and client was very different from the relationship between a lawyer and client. An attorney only had to draw out the facts. A psychiatrist was obligated to extract the feelings.

Jordan didn't want to hear Chris's feelings. He didn't want to hear Chris's dreams. That would mean getting involved personally, never a good idea when practicing law.

He had a fleeting vision of Chris, sucked dry on both accounts by Dr Feinstein and himself, blowing away like a husk.

'Why do you think you had this dream?' Dr Feinstein was saying.

'Oh – I'm not done yet. Something happened after.' Chris took a deep breath. 'I was holding this baby, see, and it was screaming. Like it was hungry, but I couldn't figure out what to feed it. It kicked harder and harder, and I talked to it, but that didn't make a difference. So I kissed it on the forehead, and then I stood up and slammed its head onto the ground.'

Jordan buried his face in his hands. *Oh, Christ*, he prayed silently. *Don't let Feinstein get subpoenaed.*

'Well. A psychoanalyst would say something about you trying to return to the so-called childhood of your original relationship,' Dr Feinstein said, smiling. 'But I'd probably say it sounds like you were frustrated when you went to bed.'

'I took this psych course at school,' Chris continued, as if Feinstein had not spoken. 'I think I can figure out why Emily turned into the baby in the dream – somehow I've got them connected in my mind. I even understand why I was trying to kill it – that guy Steve I was talking about, my cellmate? He's in here because he shook his baby to death. So that was already going around my head, too, when I went to sleep.'

Dr Feinstein cleared his throat. 'How did you feel when you woke up from the dream?'

'That's the thing,' Chris said. 'I wasn't sad. I was totally pissed off.'

'Why do you think you were angry?'

Chris shrugged. 'You're the one who said that emotions all jumble together.'

Feinstein smiled. 'So you were listening,' he said. 'In this dream, you hurt the baby. Might you be angry about the fact that Emily was pregnant?'

'Wait a second,' Jordan objected, aware that critical information was about to be revealed.

But Chris wasn't listening. 'How could I be?' he said. 'By the time I found out about it, it didn't make much difference.'

'Why not?'

'Because,' Chris said sullenly.

'Because isn't an answer,' Dr Feinstein said.

'Because she's dead,' Chris exploded. He slumped down in his chair and ran his hand through his hair. 'God,' he said softly. 'I *am* mad at her.'

Jordan leaned forward, his hands clasped between his knees. He remembered how, the day Deborah had left him, he'd gone to work at the DA's office and had picked Thomas up at day care and acted as though nothing out of the ordinary had happened. And then a week later Thomas had knocked over a cup of milk and Jordan had all but skinned him alive – he, who had never struck his son – before he realized who he was really trying to punish.

'Why are you angry at her, Chris?' Dr Feinstein asked softly.

'Because she kept it a secret,' Chris said hotly. 'She said she loved me. When you love someone you let them take care of you.'

Dr Feinstein was silent for a moment, watching his patient gather control. 'If she'd told you about the baby, how would you have taken care of her?'

'I would have married her,' he said immediately. 'A couple of years wouldn't have made a difference.'

'Hmm. Do you think Emily knew you would have married her?'

'Yes,' Chris said firmly.

'And what is it about this that scares the hell out of you?'

For a moment, Chris was speechless, his eyes set on Dr Feinstein as if he was wondering whether the man was a seer. Then he looked away and wiped his nose with the back of his hand. 'My whole life was about her,' Chris said, his voice thick. 'What if her whole life wasn't all about me?' He bowed his head at the same instant that Jordan lurched to his feet and walked out of the conference room, breaking his own rules so he would not have to listen anymore.

The Hartes' house was decorated, for the most part, in the serviceable New England WASP style that included spindly Chippendale furniture, threadbare antique carpets, and paintings of stiff-lipped subjects who were not related to the family. By contrast, the kitchen – where Jordan was currently sitting – looked as if several ethnic festivals had recently collided within it. Delft tiles decorated the splashboard of the sink; Colonial ladderback chairs offset a marble-topped ice cream parlor table; a shoji screen blocked off the doorway to the dining room. Rainbow-hued Zapotec Indian place mats surrounded a German Hofbrauhaus beer stein, which held a mismatched assortment of silverware and plastic utensils. The eclectic surroundings set off Gus Harte beautifully, Jordan thought, as he watched her pour him a glass of cold water. As for James – he turned his attention to the man, hands shoved in his pockets as he stared out the window at a bird feeder – well, he probably spent his time in the rest of the house.

'There you go,' Gus said, drawing up the second chair to the tiny round table. She frowned at its surface. 'Do we need to move?' she asked. 'There isn't much room here.'

They should have moved; Jordan had brought a crate full of papers. But there was something about being in one of the more staid, conservative rooms that didn't appeal to Jordan, not when it came to discussing a case that required nearly gymnastic flexibility. 'This is fine,' he said, steepling his hands. He looked from Gus to James. 'I came today to talk about your testimonies.'

'Testimonies?'

It had been Gus's question; Jordan let his eyes touch on her face. 'Yes,' he said. 'We're going to need you as a character witness for Chris. Who knows him better than his own mother?'

Gus nodded, her face pale. 'What do I have to talk about?'

Jordan smiled sympathetically. It was quite common for people to be afraid of going up on the stand; after all, every eye in the courtroom was focused on you. 'Nothing you won't have heard before, Gus,' he assured her. 'We'll talk about the questions I'm going to put to you before the actual testimony. Basically we'll cover Chris's character, his interests, his relationship with Emily. Whether, in your esteemed opinion, your son could ever have committed murder.'

'But the attorney general – doesn't she get to ask questions too?'

'She does,' Jordan said smoothly, 'but we can probably figure out what they're going to be.'

'What if she asks me if Chris was suicidal?' Gus blurted out. 'I'd have to lie.'

'If she does, I'll object. On the grounds that you're not an expert in teen suicide. So then Barrie Delaney will rephrase, and ask whether Chris ever mentioned anything to you about killing himself, to which you'll simply say no.'

Jordan pivoted in his seat to address James, who was still

looking out the window. 'As for you, James, we're not going to use you as a character witness. What I'd like to get out of you is the possibility that Emily might have taken the gun herself. Did Emily know where the guns were kept in your household?'

'Yes,' James said softly.

'And did she ever see you take one from the gun cabinet? Or Chris, for that matter?'

'I'm sure she did,' James said.

'So is it possible, since you weren't there to actually see it happen, that it was Emily and not Chris who removed the Colt from the safe?'

'It's possible,' James said, and Jordan broke into a smile.

'There,' he said. 'That's all you'll have to say.'

James lifted a finger and set a stained-glass angel sun catcher swinging in the window. 'Unfortunately,' he said, 'I won't be taking the stand.'

'Excuse me?' Jordan sputtered. He'd believed, until this moment, that the Hartes would condone anything short of and possibly including bribery to get their son free. 'You won't take the stand?'

James shook his head. 'I can't.'

'I see,' Jordan said, although he didn't. 'Could you tell me why?'

The cuckoo clock on the wall came obscenely to life, its small dweller slipping out like a tongue seven consecutive times. 'Actually,' James said, 'no.'

Jordan was the first to recover his voice. 'You do understand that all the defense has to do to vindicate Chris is present a reasonable doubt. And that your testimony, as the owner of that gun, would almost singlehandedly do that.'

'I understand,' James said. 'And I refuse.'

'You bastard.' Gus stood in front of the shoji screen, her arms crossed. 'You selfish, rotten bastard.' She walked up to her husband, so close her anger stirred the strands of his hair. 'Tell him why you won't do it.' James turned away. 'Tell him!' She whipped around to face Jordan. 'It has nothing to do with stage fright,' she said tightly. 'It's because if James gets up at the trial, he can't pretend that this was all a nasty nightmare. If he gets up at the trial, he's actively involved in defending his son . . . which would mean there was a problem in the first place.' She snorted in disgust, and James pushed past her and left the room.

For a moment both Jordan and Gus were quiet. Then she sat down in the chair across from him once again, her hands toying with the collection of silverware in the beer mug, making it clink against the ceramic lip. 'I can put him on the witness list,' Jordan said, 'in case he changes his mind.'

'He won't,' Gus said. 'But you can ask me the questions you were going to ask him.'

Surprised, Jordan lifted his brows. 'You've seen Emily with Chris when he was getting into the gun cabinet?'

'No,' Gus said. 'Actually, I don't even know where James keeps the key.' She scrubbed her thumbnail over the engraved design of the mug. 'But I'll say anything you need me to, for Chris.'

'Yes,' Jordan murmured. 'I imagine you would.'

The unwritten rule in the jail was that baby killers got no peace. If they were showering, you threw things into the stall. If they were shitting, you walked in on them. If they were sleeping, you woke them up.

As the medium security ward population dwindled – supposedly, the huge influx occurred after the Christmas holiday – the two prisoners who'd shared a cell with Chris and Steve were moved out. One was transferred to maximum security for spitting at an officer. The other finished his sentence and was released. With these cellmates out of the picture, Hector began anew his campaign to make Steve pay for his crime.

Unfortunately, Chris still shared the cell with Steve.

One Monday when Chris was sleeping, Hector began to bang on the bars of the cell. Privacy was an illusion in jail, especially during times when they weren't locked down. But even if the door to a cell was open, you did not walk in uninvited. And if the inhabitants were asleep, you left them alone.

Steve and Chris both sat up in bed at the sound of Hector, playing xylophone across the front of the cell with the legs of a bridge chair. 'Oh,' he said, grinning, when he saw them. 'Were you guys sleeping?'

'Jesus,' Chris said, swinging his legs off the bunk. 'What is *with* you?'

'No, professor,' Hector said. 'What's with *you*?' He leaned across the threshold, his breath still stale with the night. 'Guess now it makes sense. You compare notes?'

Chris rubbed his eyes. 'What the hell are you talking about?'

Hector leaned even closer. 'How long did you think it would take me to find out that you killed the girl 'cause she was having your kid?'

'You motherfucker,' Chris said, his hands flying of their own volition around Hector's neck. Behind him, he could feel Steve pulling at his shoulder, but he shook him off easily, putting all his strength and all his concentration into strangling the asshole in front of him who'd spoken such a filthy lie.

It did not occur to him to wonder how this information had become public knowledge. Perhaps Jordan had mentioned it to the nurse, and an inmate had been washing the floors outside the medical office at the time. Maybe a guard had overheard. Maybe it had been leaked into the papers which were available for the inmates in the day room.

'Chris,' Steve said, the voice floating thin over his shoulder. 'Let go.' And suddenly Chris could not stand the fact that everyone in this – this hellhole – would be lumping him together with Steve. There was a huge difference between hanging with Steve because Chris wanted to, and hanging with Steve because there was no one else.

Hector's eyes were bulging, his cheeks puffed and eggplant purple, and Chris did not think he'd ever seen anything so beautiful. And then all of a sudden his arms were wrenched behind his back and handcuffed and he'd been driven to his knees by a blow to the neck. Hector, restrained by another officer, was getting back his color and his wind. 'You little fuck,' he shouted, as Chris was dragged out of the pod. 'I'm going to get you for this!'

It was not until Chris reached the control desk that he managed to ask where they were going. And even then, he didn't get an answer. 'You act like an animal,' the officer said, 'you get treated like one.'

He led Chris to the isolation cell. Before the officer unlocked the handcuffs, he checked beneath the mattress. There was no pillow.

Without another word, the officer freed Chris's hands and left him alone.

'Hey!' Chris said, rushing toward the door, solid metal except for the slat where his food tray would be passed in. He stuck his fingers through the slat. 'You can't do this to me. You have to have a DR for me.'

From somewhere down the hall, he could hear laughter.

He sank down on the floor and turned around bleakly. He would have his disciplinary review eventually, he supposed, sometime after he'd served his punishment. In the meantime, he was stuck in the hole for God knew how long, and the small cell had not been cleaned up from its last inhabitant. There was a puddle of vomit in the corner, and feces smeared one of the walls.

Chris sprang up, stretching to reach along the three-inch ledge at the top of the shower, just to see if anyone had left something behind. He scrabbled beneath the mattress and the nailed-down bunk, to no avail. Then he settled back in his original position, huddled against the door, his knees drawn up to his chest, gagging with every breath.

At 12:15 his lunch was shoved through the slot.

At 2:30 the maximum security inmates went to the exercise room, passing the isolation cell. One of them spat through the slot, mucus streaking across the back of Chris's shirt.

At 3:45, when the medium security men came to the exercise room, Chris took off his shirt and slid it under the door, a flat fabric puddle. He waited for something to fall onto it as the thunder of feet passed by, and then carefully drew back the shirt. Someone – Steve, he supposed – had tossed him a pen.

He tried to draw on the walls, but the ink didn't take to the cinder block. Or to the metal bunks or shower stall, which left only one thing. For the next three hours, until dinnertime, Chris drew on his prison-issue pants and shirt, wild designs that reminded him of Emily's artistic doodling.

After dinner he lay on his back and ran through every practice relay his coach had ever written on the locker room chalkboard. He crossed his arms over his chest and pictured his blood coursing from heart to artery to vein.

When he heard the squeak of crepe-soled shoes outside, he was certain that he'd imagined it. 'Hey!' he yelled. 'Hey! Who's there?'

He tried to squint out the opening, but the angle of the metal prevented him from seeing anything. Honing his senses, he made out the roll of wheels and the slush of a mop. The custodians. 'Hey,' he said again. 'Help me.'

There was a definite pause in the routine swing of the mop. Chris tilted his head against the slot again, then jumped back when something winged him in the temple.

He scrabbled at his feet, hoping for food, but felt the unmistakably thick binding of a Bible.

With a sigh, Chris crawled onto the bunk, and started to read.

Christmas vacation began on Thursday, so Selena was extremely grateful when Mrs Bertrand agreed to speak to her Wednesday afternoon. She sat uncomfortably in the small wooden chair, wondering who the hell thought this furniture was conducive to learning. Chris Harte was nearly as tall as Selena's six feet; how could he ever have jammed his legs under a table like this? No wonder today's adolescents couldn't wait to get out of school—

'I am so glad,' Mrs Bertrand said, 'that you called.'

'You are?' Selena was taken aback. In her professional career, she could count on one hand the number of people who didn't look at her funny when she said she was working for a defense attorney.

'Yes. I mean, of course I've read the papers. And the very thought of someone like Chris . . . well, it's ridiculous, that's what.' She smiled broadly, as if that was enough to acquit. 'Now, what is it I can help you with?'

Selena extracted her ubiquitous pen and pad from her coat pocket. 'Mrs Bertrand,' she started.

'Please – Joan.'

'Joan, then. What we're looking for is certain information that can be presented to a jury to make the murder charge seem . . . as you said, ridiculous. How long have you known Chris?'

'Oh, four years, I suppose. I had him in ninth-grade English, and then I sort of knew what he was doing even in the years I didn't have him – he's the kind teachers are always talking about, you know, in a good way – and then he was put in my class this year, as well.'

'You teach honors English?'

'Advanced Placement,' she said. 'The kids take the test in May.'

'So Chris is a good student.'

'Good!' Joan Bertrand shook her head. 'Chris is extraordinary. He has a gift for clarity, for getting to the heart of a complicated tangle. It wouldn't surprise me if he went on to college to become a writer. Or a lawyer,' she added. 'The thought of that sort of mind just . . . wasting for months in a jail,' she shook her head, unable to continue.

'You're not the first person to feel that way,' Selena murmured. She frowned at the filing cabinet, lettered with the alphabet.

'Student portfolios,' Joan said. 'Writing folders.' She leaped to her feet. 'I should show you Chris's.'

'Did you have Emily Gold as a student too?'

'Yes,' Joan said. 'Again, another straight-A kid. But more reserved than Chris. Certainly, they were always together – I imagine the principal could even have told you that. But I just didn't know her as well as I do Chris.'

'Did she seem depressed in class?'

'No. Very attentive to her work, as usual.'

Selena looked up. 'Could I see her folder, too?'

The English teacher brought back two manila leaves. 'Emily's,' she pointed. 'And Chris's.'

Selena opened Emily's folder first. There were poems inside – none that mentioned death – and a creative writing piece fashioned like Arthur Conan Doyle's work. Absolutely nothing useful. She closed the folder and glanced up again. 'Did Chris seem depressed?'

She had to ask, although she knew what the answer would be. It was unlikely that an outsider would have noticed suicidal tendencies that were never there. 'Oh, good Lord, no.'

'Did Chris ever come to you for help?'

'Not in schoolwork; he was capable of that on his own. He asked me about colleges, when he started applying. I wrote him a letter of recommendation, too.'

'I meant personal things.'

Joan's brow wrinkled. 'I encouraged him to come to me, after – after Emily died. I knew he'd need someone. But he didn't have a chance,' she said delicately. 'We had a memorial here for Emily. To everyone's surprise, when Chris was asked to make a speech, he started to laugh.'

Selena reconsidered the wisdom of putting Mrs Bertrand on the stand.

'Of course, knowing Chris the way I do, I chalked it all up to stress,' she said. Clearly uncomfortable with the recollection, Joan reached for Chris's folder and opened it in front of Selena. 'I told the teachers who were gossiping about it to read this,' she said, slapping her palm against an argumentative essay. 'Any mind with this much promise wouldn't be a party to murder.'

Selena didn't really agree, having met her fair share of intelligent criminals, but she politely glanced down at the essay. 'The assignment said to come down on one side of a sensitive issue,' Joan explained. 'To present convincing evidence for that side, and then to dismiss the alternative point of view. This is something, you know, that most college graduates can't even do. But Chris pulled it off beautifully.'

Chris's paragraphs were neatly aligned, justified by the computer printer. 'In conclusion,' Selena read, 'being "pro-choice" is a misnomer. There is not really an issue of choice at all. It is against the law to cut short someone's life, period. To say that a fetus is not a life is to split hairs, since all major bodily systems are in place at the time most abortions are undertaken. To say that it is a woman's right to choose is also unclear, because it is not only her body but another's as well. In a society that stands behind the best interests of a child, it seems strange indeed . . .'

Selena lifted her head and let a white grin split over her face. 'Merry Christmas, Mrs Bertrand,' she said.

It seemed archaic to offer a Bible as comfort, in a world where a vial of crack would probably have been preferred two to one, but Chris found himself entranced. He had never really read the Bible. For a brief stint, he'd gone to Sunday School, but that was because his father insisted on belonging to the local Episcopal church for the social statement it made. Eventually, they stopped attending with the exception of holidays, when one was most likely to be seen.

The familiar quotations leaped out at him, making Chris feel as if he'd populated the small cell with old friends. 'Ask and you shall receive, seek and you shall find, knock and it shall be opened to you.' He stared at the heavy door. Not bloody likely.

When the lights went out – no warnings, up here, just a misty darkness – Chris rolled off the bunk and got to his knees. The floor was freezing beneath the thin cotton of his pants, and in the new dark the smell of the shit on the wall seemed suddenly stronger, but he managed to knot his hands together and bow his head. 'Now I lay me down to sleep,' he whispered, feeling very, very young. 'I pray the Lord my soul to keep.' He furrowed his brow, trying to remember the rest of it, but couldn't.

'I haven't done this in a long time,' Chris said, feeling foolish. 'I hope You can hear me. I don't blame You for putting me in here. And I probably don't deserve any favors.' He let his voice trail off, thinking of what he most wanted. Surely, if he only asked for one thing, he had a fighting chance of getting it. 'I want to pray for Hector,' he said softly. 'I pray that he gets out of here soon.'

Chris wondered whether God had met Emily yet. He closed his eyes, imagining the long blonde hair he'd wrapped around his hands like reins; the point of her chin and the soft blue hollow of her throat where he could touch his lips to her pulse. He remembered something he'd read that night: 'A new heart also I will give you, and a new spirit will I put within you.' He hoped, now, Emily had that.

As he drifted off to sleep, still kneeling on the floor like a penitent, Chris heard God. He came on the sounds of footsteps, of key turns and disembodied whistles. And He murmured, stirring the fine hairs on the back of Chris's neck: 'Forgive, and you shall be forgiven.'

Gus was awakened by a heavy object falling across her chest. Startled, she began to fight her way out, only to realize that it was Kate pinning her. 'Get up, Mom,' she said, her eyes shining, her smile so infectious that Gus momentarily forgot waking meant she'd have to get through another day.

'What?' she asked groggily. 'Did you miss the bus?'

'There is no bus,' Kate said. She sat up, cross-legged. 'Come on downstairs.' She poked under the covers, receiving a grunt from her father. 'You too,' she said, and ran from the room.

Ten minutes later, Gus and James walked into the kitchen,

dressed and bleary-eyed. 'You want to start the coffee,' Gus asked, 'or should I?'

'You can't start the coffee,' Kate said, bouncing in front of them. She grabbed each of their hands and drew them toward the shoji screen that separated the kitchen from the living room. 'Ta-da!' she trilled, stepped away to reveal a scraggly, potted eucalyptus tree, hastily decorated with a handful of glass balls and ornaments. 'Merry Christmas!' she sang, and wrapped her arms around her mother's waist.

Gus glanced at James over Kate's bowed head. 'Sweetheart,' she heard herself say. 'Did you do all this?'

Kate nodded shyly. 'I know it's kind of dorky, the tree from the foyer and all, but I figured if I cut down something outside you'd be pretty bummed out.'

Gus had a fleeting image of Kate pinned beneath a fallen pine. 'This is lovely,' she said. 'Really.' The Christmas lights, small and winking, were on a timer. They faded in and out, reminding Gus of the ambulance parked outside the hospital when she was summoned for Chris.

Kate walked into the living room and happily settled herself beneath the small tree. 'I figured you guys weren't around enough, with everything that's been happening, to decorate.' She held out a package to Gus, and another to James. 'Here,' she said. 'Open them.'

Gus waited while James unwrapped a new DayTimer calendar in a faux alligator-skin cover. Then she tore away the wrapping paper from her own gift, a pair of jade earrings. Gus stared at Kate, still beaming, and wondered when her daughter had been to the mall. She wondered when her daughter had decided that at all costs, she was going to celebrate a normal Christmas.

'Thanks, honey,' Gus said, hugging Kate close. And she whispered into the shell of her ear, 'For everything.'

Then Kate sat back down again, expectant. Gus fisted her hands in the pockets of her robe and glanced at James. How did you tell your fourteen-year-old you'd completely forgotten

Christmas this year? 'Your present,' she announced extemporaneously, 'isn't quite ready yet.'

The smile fell away from Kate's face in degrees.

'It's . . . being sized for you,' Gus said.

A wall went up between them, solid and unforgiving for all its transparency. 'What is it?' Kate asked.

Unwilling to lie any further, Gus turned to her husband, who only shrugged. 'Kate,' Gus pleaded, but her daughter was already on her feet and accusing.

'You don't have anything for me at all, do you?' she said thickly. 'You're lying.' She flung her arm out toward the eucalyptus. 'If I hadn't done this lame Christmas thing, you would have just moped around today like you always do.'

'Things are different this year, Kate. You know that with what's happened to Chris—'

'I know that because of what happened to Chris, you don't even know I'm around!' She grabbed the earring box out of Gus's hands and threw it against the wall. 'What do I have to do to make you see me?' she cried. 'Kill someone?'

Gus slapped Kate across the face.

A heavy shock settled over the room, the only sound the faint hiss of the lights as they glowed and faded. Kate, palm pressed to her burning cheek, whirled and ran out of the room. Trembling, cradling her hand as if it did not belong to her, Gus turned to James. 'Do something,' she begged.

He stared at her for a moment, then nodded. And walked out of the house.

It was one of those rare years when Christmas and Chanukah overlapped. The world was celebrating, which meant that Michael got the day off, and he knew exactly what he wanted to do.

He had been sleeping on the couch for months now, so he did not know if Melanie had awakened yet. But he showered in the downstairs bathroom and made himself an English muffin to take in the truck. Then he drove to the cemetery to visit Emily.

He parked some distance away, preferring the walk for the solitude and peace it offered. Snow crunched beneath his boots and the wind bit at the tips of his ears. At the cemetery gates, he paused to stare up at the wide, blue bowl of the sky.

Emily's grave was over the top of the hill, hidden by the crest. Michael walked along, thinking about what he would say to her. He had no qualms about speaking to a grave; he talked all the time to things that conventionally were considered unable to understand – horses, cows, cats. He puffed up the last bit of the long path, to the point where he could first see the grave. There were flowers there, brittle stalks now, from the last time Michael had come. And ribbons trailing, and bits of paper bleeding into the snow. And Melanie, sitting on her bottom on the frozen ground, unwrapping gifts.

'Oh, look at this,' she said, when he was close enough to hear. 'You're going to love it.' And she draped a sapphire pendant over the dead necks of the roses Michael had left behind.

Michael glanced from the glittering jewelry to the other presents, arrayed like offerings on either side of the marker. A single-cup coffee maker, a novel, several tubes of oil paint and the expensive brushes Emily favored.

'Melanie,' he said sharply. 'What are you doing?'

She turned slowly, dreamily. 'Oh,' Melanie said. 'Hi.'

Michael felt his jaw clench. 'Did you bring these things?'

'Of course,' Melanie said, as if he were the crazy one. 'Who else?'

'Who . . . who are they for?'

She stared at him, then raised her brows. 'Why, Emily,' she said.

Michael knelt down beside her. 'Mel,' he said softly, 'Emily is dead.'

His wife's eyes filled immediately with tears. 'I know,' she said thickly. 'But you see—'

'I don't see.'

'It's just that it's her first Chanukah away from home,' Melanie said. 'And I wanted – I wanted—'

Michael pulled her into his arms before he had to watch the tears streak down her face. 'I know what you wanted,' he said, 'I want it too.' He buried his face in her hair and closed his eyes. 'Will you come with me?' He felt her nod against him, her breath warm in his collar. They walked down the path of the cemetery, leaving behind the paints and the brushes, the coffee maker and the sapphires, just in case.

The Manchester airport was mobbed on Christmas Day, full of people carrying fruitcake tins and shopping bags ripping at the seams with their presents. Beside Jordan in the waiting lounge, Thomas bounced in his seat. He frowned as his son knocked the small folder with his tickets off his lap for the thousandth time. 'You're sure you remember how to make a connection.'

'Yeah,' Thomas said. 'If the stewardess doesn't take me, I ask someone else at the gate.'

'You don't go yourself,' Jordan reiterated.

'Not in New York City,' they said simultaneously.

Thomas's feet danced impatiently, kicking at the metal rungs of the brace of seats. 'Cut that out,' Jordan said. 'Everyone in this row can feel it.'

'Dad,' Thomas asked, 'do you think they have snow in Paris?'

'No,' Jordan said. 'So you'd better come back home to use those skis.' In an act of outright bribery, he'd deliberately bought Thomas a pair of Rossignols for Christmas, giving the gift to his son before he left to join Deborah for the holiday.

There had been a couple of transatlantic telephone calls, a heated exchange about whether or not Thomas was old enough to travel that far alone, and a flurry of compromise. In fact, for a few days, Jordan had refused Deborah's request. But then he awoke in the middle of the night one weekend and went in to Thomas's room to watch him sleep. He found himself thinking of Dr Feinstein's questions to Chris Harte: *What is it about this that scares the hell out of you*? And he realized that his answer was the same as Chris's had been. Up until this point, Thomas's whole life had been filled with Jordan. What if, when given an alternative, it did not remain that way?

He'd called Deborah the next morning and had given his blessing.

'Flight 1246 to New York's LaGuardia Airport, now boarding at gate three.'

Thomas jumped to his feet so quickly he tripped over the carry-on bag. 'Whoa, hang on,' Jordan said, reaching up a hand to steady him. He paused, about to lift the duffel, his eyes on his son. And Jordan realized that he would see this moment forever – one of life's gallery of pictures – Thomas with his head in profile: the soft fuzz of early adolescence on his cheeks, the concentration-camp thinness of his bony arms, the flapping orange 'youth' ticket grazing the waist of his jeans. Clearing his throat, Jordan hefted the carry-on bag. 'God, this is heavy,' he said. 'What have you got in here, anyway?'

Thomas grinned, his eyes dancing. 'Just ten or twelve *Penthouses*,' he said. 'Why?'

It had still been a sore point, something they did not talk about but rubbed sharply against every now and then when passing too close near the refrigerator or sidling out of the bathroom. With relief, Jordan felt the tension of the past week dissolve. 'Get out of here,' he said, and embraced his son.

Thomas hugged him back, hard. 'Give mom a kiss for me,' Jordan said.

The boy drew back. 'On the cheek or on the lips?'

'The cheek,' Jordan said, and gently pushed Thomas toward the boarding ramp. He took a deep breath then, and walked toward the plate-glass windows parallel with the belly of the plane. He would wait, he thought, just in case Thomas changed his mind at the last minute. With his hands in his pockets, Jordan stood sentry, watching the jet taxi to the runway and lift on the wind, until it disappeared from his range of vision.

★   ★   ★

'Merry Christmas,' the officer said, grating open the door of the isolation cell.

Chris sat up, uncurling from the floor. The Bible had fallen beneath the bunk; he quickly slipped it into the waistband of his pants. 'Yeah,' he murmured, rocking back on his heels.

The officer grunted at him. 'You want to wait till New Year's?'

Chris blinked. 'You mean that's it? I'm out?'

'Superintendent's feeling charitable today,' the officer said, holding the door open so that Chris could pass through. He walked swiftly down the corridor, stopping at the control room. 'Where now?'

'Go Directly to Jail,' the officer said, laughing at his own joke.

'I meant, which security level?'

'Usually you go back to max,' the officer said. 'But seeing as how your cellmate said you were provoked, and how you didn't have a DR before you went to the hole, we're putting you back in medium.' He opened the door for Chris. 'Oh, yeah,' he added. 'Your buddy Hector's back downstairs.'

'In maximum?' The officer nodded, and Chris briefly closed his eyes.

Steve was reading in the cell when Chris came in. He slid into his bunk and tried to bury himself under the pillow, smelling that horrible jail smell in the detergent but luxuriating in the very fact of a pillow. He could feel Steve's gaze on him, even through all these layers, deciding whether or not he should speak.

Finally, because it was coming sooner or later, Chris took the pillow off his face. 'Hey,' Steve said. 'Merry Christmas.'

'Same to you,' Chris answered.

'You all right?'

Chris shrugged. 'Thanks for telling them about Hector.' He meant it. Hector was not one to forgive someone for ratting on him.

'It was nothing,' he said.

'Well, thanks anyway.'

Steve looked away, picking at a nubby pill on the worn sleeve of his shirt. 'I've got something for you,' he said casually. 'For Christmas.'

Horrified, Chris panicked. He'd never thought about giving gifts in here, for God's sake. 'I don't have anything for you,' he said.

'As a matter of fact,' Steve said, reaching beneath his bunk, 'you do.' He extracted a nasty looking instrument, fashioned out of the shaft of a Bic pen and a long, lethal-looking needle. 'Tattoos,' he whispered.

Chris wanted to ask how he'd gotten the needle – he could not imagine any weekender sticking that up his ass – but he knew that if he was going to do this, he didn't have time. Jail tattoos – and the items used to create them – were illegal. Having one, right out in the open, raised you a notch in respect because you were flaunting your trespasses right under the officers' noses.

What Steve was really giving him for Christmas was a way to save face.

He held out his arm, unsure if he really wanted to do this but clearheaded enough to realize that if he wanted to escape AIDS, he'd damn well better go first. With a quick glance toward the officer making rounds, Steve took out a lighter – another contraband surprise – and held the needle over the flame.

Chris rested his elbow on his knee and felt the first searing burn of flesh. It smelled oddly sweet, like roasting meat, and it sent pain straight down to his groin. Clenching his fist, he watched his own blood run down his bicep as Steve heated, carved, and cut. Then he felt Steve squirt the ink cartridge from the Bic into the wound, rubbing it into the raw skin where it would permanently set. 'You can't see till you wash it off good,' Steve said, 'but it's an eight ball.' He looked up at Chris, his eyes clear and sharp. 'Because we both seem to be stuck behind it.'

Chris pulled his sleeve down as far as it would go, licking

at his fingers to rub off the residue of blood and ink. An officer drifted by the cell, and Steve pressed the lighter into his hand. 'Do one for me,' he said. 'Please.'

Chris's hands shook as he cauterized the needle and pressed it against Steve's upper arm. Steve jerked, then tightened his muscles. Chris drew the circle, the figure eight, and the black background. Then he rubbed ink into the cuts and quickly pressed the needle back into Steve's hands.

Their fingers brushed. 'Is it true,' Steve asked, without glancing up, 'about the baby?'

Chris thought of Jordan, who had told him not to say a word to anyone. He thought of these matching tattoos, branding them two of a kind. And he thought of words he'd read last night in the filth of the isolation cell: 'Listen to my voice and I shall be your God, and you shall be my people.'

Chris stared at his friend, his confidant, his congregation. 'Yes,' he said.

It had been a good visit. Michael stood up, as was his custom now, and watched Chris leave the basement of the jail. Today, he had not been planning to come. But seeing Melanie at the gravesite had unnerved him, and he wanted to tell someone about it. In the end, he hadn't told Chris – it didn't seem quite right, after all – but something about being here on Christmas Day eased his conscience. If he had not had the chance to speak to Emily that morning, at least he could talk to Chris this afternoon.

He wished the officer a happy holiday and jogged up the stairwell to the control room. It was the only way out of the jail; you were locked inside to visit with an inmate.

He stood patiently behind a woman in a camel's-hair coat, her hair concealed by a fluffy mohair cap. 'Yes,' she said to the officer. 'I'm here to visit Chris Harte.'

'Popular guy,' the officer said. He bellowed over the loud-speaker, 'Harte to Control.'

Michael felt his heart squeeze under his ribs. 'Gus,' he said, his mouth dry.

She whirled, her cap tumbling off and her bright fall of hair spilling over the lapels of her coat. 'Michael!' she gasped. 'What are you doing here?'

'Apparently,' he said, smiling wryly, 'the same thing as you.'

Her mouth worked for a moment without making a sound. 'You . . . you visit Chris?'

Michael nodded. 'I have been,' he admitted. 'Recently.'

They stared for a moment. 'How are you,' Gus asked, at the same moment Michael said, 'How has this been?' And, shaking their heads, they both smiled. A bright blush stained Gus's cheeks, and she glanced toward the staircase. 'I better go,' she said.

'Merry Christmas,' Michael answered.

'You too! Oh . . .'

'It's okay.'

'Happy Chanukah.'

'That too.' Michael smiled. Gus put her hand on the door-frame of the staircase but did not move into it. 'Do you . . . I mean, would you maybe want to get a cup of coffee after-ward?'

She smiled, her whole face lighting. 'I'd like that,' she said. 'But I . . . Chris . . .'

'I know. I'll wait,' Michael said. He leaned against the wall and folded his coat over his arm. 'I've got all the time in the world.'

3

The Truth

And ever has it been that love knows not its own depth until the hour of separation.

– KAHLIL GIBRAN
The Prophet

That a lie which is half a truth is ever the blackest of lies;
That a lie which is all a lie may be met and fought with outright;
But a lie which is part a truth is a harder matter to fight.

– ALFRED, LORD TENNYSON
The Grandmother

Now

February 1998

All in all, the Honorable Leslie F. Puckett was not a bad draw for a trial judge.

Three times in the past, as both prosecutor and defense attorney, Jordan had been involved in cases over which Puckett presided. Rumor had it that his severe approach and razor-sharp critiques of trial attorneys were grounded in his own insecurity about his given name – Leslie not being as masculine as he would have liked – but he dispensed barbs to both prosecution and defense with equanimity. That aside, the only caveat to a case with Judge Puckett was his affinity for almonds, which he kept in glass jars on his desk in both the courtroom and chambers, and cracked open loudly with his teeth.

Pretrial hearings were usually held in open court, but the severity of Chris's charge and the publicity it had attracted led everyone involved to believe the meeting was best conducted in the judge's chambers. Puckett, black robes fluttering around his ankles, strode into the room with Jordan and Barrie Delaney hurrying in his wake. All three sat down, and Puckett slid an almond out of the glass jar and popped it into his mouth.

At the hideous crunch, Jordan looked at Barrie.

Although attorneys were extremely formal in the courtroom, even the most cutthroat prosecutors and defense lawyers let their guard down outside. Jordan, as a former prosecutor, maintained a decent rapport with most of the assistant attorney generals. Barrie Delaney was another story. He'd never worked with her – she'd arrived at the AG's office after he'd left, with fists swinging – and she seemed to take it personally that Jordan had defected to the other side of the law. Hell, she seemed to take everything personally.

She was sitting like a convent school girl, hands folded, black skirt tucked around her legs and a glazed smile on her face, even as Leslie Puckett spit out the almond shell into his palm.

The judge shuffled papers on his desk. Jordan coughed to attract the prosecutor's attention. 'Nice police work, Delaney,' he said under his breath. 'Nothing like a little coercion for my client.'

'Coercion!' she hissed at Jordan. 'He wasn't even a suspect when he was in the hospital. That interview was totally aboveboard and you know it.'

'If it's totally aboveboard, how'd you know I was talking about that interview?'

'McAfee,' the judge said, 'and Delaney. You two about finished?'

The attorneys turned toward the desk. 'Yes, Your Honor,' they said in unison.

'Good,' he said sourly. 'Now, what needs to be docketed?'

'Well, Your Honor,' Barrie jumped in, 'we have a specialist looking at the blood spatters who needs some time; plus the DNA testing we're doing is backed up at the lab.' She consulted her Filofax. 'We'll be ready by the first of May.'

'Anything you're planning to hand in?'

'Yes, Your Honor. Several motions *in limine* dealing with the defendant's so-called expert witnesses and other objectionable evidence.'

The judge plucked another almond from his jar and rolled it around on his tongue, turning to Jordan. 'How about you?'

'A motion to suppress an interview that was done in the hospital with my client which clearly violated his Miranda rights.'

'That's bullshit!' Barrie cried. 'He could have walked away at any time.'

Jordan bared his teeth in a semblance of a smile. 'Blatantly illegal,' he said. 'My client didn't feel much like walking away when he'd just suffered seventy stitches to close a scalp wound and was under the influence of various painkillers. And your detective damn well knew that.'

'Keep this up,' the judge said, 'and I won't have to read the motion.'

Jordan faced Puckett again. 'I can have it for you in a week—'

'Which I'll gladly respond to,' Barrie added.

'Waste of your time, Barrie,' Jordan murmured. 'Not to mention my client's.'

'You—'

'Counselors!'

Jordan cleared his throat. 'My apologies, Your Honor. Ms Delaney gets my dander up.'

'So I see,' Puckett said. 'You'll both have these motions to me by the end of next week?'

'Not a problem,' Jordan said.

'Yes,' Barrie nodded.

'All right, then,' Puckett said, spreading his hands over his calendar, as if to divine a date. 'Let's start jury selection on May seventh.'

Jordan gathered up his briefcase and watched Barrie Delaney collect her files. He remembered that from being a prosecutor – the incredible number of files, with too little time to do justice to each case. For Chris Harte's sake, he hoped this still held true.

Out of long habit, he held the door to chambers open for Ms Delaney, although he personally rated her more on a par with a pit bull than a member of the fair sex. They walked down the hall of the courthouse, both furious and silent and filled with visions of winning. Then Barrie turned toward Jordan, blocking his progress. 'If you want a plea,' she said flatly, 'we're offering manslaughter.' Jordan crossed his arms. 'Thirty to life,' Barrie added.

When Jordan didn't even blink, Barrie shook her head slowly.

'Look, Jordan,' she said. 'He's going down, no matter what. You and I both know I've got the case locked up. You've seen the hard evidence – the fingerprints, the bullet, the trajectory through the head – and you and I both know she couldn't have shot herself like that. A jury isn't going to get far enough past those facts to even pay attention to whatever you're going to throw at them for a diversion. If you take thirty years, at least he'll be out before he's fifty.'

Jordan waited a moment, then uncrossed his arms. 'Are you finished?'

'Yes.'

'Good.' He started walking down the hall again.

Barrie ran after him. 'So?'

Jordan stopped. 'So. The only reason I am even going to tell my client about that ridiculous heap of shit you just produced as an offer is because I'm obligated to.' He stared at Barrie, a hint of a smile on his face. 'I've been around a lot longer than you have,' he said. 'In fact, I used to be on your side. I used to play the game the same exact way you are, now. Which means that I also know you aren't nearly as convinced of a conviction as you say you are.' He inclined his head briefly. 'I'll talk to my client,' he said, 'but all the same, we'll be seeing you in court.'

When Jordan finished talking, Chris drummed his fingers on the table. 'Thirty years,' he said, his voice breaking in spite of his tight rein of control. He looked up at his attorney. 'How old are you?'

'Thirty-eight,' Jordan said, knowing exactly where this was leading.

'That's, like, your whole life,' Chris said. 'And twice mine.'

'Still,' Jordan pointed out, 'it's about half a true life sentence. And there's parole.'

Chris stood and walked to the window. 'What should I do?' he said softly.

'I can't tell you,' Jordan said. 'I said there were three things you needed to decide by yourself. Whether or not to go to trial is one of them.'

Chris turned slowly. 'If you were eighteen; if you were me – what would you do?'

A grin crept across Jordan's face. 'Do I have the same kick-ass lawyer?'

'Sure,' Chris laughed. 'Be my guest.'

Jordan stood too, and settled his hands in his pockets. 'I'm not going to tell you winning's a sure thing, because it's not. But I'm not going to tell you we're flat-out going to lose either. I can tell you, though, that if you take the plea bargain, you're going to spend thirty years wondering whether or not we could have beaten them.'

Chris nodded, but did not say anything, staring out at the vista of snow outside the jail. 'You don't have to decide now,' Jordan said. 'Think it over.'

Chris splayed his hand on the cold glass, making a ghost of a shadow. 'When is the trial supposed to start?'

'May seventh,' Jordan said. 'Jury selection.'

Chris's shoulders began to shake, and Jordan moved toward him, alarmed that the thought of being incarcerated for three more months had set Chris over the edge. But when he touched his client's shoulder, he realized Chris was laughing. 'Are you superstitious?' Chris said, wiping at his eyes.

'Why?'

'May seventh is Emily's birthday.'

'You're kidding,' Jordan said, slack-jawed. He tried to imagine what Barrie Delaney would do when she pieced together that information. Probably wheel in a fucking ice cream cake for the jury to enjoy during her opening argument. He frantically tried to think of a motion he could file or a witness he could detain in order to request a continuance; he tried to evaluate how much of a bleeding heart Puckett could be.

'Do it,' Chris said, so softly that Jordan did not hear him at first.

'What?'

'The plea bargain.' Chris's lips twitched. 'Tell them to go to hell.'

There was no written rule that said Gus and Michael had to keep their weekly lunches secret, hoarded like a smile at a funeral, but they did this all the same, furtively slipping inside the delicatessen as if they'd crossed enemy lines. In a way, it was like that – a battle – and they might as well have been spies, taking comfort from someone who had every reason to betray you the minute you turned your back. But in another, very elemental way, they might have been each other's lifeline.

'Hi,' Gus said breathlessly, sliding into the booth. She smiled at Michael, who was flicking the laminated menu with his thumbnail. 'How is he today?'

'He's okay,' Michael said. 'Looking forward to seeing you, I think.'

'Is he still sick?' Gus asked. 'Last week he had that horrible cough.'

'It's much better,' Michael assured her. 'He got some Robitussin from the commissary.'

Gus settled her napkin on her lap, a thrill running through her chest and shoulders at the sight of him, like a schoolgirl with a crush. She had known Michael for twenty years, but was only beginning to really see him, as if this situation had not only changed her perception of her world, but also the people who inhabited it. How had she never noticed that Michael's voice could soothe so easily? That his hands seemed strong, his eyes kind? That he listened to her as if she were the only person in the room?

Gus was fully, guiltily aware of the fact that the conversation she was having with this man was the very conversation she should have been having with her husband. James still refused to talk about his son, as if Chris's name and the accusations against him were a great black bat, which once freed would spread its wings and shriek and refuse to go back from where it had come. She had begun to eagerly look forward to these weekly lunches, arranged around the visiting hours of the Grafton jail, because she'd have someone to speak to.

That it was Michael was sometimes odd. Since his wife had been Gus's best friend for – well, nearly forever – they knew a great deal about each other, secondhand. There were things that Melanie had told Gus about Michael, and things Melanie had told Michael about Gus. It made them uncomfortably intimate, brimming with knowledge of each other they otherwise should not have had.

'You look very nice today,' Michael said.

'Me?' Gus laughed. 'Well, thank you. So do you.' She meant it. Michael's flannel shirts and faded jeans, chosen because of his messy profession, made Gus think of soft, overstuffed words, like *comfort* and *nestle* and *snug*.

'You dress up for your visits, don't you?'

'I suppose I do,' Gus said. She glanced down at her printed dress, and smiled. 'I wonder who I'm trying to impress.'

'Chris,' Michael answered for her. 'It's how you want him to remember you, in between.'

'And how would you know that?' Gus teased.

'Because I do the same thing when I go to Emily's grave,' he said. 'Jacket and tie – can you imagine me in that? – just in case she's looking.'

Stricken, Gus lifted her face. 'Oh, Michael,' she said. 'I forget sometimes that this is so much worse for you.'

'I don't know,' Michael said. 'At least it's over for me. For you, it's just beginning.'

Gus ran her finger along the edge of her saucer. 'How come I remember the two of them catching frogs and playing tag, like it was yesterday?'

'Because it was,' Michael answered quietly. 'It wasn't all that long ago.' He glanced around the little deli. 'I don't know how we got here,' he said. 'Those days are so clear to me I can smell the grass I just mowed and see the pine tar streaking the back of Emily's legs. And then, bam. I'm visiting my daughter's grave and Chris in jail.'

Gus closed her eyes. 'It was so easy then. It never crossed my mind that something like this would happen.'

'That's because it's not supposed to happen to people like us.'

'But it has. It is. How come?'

He shook his head. 'I don't know. I keep asking myself that, thinking back. I figure it's like a root sticking out that I happened to miss the first time around, and can't help tripping over now.' He stared at Gus. 'Kids like Emily and Chris don't just decide to kill themselves, do they?'

Gus twisted her napkin. In spite of her newfound closeness to Michael, she had not confided that Chris had never been suicidal. In part, this was because she didn't want to betray her son's defense. And in part, because it would only reopen the healing wound in Michael's heart. 'Do you remember,' she said, trying to change the direction of the conversation, 'how Emily used to scream when they played tag? Chris would chase her and she'd shriek so loud that you'd come running from your house and I'd come running from mine?'

A smile wreathed Michael's face. 'Yeah,' he said. 'She made it sound like he was killing her.' As soon as the words were out, Gus's eyes flew to his. 'I'm sorry,' he said, paling. 'I . . . I didn't mean that.'

'I know.'

'Really.'

'It's okay,' Gus said. 'I understand.'

Michael cleared his throat, visibly uncomfortable. 'All right, then. What are we having?'

'The usual,' Gus said, brightening. 'I still can't get over the fact that I found New York-style pastrami in Grafton County, New Hampshire.'

'Every cloud has a silver lining,' Michael said, waving over their waitress. They ordered, and then settled into conversation, steering clear of the landmine topics that had been laid down by unspoken agreement: Melanie, James, and what they had all once been to each other.

Interestingly enough, one sanctioned topic was the upcoming trial. With Chris as a common link, they discussed the fact that Jordan wanted Michael to testify for the defense, and Michael's natural reservations. 'I don't know why I'm asking your advice,' Michael said. 'You aren't exactly nonpartisan.'

'I'm shamelessly biased,' Gus admitted. 'But you have to imagine what a jury would think, even if you barely said a word, just seeing you up on the stand on Chris's behalf.'

Michael set down his corned beef. 'That's exactly what I imagine,' he said softly. 'I think, what kind of a father am I?' He drummed the fingers of his right hand on the table. 'As much as I love Chris, could I do that to Emily?'

'Emily wouldn't want Chris to be convicted of a murder he didn't commit,' Gus said firmly.

Michael smirked. 'Ah. So that's why you come to lunch with me. You're the secret weapon in McAfee's arsenal.'

Gus's face drained of color. The secret weapon in Jordan's arsenal was that he would be lying – making the jury believe that Chris had wanted to kill himself, too. Just as she was currently allowing Michael to believe it. She settled her napkin over her unfinished lunch and reached in the far corner of the booth for her coat. 'I ought to go,' she muttered, fumbling open her purse to leave her share of the bill. 'Damn thing,' she said, her fingers slipping on the catch.

'Hey,' Michael said. 'Gus.' He reached across the table, to where Gus's fingers were furiously knotted over the clasp, and settled his hand on hers.

Gus stilled. *It is so nice*, she thought, *to be touched*.

Two bright flags of color rode high on Michael's cheekbones. 'I didn't mean it,' he said. 'About you working for the lawyer.'

'I know,' she managed.

'Then why are you rushing off all of a sudden?'

Gus looked at the edge of her plate. 'I don't tell James that I'm meeting you for lunch. Do you tell Melanie?'

'No,' Michael admitted. 'I don't.'

'Why do you think that is?'

'I don't know,' Michael said.

Gus gently pulled her hand away from his. 'Neither do I.'

James sat down behind his desk and picked up the pink telephone message slip that his secretary had given him. Palm d'Or, the restaurant was called, and it was forty miles into the middle of nowhere, although it had been given a five-star rating by most travel and restaurant guides. Of course, that was practically guaranteed with a fixed-price menu – pay seventy-five dollars a head and get whatever they feel like serving you that day. Sighing, James peered at the number of the restaurant and reached for the telephone. It was Kate's fifteenth birthday, and she had chosen the place, and he wasn't about to let her down.

He had, in fact, been very solicitous of Kate since Christmas. They'd gotten into a routine of staying at the dinner table after all the dishes were cleared and just talking. Kate, unlike her mother, was actually interested in the cases and operations that James had undertaken that day. James listened to Kate's chatter about boys, her fervent desire to have her ears pierced, her mistrust of algebraic proofs. And he fell in love with his daughter all over again. He would watch her night after night, and think: *I still have all this.*

'Hello, yes,' he said, when a voice answered at the other end of the phone line. 'I wanted to make a reservation. You do serve lunch as well as dinner? Excellent. Yes, next Saturday. The name is Harte, H-A-R-T-E.' He tapped a pencil against a stack of files on his desk. 'Oh, we're a party of four,' he said, and then winced. 'Three,' he corrected. 'Make that a party of three.'

He hung up the receiver, thinking of all the times over these past few months when he'd forgotten, and had looked into the backseat of his car expecting to see Chris's long legs folded up, or had gingerly opened Chris's bedroom door late at night to check on him sleeping.

A party of three.

Some party.

Melanie thunked a bowl of soup in front of Michael and sat down across the table, lifting up her spoon and beginning to eat without saying a word.

'So,' he said bravely. 'What did you do today?'

Melanie's eyes slowly came into focus. 'What?'

'I asked what you did today.'

She laughed. 'Why?'

Michael shrugged. 'I don't know. Polite conversation.'

'We're married,' she said flatly. 'We don't need to talk to each other.'

Michael stirred the soup, feeling the small resistances of overcooked celery and carrots. 'I, uh—' He hesitated. He'd been about to say that he'd gone to the jail to visit Chris, but realized that was not information he was ready to reveal. 'I ran into Gus today. We had lunch.'

He said it lightly, but even to Michael his words sounded too casual, so offhand they were clearly practiced. 'She's doing well,' he added.

Melanie went slack-jawed, a fine sheen of soup glistening on her lower lip. 'You had lunch with her?'

'Yes,' Michael said. 'So what?'

'So I can't believe you had lunch, willingly, with her!'

'God, Mel. She used to be your best friend.'

'That was before her son killed Emily.'

'You don't know he did,' Michael said.

'And who might have told you that?' Melanie snorted, her voice thick with sarcasm. 'Did she cry right in the middle of her salad? Or did she wait until she was finished eating to tell you the prosecutor's made a terrible mistake?'

'She didn't do anything,' Michael said quietly. 'Even if . . . even if. .' He could not bring himself to say it. 'It still wouldn't be her fault.'

Melanie shook her head. 'You're a fool. Don't you understand the lengths a mother will go to to protect her child?' She glanced up, her nostrils flared, her lips white. 'That's what Gus is doing, Michael. Which is more than I can say for you.'

The plan, the following Saturday, was for Kate and James to ride together to the Palm d'Or, and have Gus meet them after her visit with Chris. James and Kate had been sitting at the tastefully appointed table for a half hour, though, when the waiter came over for the third time. 'Perhaps,' he said, 'you would like to start without the rest of your party.'

'No, Daddy,' Kate said, frowning. 'I want to wait for Mom.'

James shrugged. 'We'll give it a few more minutes,' he said.

He slouched in his seat, watching Kate play with the delicate edges of the orchid that graced the center of the table. 'She's usually late,' Kate said, almost to herself, 'but usually not this bad.'

Suddenly Gus barreled into the tiny dining room, her camel's-hair coat nearly flying off her back into the arms of the maître d' as she hurried toward James and Kate. 'I am so sorry,' she said, leaning over Kate. 'Happy birthday, sweetie,' she said, giving her a kiss.

'James,' she greeted formally, slipping into her chair. And then, to the waiter: 'Just water, please. I'm not hungry.'

'How could you not be hungry?' James asked. 'It's lunchtime.'

Gus looked into her lap. 'I ate something on the way here,' she said dismissively. 'Now,' she smiled at Kate, 'tell me how it feels to be fifteen.'

'Daddy says,' Kate beamed, 'I can get my ears pierced if it's okay with you. Today. After lunch.'

'What a terrific idea!' Gus said, turning to James. 'Can you take her?' He did not hear Gus at first, because he was reveling in the smells that she had brought into the stuffy dining room – the wintergreen scent of the snow outside, the apple of her hair conditioner, and the lingering smell of perfume. But there was something else, something deep and tropical that he could not put a name to . . . what was it?

'Can you?' Gus asked again.

'Can I what?'

'Take Kate to the jeweler. Her ears,' Gus said, fiddling with her own lobes. Her face pinkened. 'I . . . well, I can't. I'm going back to see Chris again.'

'You were just there,' James said.

He would not have believed it possible, but Gus's cheeks burned redder. 'They have extra visiting hours today,' she said, smoothing her napkin onto her lap. 'I told Chris I'd see him again.'

James sighed and turned toward Kate. 'We'll go to the jewelry store after lunch,' he told her. He faced his wife again, intending to ask why she'd bothered coming all the way to the restaurant when she was just going right back, but was stopped again by the smell of her. Something was different, he realized. After she visited Chris she always came home smelling of jail, stale and confining, a scent that stayed in her clothes and her skin until they were scrubbed. She had been to visit Chris today, she said, but that smell was missing. There was something else in its place – that exotic element, which James suddenly recognized as the sweet, heated scent of a lie.

Chris slouched in his chair, trying not to be pissed off at his mother and failing miserably. It wasn't like he looked forward to her visits – he tried to be as nonchalant as possible about them, because if he didn't get himself psyched, then all the other days in between weren't quite so bad. But all the same, he'd been in his cell today at 10:45, which was when she always got there, and he waited and waited and didn't get the call to come down until nearly two o'clock.

'What happened to you?' he muttered.

'I'm sorry,' his mother apologized. 'We took Kate out for a birthday lunch.'

'So?' Chris said sullenly. 'You could have come before that.'

'Actually,' Gus said, 'I had a prior engagement.'

A prior engagement? Chris scowled, slouching even further down. What did she think this was, some nineteenth-century drawing room? What the hell kind of prior engagement was more important than making time to see your son, who was rotting away in a jail?

'Chris,' his mother said, touching her hand to his forehead. 'Are you sick again?'

He shied away from her palm. 'I'm fine.'

'You're not acting fine.'

'Oh, really? How am I supposed to act when I'm stuck in jail for three more months before a jury gets to lock me away for the rest of my life?'

'Is that it?' Gus asked. 'You're getting nervous about the trial? Because I can tell you—'

'What, Mom? What can you tell me?' He turned his face away, disgust distorting his features. 'Absolutely nothing.'

'Well,' Gus said, 'Michael and I both think Jordan's got a very good case.'

Chris laughed outright. 'By all means, I'd listen to Michael. The grieving father of the victim.'

'You have no right to say that! He's going out of his way to help you. You ought to be grateful to him.'

'For bringing charges against me in the first place?'

'He had nothing to do with that. It's up to the State, not the Golds.'

'Jesus, Mom,' Chris said, stunned. 'Whose side are you on?'

Gus stared at him for a moment. 'Yours,' she said finally. 'But Michael finally decided that he'll be a defense witness, which is a very good thing.'

'He told you this?' Chris asked, guardedly optimistic.

'Today,' Gus said.

At that, Chris's eyes narrowed with doubt. 'When?' he asked.

'I saw him this morning, before we took Kate out,' Gus said, her chin coming up. 'We've been meeting on the days when we're both visiting you.'

Chris's shoulders stiffened as he realized why his mother

had been late visiting today, and he turned away, feeling oddly light-boned and jealous. 'What do you talk about?' he asked quietly.

'I don't know,' Gus said. 'You. Our families. We just ... talk.' She felt the faint outline of her heart in her chest, fist-size and smooth-edged, as it pounded a little harder. 'There's nothing the matter with that,' she said defensively, before she could remember that she had nothing to answer for.

Chris stared at the scarred table for a long moment, during which the inmate beside them left. Gus kept her eyes trained on her son's face. 'You obviously have something you want to say,' she announced.

Her son turned, his expression carefully blank. 'Could you ask Dad,' Chris said, 'if he'd come to visit?'

'I wonder if working with you is going to make me old and fat before my time,' Selena said, her mouth rounding beneath an oily triangle of pizza.

Jordan looked up, surprised. 'Am I that much of a slave driver?'

'No. But your eating habits are awful. Do you even know what a salad is?'

'Sure,' Jordan said, smiling. 'It's that stuff they invented a sneeze-guard for.' He pushed aside a piece of pepperoni. 'For Thomas,' he explained.

Selena's eyes darted to the closed bedroom door. 'Oh? He hasn't been ruined by croissants?'

'No. In fact he lost some weight over there, said the food was too greasy for him.' Jordan grimaced at the pizza, soaking through the cardboard box. 'But if American junk food's what brought him back, it's okay with me.'

'Oh, he would have come back,' Selena reassured. 'He left his Nintendo behind.'

Jordan laughed. 'You're so good for my ego,' he said.

'Like you don't do a fine job all yourself,' Selena said dryly. 'You pay me to investigate, not ingratiate.'

'Mmm,' Jordan agreed. 'So what have you done lately to earn your keep?'

Selena, having finished interviewing the immediate world for the defense, was now working her way through the people on the prosecution's witness list, so that Jordan would know what he was up against. 'I really don't expect any surprises from the ME or the detective,' she said. 'And the kid they're putting on the stand – Emily's friend – should be suitably terrified and not a hell of a lot of use to Delaney. The only wild card is Melanie Gold, who I can't get close enough to interview.'

'Well, maybe we'll get lucky,' Jordan said. 'Maybe she'll have a certified breakdown in the next few months and Puckett can rule her mentally incapable of taking the stand.'

Selena rolled her eyes. 'I'm not holding my breath,' she said.

'Neither am I,' Jordan admitted. 'But stranger things have happened.'

Selena nodded, and propped her feet up beside Jordan's on the coffee table. 'Stocking feet,' she said absently, wiggling her toes. 'When I was a kid, I used to think the phrase was "stalking feet."'

'No wonder you went into PI work.'

She nudged his sneaker. 'Why did you?' she asked.

'Go into PI work?' Jordan said, grinning.

'You know what I mean.'

'I went to law school for the same reason everyone else goes to law school: I had no idea what to do with my life and my parents were paying.'

Selena laughed. 'No, I can figure out why you became an attorney – so you'd get paid to have people listen to you argue. I want to know why you switched sides.'

'From the AG's office, you mean?' Jordan shrugged. 'Pay sucked.'

Selena glanced around the well worn house. Jordan liked his creature comforts, but was never going to be ostentatious. 'The truth,' she pressed.

He swung his eyes toward her. 'You know how I feel about the truth,' he said quietly.

'Your story, then,' Selena said.

'Well,' Jordan answered, 'as a prosecutor, you've got the burden of proof. As a defense lawyer, all you have to do is introduce a tiny doubt. And how can't a jury have some doubt? I mean, they weren't there at the scene of the crime, right?'

'You're telling me you switched sides because you wanted the easy way out? I don't buy it.'

'I switched sides,' Jordan said, 'because I didn't buy it either. The idea of there being one correct story. You have to believe in that, to prosecute, or what the hell is your case all about?'

Selena shifted, turning onto her side so that her face was only inches away from Jordan's. 'Do you think Chris Harte did it?' She put a hand on his arm. 'I know you don't think it makes any difference,' she said. 'You'd still defend him, and well. But I just want to know.'

Jordan looked down at his hands. 'I think he loved that girl, and I think that he was scared shitless when the police found them. Beyond that?' He shook his head. 'I think Chris Harte is a very good liar,' he said slowly. Then he looked up at Selena. 'But not quite as good as the prosecution thinks.'

It was Thursday, a quiet day in the cemetery, so that the voice of the rabbi seemed to carry, floating up to the branches of the trees where the finches watched with their button black eyes, their beaks closing around the words as if prayers were as nourishing as thistle seed. Michael stood beside Melanie, his dress shoes no match for the cold that came up through the packed earth. *How*, he wondered, *did they get the stone in?* And for the fiftieth time that morning, his eyes wandered to the brand new pink marble headstone on Emily's grave, the purpose for this unveiling ceremony.

The stone itself did not say much: Emily's name, the dates of her birth and death. And slightly below that, in large letters, a single word: BELOVED. Michael did not remember ordering that phrase from the stonecutter, but he supposed it was possible; it had been so long ago, and his mind had been so disordered. Then again, it would not have surprised him to learn that Melanie had had that part added. He wondered, though, if it had been her idea to put the slightest of spaces between the E and the L, or if that had been a slip of the carver's hand, so that you could not be sure if the word was a description of Emily — BELOVED — or BE LOVED, a directive issued on her behalf.

He listened to the guttural run of Hebrew coming from the rabbi, and the soft sound of Melanie's tears. But his eyes kept roaming, wandering, until he saw what he had been waiting for.

Coming up over the rise of the hill was Gus, dressed in a voluminous black parka and a dark skirt, her head bowed into the wind. She met Michael's eyes squarely and took up a spot slightly behind him, on the other side of Melanie.

Michael took a step back, and then another, until he was standing beside Gus. Hidden beneath the blowing folds of her coat, he touched her gloved hand. 'You came,' he whispered.

'You asked,' she murmured in response.

And then it was over. Michael bent down and picked up a small rock, which he laid at the base of the new headstone. Melanie did the same, and then briskly walked past Gus as if she were not there. Gus knelt and found a smooth white pebble, walked toward the grave, and set her offering beside the other two.

She felt Michael's hand on her arm again. 'I'll take you to your car,' he said, turning to let Melanie know where he was going, but she'd disappeared.

Gus waited while Michael talked to the rabbi and handed him an envelope. Then she fell into step beside him, neither one speaking until they reached the car. 'Thank you,' Michael said.

'No, thank *you*,' Gus said. 'I wanted to come.' She glanced up at Michael to say good-bye, but something about his face

– the lines at the corners of his eyes, or maybe his shaky smile – made her open her arms and let him step into them. When Michael pulled back her eyes were as damp as his.

'Saturday?' he asked.

'Saturday,' she said. He looked abstracted for a moment, as if struggling internally, and then apparently came to a decision. Still holding her loosely, he leaned down, kissed her softly on the mouth, and walked away.

Gus pulled the car over a quarter mile from the cemetery. It was entirely possible that in the strain of the moment – and an unveiling was certainly stressful – Michael had not really thought about what he was doing. Then again, Gus would have staked her savings on the fact that Michael was clearly aware.

She was emotionally needy, she knew that. God, it had been months since she'd slept with James, longer since she'd really talked to him. And at the same time she'd lost her husband, her best friend had turned her back. Having some adult who wanted – wanted! – to talk about Chris was seductive.

But she wondered, feeling slightly ill, whether she looked forward to seeing Michael because she could talk about Chris, or whether she'd been using Chris as an excuse to see Michael.

They did speak of Chris, and Emily, and the trial. And it was good to get all that off her chest. But it didn't account for the way the hair on the back of Gus's neck stood up when he looked at her and smiled, or for the fact that she could close her eyes now, and picture his face in a variety of expressions with the same recall that she had once had for James.

She had known Michael for years, knew him nearly as well as she knew her own husband. It was an attraction born of close quarters, and false familiarity. It meant, she told herself, absolutely nothing.

Yet she drove home one-handed, the fingertips of her free hand gently touching her mouth, her tires sibilant on the smooth road, whispering, 'Beloved.'

*   *   *

Although neither of them had spoken of it, ever since James's forthright decision not to testify as a witness for Chris, Gus had been sleeping in a different room. Chris's room, actually. There was comfort in feeling the mattress curved beneath her where it had spooned her son's body for years; in smelling the rank collection of athletic gear fermenting on the floor of the closet, in waking up to the sound of an alarm tuned to his favorite radio station – all of which contributed to the illusion that he was still just as close to Gus as any one of these things.

It was James's late night at the hospital. Gus heard him coming in, the heavy click of the front door, the rhythm of his footsteps on the stairs. There was a slight creak as he checked on Kate, asleep hours before, and the sound of water rushing through the pipes as he turned on the shower in the master bath. He did not come to talk to Gus. He did not go near Chris's room at all.

She slipped out of the bed, her feet silent on the carpet as she shrugged into her robe.

It was strange seeing her bed. The sheets were clean and smooth, but lapped untucked from the comforter like a lolling tongue – clear evidence that she wasn't sleeping here. James liked the sheets free; on Gus's side, they always stayed tucked, the line of demarcation shifting subtly night after night.

The water in the shower stopped running. Gus imagined James stepping out of the shower and wrapping a towel around his waist, his hair standing on end from a vigorous scrubbing. Then she pushed open the bathroom door.

James turned to her immediately. 'What's the matter?' he asked, certain there was no other reason, barring emergency, for her to be there.

'Everything,' Gus said, as she untied the terry-cloth robe and let it fall.

She stepped toward him hesitantly, laid her palms flat on his chest. With amazing force, James's arms closed around her. He slid down the length of her, his mouth on her breast and her ribs, and rested his cheek on her belly.

She tugged him upright and led him into the bedroom. James fell back upon her, his heart pounding every bit as hard as hers. Gus ran her hands over the joinings of the muscles in his arms, the light furring of his buttocks, the smooth divots at the bottom of his spine – all places she needed to touch, and commit again to memory. As he entered her, she arched beneath him like a willow. James thrust again and Gus bit down hard on the skin of his shoulder, afraid of what she might say. And then as quickly as it had escalated, it was over, James straining above her, their hands ripping at the bedclothes and each other, still in silence.

With a shy smile, James went off to the bathroom, nail marks raking his back. Gus patted her breasts, rubbed raw with beard stubble, and looked down at the bed. It was a mess, sheets tangled, quilt discarded. There was even blood on the sheets, from James's back, and they'd knocked over a nightstand lamp. It did not look like the site of a reconciliation, or a bower of love. In fact, Gus thought, it did not look like anything so much as the scene of a crime.

Jordan unsnapped the rubber band from the small packet of mail. At the letterhead of the Grafton County Superior Court, he felt his pulse pick up. He ripped open the envelope to find the letter sent by the Honorable Leslie Puckett, in response to the pretrial motions he and Barrie had filed.

The prosecutor's motions, seeking to exclude two of his expert witnesses and the pro-choice English essay Selena had found, had been denied.

His own motion of suppression to bar the interview Detective Marrone had done at the hospital had been granted, on the grounds that Chris Harte had not felt he was free to leave the interview, and thus had been formally questioned without being Mirandized.

It was a small victory, but it made him smile. Jordan shuffled the letter to the back of the pile, walked back into his office, and closed the door.

★   ★   ★

When Chris saw his father standing stiffly behind the metal bridge chair down in the visitor's area, he froze. He had told his mother that he wanted James to come, but he hadn't really expected his wish to be granted. After all, when Chris had banned him from visiting months before, they all knew he was just taking the blame for something James would have done, anyway.

'Chris,' his father said, holding out a hand.

'Dad.' They shook, and Chris was momentarily shocked by the heat of his father's skin. He remembered, in a quick flash, that his father's palms had always seemed reassuringly warm, on his shoulders in a duck blind, or bracing his arms as he taught him to shoot. 'Thank you for coming.'

James nodded. 'Thank you for having me,' he said formally.

'Did Mom come with you?'

'No,' James said. 'I understood that you wanted to see me by myself.'

Chris had never said that, but that was how his mother had interpreted it. And probably, it wasn't a bad idea. 'Was there something in particular you wanted to ask me?' James said.

Chris nodded. He thought of many things at once: *If I go to prison, will you help Mom get on with her life? If I ask you, will you tell me to my face that I've hurt you more than you ever thought possible?* But instead his mouth opened, rolling over a sentence that surprised Chris as much as it did James. 'Dad,' he said, 'in your whole life, haven't you ever done anything wrong?'

James covered his startled laughter with a cough. 'Well, sure,' he said. 'I failed biology the first term of college. I shoplifted a pack of gum when I was little. And I crashed my father's car up after a fraternity party.' He chuckled, crossing his legs. 'I just never came close to murder.'

Chris stared at him. 'Neither did I,' he said softly.

James's face went pale. 'I didn't mean . . . that is . . .' Finally, he shook his head. 'I don't blame you for what happened.'

'But do you believe me?'

James met his son's gaze. 'It is very hard to believe you,' he said, 'when I'm trying so hard to pretend it never happened.'

'It did happen,' Chris said, his voice choked. 'Emily's dead. And I'm stuck in this stinking jail, and I can't change what's already been done.'

'Neither can I.' James clasped his hands between his knees. 'You have to understand – I grew up being told by my parents that the best way to get out of a sticky situation was to assume it didn't exist,' he said. 'Let the rumors fly . . . if the family isn't bothered, why should anyone else be?'

Chris smiled slightly. 'Making believe I'm in a swanky hotel doesn't make the food taste any better here, or the cells any bigger.'

'Well,' James said, his voice softer. 'There's nothing that says you can't learn from your own children, too.' He rubbed the bridge of his nose. 'As a matter of fact, now that you've got me thinking, there was one thing I've done in my life that was really awful.'

Chris leaned forward, intrigued. 'What was it?'

James smiled with so much of his heart that Chris had to look away. 'I stayed away from here,' he said, 'until now.'

Steve's murder trial had lasted four days. His lawyer was a public defender, since neither he nor his parents could afford someone more glitzy. And although he didn't talk to Chris about his case, Chris knew that he grew more and more nervous as the close of the trial drew near.

The night before the jury was supposed to return a verdict, Chris woke to the sound of a slight scratching. He rolled over in his bunk to find Steve rubbing a razor blade over the edge of the toilet.

'What the fuck are you doing?' Chris whispered.

Steve looked up. 'I'm going to prison,' he said, his voice heavy.

'You're already in prison,' Chris said.

Steve shook his head. 'This is a country club compared to the State Pen. Do you know what they do there to guys serving time for killing kids? Do you?'

Chris smiled a little. 'Make you the company whore?'

'You think it's so frigging funny? Because you could be in the same goddamned boat three months from now.' Steve was breathing harshly, trying not to cry. 'Sometimes they just beat you up, and the guards look away 'cause they think you've got it coming. Sometimes they go so far as to kill you.' He picked up the silver sliver of razor, a gleam in the half light of the cell. 'I thought I'd save them the trouble,' Steve said.

Still muzzy with sleep, it took Chris a moment to understand what Steve was saying. 'You can't do that,' he said.

'Chris,' Steve murmured, 'it's about the only thing I can do.'

Chris suddenly remembered Emily, trying to explain to him how she felt. *I can see myself now*, she said. *And I can see what I want to be, ten years from now. But I don't understand how I'm going to get from here to there.* Chris watched Steve lift a shaking hand, the blade of the razor trembling like a flame. And he jumped off his bunk and started pounding at the bars of the cell, screaming to attract the attention of an officer and do for this friend what he had not done for Emily.

Rumors flew through a jail, pervasive as gnats and just as difficult to ignore. By breakfast the next day everyone knew that Steve had been taken to the suicide cell down in maximum, where he was monitored by camera in the control room. By lunch, he was being led away by the sheriff, to the courthouse to hear the jury's decision.

At a little after three-thirty, one of the officers came into Chris's cell and started packing up Steve's things. Chris set down the book he was reading. 'Is the trial over?' he asked.

'Yup. Guilty. Sentenced to life in prison.'

Chris watched the officer pick up the broken shards of the plastic razor, the one Steve had pried apart for its blade. He pulled his pillow over his head, sobbing as he had not since the day he'd arrived at the jail. And he did not allow himself to ask whether he was crying for Steve or for himself; for what he had done, or for what was certain to happen.

At first, Barrie Delaney had called Melanie often, giving her updates on evidence that had dribbled in from the ME's office, or the forensics lab. Then the telephone calls had been made from Melanie's end, periodically, just to keep Emily on Ms Delaney's mind. Now, Melanie called maybe once a month, not wanting to take from the prosecutor any amount of precious time that would be better served preparing for the trial.

So Melanie was rather surprised when Barrie Delaney tracked her all the way to the library to talk to her.

She picked up the phone, certain that the other librarian had gotten the caller's name wrong, only to hear the prosecutor's clear, clipped voice.

'Hi,' Melanie said. 'How is everything?'

'I should be asking you that,' Barrie said. 'Actually, everything is fine.'

'Have they changed the date of the trial?'

'Oh, no. Still set for May.' She sighed into the phone. 'You see, Mrs Gold, I was wondering if you might be able to help me with a bit of research.'

'Anything,' Melanie assured her. 'What do you need?'

'It's your husband. He's agreed to testify for the defense.'

Melanie was silent so long that the prosecutor began calling her name. 'I'm still here,' she said faintly, remembering Gus at the cemetery, certain she'd put Michael up to this. She felt her head start to pound. 'What can I do?'

'Ideally, you can get him to back down,' Barrie said. 'And if he refuses, maybe you can find out what he's going to say that's so useful to the defense.'

By now, Melanie's head was bowed, her forehead grazing the reference desk. 'I see,' she said, although she did not. 'And how do I do this?'

'Well, Mrs Gold,' the prosecutor said. 'I guess that's up to you.'

The first thing Michael noticed when he entered the house, sweaty and tired and reeking of sheep dip, was that the stereo was on. After months of prolonged silence, music seemed sacreligious, and he had the absurd urge to turn it off. But then he came around the corner of the kitchen and found Melanie chopping vegetables, the jewel tones of the peppers dotting the countertop like confetti. 'Hi,' she said brightly, so much like the woman she'd been a year ago that Michael started. 'You hungry?'

'Famished,' he said, his mouth dry. He heard the swell of a horn on the CD, and resisted the desire to reach out his hand and touch Melanie to make sure she was really there.

'Go clean up,' she said. 'I've got a nice lamb ragout cooking.'

He walked up to the bathroom like an automaton, his head spinning. This was what he had heard about grief, after all – it could change a person drastically, then, one day, they'd be all right. It had certainly been that way for him. Maybe it was Melanie's turn to come back to life.

As he soaped himself in the shower and lathered his hair with shampoo, he kept envisioning Melanie as he'd seen her in the kitchen, her back to him, the curve of her spine graceful beneath her turtleneck, the highlights in her hair winking gold and roan and russet in the afternoon sun.

He came out in a towel, only to find Melanie sitting on the bed with two steaming plates and two glasses of red wine.

She was wearing a green silk robe that he remembered from a second honeymoon a million years ago, its sash slipping open. 'I thought you might not want to wait,' she said.

He swallowed. 'For what?' he asked.

Melanie smiled. 'The ragout.' She stood up, the colorful delicacy on the plates jiggling with the movement of the mattress, and lifted a glass of wine. 'Want some?' When Michael nodded, she took a sip, and then leaned up to kiss him, letting the wine run over his lips and into his throat.

He thought he was going to come, right then and there.

It had been months since he'd made love with Melanie, as long as his daughter had been dead. He would have jumped at the invitation to share a bed with her ... but this was not Melanie. In all the years they had been married, Melanie had never been one to initiate sex. He thought of her dribbling wine into his mouth, felt himself grow even harder, and then wondered what book she'd stolen that from.

Before he could stop himself, he laughed.

Melanie's eyes flickered; someone who did not know her as well as Michael might have missed the indecision that widened her pupils for that fraction of a second. To her credit – and his shock – she put the glass of wine down, reached for the back of his head, and tugged him down for a kiss.

He felt the robe open, her nipples peaked against his chest. He felt her tongue curl into his mouth and her fingers stroke the nape of his neck. And then he felt her other hand slide between them, to cup his testicles.

She had him by the balls.

Suddenly he understood why Melanie was cooking ragout, wearing silk, making love to him. She had not changed overnight. She only wanted something.

He lifted his head and drew back. Melanie made a sharp, tiny sound, and opened her eyes. 'What's the matter?' she asked.

'How about,' Michael murmured, 'you tell me.'

He saw her looking at him, felt her surprise as his penis grew flaccid in her grip. She tightened her grasp almost cruelly and then let him go, jerking the lapels of her robe closed. 'You're going to be a defense witness,' she hissed. 'Your own daughter's dead, and you're going to stick up for her killer.'

'That's what this is about?' Michael said, incredulous. 'Did you think if you fucked me you could change my mind?'

'I don't know!' Melanie cried, her hands buried in her hair. 'I thought that maybe you wouldn't do it. That you'd owe it to me.'

Michael blinked at her, stunned that in a marriage which had lasted twenty years, she could even think of using sex as a down payment, instead of a gift. Wanting to hurt Melanie as badly as she had hurt him, Michael schooled his face into a careful blank. 'You flatter yourself,' he said, and walked out of the room.

He was naked, but that didn't matter. He stalked across the house and up the connecting staircase to the offices of his veterinary practice. There he dressed in the scrubs he wore sometimes for surgeries, and sat down at his desk. He could hear the quiet clatter of Melanie in the kitchen.

His hands were shaking as he picked up the phone and dialed.

Gus walked into the Happy Family restaurant and immediately strode toward the booth in the back that they all used to frequent on Friday nights. Michael was sitting there in a pair of green scrubs, drinking what looked to be straight vodka. 'Michael,' she said, and he lifted his head.

She had seen that look before, but she couldn't quite place it. The vague set of the eyes, the small parenthetic downturns at the edges of the mouth. It took her a moment to recognize it as despair, an expression she'd seen on Chris's face before he remembered to pull his mask of indifference into place.

'You came,' Michael said.

'I said I would.'

He had called her at home, risky to begin with, and begged her to meet him right away. Trying to pick a familiar public venue that wouldn't be too busy this time of day, she suggested the Chinese restaurant. It was only as she was driving there, having lied to James and Kate, that she realized how crowded it would be with memories.

'It's Melanie,' Michael said, and Gus's eyes widened.

'She's all right?'

'I don't know. I guess that depends on your frame of reference,' he said. He told Gus what had happened.

By the time he finished, Gus's face was pink. She remembered, not so long ago, laughing with Melanie over coffee, discussing width versus length and other abstractions about sex that seemed too close for comfort right now. 'Well,' she said, clearing her throat, 'you knew she was going to find out if you testified.'

'Yeah. I don't think that's what upset me, really.' He looked up at Gus, his eyes clouded. 'It's just that this very horrible thing has happened to the two of us, you see? And I guess I always figured that if it came to this, we'd band together. Ride out the storm.' He stared down at the place mat, festively decorated with a Chinese calendar wheel: the year of the rat, of the ox, of the horse. 'Do you know what it's like to give your whole self to a person, and your whole heart to boot, until you've got nothing left to give – and then realize that it still isn't what they need?'

'Yes,' Gus said simply. 'I do know.' She reached across the table and clasped both Michael's hands, giving him strength. And they thought separately of Melanie, and of James, and of how a stream of difference between two people might, overnight, turn into a canyon.

They were still holding hands when the waiter came over to take their order. 'Missus! Mister!' he crowed, a wide smile splitting his face as Gus and Michael jumped apart. 'It be many time since you be here to eat,' he said, his voice a pidgin singsong. 'When are coming the other couple?'

Gus stared at the waiter, openmouthed. It was Michael who realized the mistake that had been made. 'Oh . . . no,' he said, smiling. 'We're not married. We are, that is, but not to each other.'

Gus nodded. 'The other two, the ones who aren't here—' she said, and then broke off as the waiter smiled beatifically at them, unwilling or unable to understand.

Michael rested his palm on the menu. 'Chicken and broccoli,' he said. 'And more vodka.'

In the awkward silence that followed the waiter's disappearance to the kitchen, Gus slid her hands under the table, still tingling with Michael's touch. Michael tapped his chopsticks against the edge of the vodka glass. 'He thought that you and I were—'

'Yes,' Gus said. 'Funny.' But she was staring down at her place mat, at the odd Chinese calendar, and wondering if the waiter was not the only one who had thought that spouses were interchangeable. It was a logical mistake, after all; anyone who'd seen the Hartes and the Golds here for years, and the rapport between the four of them, could have come to the same conclusion.

Gus peeked at Michael over the edge of her teacup, considering his thick silver hair, his capable, square hands, his heart. She had come to Michael tonight because he'd needed her. It felt perfectly natural – after all, he was almost a member of the family.

Which was, in itself, a little horrifying.

And incestuous.

The heavy china cup clanked onto the table as it slipped out of Gus's hand. Both she and Michael had felt the odd, simultaneous ease and discomfort of this attraction. But they were old enough to move away from each other, when reality – in the form of a Chinese waiter – intruded. It might not be as simple, for someone younger.

Who was to say that Emily hadn't felt it, too, blithely pushed into a romance with a boy who might as well have been her brother?

Pregnant with his child?

Gus closed her eyes and offered up a quick prayer, suddenly realizing what no one else had been able to for many months – why the bright, lively, intelligent Emily Gold might have been confused enough to take her own life.

Then

October 1997

The first time Emily told Chris she wanted to kill herself, Chris laughed.

The second time, he pretended he didn't hear.

The third time, he listened.

They had been driving home from a late movie, and Emily had fallen asleep. She was doing that a lot these days, Chris realized – nodding off in the middle of the evening, sleeping so late in the morning Chris had to wake her up before driving her to school, once even dozing off in class. Her head was balanced lightly on his shoulder as he drove, her body canted sideways over the stick shift between the bucket seats. Chris kept his left hand on the wheel, his right bent at a strange angle to cradle Emily's head and keep it from bobbing all over the place.

He needed both hands to get off the highway, and he let go of Emily only to have her slip off his shoulder and settle in his lap, her ear pressed against the ring of his belt, her breasts nestled against the gear shift, her nose an inch from the steering wheel. Her head was heavy and warm, and as he drove through the silent streets of Bainbridge he rested his hand on it, brushing her hair back from her face. He turned into her driveway and cut the motor and the lights, watching her sleep.

He traced the pink of her ear, so fragile that Chris could see the slight blue veins webbing it, could imagine the traveling blood. 'Hey,' he said softly. 'Wake up.'

She did, with a start, and would have smashed her head on the steering wheel if Chris's hand wasn't there to stop her. She struggled upright, Chris's hand still on the back of her neck.

Emily stretched. There was a deep red furrow on her left cheek, a scar carved by the edge of his belt. 'Why didn't you wake me up before?' she said, her voice husky.

Chris smiled at her. 'You looked too cute,' he said, and he tucked a strand of hair behind her ear.

It was nothing, a compliment like a thousand others he'd given her, and yet she burst into tears. Stunned, Chris reached across the stick shift, trying as best as he could to gather her into his arms. 'Emily,' he said, 'tell me.'

She shook her head; he felt the slight movement against his shoulder. Then she drew back, wiping her nose with the back of her sleeve. 'It's you,' she said. 'You're what I'm going to miss.'

It seemed a strange way to say it – 'I miss you' would have made more sense – but Chris smiled. 'We can visit,' he said. 'That's why colleges have long breaks, you know.'

She laughed, although it might have been a sob. 'I'm not talking about college. I keep trying to tell you,' Emily said haltingly. 'But you don't listen.'

'Tell me what?'

'I don't want to be here,' Emily said.

Chris reached for the ignition key. 'It's early. We can go somewhere else,' he said, a thrum of alarm working its way up his spine.

'No,' Emily said, turning to him. 'I don't want to *be*.'

He sat in silence, his throat working, his mind replaying the other, dismissed things Emily had said that had been leading up to this. And he saw what he had been trying so hard not to see: for someone who knew Emily as well as he did, he saw that she'd been acting different. 'Why?' he managed.

Emily bit her lip. 'Do you believe that I would tell you everything I could?' Chris nodded. 'I can't take it anymore. I just want it to be over.'

'Want what to be over? What is it?'

'I can't tell you,' Emily choked out. 'Oh, God. We've never lied, you and me. We maybe haven't always told each other everything, but we've never lied.'

'Okay,' Chris said, his hands trembling. 'Okay.' He felt himself spinning out of his body, like the time he'd smacked his head on the edge of the high-diving board and had passed out – grasping at the most ordinary things, like the air and the view right in front of his eyes, and knowing he wasn't going to be able to keep it from dissolving. 'Em,' he said, swallowing, his voice just another shadow in the car. 'Are you . . . is this about killing yourself?' And when Emily looked away, his lungs swelled up like balloons and the bottom dropped out of his world.

'You can't,' Chris said after a minute, stunned that he'd made any sound at all, with his lips so rubbery and thick. *I am not talking about this*, he thought. *Because if I talk about it, it will really be happening.* Emily wasn't sitting across from him, pale and beautiful, discussing suicide. He was having a nightmare. He was waiting for the punch line. Yet he could hear his own voice, high and freaked out, already believing. 'You – you can't do this,' he stammered. 'You don't just go and kill yourself because you're feeling crappy one day. You don't decide something like that out of the blue.'

'It's not out of the blue,' Emily said evenly. 'And it's not one day.' She smiled. 'It feels good to talk about it. It isn't so bad to think about, when I say it out loud.'

Chris's nostrils flared, and he yanked open his car door. 'I'm going to talk to your parents.'

'No!' Emily cried, so much fear in that one word that Chris immediately stopped. 'Please don't,' she murmured. 'They won't get it.'

'I don't get it,' Chris said heatedly.

'But you'll listen,' she said, and for the first time in five minutes, something made sense to Chris. Of course he'd listen; he'd do anything for her. And her parents . . . well, she was right. At seventeen, the smallest crises took on tremendous proportions; someone else's thoughts could take root in the loam of your own mind; having someone accept you was as vital as oxygen. Adults, light-years away from this, rolled their eyes and smirked and said, 'This too shall pass' – as if adolescence was a disease like chicken pox, something everyone recalled as a mild nuisance, completely forgetting how painful it had been at the time.

There were mornings Chris woke up in a sweat, full to bursting with life, panting as if he'd run all the way up to the top of a cliff. There were days when he felt like he could not fit inside his own skin. There were nights when he was terrified of living up to the model of what he was turning out to be, needing more than anything to breathe in the drugging shampoo scent of Emily's hair, and just as unwilling to admit it. But he could not explain this to anyone, least of all his parents. And Emily, just because she was Emily, clung to him and rode out the storm until he could come up for air.

He was all at once panicked and proud that Em would take him into her confidence. It escaped him, for the moment, that she had not been able to tell him what was bothering her in the first place. Riding on the crest of her faith, he was tugged by the glory of shutting everyone else out, of being Emily's savior.

Then he thought of her cutting her wrists open and felt something crack in his chest. This was much bigger than the two of them. 'There has to be someone,' he said. 'A psychiatrist or something.'

'No,' Emily said again softly. 'I let you in on this because I've always told you everything. But you can't—' her voice faltered. 'You can't ruin this for me. Tonight is the first night in – God, I don't know how long – that I've felt like I can handle this. It's like a really bad pain that you can take, you know, because you've already swallowed the medicine and you can see that it's going to stop hurting soon.'

'What hurts?' Chris asked thickly.

'Everything,' Emily said. 'My head. My heart.'

'Is it . . . is it because of me?'

'No,' she said, her eyes shining again. 'Not you.'

He grabbed her then, oblivious of the hard knot of the stick shift between them, and crushed her against his chest. 'Why would you tell me, unless you want me to help you?' he whispered.

Emily panicked. 'You won't tell?'

'I don't know. Am I supposed to just sit around and pretend everything's okay until you go and do it? And then say, "Oh, yeah . . . she did mention something about killing herself."' He drew back, his hand over his eyes. 'Christ. I cannot believe I'm even talking about this.'

'Promise me,' Emily said, 'you won't tell anyone.'

'I can't.'

The tears that had welled in Emily's eyes spilled over. 'Promise,' she asked again, her hands grabbing small fistfuls of his shirt.

For years he'd been cast as Emily's future protector, as her other half – and although he never imagined himself to be any less than that, he didn't really understand how to fully grow into the role. He suddenly realized that this was his test as much as Emily's, his chance to carry Em safely away. If she trusted him, he could damn well be worthy of it . . . even if that meant something very different to each of them. He had time. He would get her to talk. He would find out this horrible secret and show her there was another, better way; and eventually everyone – Emily included – would praise him for it. 'Okay,' Chris whispered. 'I promise.'

Yet even with Emily pressed against him, he felt a wall come up, so that skin to skin, he could no longer really feel her. As if she sensed it, too, Emily burrowed closer. 'I told you,' she said quietly, 'because I didn't know how not to.'

Chris looked into her eyes, realizing the strength of her statement. But what difference was there between having Emily try to explain what she wanted to happen, or finding out from a knock at the door that Emily had committed suicide, when the end result was the same?

'No,' he said calmly, filled with purpose. He took her arms lightly in his hands and shook her. 'I am *not* giving you up.'

Emily looked at him, and for just a moment he could read her thoughts. Melanie used to say they were like twins, with their own secret, silent language. In that instant, Chris felt her fear and her resignation, and the knotty pain of coming up against a brick wall again and again. She glanced away, and he could breathe again. 'The thing is, Chris,' Emily said, 'it's not your choice.'

Chris lunged through the water, warming up at swim practice with four laps of freestyle. Swimming had always been good for his mind – there was not much to do in fifty meters but think. He'd memorized the periodic table while swimming his laps, and SAT vocabulary, and he'd even rehearsed the things he'd say to Emily to get her to sleep with him. Most of the time he could keep a lazy rhythm without breaking stride. But thinking about dying – and Emily – made his arms wheel faster and his legs strike the water punishingly, as if he could outrace his thoughts.

Finishing, he hoisted himself out of the pool, his heart thundering. He stripped off his goggles and swim cap and scrubbed his towel over his hair, then went to sit on one of the benches that lined the pool. His coach walked up to him, a smirk on his face. 'We try to save the record-breaking times for competitions, Harte,' he said. 'It's just practice. Don't kill yourself.'

Don't kill yourself.

He couldn't let Emily do it; it was that simple. And maybe it was for purely selfish reasons, but surely one day she'd thank him for saving her life. Whatever it was that was bothering her – and what the hell could it be that she wasn't able to tell him? – could surely be resolved. Especially if he was there to help her.

His eyes widened. That was it. Em wanted his understanding, and his silence. If he played along, he'd have a chance to talk her out of doing it. Even up to the last minute. He'd pretend that this crazy idea of killing herself was acceptable, and then, like a white knight, he'd sweep down and save Emily from herself. No one else would ever have to know what had almost happened. And he wouldn't have to break his promise to her about keeping the whole horrible plan to himself. The ends justified the means.

It did not occur to Chris that he might not succeed.

Feeling much better, he stood up at the sound of his coach's whistle and sleeked into the pool again for another drill.

Emily was waiting for him after practice. She stayed late at school, too, usually taking up residence at her easel in the art room, and finishing in time to meet Chris after swimming so that he could drive her home. She was waiting for him on a chair beside the water fountain outside the boys' locker room, her hands smelling faintly of turpentine and her coat bunched in a heap at her feet, like a lapdog. 'Hi,' Chris said, his duffel bag slung over his shoulder as he crossed to her.

He bent down to kiss her cheek, and she breathed him in, that wonderful mixture of Safeguard and chlorine and laundry detergent. His sideburns were still dripping water from his shower; he was close enough that she could put out her tongue and catch a drop. Emily closed her eyes, sketching the picture into her mind so that she would be able to take it with her.

She fell into step beside him on the way to the students' parking lot. 'I've been thinking,' Chris began. 'About what you said Saturday night.'

Emily nodded, but kept her eyes trained on her shoes.

'And I want you to know, for the record, that this is like the last thing in the world I want to happen,' Chris said. 'I'm going to do everything I can to change your mind.' He took a deep breath and squeezed her hand. 'But if it . . . comes to that,' he said, 'I would like to be there with you.'

Emily realized as he said the words that apparently she had not lost all hope, not when she'd subconsciously been wishing so hard for this. 'I'd like that,' she said.

Chris began a subtle, undeterrable campaign to show Emily

what she would be missing. He took her out to restaurants where dinner cost a hundred dollars; he drove her to watch the sun set over the jetties that glided into the Atlantic. He dug out old notes they'd passed back and forth on a tin-can pulley system that worked exactly three times before tangling irreparably in the pines between the houses. He made her look through his stacks of college application materials, as if her input was imperative to his decisions. And he made love to her, offering his body in both tenderness and anger, unsure which was the best way to pass her bits of his soul so that she could patch her own with it.

And Emily suffered it. That was the best way Chris could describe it, really; she endured whatever he set in her path but from a distance, as if she were watching from on high and had long ago set her mind.

To his astonishment, Emily didn't give an inch. He tried to figure out what her problem was with all the fortitude and strategic delicacy of a general mounting a land invasion. In the wake of her silence, he dreamed of the worst things he could imagine: She was a drug addict; she was a lesbian; she had cheated on the SATs – all things that would not make him stop loving her.

He tried teasing her secret out of her; he tried Twenty Questions; he tried bullying. It only made Emily tighten her mouth and curl away, so that Chris panicked about losing her sooner rather than later. He could only press to a certain point, because if she started to think he wouldn't truly help her kill herself, his charade – and his valiant chance to save her – would be blown.

'I can't talk about it,' she'd say.

'You *won't*,' Chris corrected.

Frustrated, Emily would say that by bringing it up, Chris was only making it hurt more. If he really loved her, he'd stop asking.

And Chris, just as wearied by the stalemate, would shake his head. 'I can't,' he'd tell her.

'*Won't*,' Em parroted, shaming him into dropping the subject once again.

They lay on their bellies in the living room of the Gold house, their math textbooks open in front of them, derivatives and differential equations curled like a foreign tongue over the pages. 'No,' she said, pointing out a spot where Chris had made an error. 'It's $2xy-x$,' she corrected. Then she rolled onto her back, staring up at the ceiling. 'Why is it so important to me to get an A,' she mused, 'when I'm not even going to be here to get a report card?'

She sounded so matter-of-fact about it that Chris felt nauseated. 'Maybe it's because you don't really want to kill yourself,' he pointed out.

'Thanks, Dr Freud,' Emily said.

'I mean it,' Chris said, coming up on an elbow. 'What if we said you'd wait six months, and see how you felt.'

Emily's face froze. 'No,' she said.

'That's it? Just *no*?'

She nodded. 'No.'

'Oh, well, that's great,' Chris said, slamming the textbook. 'That's just wonderful, Em.'

Emily narrowed her eyes. 'I thought you were going to help me.'

'Sure,' Chris said angrily. 'What would you like me to do? Push you off the chair when the rope's around your neck? Pull the trigger?'

Emily's face flushed red. 'Do you think it's easy for me to talk about it?' she asked tightly. 'Because it isn't.'

'It's easier for you than it is for me,' Chris exploded. 'You don't even get where I'm coming from. I look at you and I see this amazing, beautiful thing. All these books and songs are written about people looking for the love of their life and never finding it, and we've got it and it isn't worth a damn to you.'

'It is worth a damn to me,' Emily said, covering Chris's

hand with her own. 'It's the only thing worth a damn. All I'm trying to do is to keep it that way, forever.'

'Hell of a way to do it,' Chris said bitterly.

'Really?' Emily asked. 'Would you rather spend the rest of your life thinking about us, and remembering it as something totally perfect, or would it be better to let it get all screwed up and have that as your memory?'

'Who said we'd ever get all screwed up?'

'We would,' Emily said. 'It happens.'

'Don't you see?' Chris said, trying to keep the tears out of his voice. 'Don't you understand what you'd be doing to me?'

'I'm not doing it to you,' Emily answered softly. 'I'm doing it for me.'

Chris stared at her. 'What,' he said, 'is the difference?'

To his surprise, the more Emily brought up the subject of suicide, the less shocking it became. Chris stopped arguing with her about it, because that only made her more set in her ways, and took up a new tack: exploring her options thoroughly, so that she might see how completely ludicrous the idea was.

He turned to her one night in the middle of a TV-movie and asked her how she was going to do it.

'What?' It was the first time Emily had ever heard Chris bring it up; usually she was one to broach the topic.

'You heard me. I figure you must have been thinking it over.'

Emily shrugged, gave a quick glance over her shoulder to make sure her parents were still upstairs. 'I have,' she said. 'Not pills.'

'Why not?'

'Because it's too easy to do it wrong,' she said. 'You wind up with your stomach pumped, in a psychiatric ward.'

He rather liked that idea, actually. 'So what's your alternative?'

'There's carbon monoxide poisoning,' she said, and then

smiled. 'But I'd probably have to use your Jeep. And slashing wrists seems . . . deliberate.'

'I think killing yourself in general is pretty deliberate,' Chris said.

'It might hurt,' Emily said meekly. 'I just want it to be over right away.'

Chris looked at her. *Before you can change your mind*, he thought, *or I can change it for you.*

'I was thinking of a gun,' she said.

'You hate guns.'

'Well, what does that have to do with it?'

'Where are you going to get a gun?' Chris said.

Emily looked up at him. 'Maybe from you,' she suggested.

His eyebrows raised. 'Oh, no. Absolutely not.'

'Please, Chris,' she said. 'You could just give me the key to the cabinet. Tell me where to find the bullets.'

'You're not going to shoot yourself with a hunting rifle,' Chris muttered.

'I was thinking of the little one. The Colt.'

She saw him put up a wall, and her chest spasmed. Chris had seen that look before – wide and resigned, backed into a corner – like a doe, the moment before he took it down. And he realized that this was Emily now, that the only time she seemed happy was when she was planning the way she would die.

Tears were running down her face, thickening his own throat and making Chris cry the same way her orgasm sometimes triggered his. 'You used to say you'd do anything for me,' Emily pleaded.

Chris looked down at their hands, linked over the textbooks, and accepted for the first time that – for whatever reason – he might fail, that this might really happen. 'I would,' he said, his heart breaking beneath the weight of the truth.

They sat in the dark of the movie theater, holding hands. Whatever they'd gone to see – Chris couldn't even remember the title – was long finished. The credits had rolled, the other patrons had left. Around them one or two ushers swept empty popcorn containers out of the aisles, moving in a hushed rhythm and doing their best to ignore the couple still curled in the back of the theater.

Sometimes he was certain that he'd come away a hero, and one day he and Emily would find this all very funny. And other times he believed that he would be only what he'd promised Emily: someone there to witness her, as she went.

'I don't know what I'd do without you,' Chris whispered.

He could see Emily turn to him, her eyes shine in the dark. 'You could do it with me,' she said, and swallowed, the suggestion still bitter in her throat.

Chris did not respond, purposely letting her feel sick to her stomach at the thought. He wondered silently, *What makes you so sure we would still be together, after? How do you know it works like that?*

'Because,' Emily said, as clearly as if she'd heard him. 'I can't picture it any other way.'

One night he went into the basement and took the key from his father's workbench. The gun cabinet was locked, as always, to keep out children. Not teenagers like Chris, who knew better.

He opened the cabinet and took out the Colt, because he knew Emily well enough to be certain that the first thing she'd ask was to see the pistol. If he didn't bring it, she'd realize something was up, and stop trusting him before he had a chance to keep her from going through with it.

He sat there, the weight of the gun cradled in his hands, remembering the acrid smell of Hoppe's Solvent #9 and the way his father's hands, gifted and precise, had rubbed the shaft and the barrel with a silicone cloth. *Like Aladdin's lamp*, Chris had once thought, expecting magic.

He remembered the stories his father had told about the piece, about Eliot Ness and Al Capone, about speakeasies and secret raids and sloe gin fizzes. He told Chris that this gun had driven home justice.

Then he remembered his first deer hunt, which had not been a clean kill. Chris and his father had tracked the animal into the woods, where it lay on its side taking great, heaving breaths. *What do I do?* Chris had asked, and his father had lifted his rifle and fired. *Put it out of its misery,* he said.

Chris reached into the bottom of the gun cabinet and drew out the bullets for the .45. Emily was no fool; she'd ask to see these too. He closed his eyes and made himself imagine her lifting the tarnished silver barrel to her forehead; made himself picture his own hand coming up and drawing the gun away from her head, if it came down to that.

It was selfish, but it was simple: he could not let Emily kill herself. When you'd been with someone your whole life, you could not imagine living in a world that did not have her in it.

He would stop her. He would.

And he did not let himself wonder why he'd slipped two bullets into his pocket, instead of just the one.

Now

May 1998

Gus sat on the edge of her bed and smoothed her panty-hose up her legs. *Next*, she thought woodenly, *clothes*. She stepped into the closet to retrieve a simple navy dress and a pair of matching low-heeled pumps. She would wear her pearls, too – elegant and understated.

She was not allowed in the courtroom. Witnesses were sequestered until they gave their testimony. In all likelihood, she would not be called to the stand today, maybe not even tomorrow. She was dressing up on the off chance that she might see Chris, even in passing.

Gus heard the water running in the bathroom as James shaved. It was as if they were going to a dinner party, or a conference with one of the children's teachers. Except they weren't.

And so James emerged from the bathroom to find Gus sitting on the bed in her bra and pantyhose, her eyes closed and her body bent, taking small shallow breaths as if she'd been running forever.

Melanie and Michael walked out of the house together. Her feet sank into the soft earth, mucking up her heels. She opened the door of her car, and without saying a word, got inside.

Michael got into his own truck. He followed his wife all the way down Wood Hollow Road, staring at the rear end of her car. There were two high brake lights on each side of the wide back window, and a low strip of lights across the bumper of the car as well. Every time Melanie stepped on the brake, they all flashed, making it seem as if the car were smiling.

*   *   *

Barrie Delaney's cat knocked over her cup of coffee the minute she was scheduled to leave for the courthouse. 'Shit, shit, *shit*,' she muttered, pushing the yowling cat away from the mess and soaking it up with a dishtowel. It was not enough, the coffee was still running in rivulets beneath the kitchen table. Barrie glanced quickly at the sink, deciding that she did not have time to clean up.

It was not until days later that she realized coffee would stain her white vinyl flooring, that for the next ten years she'd come into her kitchen and think about Christopher Harte.

Jordan set his briefcase down on the kitchen counter. Then he spun around toward Thomas, one hand flattening his tie. 'So?'

Thomas whistled. 'Looking good,' he said.

'Good enough to win?'

'Good enough to kick some ass,' his son crowed.

Jordan grinned and slapped Thomas on the back. 'Watch your mouth,' he said half-heartedly, and lifted the box of Cocoa Krispies, his face falling. 'Oh, Thomas. You didn't.' His brows drew together as he peered into the dark, empty recesses of the cereal box.

Thomas, in the middle of a mouthful, let his jaw drop open. 'Isn't there some left? I swear, Dad, I thought there was.'

Every morning before a trial, Jordan had Cocoa Krispies. It was a sorry superstition, one with no more meat to it than a baseball pitcher who didn't shave for consecutive wins, or a cardsharp with a rabbit's foot sewn into the lining of his jacket. But it was his superstition, dammit, and it worked. Eat the Krispies, win the trial.

Thomas squirmed under his father's glare. 'I could run out and get some more,' he suggested.

Jordan snorted. 'With what vehicle?'

'My bike.'

'So you'll be back in time for . . . oh, maybe lunch.' Jordan shook his head. 'I just wish,' he said, trying to keep his temper in check, 'that sometimes you'd think before you acted.'

Thomas stared into his bowl. 'I could go next door and see if Mrs Higgins has some.'

Mrs Higgins was seventy-five if she was a day. Jordan highly doubted that Cocoa Krispies was a pantry staple for her. 'Forget it,' he said irritably, reaching into the refrigerator for an English muffin. 'It's too late.'

It felt weird, being in a suit. An officer had brought Chris the clothes with his breakfast; the jacket and slacks he hadn't seen since his arraignment seven months before. He remembered when he and Em and his mother had gone shopping for the suit. The store had smelled of money and worsted wool. He'd stood on the inside of the dressing room booth, hopping around to get the pants on, while Em and his mom chattered about ties, their voices coming through the door like the pipe of finches.

'Harte,' an officer said, standing at the door of the cell. 'Time to go.'

He walked through the pod in his suit, sweat beading at his temples, aware of the conspicuous silence from the occupants of other cells. It hit too close to home, was all. You could not watch someone march off to trial without thinking what might happen to you.

When the heavy door was locked behind him again, the officer led him to a deputy sheriff, one of several stationed at the Grafton County Courthouse. 'Big day,' he said, cuffing Chris and then attaching the links to a waist chain. He waited for the officer to unlock the jail's main door and led Chris out of the prison, one hand firmly on his upper arm.

It was the first time in seven months that Chris had stood outside, fenced in only by the mountains and the lazy strip of the Connecticut River. The farm beside the jail reeked of manure. He took a deep breath and lifted his face, the sun soaking his cheeks and the bridge of his nose, his knees buckling under the tentative weight of freedom.

'Let's go,' the deputy said impatiently, yanking him toward the courthouse.

*   *   *

The courtroom was conspicuously empty, most of the players in the drama having been pulled aside as future witnesses. James sat stiffly in the row of seats just behind the defense table. Jordan, who had arrived a few minutes earlier, was talking to a colleague, his foot braced up on a chair. He stopped speaking when a side door opened, and James followed his gaze to see Chris being brought inside.

A bailiff led Chris to the defense table. James felt his throat close at the sight of his son, and before he could remember himself he reached over the divider and tried to touch Chris's arm.

Chris was directly in front of James, but a foot out of reach. *They built it this way*, James thought, *on purpose*.

'I don't *think* so,' Jordan was yelling, pointing to the handcuffs, which were horrible but had been expected. In fact Jordan had been the one to mention it to the Hartes, so James didn't see why he was so surprised. He gesticulated wildly, striding with the prosecutor toward the judge's chambers.

Chris turned around in his chair. 'Dad,' he said.

James reached out his hand again. For the first time in his life he was completely oblivious to an entire room of people looking on. He straddled and swung his legs over the divider, sitting down in the chair Jordan had vacated. Then he embraced his son, his body enveloping Chris's, so that the reporters and onlookers who poured into the courtroom to ogle the defendant could not even see that he was fettered.

In chambers, Jordan exploded. 'For God's sake, Your Honor,' he said. 'While we're at it, why don't I put him in dreadlocks and have him grow a beard and – hell, let's put a skinhead tattoo on his forehead so the jury *really* forms a bias before we've even started the trial!'

Barrie rolled her eyes. 'Your Honor, it's perfectly within precedent to have an alleged murderer brought to trial in handcuffs.'

Jordan rounded on her. 'What do you think he's going to do here? Start hammering someone to death with a Bic pen?' He turned to the judge. 'The only reason for the shackles, as we all know, is to make everyone think he's dangerous.'

'He *is* dangerous,' Barrie pointed out in an undertone. 'He killed a person.'

'Save it for the jury,' Jordan muttered beneath his breath.

'Jesus God,' Puckett said, spitting an almond shell into his hand. 'Is this what I have to look forward to?' His lids drifted shut as he rubbed his temples. 'It may be precedent, Ms Delaney, but I'm going to go out on a limb and assume that Chris Harte isn't planning to go off on a murderous rampage. The defendant can remain uncuffed for the duration of the trial.'

'Thank you, Your Honor,' Jordan said.

Barrie turned, bumping shoulders with Jordan on her way out the door. 'Must be a pretty feeble defense,' she whispered, 'if you're already begging favors from the bench.'

Jordan smiled confidently at Chris, who was still rubbing his wrists. 'This,' he said, nodding down at Chris's newly freed state, 'is a terrific sign.'

Chris didn't really see why, since even an honest-to-God murderer would have to be a total idiot to attack someone in the middle of a court of law. He knew and Jordan knew – hell, everybody knew – that the only reason he'd been brought in, cuffed, was to strip him of his dignity.

'Don't look at the prosecutor,' Jordan continued. 'She's going to say some awful things – you're allowed to do that in an opening argument. Ignore her.'

'Ignore her,' Chris repeated dutifully, and then some skinny guy with an Adam's apple as big as an egg told everyone to rise. 'The Honorable Leslie F. Puckett presiding,' he announced, and a man in a flowing robe entered from a side door, his teeth cracking audibly against something.

'Be seated,' the judge said, opening a file. He plucked a nut out of a squat, square jar in front of him, and sucked it through his lips, like krill being drawn through a whale's baleen. 'The prosecution,' he said, 'may begin.'

Barrie Delaney stood up and faced the jury. 'Ladies and gentlemen,' she said. 'My name is Barrie Delaney, and I'm here to represent the State of New Hampshire. I want to thank each one of you for taking on a very important job. The twelve of you are here to make sure that justice is done in this court-room. And in this case, justice means that you will find that man' – she raised a finger and pointed – 'Christopher Harte, guilty of murder.

'Yes, murder. It does sound shocking, and it's probably even more shocking to you that I'm pointing at a good-looking young man. I bet you're even thinking, "He doesn't look like a murderer."' She turned to examine Chris with the other members of the jury. 'He looks like . . . well, a prep-school kid. He doesn't fit the Hollywood image of a murderer. But ladies and gentlemen, this isn't Hollywood. This is real life, and in real life, Christopher Harte killed Emily Gold. Before this trial is over, you will know the defendant for what he really is, beneath that fancy jacket and that nice blue tie – a cold-blooded murderer.'

She flicked a glance toward Jordan. 'The defense is going to try to play on your emotions, and tell you that this was a botched double suicide. That's not what happened. Let me tell you what did.' She turned around, her hands spread on the rail of the jury box, directing her attention at an elderly blue-haired woman in a flowered cotton dress. 'On the night of November seventh, at six P.M., Christopher Harte went into the locked gun chest in the basement of his house and took out a Colt .45 revolver. He put it in his coat pocket and picked up his girlfriend, Emily. He took her to the carousel on Tidewater Road. The defendant also brought liquor. He and Emily drank, had sex, and then, while the defendant still had Emily in his arms, he took out the gun. After a brief struggle,

Christopher Harte put the barrel of that revolver up to Emily's right temple and shot her.'

She paused, letting that sink in. 'Ladies and gentlemen, you'll hear from Detective Anne-Marie Marrone. She will tell you that we have the gun, with the defendant's fingerprints all over it. You'll hear the county medical examiner say that the angle of the wound would make it virtually impossible for Emily to have pulled the trigger herself. You'll hear from a jeweler in town that Emily had bought a five-hundred-dollar watch to give to Chris for his birthday, which was the month after she died. And both a friend of Emily's and her own mother will tell you that Emily was not suicidal.

'You'll also hear Christopher Harte's motive: why on earth he would have shot his girlfriend. You see, ladies and gentlemen, Emily was eleven weeks pregnant.' At the quiet gasp of a juror, Barrie hid a smile. 'This young man had big plans for his future, and didn't need a baby or a high-school sweetheart ruining them, so he decided to – quite literally – get rid of the problem.'

She stepped back from the jury box. 'The defendant is charged with murder in the first degree. A person is guilty of first-degree murder when he purposely causes the death of another, and when his actions toward that end are premeditated and deliberate. Did Christopher Harte kill Emily Gold on purpose? Absolutely. Were his actions that night premeditated and deliberate? Absolutely.' She turned on her heel, her cold green eyes pinning Chris's. 'In the Bible, ladies and gentlemen, the Devil comes in many disguises. Don't let his latest one fool you.'

'Nice speech. Ms Delaney did a fine job, didn't she?' Jordan stood and sauntered toward the jury. 'Unfortunately, she was right about only one thing: the fact that Emily Gold . . . is dead.' He spread his hands. 'That is a tragedy. And I'm here to make sure that you don't allow another tragedy to occur – that you don't let this young man get put away for a crime he did not commit.

'Imagine for a moment the terrible pain of losing a loved one. It's happened to you,' Jordan said, looking at the same blue-haired lady Delaney had singled out. 'And you,' he said to a dairy farmer, with a face so creased it seemed again smooth. 'We've all lost someone. And recently, Chris did too. Think of how you felt when it happened to you – the pain, the rawness of it – and then imagine the horror of being charged with that same person's murder.

'The State says that Christopher Harte committed murder, but that's not what happened. He almost committed suicide. He watched his girlfriend do it, then he fainted before he could do it himself.

'All of the evidence the State was talking about is consistent with a double suicide. I'm not going to bore you with contradictions. I'm just going to ask you, now, to listen very carefully to all the witnesses, and look very carefully at all the evidence . . . because everything the State is using as proof of murder has been twisted.

'Ladies and gentlemen – in order to find Chris Harte guilty of murder, you have to be convinced beyond a reasonable doubt that the scene Ms Delaney painted for you was the real one. But that's all the State has – a painted scene.' He walked back to the defense table and placed his hand on his client's shoulder. 'When this trial is finished, you'll have more than a reasonable doubt – and you'll know that this isn't about murder. Emily Gold wanted to kill herself, and Chris decided to join her. He loved Emily so much that life wasn't worth living without her.' Jordan shook his head and turned toward Chris. 'That's not a crime, ladies and gentlemen. That's a tragedy.'

'The prosecution calls Detective Anne-Marie Marrone to the stand.'

There was a slight buzz as the first witness was sworn in. She settled down with the ease of someone who's played a particular house before, her gaze level on the jury.

Anne-Marie Marrone was wearing a simple black suit; her

hair was twisted up in a knot at the back of her head. With the exception of the holster peeking out from beneath her jacket, it was easy to forget she was a policewoman.

Barrie Delaney crossed in front of the witness stand. 'Please state your name and address for the court.' The detective complied, and Barrie nodded. 'Could you tell us in what capacity you're employed?'

'I'm a detective-sergeant with the Bainbridge police.'

'How long have you worked there?'

'Ten years.' She smiled. 'This June.'

There was a brief exchange about her training, her work at the police academy, and her experience within the police force. Then Barrie stopped pacing, her hand on the railing of the witness stand. 'Who was in charge of the investigation surrounding the death of Emily Gold?'

'I was,' the detective said.

'Did you determine the cause of death?'

'Yes. A gunshot wound to the head.'

'So there was a weapon involved in this case.'

'A Colt .45.'

'And were you able to retrieve the weapon?'

Anne-Marie nodded. 'It was at the scene of the crime,' she said. 'Lying on a carousel. We took the gun and ran a variety of ballistics tests on it.'

'Is this the gun you retrieved from the scene of the crime?' Barrie asked, holding up the Colt .45.

'That's it,' Detective Marrone said.

'Your Honor,' Barrie said, 'I'd like to enter this as Exhibit A.' She went through the customary procedure, showing the gun to Jordan, who dismissively waved it away. Then she turned back to the detective. 'Did you determine where the gun came from?'

'Yes. It was traced back to its owner, James Harte.'

James, behind the defense table, started at the sound of his name. 'James Harte,' the prosecutor said. 'Is that any relation to the defendant?'

'Objection,' Jordan called out. 'Relevance?'

'I'll allow it,' the judge said.

The detective looked from the judge to Barrie Delaney. 'It's his father.'

'Did you have a chance to interview James Harte?'

'Yes. He said that the gun was a collector's item, but still used for target practice. His also said his son was familiar with the gun, had access to it, and used it as well for target shooting.'

'Can you tell us about the tests you ran on the weapon?'

Detective Marrone shifted in her chair. 'Well, we determined that there was one bullet fired, which went into the victim's temple, exited the victim's head, and lodged in the wood of the carousel. We found the casing from that bullet still in the chamber of the gun, as well as a second bullet that had not been fired. Christopher Harte's fingerprints were on both of those bullets.'

Barrie pointed. 'By Christopher Harte, you mean the defendant.'

'Yes,' Detective Marrone said.

'Hmm.' Barrie turned to the jury, as if she was deliberating over this tidbit for the first time. 'So his fingerprints were on both bullets. Did you find anybody else's fingerprints on the bullets?'

'No.'

'And what, in your expert opinion, does that suggest?'

'He was the only one who handled the bullets.'

'I see,' Barrie said. 'Were there any other tests done on the weapon?'

'Yes, a standard ballistics test checked for fingerprints on the gun itself. We found both Christopher Harte's and Emily Gold's fingerprints on the gun. However, Mr Harte's fingerprints were all over it. The victim's fingerprints were only on the barrel of the gun.'

'Can you show us what you mean?' Barrie asked, picking up the Colt, with its new exhibit tag.

The detective easily palmed the gun. 'Mr Harte's fingerprints were here, here, and here,' she said, pointing. 'Emily Gold's fingerprints were only in this region.' She scraped her fingernail along the blunt steel barrel.

'But to shoot this gun, Detective Marrone, you would have to have your hand where?' She waited for Anne-Marie to indicate the butt of the gun. 'And Emily's fingerprints were not there.'

'No.'

'Yet Mr Harte's were.'

'Objection,' Jordan said lazily. 'Asked and answered.'

'Sustained,' Puckett said.

Barrie turned her back on Jordan. 'Was any other testing done at the crime scene?'

'Yes. We did a Luminol test, a fluorescent spray that detects blood spatter patterns. Based on that, as well as the angle of the bullet that eventually lodged in the carousel, we deduced that Emily Gold was standing up when the bullet was fired, and that someone else was standing very close and slightly in front of her. We also know that she lay on her back and bleeding for several minutes before she was moved into the position in which officers first found her when arriving at the scene of the crime.'

'Which was?'

'Bleeding profusely with her head in the defendant's lap.'

'And did the Luminol pick up anything else?'

'Yes. A large stain not tied to the spatter pattern of the bullet wound, where the defendant supposedly struck his head.'

'Objection.' Jordan gestured at Chris. 'Would you like to see the scar?'

Puckett gave Jordan a measured glance. 'Continue, Ms Delaney,' he said.

'From that stain, is it possible to determine how or why the defendant fell down?' Barrie asked.

'No,' the detective said. 'It only shows that he lay still there for about five minutes, bleeding.'

'I see. Any other tests?'

'There was gunpowder residue found on both the victim's and the defendant's clothing. We also tested the corpse of the victim for gunpowder residue on the fingers.'

'And what did you find?'

'There was no gunpowder residue on Emily Gold's fingers.'

'In a suicide, with a victim holding the gun in her hand when she shot herself, would you normally find gunpowder residue on the hands?'

'Definitely. That's why I started to think Emily Gold did not kill herself.'

Barrie was silent for a moment, assessing the faces of her jury. And they were hers now. Every single one of the twelve sat on the edge of his or her seat; several were taking careful notes on the provided pads of paper. 'Was there anything else you found at the scene of the crime?'

'We found a bottle of Canadian Club. Liquor.'

'Ah . . . underage drinking,' Barrie said, smiling.

The detective grinned, too. 'It wasn't my biggest concern at the time.'

At this, Jordan objected. 'Your Honor,' he said, 'if there was a question somewhere in there, I missed it.'

Puckett rolled an almond about on his tongue, neatly tucking it into the pouch of his cheek. 'Watch yourself, counselor,' he warned Barrie.

'Was there anything that stood out in the autopsy report?'

Anne-Marie nodded. 'The victim was eleven weeks pregnant.'

The prosecutor walked the detective through the interviews she'd done with the friends of Emily Gold, her neighbors – with one glaring exception, her parents, her teachers. 'Detective Marrone, did you also have a chance to speak to the defendant?' Barrie made sure to catch Anne-Marie's eye. The detective was good, a professional, but she'd been forewarned to not mention the conversation she'd had with Chris at the hospital. Ruled inadmissible, even its mention could be cause for a mistrial.

'Yes, I did. He came down to the police station on November eleventh. I read him his rights, and he waived them.'

'Is this the police report transcribing the conversation on November eleventh?' The prosecutor held up a file, emblazoned with the logo of the Bainbridge police.

'It is,' the detective said.

'How soon, Detective, after your meeting with Christopher Harte, did you write this report?'

'Immediately after he left.'

'What was the gist of that conversation?'

'Mr Harte basically told me he brought the gun to the scene of the crime, went to the scene of the crime, and watched Emily Gold shoot herself.'

'Did that add up to the evidence you'd seen?'

'No.'

'Why not?'

Detective Marrone cocked her head, staring at Chris. He felt his cheeks redden, and forced himself to keep his gaze steady and direct. 'If it was just one of those things, instead of all of them. . .if it was only that the bullet traveled through the victim's head at a weird angle—'

'Objection!'

'Or if there were bruises on her wrist, but everything else seemed consistent with suicide—'

'Objection!'

'—or if even one person described her as troubled. But too much just didn't add up.'

'*Objection, Your Honor!*'

The judge narrowed his eyes at Jordan. 'Overruled,' he said.

Barrie's heart was pounding. 'So it wasn't a suicide, in your expert opinion, in spite of what the defendant told you. From what you had seen of the evidence – the fingerprints, the blood spatter patterns, the gunpowder residue, the liquor bottle, the interviews – did you form an alternative theory of what happened?'

'Yes,' Detective Marrone said firmly. 'Christopher Harte murdered her.'

'How did you come up with that?'

Anne-Marie began to speak, weaving a picture that hung in the courtroom like a tapestry, rich in detail and impossible to ignore. 'Emily was a happy kid that no one – not teachers, not parents, not friends – considered depressed in any way. She was pretty, popular, had a great relationship with her parents – a model daughter. She was eleven weeks pregnant with her boyfriend's child. And Chris was a senior in high school, about to go off to college, already applying – he was certainly at a point where he didn't need a baby in his life, or a girlfriend who was clinging to him.'

Jordan considered objecting – this was all speculative – but realized that would only hurt him, and make the detective's testimony take on more importance than he wanted it to. He sighed loudly, hoping to convey to the jury how ludicrous he found Marrone's theory.

The detective lowered her voice, and the jury strained forward to listen. 'So he arranged to go to the carousel for some kind of romantic rendezvous. He gave her something to drink, trying to get her intoxicated so that she wouldn't fight him when he pulled out the gun. They had sex, they got dressed, he pulled her into an embrace, and before she knew what was happening, there was a gun pressed to her head.' Anne-Marie raised her own hand to her temple, then brought it down. 'She fought him, but he was a lot bigger and stronger than she was, and he shot her. That,' she said, sighing, 'is how I see it.'

Barrie headed back to her table, almost ready to relinquish her witness. 'Thank you, Detective. Oh, one last question. Was there anything else important that came out of your interview with Christopher Harte at the police station?'

Anne-Marie nodded. 'He had to sign a paper to agree to the interview, it's standard procedure. And he picked up the pen with his left hand. So I asked him about it, and he told me that he was indeed a lefty.'

'And why was that significant, Detective?'

'Because we know from the path of the bullet and the pattern of the blood spatter that someone else was there, facing Emily. And if that person shot her in the right temple, he had to have done it with his left hand.'

'Thank you,' Barrie said. 'Nothing further.'

When Jordan stood up for his first cross-examination, he smiled at Anne-Marie Marrone. 'Detective,' he said, 'we all heard you tell Ms Delaney that you've been with the police force for ten years. Ten years.' He whistled. 'That's a long time to be in the public service.'

Anne-Marie nodded, too smart and too practiced at this to relax, as Jordan intended. 'I like what I do, Mr McAfee.'

'Yeah?' Jordan said, grinning widely. 'Me, too.' In the jury box, someone snickered. 'In ten years, Detective, how many homicides have you worked on?'

'Two.'

'Two,' Jordan repeated. 'Two homicides.' He wrinkled his brow. 'This is the second?'

'Correct.'

'So you've only worked on one before this?'

'Yes.'

'Well, then, why did they pick you to be in charge of this investigation?'

High color rose in Anne-Marie's cheeks. 'It's a small department,' she said, 'and I'm the head detective. It falls to me.'

'So. It's your second murder,' he said, stressing the utter lack of this expert's expertise. 'And you started off by looking at the gun. Is that right?'

'Yes.'

'And you found two sets of fingerprints on it.'

'Yes.'

'And you found two bullets.'

'Yes.'

'But if someone was going to shoot you at very close range, he wouldn't need two bullets, would he?'

'That depends,' the detective said.

'I realize this is somewhat new to you, Detective,' Jordan said, 'but yes or no will do.'

He saw Anne-Marie set her jaw. 'No,' she gritted out.

'On the other hand,' Jordan continued breezily, 'wouldn't it make sense that if you and a friend were planning to commit a double suicide, you'd need two bullets?'

'Yes.'

'And Chris's fingerprints were on those bullets?'

'Yes.'

'Is it consistent with a double suicide that Chris's fingerprints be the only ones on the bullets if, by Chris's own admission, it was his father's gun and he brought that gun?'

'Yes.'

'In fact, wouldn't it be unusual to see Emily's fingerprints on the bullets loaded into the chamber since she had no experience with guns at all?'

'I guess so.'

'Wonderful. You also told Ms Delaney you did some testing on that gun.'

'That's correct.'

'You found Emily's fingerprints on the gun, along with Chris's, didn't you?'

'Yes.'

'Isn't it true that you found additional fingerprints on the gun?'

'Yes. Some that matched up with James Harte, the defendant's father.'

'Really. But he wasn't under suspicion during your investigation.'

Anne-Marie sighed. 'That's because his fingerprints were the only evidence that placed him at the scene of the crime.'

'So you can't only rely on fingerprint evidence, can you? Just because someone's fingerprints are on a gun doesn't mean they happened to be touching it that particular night?'

'That's correct.'

'Ah. You found Emily's fingerprints on the top of the gun,'

Jordan said, walking over toward the display of evidence. 'Any objection to me picking this up?' he asked, gesturing to the Colt. He lifted it in his hand gingerly. 'And you found Chris's fingerprints around here, on the bottom.'

'That's right.'

'But you found no conclusive fingerprints on the actual trigger of the gun.'

'No, we did not.'

Jordan nodded thoughtfully. 'Is it true that you need only a quarter inch of a fingerprint, a very small area indeed, to make a conclusive match?'

'Well, yes,' Anne-Marie said, 'but it has to be the right quarter inch. A particular spot.'

'So fingerprints aren't as easy to pick up as it looks in the movies?'

'No, they're not.'

'Can they get smudged by newer fingerprints?'

'Yes.'

'In fact, Detective, testing for fingerprints is far from an exact science, wouldn't you say?'

'Yes.'

'If I pick up this gun and fire, and then you pick it up and fire, is it possible that my fingerprints would not show up on that trigger?'

'Maybe not,' Anne-Marie conceded.

'So is it possible that Emily pulled the trigger, and then when Chris picked up the gun he erased, if you will, her original fingerprints?'

'It's possible.'

'Let me recap: even though Emily's fingerprints were not identified on the trigger during your testing, Detective Marrone, can you say without a doubt that she never touched that trigger?'

'No – but then again Chris could have touched it too, without it showing up.' She smiled neatly at Jordan.

Jordan drew in his breath. 'Let's talk about the Luminol,'

he said. 'You said that the blood spatter pattern on the carousel indicated a spot where the defendant was bleeding.'

'I assume so. He was bleeding from a scalp wound when officers arrived.'

'Yet you say it's not proof that Chris fainted. So are you telling me,' he said scornfully, 'that Chris lay down on the carousel floor, smacked his head on the edge, and then lay there for several minutes to let a pool of blood form?'

Anne-Marie looked down her nose at him. 'It's been done before.'

'Really?' Jordan asked, with true surprise. 'I assume that was during your one previous murder case?'

'Objection!' Barrie said.

'Sustained.' Puckett glared at Jordan. 'I don't have to warn you, Mr McAfee.'

Jordan walked to the exhibit table. 'Is this the transcript of your interview with Chris Harte?'

'Yes.'

'Can you read this line...right here?' He brought the papers to the detective and pointed.

Anne-Marie cleared her throat. '"We were going to kill ourselves together."'

'That's a direct quote of something that Chris Harte said to you.'

'Yes.'

'He told you outright that this was a double suicide.'

'Yes, he did.'

'And can you tell me what this says, on page three?'

The detective glanced at Barrie Delaney. 'There was a pause in the tape.'

'Hmm. Why?'

'I had to shut the recorder off because the subject was crying.'

'Chris was crying? How come?'

Anne-Marie sighed. 'We were talking about Emily, and he got very upset.'

'In your expert opinion, is that consistent with genuine grieving?'

'Objection,' Barrie said. 'My witness is not an expert on grief.'

'I'll allow it,' said the judge.

The detective shrugged. 'I suppose so,' she said.

'So let me get this straight. In the middle of this interview, an interview where Chris Harte waived his right to have me present and said, flat-out, that he and Emily were going to commit suicide together, he started crying so hard that you had to actually stop the tape?'

'Yes,' Anne-Marie said pointedly. 'But we didn't have a lie detector hooked up, either.'

If Jordan heard her, he showed no sign of it. 'You mentioned that in your theory, Chris was trying to get Emily drunk.'

'Yes, I believe that.'

'The idea being that she would be submissive,' Jordan clarified.

'Correct.'

'Did you, by any chance, have the coroner check Emily's blood/alcohol level?

'They do that automatically,' the detective said.

'Did you find out what it was?'

'Yes,' she said grudgingly. '.02.'

'Which would be consistent with what, Detective?'

Anne-Marie coughed. 'One drink. Maybe one shot for a small girl.'

'She had one shot of alcohol out of that whole bottle.'

'Apparently, yes.'

'And the legal level for driving in this state is what, Detective?'

'.08.'

'What was Emily's, again?'

'I told you,' Anne Marie said. '.02.'

'Considerably less than the legal limit for driving while intoxicated. Would you say that she was drunk, then?'

'Probably not.'

'You mentioned evidence of gunpowder on both Emily's

and Chris's clothes,' Jordan said. 'Isn't it true that if you find gunpowder on the shirt all it really proves is that the fabric was in close contact when the gun was fired?'

'That's correct.'

'Can you determine from gunpowder residue on clothing who actually shot the gun?'

'Not conclusively. But we didn't find any gunpowder residue on the victim's hands either. And the perpetrator of a suicide would have had some sort of trace of powder on her skin.'

Jordan seized on that. 'Is it consistent with a murder investigation to immediately bag the hands of the victim?'

'Ordinarily yes, but—'

'When was the gunpowder test performed on the corpse?'

Anne-Marie looked at her lap. 'November ninth.'

'You're saying you didn't test Emily's hands at the scene of the crime, and you didn't test her on the way to the hospital, and you didn't even test her in the morgue until two days after she'd died? Is it possible that during that block of time, someone had tampered with Emily's hands?'

'Well, I—'

'Yes or no?'

'It's possible,' Anne-Marie said.

'Could someone have touched Emily's hands during the trip from the crime scene to the hospital?'

'Yes.'

'Such as medics, or uniformed officers?'

'Either would be possible.'

'In the emergency room of the hospital, might someone have touched her hands?'

'Yes.'

'For example, maybe nurses or doctors?'

'I suppose so.'

'In the emergency room might she have been swabbed down, since there were no instructions otherwise?'

'Yes,' the detective said.

'So any number of people might have tampered with

important evidence before you got around to collecting it from Emily's hands?' Jordan summarized.

'Yes,' Marrone admitted.

'Wouldn't it also be consistent with a murder investigation to immediately test the hands of the perpetrator for gunpowder residue?'

'That's standard procedure.'

'When you first saw Chris at the scene of the crime, did you test his hands for gunpowder residue?'

'Well, no. But he wasn't under direct suspicion then.'

Jordan's eyes widened. 'Really, Detective Marrone? He wasn't a suspect when the police got to the scene of the crime?'

'No.'

'So when did it dawn on you that he was a suspect?'

'Objection!' Barrie called.

'Counselor, why don't you rephrase that question,' Puckett said dryly.

'I'll move on. Did you test him at the hospital?' Jordan hammered.

'No.'

'Did you test him the next day, when you went to gather more information?'

'No.'

'Did you test Chris the day he came into the police station for that interview?'

'No.'

Jordan snorted. 'So he was never tested for gunpowder residue – not at first when he was not a suspect and not later, when you decided he was a murderer?'

'He was never tested.'

'Isn't it possible that if you had managed to test Emily's hands before someone tampered with them, you might have found gunpowder residue on them?'

'That's possible.'

'And that would have indicated that she'd fired the gun.'

'Yes, it would,' Anne-Marie said.

'And if you had tested Chris for gunpowder residue right at the scene of the crime, you might not have found any on his hands, either?'

'That's right.'

'And that would have indicated that he hadn't fired the gun?'

'Correct.'

And then none of us would have to be here. Jordan did not have to say the words. He walked to the jury box, standing at the end as if he was one of its members. 'Okay, Detective. Your theory is that Chris was at the scene of the crime. He put two bullets in the gun in case he missed the first time from an eighth of an inch away. He unsuccessfully tried to get Emily drunk, had sex with her, went for the gun. Emily saw him going for the gun, they wrestled, and then he shot her. You absolutely believe this is what happened?'

'Yes, I do.'

'Not a single doubt in your mind?'

'None.'

Jordan moved closer to the witness stand. 'Couldn't the fact that there were two bullets in the gun that night have meant that there was going to be a double suicide?'

'Well—'

'Couldn't it?'

'It could,' Anne-Marie sighed.

'And couldn't the Canadian Club have been there to take the edge off a suicide attempt?'

'Maybe.'

'And might there have been fingerprints on that gun that weren't in the right spot, or clear enough, to have been picked up by that test of yours?'

'Yes.'

'And might another gunpowder test – one that for whatever reason, wasn't done – have shown that Chris Harte did not fire that gun?'

'Maybe.'

'So you're saying, Detective, that in your expert opinion, there might be another way to look at this.'

Anne-Marie Marrone exhaled through her mouth. 'Yes,' she said.

Jordan turned his back. 'Nothing further,' he said.

The jury – not to mention the judge – was getting glassy-eyed; a common enough response to heavily detailed police testimony. Judge Puckett called for a ten-minute recess, during which the courtroom emptied.

Selena grabbed Jordan's arm on his way back from the men's room. 'Nice work,' she praised. 'You've got Juror Five for sure, and I think Juror Seven.'

'It's early yet.'

'Still.' She shrugged, rubbing his arm lightly. 'On the other hand, your client is falling apart.' She gestured toward Chris, visible through the courtroom's doors. Chris was still seated at the defense table, two bailiffs and a sheriff's deputy standing guard behind him with their arms crossed, a physical barrier to contact. 'He's just spent an hour hearing what a sociopath he is, and there isn't even a friendly face in the courtroom.'

Jordan peered at Chris, his body hunched slightly over the table. 'His father's here,' he told Selena.

'Yeah, but Ward Cleaver he's not.'

Jordan nodded and ran a hand through his hair. 'All right,' he said. 'I'll talk to him.'

'You should. Unless you want him to pass out cold at the ME's testimony.'

Jordan laughed. 'Yeah. He'd probably crack his head open on Barrie Delaney's chair rollers, and she'd still find a way to make it look like Chris was faking.' With a light squeeze of Selena's hand, Jordan made his way back into the courtroom. He nodded at the entourage surrounding his client. 'Gentlemen,' he said, slipping into his chair and waiting for them to disappear.

'It's going well,' he said to Chris. 'Really.'

To his surprise, Chris laughed. 'I hope so,' he said. 'Because it seems a little early to throw in the towel.' Then the smile fell away from his face, revealing – as Selena had said – the tightly drawn mouth and pale countenance of a very frightened teenager.

'You know,' Jordan said, 'I realize it's hard to hear yourself described as a monster. The prosecutor is allowed to say whatever she wants . . . but so are we. We just haven't had our turn yet, and we've got the better story.'

'That's not it.' Chris ran his finger over the blue lines of a legal pad. 'It's that . . . the prosecutor's making it real. It's been seven months, you know? But there's all this technical stuff and the blood and where Emily was and where I was and—' He paused, burying his head in his hands. 'She's making me live it all over again, and I could barely survive it that once.'

Jordan – who could confidently slay any prosecution's witness with his words, who had a thousand answers for any of Barrie Delaney's questions – stared at his client, speechless.

The medical examiner for Grafton County – Dr Jubal Lumbano – was a thin, bespectacled man who looked far more suited to chasing butterflies with a large collector's net than rooting around elbow-deep in the innards of a corpse. It took Barrie Delaney a full ten minutes to get Lumbano's credentials down on the record, and to make certain the jury knew that here, at least, was a witness with experience – the unprepossessing Dr Lumbano had completed over five hundred autopsies during his career.

'Dr Lumbano,' Barrie began, 'did you do the autopsy on Emily Gold?'

'Yes,' the medical examiner said, his nose bumping against the microphone with a screech. Leaning back, he smiled apologetically. 'Yes, I did.'

'Can you tell us what was the cause of death?'

'All findings were commensurate with the cause of death being a forty-five caliber bullet fired against the skull into the brain; more precisely, entering the right temporal lobe – missing the frontal lobe – and exiting from the right rear occipital lobe.'

Barrie admitted a chart into evidence showing the outline of a three-dimensional head surrounding a brain. Then she turned to the jury with a helpless smile. 'Dr Lumbano, for those of us not as – intimate – with occipital and temporal lobes, could you use this chart to show us where that bullet went?'

She handed the medical examiner a Magic Marker – blood red – and the doctor carefully set it against the drawing. 'The bullet went in here,' he said, making an X at the right temple. 'Then it traveled this approximate path, and exited above the neck, here.' Another X, behind the right ear. The line between them ran almost parallel to the side of the diagrammed head.

'Can you tell us how long it took for Emily Gold to die?' Barrie asked.

'It wasn't immediate,' Dr Lumbano said. 'She was still alive when the medics got to her. She may even have been conscious for some of that time.'

'Conscious . . . and able to feel pain?'

'Certainly.'

Barrie looked appropriately horrified. 'So . . . Emily lingered, possibly in pain, for how long?'

'I would say a half hour or so.'

'Doctor Lumbano, did you find any other marks on Emily Gold's body?'

'Yes.'

'Did they indicate violence?'

'Your Honor, she's leading,' Jordan cut in. 'It remains to be proved that any violence occurred.'

'Sustained.' Puckett nodded at the prosecutor. 'Ms Delaney, don't lead your witness.'

'Were there any distinguishing marks on Emily Gold's body, Doctor?'

'Yes. There were bruises on her right wrist.'

'What did that lead you to believe?'

'That some violence may have occurred.'

'Might they have been caused by someone pulling at her wrist?' Out of the corner of her eye, Barrie saw Jordan open his mouth. 'Let me rephrase that,' she said, before he could object. 'What would you, as a medical expert, attribute as the cause of those bruises?'

'It's possible that they were caused by someone who'd grabbed her wrist.'

'How soon before death would you say those bruises were formed?'

'Within an hour premortem,' Dr Lumbano said. 'The blood had just begun to rise to the surface of the skin.'

'Was there anything else you discovered during the autopsy?'

'There was evidence of semen, which, with the condition of vaginal tissues, suggested recent sexual activity – approximately a half hour before death. And there was also skin under the victim's fingernails, cell samples of which did not match up with the victim's own skin.'

'Which indicates what?'

'She scratched someone.'

'Did you determine whose skin was under her fingernails?'

'Yes, the tissue samples matched those taken from Chris Harte and brought in by the detectives.'

Barrie nodded. 'Could you tell whether Emily was left- or right-handed?'

'Yes. All of the calluses were on her right hand, heavy calluses on the left side of the middle finger and the right side of the second finger. In my medical opinion, I would say the victim was right-handed.'

'And the gunshot wound was through the right temple.'

'Yes, it was.'

Barrie nodded thoughtfully. 'Have you seen a lot of suicides, Doctor?'

'Oh, a fair number. Sixty to seventy.'

'Were any of those caused by a gunshot wound to the head?'

'Thirty-eight,' Doctor Lumbano said. 'It's a popular method, I'm afraid.'

'Of those thirty-eight suicides, how many used a pistol or revolver?'

'Twenty-four,' Dr Lumbano said.

'And how did those twenty-four suicides shoot themselves?'

'I'd say ninety percent shoot themselves in the mouth, because that's what works. The other ten percent shoot themselves through the temple. Although I did see one strange case where a man shot a bullet up his nose.'

'In the ten percent of people who point the gun at the temple, where is the exit wound?'

'On the opposite temporal lobe.' He pointed at both of his temples.

'And where did Emily Gold's bullet exit?'

'From the same side occipital lobe.' Moving his left hand behind his head, he pointed to a spot behind his right ear.

'Did you find that unusual?'

'Yes, as a matter of fact,' the medical examiner said, his cheeks pinkening with excitement. 'I've never seen anything like it. It would be very difficult to hold a gun to your right temple and have the bullet exit the right rear of the head. It requires the angle of the gun to be something like this.' Dr Lumbano lifted his right hand, pointed his finger like the barrel of a gun, and held it up against his right temple almost parallel to his head, twisting his wrist in a forced, unnatural position. 'In my opinion, that's not—'

'Objection!'

'—a typical position—'

'*Objection!*'

'Sustained,' Puckett said.

'Took your sweet time,' Jordan muttered beneath his breath.

'What was that, counselor?' The judge slid a nut into his mouth. 'Did you say something? No?' He turned to the jury. 'Please ignore Dr Lumbano's last statement.'

Barrie approached her witness. 'In your medical opinion, Dr Lumbano, what did that lead you to believe?'

'Speculative!' Jordan yelled again. 'Come on!'

'Your Honor, request permission to approach the bench.' Barrie said, nodding at Jordan, who joined her in front of the judge's high desk.

'Ms Delaney,' Puckett said, 'the only way you could lead this witness any more would involve putting a collar around his neck.'

Barrie bit her lip. 'If my witness can't speculate on this, I'd like to be able to show the jury what I'm trying to get at . . . but I'll need the assistance of the defendant.'

Jordan looked from Barrie to the judge. He had no idea what the hell she was going to do, and he wasn't about to give her free rein with his client. 'I want to know what she's up to,' he said.

Puckett turned toward the prosecutor. 'Delaney?'

She spread her hands. 'A little demonstration, Your Honor. I want to show the jury how Chris could have done this.'

'Absolutely not,' Jordan hissed. 'That's completely prejudicial.'

'Look, Your Honor,' Barrie said. 'I'm going to make my point. I'll use the doctor or a bailiff, if necessary. I just need a body – why not use the one allegedly involved?'

Puckett cracked an almond. 'Proceed with caution, counselor, or we'll be right back up at the bench.'

'What!' Jordan exploded.

'I've ruled,' Puckett said firmly. And to Barrie, 'Go ahead.'

Jordan walked back to the defense table, thinking that at least now he had an appealable issue. Sliding into his seat, he touched Chris's shoulder. 'I'm not sure what's up her sleeve,' he whispered. 'Just look at me and I'll nod, or object if she's out of line.'

At this point, Barrie was walking toward Chris. 'Okay, Dr Lumbano. I'm going to have the defendant help me out here.' She smiled at Chris. 'Would you please stand up, Mr Harte?'

Chris glanced at Jordan, who nodded imperceptibly. He stood.

'Thank you. Could you come over here?' She gestured to a

spot directly in between the jury box and the witness stand. 'Now, Mr Harte, if you'd extend your arms out in front of you.' She gestured, like a Frankenstein monster, until Chris hesitantly raised his arms.

And Barrie Delaney walked right into them.

Chris started as she embraced him, her hands coming around to the tails of his jacket and her body flush against his. He stood stiff as a board as her head tucked onto his right shoulder, falling onto the same spot Emily's had when he used to hug her. *What*, he thought, *is going on?*

'Mr Harte,' Barrie said, her voice slightly muffled against the weave of his blazer. 'Could you put your arms around me?' Chris looked at his lawyer, who nodded tightly. 'Now, could you take your left hand and put it up to my right temple?'

With his eyes trained on Jordan, who for all his recent objecting was now sitting as still as a damn stone, Chris complied.

They were facing in such a way that the jury had a clear view of Chris leaning back maybe eight inches, just enough to put his left hand up to the right side of the prosecutor's head, while his right arm still embraced her. 'Now Dr Lumbano,' Barrie said, 'if there was a gun in Mr Hart's hand right now, how likely would it be that the trajectory of a bullet fired at my temple at this point might exit at the right rear occipital lobe?'

The medical examiner nodded. 'I'd say there's an excellent chance that would happen.'

'Thank you,' Barrie said, her arms falling away from Chris, her brisk footsteps leaving him standing alone in the middle of the courtroom.

'Jesus,' Chris hissed, his face red as a beet as he slipped into the seat beside Jordan. 'Why didn't you do something?'

'I couldn't,' Jordan said through his teeth. 'If I jumped up, the jury would think you had something to hide.'

'Oh, well, great. As opposed to what they think now – that I'm a fucking murderer?'

'Don't worry. I'm going to take care of it on the cross.' He stood, assuming that after that debacle there was little else Delaney could want with her witness, but was stopped by her voice.

'One more question,' Barrie said. 'Was there anything else about Emily's physical condition that you noticed during the autopsy?'

'Yes,' Dr Lumbano said. 'On the night Emily Gold died, she was eleven weeks pregnant.'

Jordan closed his eyes, and sat back down.

'We all appreciate you being here today, Dr Lumbano,' Jordan said a few minutes later. 'And we all know you've worked on thirty-eight suicides. We heard you say that there was evidence of semen, evidence of bruising, and skin beneath Emily's fingernails. Now let's put that into perspective. The semen, that shows there was intercourse, right?'

'Yes.'

'Do you know whether or not Emily bruised easily?'

'No,' Dr Lumbano said. 'Aside from the fact that she was rather fair, which suggests she might bruise easily.'

'Could these bruises have occurred during . . ?' He coughed delicately and smiled at the jury. 'A particularly ardent point in intercourse?'

'They could have,' the medical examiner said, straight-faced.

'And the skin beneath the fingernails, Doctor. Is it possible that you can get someone's skin cells beneath your fingernails by gently scratching his back?'

'Yes.'

'How about by raking his shoulder in a frenzy of passion? Could that produce skin beneath your fingernails?'

'Absolutely.'

'And what if you caressed someone's cheek and jaw?'

'It's possible.'

'So you're telling me that there are a number of different ways that Emily could have Chris's skin under her fingernails, and that many of those different ways could be consistent with nonviolent, passionate lovemaking. Is that right?'

'Yes.'

'You can't tell me with any certainty that there was any violence that night between Emily and Chris, can you?'

'No, not precisely. But there was a bullet wound in the victim's head.'

'Ah, yes,' Jordan said. 'We all saw what Ms Delaney did with Chris. But a lot of things could have happened that night, right? Let's work through a couple other scenarios to see how else that wound might have been inflicted.' He turned suddenly toward his client. 'Chris? If you don't mind . . . again?'

Bewildered, Chris stood up and walked toward Jordan, to almost exactly the same spot where the prosecutor had brought him before. Then Jordan walked over to the exhibit table and picked up the gun. 'All right if I use this?' Without waiting to see if Barrie had agreed, he casually carried the pistol back toward Chris. 'Now.' With a grin at the jury, he took Chris's hands and settled them on his waist. 'You're going to have to use your imaginations here, because I don't make quite as convincing a female as Ms Delaney.' He nodded to Chris, whose neck turned crimson as he loosely embraced Jordan.

There was a murmur in the gallery as Jordan pressed the gun up against his own head. He smiled, knowing he'd just presented the jury with an even more shocking mental image than the one of Chris with Barrie Delaney. 'What if, Doctor, Emily was holding the gun like this, like someone would normally hold a gun, but since she had no experience with guns she sort of twisted the barrel toward her?' Leaning back slightly in Chris's arms, Jordan directed the gun at his temple in the same uncomfortable angle the medical examiner had posited earlier. 'If the gun was up against her head like this, would the bullet trajectory have been consistent with what you found in the autopsy?'

'Yes, I believe so.'

'Doctor, what if she was holding the gun like this, to the

side of her temple like all those other ten percent of pistol suicides you've seen, but then her hand was shaking so badly that it jumped as she pulled the trigger? Is it possible the trajectory might change?'

'It is possible.'

'And what if Emily was so uncomfortable with the very idea of holding a gun that she picked it up like this?' He wrapped both hands around the barrel of the gun and held it up to his head, almost parallel against his temple, thumbs dangling at the trigger. 'If she'd held the gun like this and used her thumb to pull the trigger, could the bullet match that odd trajectory?'

'Yes.'

'So you are saying, Doctor, that there are a variety of possibilities that might have accounted for the strange path of that bullet.'

'I suppose so.'

'And Doctor Lumbano,' Jordan finished, turning in his client's embrace, 'in any of these alternative scenarios, have you seen Christopher Harte's hands on the trigger of that gun?'

'No.'

Jordan broke away from Chris and set the gun back on the exhibit table, his fingers resting on the metal for a moment. 'Thank you,' he said.

The bleached blonde on the witness stand looked longingly at the jar of almonds in front of the judge, and raised her hand. Startled, Barrie looked up from her notes. 'Um . . . yes?'

'I was wondering, if he can have those, maybe it wouldn't be so bad if I could just have a little piece of gum? I mean, I know what you said and all, but since a cigarette's out of the question, and I'm a little freaked about this whole thing . . .' She blinked owlishly at the prosecutor. 'So?'

To everyone's surprise, Judge Puckett laughed. 'Just maybe, Ms DiBonnalo,' he said, 'I'll take you up on that cigarette.' He signaled a bailiff to carry the jar of nuts toward the witness.

'I'm afraid that chewing gum might make your testimony hard to understand. But I'm willing to share.'

The woman relaxed a little, until she realized there was nothing to crack the nuts with. But by that time, Barrie was ready to question her witness. 'Could you state your name, address, and occupation for the record?'

'Donna DiBonnalo,' she said loudly into the microphone. 'Four-fifty-six Rosewood Way, Bainbridge. And I work at the Gold Rush.'

'What sort of establishment is the Gold Rush?'

'A jewelry store,' Donna said.

'Did you ever come in contact with Emily Gold?'

'Yes, she came into the store to buy a birthday present for her boyfriend. A watch, she wanted to have it engraved.'

'I see. What did she want engraved on it?'

'The name Chris,' Donna said, her eyes sliding toward the defense table.

'And how much did it cost?'

'Five hundred dollars.'

'Wow,' Barrie said. 'Five hundred dollars? That's a lot of money for a seventeen-year-old.'

'It's a lot of money for anyone. But she said she was really excited about it.'

'Hearsay,' Jordan objected.

'Sustained.'

'Did she tell you why she was making the purchase?' Barrie asked.

Donna nodded. 'She said that the watch was for her boyfriend's eighteenth birthday.'

'Did she leave any specific instructions?'

'Yes. They were written on the receipt. If we had to call to tell her anything about the watch – like when it came in – we were only supposed to ask for Emily and say nothing about the jewelry store or the watch.'

'Did she tell you why she wanted to keep it a secret?'

'She said it was going to be a surprise.'

'Again,' Jordan called. 'Hearsay.'

The judge nodded. 'Approach the bench.'

Jordan and Barrie stood shoulder to shoulder, jockeying for position. 'Either you find another way to get that in,' Puckett told the prosecutor, 'or it's stricken from the record.'

Barrie nodded and turned back to her witness as Jordan sat down again. 'Let me rephrase that,' she said. 'What exactly did those instructions say?'

Donna furrowed her brow, thinking. '"Call to the house – ask for Emily. This is private. Don't say what it's about."'

'Did Emily tell you when her boyfriend's birthday was?'

'Yeah, because we had to get it done in time. It came special-ordered from London. We had to have it finished by November.'

'Any specific date?'

'Well, the watch was supposed to be engraved with the birthday, too. November twenty-fourth. She wanted me to have it in the store by November seventeenth, to give us a week just in case anything went wrong, because she planned to give it to him on the twenty-fourth.'

Barrie leaned against the jury box. 'Were you expecting Emily to pick up that watch on November seventeenth?'

'Oh, yeah.'

'Did she?'

'No.'

'Did you find out why not?'

Donna DiBonnalo nodded gravely. 'She died the week before.'

Jordan sat at the defense table for a minute, after the witness had been turned over to his cross-examination. There wasn't a hell of a lot he was going to get out of her. He stood up slowly, knees creak. 'Ms DiBonnalo,' he said pleasantly. 'When did Emily Gold place her order?'

'On August twenty-fifth.'

'And was that the first time you saw her?'

'No. She'd come in to look around about a week before.'

'Did she pay you when she placed the order?'

'Yes, in full.'

'How did she seem to you when you met her in August – happy? Cheerful?'

'Sure. She was psyched about finding the watch as a birthday present.'

'When did the watch come in, Ms DiBonnalo?'

'On November seventeenth.' She smiled. 'Nothing went wrong.'

Depends on your point of view, Jordan thought, but he smiled back evenly. 'And when did you call the Gold household?'

'On November seventeenth, for the first time.'

'So you had no contact with Emily between August twenty-fifth and November?'

'No.'

'When you called the Gold house, what kind of response did you get?'

'Well, actually, her mother was really rude to me!'

Jordan nodded sympathetically. 'How many times did you have to call?'

'Three,' Donna sniffed.

'On the third time, did you finally tell Mrs Gold about the watch?'

'Yeah, after she told me that her daughter was dead. I was shocked.'

'So Emily seemed perfectly happy in August . . . and then you didn't have any contact with her until November, which was when you found out she had died.'

'Yeah,' Donna said.

Jordan slid his hands into his pockets. It looked like a pointless cross, but he knew better. He'd use the testimony in his closing, to point out that three short months before her death, Emily Gold did not appear suicidal. In fact, it might have been fairly sudden. Which was only a short step away from explaining why Emily's teachers, her friends – her own mother – hadn't seen it coming. 'That's all, ma'am,' Jordan said, and sank back into his chair.

*   *   *

Judge Puckett's scheduled dental cleaning brought the testimony to an end shortly after two o'clock. Jurors were dismissed with a reminder not to speak about the case to anyone; witnesses who had not yet been called to the stand were told to return tomorrow at nine A.M.; and Chris was handcuffed again and led to the sheriff's offices in the basement of the courthouse.

James met Gus in the lobby of the courthouse. He knew that legally, he was not supposed to talk to his wife about what had transpired in the courtroom that day. He also knew that Gus would not let a little thing like the justice system stop her from finding out how the trial was going so far. So he was surprised when Gus fell into step beside him, deep in thought and oddly silent.

It was raining outside. 'I'll get the car,' James said, with a glance at Gus's high heels. 'You wait here.'

She nodded, standing with her hand pressed up against the wide glass window of the entrance as James leaped over puddles. At the feel of a hand on her upper arm, Gus whirled around. 'Hi,' Michael said, his touch making her skin tingle, and making her want to draw away at the same time.

She forced herself to smile. 'You look as bad as I feel.'

'Thanks a lot.'

Gus watched James unlock the car door. 'I saw you with Melanie.' They'd been sitting in the lobby, sequestered as she was, a few rows away.

Michael placed his hand against the window beside Gus's. 'It's hard, isn't it? Trying to imagine what's going on inside?'

Gus didn't answer. In the parking lot, the Volvo pulled out of its spot.

'Tomorrow,' he said, 'let's wait together.'

She did not let herself look at him. 'I have to go,' she said, and she ran into the chill of the rain.

Selena hurried through the door while Jordan shook out the umbrella they'd been sharing. 'Got to get a bigger one of those,' she laughed, her hair soaked.

'Got to get a smaller investigator,' Jordan countered, grinning at Selena. 'It took me years to find an umbrella that I liked.'

They stumbled together from the small mud room vestibule into the living room, where Thomas was waiting with his arms crossed. 'Well?' he demanded.

Selena grinned. 'Your dad's a master,' she said.

A wide smile split Thomas's face. 'Knew it,' he said. He high-fived Jordan and flopped onto an overstuffed chair. 'This means you're in a good mood, right?'

'Why?' Jordan answered guardedly. 'What did you do?'

'Nothing!' Thomas said, affronted. 'I'm just hungry, is all. Can we order in a pizza?'

'At three-thirty? Isn't that early for dinner?'

'Call it a snack,' Thomas suggested.

Jordan rolled his eyes and walked into the kitchen, still wearing his mackintosh. 'Get a snack out of the refrigerator,' he said, swinging the door of the appliance open. 'Oh. Or maybe not,' he said, throwing a Saran-wrapped package into the trash. 'Isn't there anything else in here?'

'Beer,' Thomas said. 'And milk. Everything else is growing penicillin.'

Selena slung her arm around Thomas's thin shoulders. 'You want pepperoni or sausage?'

'Anything but anchovies,' Thomas said. 'You going to call?'

Selena nodded. 'I'll let you know when the pizza guy gets here.'

Thomas, taking his cue, retreated to his room. Selena reached past Jordan into the refrigerator and pulled out a beer. 'Consider yourself lucky he didn't just drink these. You want one?'

Jordan looked at his watch, thought better of it, and then watched Selena wrench the twist-off top from her bottle. 'Sure,' he said.

They settled down in the living room after calling the pizza place. Jordan took a long pull of beer and winced. 'What I really need,' he said, 'is Tylenol.'

'Here,' Selena said, patting her lap. 'Lie down.'

He did, gratefully, setting his bottle of Samuel Adams on the floor. Selena's long fingers brushed the hair off his forehead and sleeked over his temples like waterfalls. 'You're being awfully accommodating,' he murmured.

Selena gently rapped his skull. 'Gotta keep that brilliance flowing.'

He closed his eyes, letting her hands travel over pulse points. When Selena stopped, he reached up and touched her wrist, urging her on, and immediately pictured Barrie Delaney lifting Chris's hand to her own temple.

Jordan groaned, his headache returning with a vengeance. If he was still thinking of that, what could he expect of the jury?

Chris was strip-searched, his good clothes taken away for safekeeping until the next morning. As he pulled the drawstring pants on, and the soft short-sleeved shirt, he relaxed. These clothes, worn and faded and smelling of jail, were a thousand times more comfortable than the restricting pleated pants and noosed necktie he'd been forced to wear all day.

But then again, it had been seven months. Today he'd discovered that there were many things he was unaccustomed to: direct sunlight; human contact; even Pepsi. The can that Jordan had bought for him – the drink he'd craved so badly for so long – had fizzed up in his stomach and given him the runs.

Chris crawled into his bunk, with the unwelcome realization that even if he was given leave to rejoin the real world, he might no longer fit in.

In the middle of the night, with the shades drawn and the bedroom an airless cocoon, Gus turned to James. Like her, he'd been lying in bed perfectly still, as if immobility might segue into sleep, but Gus knew that he was every bit as awake as she was. She took a deep breath, thankful for the darkness that kept her from seeing his face and knowing whether or not he was lying.

'James,' she said, 'is it going all right?'

He did not pretend to misunderstand, but beneath the covers, blindly reached for and covered her hand. 'I don't know,' he said.

The next morning, Jordan showered and shaved and dressed. He walked into the kitchen, his mind already running through his cross-examinations of the day. Heather Burns, a friend of Emily's, he could do in his sleep. Melanie Gold was a different story.

It was not until he sat down that he noticed Thomas smiling at him from across the table. And at his place, a clean bowl and spoon, a jug of milk, and a brand new box of Cocoa Krispies.

Heather Burns trembled so badly on the witness stand that the slightly uneven legs of the chair beat a quick tattoo on the floor. Seeking to put the girl at ease, Barrie Delaney walked toward her, blocking out Heather's view of everything but Barrie herself. 'Relax, Heather,' she said in an undertone. 'Remember? We've already been through all the questions.'

Heather nodded bravely, her face a stark white. 'Heather,' Barrie said, 'I understand you were Emily's best friend.'

'Yes,' she said in a tiny voice. 'We've been friends for about four years.'

'That's a long time. Did you meet in school?'

'Uh-huh. We had a bunch of classes together. Health, and Calculus. And some art classes, too . . . but Emily was a lot better than me when it came to art.'

'How often did you see her?'

'Every day, at least in class.'

'And did she tell you what her plans were for the future?'

'She wanted to go to college and learn to be a better painter.'

'Did you know Emily when she began to date Chris?'

Heather nodded. 'She was dating Chris when I met her. They were, like, always together.'

'Always?'

'Well, one time sophomore year they broke up for a couple of months. Chris was seeing someone else, and Emily got really upset about it.'

'So there wasn't always perfect harmony between them.'

'No.' Heather looked down. 'But they did get back together.'

Barrie smiled sadly. 'Yes. So they did. Can you tell me, Heather, what Emily was like this November – her personality?'

'She was usually pretty quiet – she always had been. But she certainly wasn't, like, crying all the time or saying she was going to kill herself. She was just acting like Emily, and hanging around with her boyfriend. That's why . . .' Her voice trailed off, and her eyes, for the first time during her testimony, drifted toward Chris. 'That's why it was such a shock to hear what happened.'

Jordan smiled engagingly at Heather Burns. She was a little sparrow of a girl, with brown hair hanging midway down her back and a silver ring on every finger. 'Heather, thanks for being here. I know this is difficult,' he said, and then grinned. 'But at least it gets you out of school.'

Heather giggled, warming toward the defense attorney, looking nowhere near as close to fainting as she had a minute before. 'You saw Emily every day in school,' he said. 'How about outside of school?'

'Not so much,' Heather said.

'You didn't run into her at the Gap, or at the movies on weekends?'

'No.'

'You didn't make plans to go hang out together?'

'Hardly ever,' she said. 'It wasn't that I didn't want to, but Emily was always with Chris.'

'So even though you were her best friend, you really didn't see her often outside of school?'

'I was her best girlfriend,' Heather admitted. 'But Chris knew her better than anyone else.'

'Did you see Chris and Emily together?'

'Yes.'

'What was their relationship like?'

Heather's eyes clouded. 'I used to think it was really romantic,' she said. 'I mean, they'd been together forever, and it was sometimes like they couldn't hear anything but each other's voices or see anything but each other's faces.' She bit her lip. 'I used to think that Emily had what all of us wanted.'

Jordan nodded gravely. 'And Heather, based on the relationship you saw between Chris and Emily, can you picture him ever hurting her?'

'Objection,' Barrie called.

'Overruled.'

At Jordan's nod, Heather looked directly at Chris, her eyes wide and liquid. 'No,' she whispered. 'I can't.'

Melanie Gold was wearing black. On the witness stand, with her hair pulled back severely and the padded shoulders of her suit jacket stretched wide, she looked like an implacable mother superior, or maybe even an archangel. 'Mrs Gold,' Barrie said, laying a hand over her witness's. 'Thank you for being here. I'm so sorry to put you through this formality, but I need a few facts for the record. Could you state your name?'

'Melanie Gold.'

'What was your relationship to the victim?'

Melanie stared directly at the jury. 'I was her mother,' she said softly.

'Can you tell us about your relationship with your daughter?'

Melanie nodded. 'We spent a lot of time together.' She began to talk, her words brush strokes, bringing Emily back to life with the same artistic elegance that Emily had possessed. *She would spend time with me after school, when I was at the library working. We'd go shopping together on the weekends. She knew she could turn to me.*

'What sorts of things did Emily talk to you about?'

Melanie started, and directed her attention back to the prosecutor. 'We'd been discussing college a lot. She was getting ready to apply.'

'What were her feelings about going to college?'

'She was very excited,' Melanie said. 'She was a wonderful student, and an even better artist. As a matter of fact, she was applying at the Sorbonne.'

'Wow,' Barrie said, 'that's impressive.'

'So was Emily,' Melanie said.

'When did you first find out that something had happened to Emily?'

Melanie wilted in the chair. 'We were called in the middle of the night and told to come down to the hospital right away. All we knew was that Emily had gone on a date with Chris. By the time we got there, Emily had died.'

'What were you told about the death?'

'Not very much. My husband went in to identify . . . Emily. I . . .' She looked up at the jury. 'I couldn't. And then Michael came back out and told me that she'd been shot in the head.'

'What did you think, Mrs Gold?' Barrie asked gently.

'I thought, *Oh, my God – who did this to my baby?*'

The stillness that comes on the heels of true grief settled over the courtroom, so that the jury could hear the scratch of Jordan's pen, the tick of the bailiff's watch, Chris's labored breathing. 'Did you ever think for a moment, Mrs Gold, that it might have been a suicide?'

'No,' Melanie said, her voice firm. 'My daughter was not suicidal.'

'How do you know?'

'How wouldn't I know? I'm her mother. She wasn't sad; she wasn't depressed; she wasn't crying. She was the same wonderful young woman we'd always known. And she'd never used a gun in her life; she didn't know anything about them. Why would she have tried to shoot herself with one?'

'Did a jeweler start calling you after Emily's death?'

'Yes,' Melanie said. 'At first I didn't know who it was. The woman just kept asking for Emily, and it seemed like a bad joke. But then she finally told me about a watch that Emily had bought for Chris and I went down to pick it up. It was a five-hundred-dollar watch – fifty dollars more than she'd made the entire summer working at a camp. Emily knew we would have been very upset to find out that she'd spent that amount of money on a surprise birthday gift for Chris; it was far too extravagant, and we would have made her return it.' She took a deep breath, then continued. 'After I went to the jeweler's, I took that watch home and I realized it was Emily's way of telling me to look more closely at what happened.' She stared at the jury. 'Why would Emily have bought a watch to give to Chris at the end of November, if she knew they were going to kill themselves before then?'

Barrie walked toward the defense table. 'As you know, Mrs Gold, the only other person at the carousel that night was Christopher Harte.'

Melanie's eyes flicked over him. 'I know.'

'Do you know the defendant well?'

'Yes,' Melanie said. 'Chris and Emily grew up together. We've lived next door to his family for eighteen years.' Her voice thickened, and she glanced away. 'He was always welcome in our house. He was like a son to us.'

'And you know that he's here because he's charged with murder? The murder of your daughter?'

'Yes.'

'Do you believe that Chris could have been violent toward your daughter?'

'Objection,' Jordan said. 'This witness is biased.'

'Biased!' Barrie sputtered. 'The woman's child is dead and buried. She can have any bias she pleases.'

Puckett rubbed his temples. 'The prosecution has the right to put on any witness it wishes. We'll give Mrs Gold the benefit of the doubt.'

Barrie turned back toward Melanie. 'Do you believe,' she

repeated, 'that Chris could have been violent toward your daughter?'

Melanie cleared her throat. 'I think he killed her.'

'Objection!' Jordan yelled.

'Overruled.'

'You think he killed her,' Barrie restated, letting Melanie's words settle, a gauntlet thrown. 'Why?'

For a moment, Melanie stared at Chris. 'Because my daughter was pregnant,' she spat out, forgetting the prosecutor's warning to stay calm. 'Chris was going off to college. He didn't want his career and his education and his swimming future ruined by some baby and a hometown girl.' Melanie saw Chris startle, then begin to shake. 'Chris was the one who knew about guns,' she said tightly. 'His father had his own arsenal. They were hunting all the time.' She pinned Chris with her gaze, her words solely for him. 'You put two bullets in the gun.'

Jordan leaped to his feet. 'Objection!'

'You thought the whole thing out. But you couldn't keep her from bruising when she fought you—'

'Objection, Your Honor! This is inappropriate!'

Melanie stared at Chris, unstoppable. 'You couldn't guarantee the angle of the bullet. And you couldn't do a thing about the watch, because you didn't even know about it.' Her hands flexed on the railing of the witness stand, knuckles white.

'Mrs Gold,' the judge interrupted.

'You killed her,' Melanie shouted. 'You killed my baby, and you killed your baby.'

'Mrs Gold, you will cease immediately!' Puckett yelled, banging his gavel. 'Ms Delaney, control your client!'

The tips of Chris's ears were flame red. He shrank down beside Jordan. 'Your witness,' Barrie said, offering up the sobbing, heartsick woman.

'Your Honor,' Jordan said tightly. 'Perhaps we should take a short recess.'

Puckett glared at the prosecutor. 'Perhaps we should,' he said.

*   *   *

When Melanie took the stand again, her eyes were red and high flags of color rose on her cheekbones, but for all intents and purposes she was again composed. 'It sounds like Emily was quite a daughter, Mrs Gold,' Jordan said, still seated at the defense table, as casual as if he'd invited the woman over for lunch. 'Talented, beautiful, and she confided in you. What else could you possibly want in a child?'

'Life,' Melanie said coldly.

Momentarily flustered – Jordan hadn't expected her to be quite so sharp – he mentally took a step back. 'How many hours a week did you spend with Emily, Mrs Gold?'

'Well, I work three days a week, and Emily was in school.'

'So . . . ?'

'I'd say two hours at night, on weeknights. Maybe more on weekends.'

'How much time did she spend with Chris?'

'Quite a lot.'

'Could you be more specific? More than two hours at night, and some extra on weekends?'

'Yes.'

'So she spent more time in Chris's company than in yours.'

'Yes.'

'I see. Did Emily have high expectations for her future?'

Surprised at the change of topic, Melanie nodded. 'Very.'

'You must have been very supportive parents.'

'We were. We certainly praised academic success and helped her further her interest in art.'

'Would you say it was important to Emily to meet your expectations?'

'I think so. She knew we were proud of her.'

Jordan nodded. 'And you said that Emily confided in you, as well.'

'Absolutely.'

'I've got to tell you, Mrs Gold,' he said. 'I'm a little bit jealous.' He turned to the jury, inviting them into confidence. 'I've got a thirteen-year-old son, and it's not that easy to keep the lines of communication open.'

'Maybe you don't make yourself available to listen,' Melanie said sarcastically.

'Ah. So that's what you did, those two hours every weeknight? Make yourself available to listen to whatever Emily had to say?'

'Yes. She told me everything.'

Jordan leaned against the jury box. 'Did she tell you that she was pregnant?'

Melanie's lips pressed together. 'No,' she said.

'In her eleven weeks of pregnancy, during all those heart-to-hearts, she never mentioned it to you?'

'I said no.'

'Why didn't she tell you?'

Melanie smoothed the fabric of her skirt. 'I don't know,' she said softly.

'Might she have thought that being pregnant would mean not living up to your very high expectations of her? That she might not be able to become an artist, or even go to college?'

'Maybe,' Melanie said.

'Might she have been so upset about not meeting your expectations, about not being the perfect daughter anymore, that she was too afraid to tell you?'

Melanie shook her head, tears coming easily now. 'I need an answer, Mrs Gold,' Jordan said gently.

'No,' she said. 'She would have told me.'

'But you just told us she didn't,' Jordan pointed out. 'And Emily isn't here to answer for her reasons. So let's look at the facts: you're saying that Emily was so close to you she told you everything. But her pregnancy – she didn't tell you about that. If she hid something that important from you, isn't it possible that she could have hidden other things as well – for example, the fact that she was thinking of killing herself?'

Melanie covered her face with her hands. 'No,' she murmured.

'Isn't it possible that the pregnancy triggered the suicidal feelings? That if she couldn't live up to your expectations, she didn't want to live?'

The blame squarely set on Melanie's shoulders, she began to crumble. She sank in the witness stand, curling into herself the same way she had when she'd first found out that her daughter had died. Jordan, realizing he could not push any further without looking bad, walked toward the witness stand and put his hand on Melanie's arm. 'Mrs Gold,' he said, handing her his own clean handkerchief. 'Ma'am. Allow me.' She took the paisley cloth and wiped at her face while Jordan continued to pat her on the shoulder. 'I'm very sorry to upset you like this. And I know how devastating it must be to even consider these possibilities. But I do need you to answer me, for the record.'

With a supreme effort of will, Melanie drew herself upright. She wiped at her nose and tucked Jordan's handkerchief into her clenched fist. 'I'm sorry,' she said with dignity. 'I'll be all right now.'

Jordan nodded. 'Mrs Gold,' he said. 'Isn't it possible that Emily's pregnancy was what caused her to feel suicidal?'

'No,' Melanie said firmly, in a voice that carried. 'I know the kind of relationship my daughter and I had, Mr McAfee. And I know that Emily would have told me everything, in spite of the lies that you're trying to spread. She would have told me if something was bothering her. If she didn't tell me, it was because she wasn't upset about it. Or perhaps she didn't even know for certain, herself, that she was going to have a baby.'

Jordan tipped his head to the side. 'If she didn't know about the baby, Mrs Gold, then how could she tell Chris?'

Melanie shrugged. 'Maybe she didn't.'

'You're saying he might not have known she was pregnant.'

'That's correct.'

'Then why,' Jordan asked, 'would he want to kill her?'

There was a stir in the courtroom as Melanie got off the stand. She walked slowly down the center aisle, escorted by a bailiff.

As soon as the doors closed behind her, a volley of questions and comments broke out among the gallery, as pervasive and quick as the spread of a fever.

Chris was smiling as Jordan took his seat again. 'That,' he said, 'was awesome.'

'Glad you liked it,' Jordan said, smoothing his tie.

'What happens next?'

Jordan opened his mouth to tell Chris, but Barrie did it for him. 'Your Honor,' she said, 'the prosecution rests.'

'Now,' Jordan murmured to his client, 'we put on a show.'

Then

Emily rubbed the towel down her body and wrapped it around her hair. When she yanked open the bathroom door the cold air of the hall rushed in. She shuddered, careful not to look at the flat plane of her stomach in the mirror as she left.

There was no one in the house, so she walked to her bedroom nude. She straightened her bed and tucked Chris's sweatshirt, the one that smelled like him, around her pillow. But she left her dirty clothes piled on the floor, to give her parents something familiar to come home to.

She sat down at her desk, the towel loose now around her shoulders. There was a stack of art school applications – Rhode Island School of Design, and the Sorbonne, right on top. A blank pad, used for homework.

Should she leave a note?

She picked up a pencil and pressed the tip to the paper, digging hard enough to leave a mark. What did you say to the people who had given you life, when you were about to intentionally throw that gift away? With a sigh, Emily threw down the pencil. You didn't. You didn't say anything, because they'd read between the lines for what you left out, and believe that it was all their fault.

As if that reminded her, she dug in her nightstand for a small, clothbound book, and took it over to the closet. Inside, behind the stack of her shoeboxes, was a small hole, eaten away by squirrels years ago and used, when she and Chris were little, for the stash of secret treasures.

As she reached inside, she found a folded piece of paper. A

lemon-juice message, invisible ink that had been revealed when held over a candle flame. She and Chris must have been about ten. They'd passed notes in a tin-can pulley system linked between their bedroom windows, before the fishing line had tangled in the branches of the trees. Emily ran her finger over the torn edges of the paper and smiled. *I am coming to save you*, Chris had written. If she remembered right, she'd been grounded at the time. Chris had scaled the rose trellis on the side of the house, planning to enter the bathroom window to spring her from her cell – but he'd fallen and broken his arm instead.

She crumpled the paper into her fist. So. This wasn't the first time he'd be saving her by letting her go.

Emily wound her hair into a French braid and went to lie down on the bed. And she stayed that way – naked, the message tight in her palm – until she heard Chris start his car in the driveway next door.

When Chris turned fifteen, the world had become unfamiliar. Time moved too quickly and impossibly slow all at once; no one seemed to understand what he was saying; ebbs and surges tingled his limbs and stretched his skin. He remembered one summer afternoon, when he and Em had been lazing on a raft in the pond; he had fallen asleep in the middle of one of her sentences and woke up with the sun lower and hotter and Emily still talking, as if both everything and nothing at all had changed.

It was like that, again, now. Emily, whose face Chris could trace with his eyes shut, was suddenly unrecognizable. He'd wanted to give her time to see how crazy this idea was, but all the time had run out and the whole nightmare had snowballed, huge and unwieldy, impossible for Chris to stop in its path. He wanted to save her life – so he was pretending to help her to die. On the one hand, he felt powerless in a world too big for him to alter; on the other hand, his world had shrunk to the head of a pin with room for nothing but him and Emily and their pact. He was paralyzed by indecision – believing with all the unshakable drama of adolescence that he could handle something as enormous as this, and at the same time wanting to whisper the truth in his mother's ear so that she could make it go away.

His hands shook so much he had taken to sitting on them, and there were moments when he was convinced he was losing his mind. He thought of this as a competition he simply had to win, and in the same moment reminded himself that no one died at the end of a race.

He wondered how time had moved so quickly since the night Emily had told him. He wished it would move faster, so that he would be an adult, and like all other adults, would be unable to remember this time of his life clearly.

He wondered why he felt like the road was crumbling beneath him, when he'd only been trying to drive slowly through a safety zone.

She slid into the passenger seat, in a motion so familiar that Chris had to close his eyes against the sight of it. 'Hi,' she said, like always. Chris pulled out of her driveway feeling as if someone had changed the plot of a play he was acting in, forgetting to mention it to him.

They had just rounded the curve of Wood Hollow Road when Emily asked him to pull over. 'I want to see it,' she said.

Her voice had that high note of excitement, and her eyes, now that he could see them, were glassy and bright. Like she had a fever. And Chris wondered if this wasn't, after all, something that was running through her blood.

He reached into his coat and withdrew the gun, wrapped in a chamois. Emily held out her hand, hesitating to touch it. Then she ran her forefinger down its barrel. 'Thank you,' she whispered, sounding relieved. 'The bullet,' she said suddenly. 'You didn't forget it?'

Chris patted his pocket.

Emily stared at his hand, covering the heart of his shirt, and then at his face. 'Aren't you going to say anything?'

'No,' Chris said. 'I'm not.'

It had been Emily's idea to go to the carousel. In part, because she knew it was likely to be deserted at this time of year, and in part because she was making a conscious effort to take with her all the best things about the world she wanted to leave, just in case memories could be carried in one's pockets and used to plot out the course of whatever it was that came next.

She had always loved the carousel. The past two summers, when Chris had run it, she'd met him here often. They had christened the horses: Tulip and Leroy; Sadie and Starlight and Buck. Sometimes she'd come during the day and help Chris hoist the thick, damp weights of toddlers onto the carved saddles; sometimes she'd arrive at dusk to help him clean up. She'd liked that best. There was something impossibly lovely about the big machine running itself down, horses moving in slow motion to the creak and whir of the gears.

She didn't feel frightened. Now that she'd found a way out, even the thought of dying didn't scare her. She just wanted to end it before other people she loved were hurt as badly as she was.

She looked at Chris, and at the small silver box that contained the mechanism that activated the carousel. 'Do you still have your key?' she asked.

The wind whipped her braid against her cheek, and her arms were crossed in an effort to keep warm. 'Yeah,' Chris said. 'You want to go on?'

'Please.' She climbed onto the carousel, passing her hand against the noses of the sturdy horses. She picked the one she'd named Delilah, a white horse with a silver mane and paste rubies and emeralds set into her bridle. Chris stood by the silver box, his hand on the red button that started the machine. Emily felt the carousel rumble to life beneath her, the calliope jangling as the merry-go-round picked up speed. She slapped the cracked leather of the reins against the horse's neck and closed her eyes.

She pictured herself and Chris, little children standing side by side on a backyard boulder, holding hands and leaping together into a high pile of autumn leaves. She remembered the jewel tones of the maples and oaks. She remembered the yank of her arm against Chris's as gravity tugged at them. But most of all she remembered that moment when they were both convinced they were flying.

He stood on level ground and watched Emily. Her head was thrown back and the wind had pinked her cheeks. Tears were streaming from her eyes, but she was smiling.

This, he realized, *is it*. Either he let Emily have what she wanted more than anything, or he let himself have what he wanted. It was the first time he could remember those two things not being the same.

How could he stand by and watch her die? Then again, how could he stop her, if she was hurting so badly?

Emily had trusted him, but he was going to betray her. And then the next time she tried to kill herself – because there would be a next time, he knew – he wouldn't find out until after the fact. Like everyone else.

He felt the hairs stand up on the back of his neck. Was he really considering what he thought he was?

He tried to clear his head the way he did before a meet, so that the only thing in his mind was the straightest, fastest path from here to there. But this time, it would not be that easy. There was no right way. There was no guarantee that both of them would make it to the other side.

Shivering, he focused on the long, white line of her throat, the beat at its hollow. He kept his eyes on her pulse as she disappeared out of his range of vision to the far side of the carousel, holding his breath until he saw her coming back to him.

*   *   *

They sat on the carousel bench where mothers rode with the tiniest babies, the wood bubbly and thick beneath their hands from consecutive coats of paint. The bottle of Canadian Club rested between Chris's feet. He felt Emily shaking beside him, and preferred to think that she might be cold. Leaning over, he buttoned her jacket all the way. 'You don't want to get sick,' he said, and then, considering his words, felt queasy. 'I love you,' he whispered, and that was the moment he knew what he was going to do.

When you loved someone, you put their needs before your own.

No matter how inconceivable those needs were; no matter how fucked up; no matter how much it made you feel like you were ripping yourself into pieces.

He did not realize he'd begun to cry, partly in shock and partly in acceptance, until he tasted himself, slick and salty, on Emily's lips. It was not supposed to be this way; oh, God, but how could he be a hero when saving Em would only make her hurt more? Out of comfort, Emily's hands began to stroke his back, and he wondered, *Who is here for whom?* Then suddenly he had to be inside her, and with an urgency that surprised him he found himself ripping at her jeans and shoving them down her thighs, wrapping her legs around him as he came.

Take me with you, he thought.

Emily straightened her clothes, her cheeks flaming. Chris could not stop apologizing, as if the fact he'd forgotten a condom was something she'd hold against him for eternity. 'It doesn't matter,' she said, tucking in her shirt, thinking, *If you only knew.*

He sat a few feet away from her, his hands clasped in his lap. His jeans were still unbuttoned, and the smell of sex carried on the wind. He felt unnaturally calm. 'What do you want me to do,' he said, 'afterward?'

They hadn't talked about it; in fact, until this moment Emily was not entirely sure that Chris wasn't going to do something completely stupid, like throw the bullets into the shrubbery when he went to load the chamber, or knock the gun out of her hand at the last minute. 'I don't know,' she said, and she didn't: she'd never gotten this far in her thoughts. There was the planning, and the organization, and even the act itself – but the truth of being dead was not something she'd pictured. She cleared her throat. 'Do anything,' she said. 'Whatever you need to.'

Chris traced a pattern on the floorboards with his thumbnail, a sudden stranger. 'Is there a time?' he asked stiffly.

'Just not yet,' Emily whispered, and at the reprieve Chris buttoned his jeans and pulled her onto his lap. His arms closed around her and she leaned into him, thinking, *Forgive me.*

His hands were shaking as he snapped open the chamber of the gun. The Colt would hold six bullets. After one was fired, the shell remained in the revolver. He explained all this to Emily as he fumbled in his shirt pocket, as if reciting the sheer mechanics of the act would make it that much less painful.

'Two bullets?' Emily said.

Chris lifted a shoulder. 'Just in case,' he answered, daring her to ask him to explain something he did not really understand himself. *Just in case one bullet didn't do the trick? Just in case he found that with Emily dead, he'd want to die, too?*

Then the gun lay between them, a living thing. Emily picked it up, its weight bending her wrist.

There was so much Chris wanted to say. He wanted her to tell him what this horrible secret of hers was; he wanted to beg her to stop. He wanted to tell her she could still back out of this, although he felt things had gotten so far he did not quite believe it himself. So he pressed his lips against hers, hard – a brand – but then his mouth curled around a sob and he broke away before the kiss was finished, his body folding like he'd been punched. 'I am doing this,' he said, 'because I love you.'

Emily's face was still and white with tears. 'I am doing this because I love you, too.' She gripped his hand. 'I want you to hold me,' she said.

Chris moved her into his arms, her chin on his right shoulder. He committed to memory the solid weight of her, and the life that ran like a current, before pulling back slightly to give Emily room to place the gun to her head.

Now

May 1998

Randi Underwood apologized to the jury. 'I work nights,' she explained, 'but they didn't want to keep all of you up during the time I'm usually most lucid.' She'd just come off a thirty-six hour stint at the hospital, where she was a physician's assistant in the emergency room. 'Just let me know if I don't make any sense,' she joked. 'And if I try to intubate someone with a pen, slap me.'

Jordan smiled. 'We certainly appreciate you being here, Ms Underwood.'

'Hey,' the witness grinned. 'What's a little sleep?'

She was a large woman, still dressed in hospital scrubs that had small green snowflakes printed all over them. Jordan had already established her identity for the record. 'Ms Underwood,' he continued, 'were you on duty the night of November seventh, when Emily Gold was brought into the emergency room of Bainbridge Memorial?'

'Yes, I was.'

'Do you remember her?'

'I do. She was very young, and those are always the most terrible to see. There was a lot of activity around her at first – she was arresting as the medics brought her in – but apparently that was over in a matter of seconds, and she was pronounced dead by the time she was in the ER cubicle.'

'I see. What happened next?'

'Well, standard procedure is to have someone identify the body before it's moved to the morgue. We had been told that the parents were on their way. So I started to clean her up.'

'Clean her up?'

'It's customary,' she said. 'Especially when there's a great deal of blood; it's harder on the relatives to see that. Basically I wiped off her hands and her face. Nobody told us not to wash her.'

'What do you mean?'

'In police investigations, evidence is evidence, and a corpse qualifies. But the officers who brought her in said it was a suicide. No one from the police told us to treat it differently; no one came in to do tests or anything.'

'You specifically washed her hands?'

'Yes. I remember that she had on a pretty gold ring – one of those Celtic knots, you know?'

'And when did you leave the cubicle?'

'When the girl's father came in to ID the body,' she said.

Jordan smiled at the witness. 'Thank you,' he said, 'nothing further.'

As Jordan had expected, Barrie Delaney declined to cross-examine the physician's assistant. There was very little she could ask without making her star witness, Detective Marrone, look like a bumbling fool. So Jordan put Dr Linwood Karpagian on the stand, thinking as he watched the man that he owed Selena a dozen roses for finding him.

The jury could not take their eyes off him. Dr Karpagian looked like Cary Grant in his prime, with silvered hair waving off his temples and finely manicured hands that looked capable of holding your confidence, much less anything more conventionally substantial. He sat easily on the stand, accustomed to being the center of attention.

'Your honor,' Barrie said, 'request permission to approach.'

Puckett waved the lawyers closer, and Jordan raised his brow, waiting to hear what Barrie had to say. 'For the appellate record, we still have an objection to this witness.'

'Ms Delaney,' Judge Puckett said, 'I already ruled on this in your pretrial motion.'

As Barrie stomped back to her table, Jordan walked Dr

Karpagian through his credentials, further impressing the jury. 'Doctor,' he said, 'how many teens have you worked with?'

'Thousands,' Dr Karpagian said. 'I couldn't begin to narrow that down.'

'And how many with suicidal natures?'

'Oh, I've counseled upwards of four hundred teenagers who were suicidal. And that of course doesn't count the profiles of other suicidal teens who were featured in the three books I've written on the subject.'

'So you've published your findings?'

'Yes. Beside the books, I've had studies published in the *Journal of Counseling and Clinical Psychology*, and the *Journal of Abnormal Child Psychiatry*.'

'Since we're not nearly as familiar as you are with the phenomenon of teen suicide, could you just give us a general overview of its characteristics?'

'Certainly. Teen suicide is an alarming epidemic, increasing every year. To an adolescent, suicide is seen as a joint statement of strength and despair. Teenagers need, more than anything, to be taken seriously. And the world of a teenager revolves around himself. Now, imagine a troubled teenager with a problem. His parents brush him off, because they either don't want to accept that their child is upset or don't have time to listen. And in response, the teenager thinks, "Oh, yeah? Well, watch what I can do." And he kills himself. He's not thinking of being dead. He's thinking of suicide as a way to solve the problem, to end the pain, and to say, "So there!" all at once.'

'Is there a percentage breakdown for male versus female suicides?'

'Girls try to kill themselves three times more frequently than boys, but boys succeed far more often.'

'Really?' Jordan feigned amazement. In reality, he and Dr Karpagian had fine-tuned this testimony for hours the previous week, and there was nothing the good doctor could say that was going to surprise him. 'Why is that?'

'Well, when girls try to commit suicide, they often use less decisive methods. Pills, or carbon monoxide poisoning – both of which require a long period of time to do their work, during which the victim is often found alive and taken to the hospital. Sometimes they slash their wrists, but most draw the razor across laterally, not realizing that the quickest way to die is to slash vertically, along the artery. On the other hand,' he said, 'boys tend to use guns, or to hang themselves. Both methods are fast, death occurring before someone can save them or stop them.'

'I see,' Jordan said. 'Is there a certain type of teenager that is more likely than another to kill him- or herself?'

'That's the intriguing thing,' Dr Karpagian said, his eyes snapping with the interest of a scholar. 'A poor teenager is just as likely to try as a wealthy one. There is no real socioeconomic profile to suicidal teens.'

'Are there any behaviors that just jump out and say, "Whoa – this kid's about to kill himself!"'

'Depression,' Karpagian said bluntly. 'It may be something that has been going on for years; it may happen rather quickly in a matter of several months. The actual suicide is often triggered by a certain event, which – coupled with the depression – seems too overwhelming to accept.'

'Would this depression be obvious to people who knew the teenager?'

'Well, you know, Mr McAfee, that's one of the problems. Depression can manifest itself in many different ways. It's not always noticeable to friends and family. There are certain signs of suicidal behavior that psychologists recognize and that should be taken seriously, if they occur. But some teens show none of them, and some show all of them.'

'What are these signs, Doctor?'

'Sometimes we see a preoccupation with death. Or a change in eating or sleeping habits. Rebellious behavior. Withdrawal from people, or outright running away. Some suicidal teens act persistently bored, or have difficulty concentrating. There may be evidence of drug or alcohol abuse, falling grades. They may neglect their appearance, exhibit personality changes, or have psychosomatic complaints. Sometimes we see kids giving away prized possessions, or joking about killing themselves. But, as I said, sometimes we don't see any of this.'

'Sounds like some perfectly normal teens I know,' Jordan said.

'Exactly,' the psychologist said. 'That's what makes it so hard to diagnose beforehand.'

Jordan lifted a document, a collection of Emily Gold's medical information and interviews with neighbors, friends, and family by both Selena and the police. 'Doctor, did you have a chance to look at Emily Gold's profile?'

'I did.'

'And what did her friends and family say about her?'

'For the most part, her parents were unaware of any depression. Likewise her friends. Her art teacher's comments suggested that although Emily wasn't talking about being upset, her artwork had taken a turn toward the macabre. It seems to me, reading between the lines, that Emily was withdrawing in the weeks before her death. She was spending quite a lot of time with Chris, which is also consistent with a suicide pact.'

'A suicide pact. What does that mean, exactly?'

'Two or more deaths planned together. It's an extraordinary thought to an adult, actually – the idea of holding enough sway over someone to get them to take their life, too.' He smiled sadly at the jury. 'Most of you have forgotten – probably for good reason – what it was like when you were sixteen and seventeen; how crucially important it was to have someone understand you and admire you. You grow up, and things get more relative. But when you're an adolescent, that one close relationship is all consuming. You are so bonded to that peer that you wear the same kinds of clothes, you listen to the same kinds of music, you do the same kinds of things for fun, and you think alike. It only takes one teenager to conjure up the idea of suicide. It takes a variety of psychological reasons for a second teen to decide it's a good idea.'

Dr Karpagian looked at Chris, as if analyzing him now. 'Teens who decide to commit suicide together are usually close. But once the decision to kill themselves is made, that small world grows even smaller. The only people they want to confide in is each other. The only people they want to see is each other. And everything narrows until the only thing that matters is the act of committing suicide: the planning, the event itself. They're going to make a collective statement to all the people who are on the outside of that very small world, the people who don't understand them.'

'Dr Karpagian, based on Emily's profile, did she seem suicidal?'

'Not having met her, the best I can say is that it is entirely possible she was depressed enough to commit suicide.'

Jordan nodded. 'You're saying there doesn't have to be a blatant red flag on that profile? That a girl who looks like a pretty normal teen but is just a little bit withdrawn might be suicidal?'

'It's happened before,' Dr Karpagian said.

'I see.' He turned toward his notes. 'Did you have a chance to look at the profile of Chris?'

It had been at Jordan's insistence that Selena created a profile, in much the same way one had been constructed for Emily, by talking to family and friends and eliciting comments. Knowing – albeit grudgingly – that Chris had never been suicidal, it wouldn't work to get him face-to-face with an expert, and then put that expert on the stand sworn to tell the truth.

'I did look it over. And the most important thing I saw in Chris Harte's profile was his preoccupation with Emily Gold. I was a psychologist long before I was an expert on suicide, you know, and there's a specific term for the kind of relationship that had developed between Chris and Emily over the years.'

'What's that?'

'Fusion.' He smiled at the jury. 'Just like the physicists. It means that two personalities have bonded together so strongly that a whole new personality is created, and the separate ones cease to exist.'

Jordan raised his eyebrows. 'Could you run that by me again?'

'In plain English,' Dr Karpagian said, 'it means that Chris and Emily's minds and personalities were so connected there really was no distinction between them. They grew up so close that they couldn't function without each other. Anything that happened to one of those kids was going to affect the other. And in the case of the death of one of them, the other one literally would not be able to go on living.' He looked at Jordan. 'Does that make more sense?'

'It's more clear,' Jordan said, 'but it's hard to accept.'

Dr Karpagian smiled. 'Congratulations, Mr McAfee. That simply means you're mentally healthy.'

Jordan grinned. 'Don't know that Ms Delaney would agree, sir, but I thank you.' The jury tittered behind him. 'So in your expert opinion, Dr Karpagian, did you come to any conclusions about Chris Harte and Emily Gold?'

'Yes. I see Emily as being the one who was suicidal for whatever reason. And – it's important to note this – we may never know what that reason was. But something made her depressed and death seemed a way out. She turned to Chris because he was the person closest to her by far, and she told him she was going to commit suicide. But once she confided in Chris, he realized that if Emily was dead, there would be no reason for him to be alive.'

Jordan stared at the jury. 'So what you're saying is that whatever made Emily suicidal was not the same thing that made Chris suicidal?'

'No. It was most likely the simple fact that Emily was going to kill herself that made Chris agree to a suicide pact.'

Jordan closed his eyes briefly. To him, that was the biggest hurdle in his defense – getting the jury even to believe that two kids could have come up with this awful idea together. The good doctor, thank God – or Selena, who'd found him – had made it seem possible. 'One more thing,' Jordan said. 'Emily purchased a very expensive gift for someone several months before her suicide. What would you say about that kind of behavior?'

'Oh, that would be a giveaway,' Dr Karpagian said. 'Something she was planning to leave behind for someone, to make sure she was remembered.'

'So Emily bought this gift to let the world know she was planning on killing herself?'

'Objection,' Barrie called. 'Leading.'

'Your Honor, this is very important,' Jordan countered.

'Then rephrase, Mr McAfee.'

Jordan turned back to Dr Karpagian. 'In your expert opinion, why would Emily purchase an expensive gift like that watch, if she was indeed suicidal?'

'I'd say,' the psychologist mused, 'that Emily bought the watch before she decided to kill herself and involve Chris in a suicide pact. And it may indeed have been expensive, but that didn't matter.' He smiled sadly at the attorney. 'When you're going to kill yourself, the last thing on your mind is getting a refund.'

'Thank you,' Jordan said, and sat down.

Barrie's head was spinning. She had to make an expert look like an idiot, and she had absolutely no grounding in his field. 'Okay, Doctor,' she said gamely, 'you looked at Emily's profile. And you mentioned a lot of characteristics that teenagers some-times exhibit when they're suicidal.' She picked up her legal pad, covered with notes. 'Sleeplessness is one?'

'Yes.'

'And did you see that in Emily's profile?'

'No.'

'Did you find unexplained changes in eating behavior in the profile?'

'No.'

'Did Emily act rebellious?'

'Not that I could see, no.'

'How about running away?'

'No.'

'Was she preoccupied with death?'

'Not overtly.'

'Did she appear to be bored, or have difficulty concentrating?'

'No.'

'Was she abusing alcohol or drugs?'

'No.'

'Was she failing any classes?'

'No.'

'Was she neglecting her appearance?'

'No.'

'Was she complaining of psychosomatic illnesses?'

'No.'

'Did she joke about suicide?'

'Apparently not.'

'So the only characteristics that led you to believe Emily might have been suicidal were that she was slightly withdrawn and out of sorts. Isn't that fairly normal for ninety-nine percent of women at least once a month?'

Dr Karpagian smiled. 'I have it on authority that that's true,' he said.

'So isn't it possible that since Emily didn't exhibit most of these traits, she was not suicidal?'

'It is possible,' the psychologist said.

'The few signs Emily did exhibit, would you say they are normal behaviors for a teenager?'

'Yes, often.'

'All right. Now, you worked from a profile of Emily, is that correct?'

'Yes.'

'Who made up this profile?'

'I understand the defense's investigator, Ms Damascus, collated it. They were a series of interviews done by herself or by the State, with friends and families of the teenager in question.'

'By your own testimony, Chris Harte was the closest person to Emily Gold. Were his observations part of her profile?'

'Well, no. He wasn't asked.'

'But he was the one Emily turned to the most during those last weeks?'

'Yes.'

'So he may have been able to tell you whether or not she had any of those characteristics we just listed. He probably would have seen more than anyone else.'

'Yes.'

'Yet you didn't speak to him when he was obviously your best source?'

'We were trying to make a judgment without Chris's input to keep it completely unbiased.'

'That wasn't the question, Doctor. The question was, *Did you interview Chris Harte?*'

'No, I did not.'

'You did not interview Chris Harte. He was alive and available and yet never even consulted, even though he was the best witness you had on Emily's behavior prior to her death. Short of Emily herself, that is.' Barrie pinned the witness with her gaze. 'And you couldn't interview Emily, could you?'

Kim Kenly appeared for her brief sojourn in court wearing a tie-dyed caftan, stamped with a hundred small handprints. 'Isn't this great,' she said to the bailiff escorting her to the stand. 'The kindergartners gave it to me.'

Jordan established her credentials and then asked how Ms Kenly knew Emily Gold. 'I taught her art throughout high school,' she said. 'Emily was incredibly talented. You have to understand, as a specials teacher, I see five hundred kids a day. Most of them just parade through the art room and leave a mess. There are a handful who stick with it, and have a true affinity for the subject. Maybe one or two of them even has talent. Well, Emily was the rarest of jewels. They come along once every ten years, I figure: a student who not only loves art but knows how to use her abilities to their best advantage.'

'She sounds very special.'

'Talented,' Kim said. 'And dedicated. She spent all her free time in the art room. She even had her own easel stand in the back.'

Jordan lifted a series of canvases that the bailiff had brought in along with Ms Kenly. 'I have here several paintings to enter into evidence,' he said, waiting until they were examined by Barrie and duly tagged by the clerk. 'Can you walk us through these paintings?'

'Sure. The boy with the lollipop is one she did in ninth grade. The tenth-grade picture – the mother and child – is more developed, you see, in the facial structure? More lifelike? The subjects are also more three dimensional. This third painting, well, it's clear that Chris was the subject.'

'Chris Harte?'

Kim Kenly smiled. 'Mr McAfee,' she said, 'can't you tell?'

'I can,' he assured her. 'But the court record can't.'

'Well, then, yes. Chris Harte. Anyway, Emily captured the expression on the subject's face, as well as the realism of the features. As a matter of fact, Emily's work always reminded me a little of Mary Cassatt.'

'Okay,' Jordan said. 'Now you've lost me. Who's Mary Cassatt?'

'A nineteenth-century painter who often used mothers and children as subjects. Emily did too, and she also showed the same attention to detail and emotion.'

'Thank you,' Jordan said. 'So Emily's paintings developed fairly logically as she went through high school?'

'Technically, yes. There was a lot of heart there from day one, but as she progressed from ninth grade to twelfth grade, I stopped seeing what she was thinking of her subjects, and saw instead what the subject was thinking of being a subject. That's something you rarely see in amateur painters, Mr McAfee. It's a measure of real refinement.'

'Did you notice any changes in Emily's style?'

'Well, as a matter of fact I did. Last fall she was working on a painting that was so dramatically different from her usual work, it really surprised me.'

Jordan drew out the final painting to enter into evidence. The free-form skull, with its storm-clouded eye sockets and lolling tongue, caught the jury's attention. One woman covered her hand with her mouth, and said, 'Oh, my.'

'That's what I thought, too,' Kim Kenly said, nodding at the juror. 'As you can see, this isn't realism anymore. It's surrealism.'

'Surrealism,' Jordan said. 'Can you explain that to us?'

'Everyone's seen surrealist paintings. Dali, Magritte.' At Jordan's blank look, she sighed. 'Dali. The guy who painted the dripping clocks?'

'Oh, that's right.' He glanced swiftly at the jury. Like any random group from Grafton County, its makeup was a study in contradictions. A Dartmouth economics professor was seated beside a man Jordan would bet had never in his life left his Orford dairy farm. The Dartmouth professor looked bored, and probably had known who Dali was the whole time. The farmer was scribbling on his note pad. 'Ms Kenly, when did Emily paint this?'

'She began at the end of September. She wasn't completely finished when she . . . died.'

'No? But it's signed.'

'Yes,' the art teacher said, frowning. 'And titled. She obviously thought she was rather close to finishing.'

'Can you tell us what Emily titled this picture?'

Kim Kenly's long red fingernail hovered over the line of the skull, across the wide tongue and the roiling clouds in the eye sockets, coming to rest on the words beside the artist's signature. 'Right here,' she pointed. '*Self-portrait.*'

For a minute Barrie Delaney stared at the painting, her chin resting in her hand. Then she sighed and stood up. 'Well, I can't make much sense of it,' she admitted to Kim Kenly. 'Can you?'

'I'm no expert . . .' Kim began.

'No,' Barrie interrupted. 'But rest assured, the defense has found one. I wonder, though, as Emily's art teacher, if you asked her why she was painting something so disturbing.'

'I did mention that it looked very different from her usual stuff. And she said that it was what she felt like painting at the time.'

Barrie began to pace back and forth in front of the witness stand. 'Is it unusual for painters to try different mediums, and styles?'

'Well, no.'

'Did Emily ever try her hand at sculpting?'

'Once, briefly, in tenth grade.'

'How about throwing pottery?'

'A bit.'

Barrie nodded, encouraging. 'What about watercolors?'

'Yes, but she preferred oils.'

'But occasionally Emily would do a painting that was out of character?'

'Sure.'

Barrie slowly walked toward the portrait of the skull. 'Ms Kenly, when Emily first tried watercolors, did you notice anything different about her demeanor?'

'No.'

'The time she attempted sculpting, did you notice any change in her behavior?'

'No.'

Barrie lifted the skull portrait. 'At the time she painted this painting, Ms Kenly, was she acting markedly different from the way she usually did?'

'No.'

'Nothing further,' Barrie said, and she placed the painting on the exhibit table again, face down.

★   ★   ★

In the lobby of the courthouse was a large swath of chairs, set like a joint between the two courtrooms. On any given day the chairs were filled with harried attorneys, people awaiting arraignments, and witnesses who'd been warned not to speak to each other. The previous two days, Michael had been seated at one end of the lobby with Melanie; Gus had been seated at the other. But today was the first day Melanie would be allowed into the trial, having given her testimony. Gus had taken her customary seat, trying desperately to read the newspaper and not notice the moment Michael came in.

As he sat down next to her, she folded the paper. 'You shouldn't,' she said.

'Shouldn't what?'

'Sit here.'

'Why? As long as we say nothing that has bearing on the case, it's okay.'

Gus closed her eyes. 'Michael, the two of us breathing the same air in this room has bearing on the case. Just the fact that you're you, and I'm me.'

'Have you seen Chris?'

'No, I'm going tonight.' Gus turned, an afterthought. 'Are you?'

'I don't think it would be right,' he said. 'Especially if I testify today.'

Gus smiled faintly. 'You have a strange notion of morality.'

'What's that supposed to mean?'

'Nothing. It's just that you're already testifying for the defense. Chris would want to thank you personally for that.'

'Exactly. I'm testifying for the defense. And tonight I'll probably go out and get drunk so I can forget I did it.'

Gus turned in her seat. 'Don't,' she said, laying her hand on his arm.

They both looked down at it, radiating heat. Michael covered her hand with his own. 'Will you come out with me instead?' he asked.

Gus shook her head. 'I have to go to the jail,' she said gently. 'For Chris.'

Michael glanced away. 'You're right,' he said evenly. 'You should always do what's right for your child.' And he stood up and walked down the hall.

'Ms Vernon,' Jordan said, 'you're an art therapist.'

'That's right.'

'Can you tell me what that is?' He smiled engagingly. 'We don't get a lot of art therapists here in New Hampshire.'

In fact, Sandra Vernon had been flown in from Berkeley. She had a California tan, short platinum hair, and a Ph.D. in psychology from UCLA. 'Well, we work in the mental health field. Usually we're called in and we issue directives where we ask the client to draw something specific, like a house or a tree or a person. And based on what they draw and the style in which they complete the drawing, we can tell things about their psychological health.'

'That's incredible,' Jordan said, truly amazed. 'You can look at stick figures and see what's going on in someone's mind?'

'Absolutely. With very young children, who don't have the words to tell us things, we can discover whether they're being sexually or physically abused, things like that.'

'Have you worked with teens?'

'On occasion, yes.'

Jordan moved behind Chris, quite intentionally placing his hand on Chris's shoulder. 'Have you worked with deeply depressed and suicidal teens?'

'Yes.'

'Can you look at an adolescent's drawing and find suggestions of sexual abuse or suicidal tendencies?'

'Yes,' Sandra said. 'Pictures can sometimes depict unconscious feelings that are being repressed, too raw to come to the surface in any other way.'

'So you may meet a child who is not acting out, but then look at one of her pictures and see there is a huge disturbance in her life.'

'Certainly.'

Jordan walked to the exhibit table and picked up the painting that Emily had done of a mother and child in tenth grade. 'Could you tell me the frame of mind of the person who painted this picture?'

Sandra pulled a pair of cat's-eye glasses from her pocket and settled them on her nose. 'Well, this looks like the work of a stable, well-adjusted person. You can see that the face and hands are all well-proportioned; that there's a strong element of realism; that nothing seems to be truly out of the ordinary or exaggerated; there are bright colors used.'

'Okay.' Jordan lifted the portrait of the skull. 'How about this one?'

Sandra Vernon raised her brows. 'Well,' she said. 'This is very different.'

'Can you tell us what you see in it?'

'Sure. First off, there's a skull. That would immediately say to me that there's a possible preoccupation with death going on here. But even more telling is the way the colors red and black are juxtaposed in the background – that's a documented hint about suicide, in many art therapy studies. Also, there's a cloudy sky. Often we see paintings of clouds or rain when people are depressed and/or suicidal. . .but what's even more disturbing is the way the artist put the clouds inside the space where the eyes should have been. The eyes are symbolic of a person's thoughts. I'd say that the artist's choice here of putting a gathering downpour in the eye sockets strongly suggests there are thoughts of suicide going on in his or her own head.'

She leaned over the railing of the witness box. 'Could I . . . could you bring it closer?' Jordan walked the painting over and propped it between Sandra and the judge. 'What's really disturbing, too, are some of the details in the picture. It's in the surreal style—'

'Does that make a difference?'

'Not really, no. But the way the items are put together in this picture does. You can see here that although it is a bony skull, there are also long developed eyelashes, and a highly realistic tongue coming out of the mouth. Those things send off warning signals in me about sexual abuse.'

'Sexual abuse?'

'Yes. Victims of abuse fixate on tongues, eyelashes, and wedge-shaped objects. Also belts.' She squinted at the painting, considering. 'And the skull is floating in the sky. Usually when we see someone who draws a floating image of a body with no hands or a detached head, it indicates that they don't have a feeling of control in their life. Their feet aren't on the ground, so to speak, so they can't walk away from whatever is bothering them.'

Jordan set the painting back on the exhibit table. 'Ms Vernon, if you saw this painting in a professional capacity, what would be your clinical recommendation for the artist?'

Sandra Vernon shook her head. 'I'd be very concerned about the mental state of the artist, with regard to issues of depression and even suicide,' she said. 'I'd suggest seeing a therapist.'

Melanie shifted in her seat. It was the first day she'd been allowed to hear testimony, since her own stint as a witness was over. And of all the testimonies she wanted to hear, this woman from Berkeley had to be the most upsetting. *Tongues. Eyelashes. Wedge-shaped objects.*

Warning signals; sexual abuse.

Her hands clenched in her lap, and she clearly remembered the feel of Emily's journal, the one that she'd found tucked behind the rotted panel of the closet. The one she'd fed to the fire.

The one she'd read through to the end.

Melanie pushed past the other people in her row and stumbled out of the courtroom, past Gus Harte and her husband and a hundred other people, until she reached the ladies' room and was sick all over the floor.

'Ms Vernon, did you go to art school?'

'Yes,' Sandra said, grinning at the prosecutor. 'Back when the dinosaurs were still around.'

Barrie did not crack a smile. 'Isn't it true that you need to gather fifteen to twenty slides of your artwork to send to an art school with your application?'

'Yes.'

'Could this painting be illustrating an alternative style to that art school, to exhibit the artist's range?'

'Actually, schools prefer to know that an artist is fairly consistent.'

'But it is possible, Ms Vernon?'

'Yes.'

Barrie walked over and extracted two small plastic squares from her briefcase. 'I'd like to enter these into evidence,' she said, placing the two compact discs on the exhibit table to be tagged. 'Ms Vernon, these are CDs taken from Emily Gold's bedroom. Can you describe them to us?'

The art therapist took the discs from the prosecutor's outstretched hand. 'One's a Grateful Dead CD,' she said. 'A mighty good one, I should add.'

'What do you see on the cover?'

'A skull, floating on a psychedelic background.'

'And what about the other one?' Barrie asked.

'The Rolling Stones. With the cover art of a mouth, and a long tongue.'

'Have you ever known teenagers to reproduce artwork that is important to them, Ms Vernon?'

'Yes, we see that quite often. It's part of adolescence.'

'So it is entirely possible that the artist who painted the skull might only have been copying elements from the cover art of some favorite CDs?'

'That's definitely possible.'

'Thank you,' Barrie said, taking back the music. 'You also mentioned that you were disturbed by certain elements that you saw in the painting. Can you cite a specific source for me that says that clouds mean suicide?'

'Well, no. It's not one specific source, it's the result of studies of many directives issued to children.'

'Can you give us the name of a study, then, that says a tongue coming out of the mouth indicates sexual abuse?'

'Again, it was a compilation of different cases.'

'So you couldn't really say with any specificity that because there is red and black in a painting, this person is going to kill herself.'

'Well, no. But in ninety out of one hundred paintings where there is red and black like that, we have found that the artists felt suicidal.'

Barrie smiled. 'How interesting that you should say that.' She pulled out a poster, and held it up for Jordan.

'Objection,' he said immediately, walking up to the bench. 'What the hell is that?' he asked Barrie. 'And what does it have to do with this case?'

'Come on, Jordan. It's a Magritte. I know you're a cretin when it comes to culture, but even you can see where I'm going to go with this.'

Jordan turned to the judge. 'If I knew she was going to put a goddamn Magritte up there, I would have done some research on the subject.'

'Oh, give it up,' Barrie said. 'This just came to me last night. Let me have a little leeway.'

'If you put that thing up on the stand,' Jordan said, 'then I want leeway too. I want time to find out whatever I can about Magritte.'

Barrie smiled sweetly. 'With your knowledge of art, by then your client could be seventy.'

'I want time to research Magritte,' Jordan repeated. 'He was probably seeing frigging Freud.'

'I'm going to allow it,' Puckett said.

'What?' Barrie and Jordan spoke in unison.

'I'm going to allow it,' he said. 'You're the one who brought in an art expert, Jordan. Let Barrie give her something to cut her teeth on.'

As Jordan stalked back to his table, Barrie entered the Magritte poster into evidence. 'Do you recognize this painting?'

'Of course. It's a Magritte.'

'Magritte?'

'He was a Belgian painter,' Sandra explained. 'He did a number of variations on that particular work.' She gestured toward the image of a silhouetted man, his conservative bowler filled with clouds.

'Can you see similarities between this poster and the painting Mr McAfee asked you to examine?'

'Sure. There are clouds, although Magritte's aren't quite as stormy, which fill not only the eyes but the entire head.' Sandra smiled. 'You've gotta love Magritte.'

'Someone does,' Jordan muttered.

'Was Magritte in therapy?' Barrie asked.

'I don't know.'

'Did he receive therapy after painting this?'

'No idea.'

'Was he depressed when he painted this?'

'I couldn't say.'

Barrie turned toward the jury quizzically. 'What you're telling me, then, is that art therapy is not conclusive. You can't look at a painting and say, without a doubt, that if someone paints a realistic tongue, therefore she was sexually abused. Or if someone paints a storm where her eyes should be, therefore she is suicidal. Isn't that true, Ms Vernon?'

'Yes,' the therapist conceded.

'I have another question for you,' Barrie said. 'In art therapy, you issue a directive to a child or teenager, correct?'

'Yes. We ask them to draw a house, a person, or a scene of some kind.'

'Are most of the studies that have been done in art therapy based on directives?'

'Yes.'

'Why are you supposed to issue a directive?'

'Part of art therapy,' Sandy explained, 'involves watching

the person create. That's just as important as the finished product for divining what's troubling them.'

'Can you give us an example?'

'Sure. A girl who is asked to draw a picture of her family and who hesitates drawing the father or completely skips drawing his lower half is possibly indicating signs of sexual abuse.'

'Ms Vernon, did you see Emily Gold painting that portrait of a skull?'

'No.'

'Had you issued her a directive, to draw a self-portrait?'

'No.'

'So the fact that you are being presented with this picture now, for the first time, might change the level of certainty with which you can make assumptions about this painting?'

'I'd have to say yes.'

'Could it be possible, then, that Emily Gold was not suicidal when she did this painting, and that she was not sexually abused, and that . . . perhaps like Mr Magritte over there . . . she was only having a bad day?'

'It is possible,' Sandra said. 'But then again, this was a painting that was produced over a series of a couple of months, I'd wager. That's a heck of a lot of consecutive bad days.'

Barrie's mouth tightened at the unintended verbal slap. 'Your witness.'

'I'll redirect,' Jordan said. He stood up, walking toward the art therapist. 'You told Ms Delaney that you cannot say conclusively that any one of the disturbing things in Emily's painting proves that there's been sexual abuse or suicidal thoughts. This could be just another style she was attempting in order to get into the Sorbonne. But in your expert opinion, what's the likelihood of that?'

'Pretty slim. There's a lot of strange stuff going on in that picture. If it was just one or two things,' Sandra said, 'like a melting clock, or an apple in the middle of the face – I'd say she was trying surrealism on for size. But there's a way to show off your range without throwing in a handful of different things that raise the hackles on an art therapist's neck.'

Jordan nodded, then walked toward the exhibit table and gingerly lifted the Magritte poster by his fingertips. 'Now, I think if anything's been proven in this trial, it's my own absolute dearth of knowledge when it comes to art.' The therapist smiled at him. 'So you've definitely got me at a disadvantage here. But I'll take your word . . . and Ms Delaney's . . . that this is a Magritte.'

'Yes. He was a wonderful painter.'

Jordan scratched his head. 'I don't know. I wouldn't hang it in my house.' He turned to the jury, holding the poster up for their perusal. 'Now, even *I* know that van Gogh cut his ear off, and Picasso's faces didn't match up, and that as a group, artists are often very emotional people. Do you know if Mr Magritte was seeing a psychologist?'

'No.'

'So he might have been mentally disturbed.'

'I suppose so.'

'Might he have been sexually abused?'

'It's possible,' Sandy said.

'Unfortunately,' Jordan continued, 'I haven't had any time to do any research on Magritte, but what you're saying here is that Magritte looks, to an art therapist, like he might have had some emotional problems. Right?'

Sandy laughed. 'Sure.'

'You also told Ms Delaney that most of your studies deal with directives. Is that to say you never look at random pictures to see if there might be a problem for a particular child?'

'No, we do that every now and then.'

'A parent who's concerned might bring in a piece of artwork done by a child?'

'Yes.'

'And can you determine from those pieces of artwork if a child has a problem?'

'Often, yes.'

'When you look at non-directive-issued artwork, how often do you diagnose problems and later discover the artist did in fact need help?'

'Oh, nine out of ten times,' Sandra said. 'We're pretty discerning.'

'Unfortunately,' Jordan said, 'Emily is not here for you to give a directive to. Maybe if she was, you could have helped her. But in lieu of that, and having seen this piece of artwork, would you as a certified art therapist have been concerned about Emily's mental health?'

'Yes, I would have.'

'Nothing further.' Jordan sat down, smiling at Chris.

'I'd like to recross, Your Honor.' Barrie stepped in front of Sandra Vernon. 'You just told Mr McAfee that you occasionally do preliminary assessments from art that isn't directive-issued.'

'Yes.'

'And you said that nine out of ten pictures which have disturbing elements wind up pointing to someone with mental problems that need to be resolved.'

'Yes.'

'What about the other one?'

'Well,' Sandra said. 'He or she is usually just fine.'

Barrie smiled. 'Thank you,' she said.

Joan Bertrand was a plain, middle-aged woman whose dreamy green eyes spoke of hours spent recasting herself in the world's greatest novels or even, perhaps, with her favorite male students. Within moments of taking the stand for the defense, Chris's English teacher managed to convey that he was not only a beloved pupil, but quite possibly – in her opinion – one of next great minds of the twentieth century. Jordan gritted his teeth around a smile. Off the stand, when her only props were a chalkboard and rows of student desks, Bertrand hadn't been quite the zealot she appeared to be in a courtroom.

'What kind of student is Chris?'

Joan Bertrand clasped her hands to her heart. 'Oh, excellent. I don't think I've ever given him less than an A. He was the sort of student the faculty discussed in the teacher's lounge – you know, 'Who's got Chris Harte for social studies this term?' and things like that.'

'Was he in your class last fall?'

'Yes, for three months.'

'Mrs Bertrand, do you recognize this?' Jordan held up a neatly typed essay.

'Yes,' she said. 'Chris wrote this for Advanced Placement English. It was handed in the last week of October.'

'What was the assignment?'

'To craft an argumentative essay. I told the students to take a confrontational issue, a very hot topic, and to come down on one side of it using their own personal beliefs. They were required to state a thesis, find support for it, disprove the antithesis, and come to a conclusion.'

Jordan cleared his throat. 'I did almost as poorly in English as I did in art,' he said, full of sheepish charm. 'Could you run that by me again?'

Mrs Bertrand simpered. 'They had to take an issue, state the pros and cons, and come to a conclusion.'

'Ah,' Jordan said. 'I understand that much better.'

'Most college sophomores couldn't do this. Yet Chris did a wonderful job.'

'Could you tell us what Chris's essay was about, Mrs Bertrand?'

'Abortion.'

'And what side did he favor?'

'He was very impassioned about being pro-life.'

'Were the students required to actually believe in the issues they wrote about?'

'Yes. Some of them didn't, of course, but we met several times during writing conferences, and I can tell you from speaking to Chris that he was quite strong in his convictions.'

'Could you read, Mrs Bertrand, the part that's marked off on the bottom of page four?'

The teacher held the paper at arm's length, squinting. '"There is not really an issue about choice at all. It is against the law to cut short someone's life, and that law must apply universally. To say that a fetus is not a life is to split hairs, since most bodily systems are in place at the time most abortions are undertaken. To say that it is a woman's right to choose is also unclear, because it is not only her body but another's as well."' She glanced up, waiting.

'You're right; that is pretty clear. In your opinion, Mrs Bertrand, would Chris Harte have killed his girlfriend because he found out she was pregnant?'

'Objection,' Barrie said. 'She's an English teacher, not a mind reader.'

'I'll allow it,' Puckett answered.

Jordan glanced at Barrie. 'Would you like me to repeat that question, Mrs Bertrand? In your opinion, would Chris Harte have killed his girlfriend because he found out she was pregnant?'

'No. He never would have done that.'

Jordan flashed his dimples. 'Thanks,' he said.

Joan Bertrand stared after him. 'No problem,' she sighed.

Barrie stood up immediately. 'Unlike Mr McAfee,' she said, 'I used to love English. It sounds like Chris did, too. And that he was certainly one of your favorite students.'

'Oh, yes.'

'You can't imagine him doing something as horrible as committing murder.'

'Absolutely not.'

'And, of course, based on that very impressive essay, you can't imagine him taking a baby's life, or shooting his girlfriend in cold blood?'

'No, I can't imagine him killing anyone.'

'Not even himself?'

'Oh,' Mrs Bertrand shook her head vigorously. 'Certainly not.'

'Well. Let me just recap, then.' Barrie began counting off on her fingers. 'He wouldn't have taken a life. He wouldn't have taken Emily's life, he wouldn't have let Emily take her own life, and he certainly wouldn't have killed himself. But on the other hand, we have a dead body; we have a confession from Chris saying that Emily was going to kill herself and then he was going to do the same thing; and we have all sorts of evidence placing Chris at the scene of the crime.' She tipped her head to the side. 'So, Mrs Bertrand. What's your theory?'

'Objection!' Jordan roared.

'Withdrawn,' Barrie said.

During lunch, Chris was taken downstairs to the sheriff's office. Jordan brought him a turkey sandwich and ate his own on a folding chair outside the cell. 'I felt bad for her,' Chris said, his mouth full. 'Mrs Bertrand.'

'She's a nice lady.'

'Yeah. Unlike the prosecutor.'

Jordan shrugged. 'Different jobs call for different styles,' he said. 'I was just as cutthroat as she was when I was an AG.'

Chris smiled faintly. 'You mean, as opposed to now, when you've gone all soft.'

'Hey,' Jordan said, holding his hand up to the bars of the lockup. 'You're not starting to doubt me, are you?' When Chris didn't answer, Jordan snorted. 'O ye of little faith.'

At that, Chris looked up, quite serious. 'I have faith,' he said, 'I'm just not sure in what.' He set his unfinished sandwich into the foil and balled it up, discarded. 'What happens,' he asked, 'if I'm found guilty?'

Jordan met his gaze. 'You'll have a sentencing hearing,' he said. 'And based on that, you'll be transported down to Concord.'

Chris nodded. 'And that's it.'

'No. We'll appeal the decision.'

'Which could take forever, and go nowhere.'

Jordan looked down at his sandwich, which suddenly tasted like sawdust, and did not say anything.

'You know, it's funny,' Chris said. 'You don't want honesty from me. And all I want is honesty from you.' He turned away, running his thumbnail over the bars of the cell. 'But I don't think either of us is all too damn happy with what we're getting.'

'Chris,' Jordan said, 'I'm not giving out false hope. But your two best witnesses are still to come.'

'And then what, Jordan?'

His attorney stared at him, face perfectly blank. 'I don't know.'

There was a slight hubbub in the afternoon when Stephanie Newell took the stand, and someone sitting in the back row of the courtroom threw a rotten tomato that landed square on her blouse, yelling, 'Murderer!' before he ran out the door. Following a minor recess, during which Stephanie was given a clean shirt and the police were called in to deal with the small-scale anti-abortion display, the court reconvened. By the time Stephanie Newell actually got on the witness stand and stated her credentials, most of the jury had already deduced that Emily Gold had come to Planned Parenthood looking for an abortion.

'I was the counselor,' she said, 'assigned to Emily's case.'

'Do you have a file on her?' Jordan asked.

'Yes.'

'When did you meet with Emily?'

'I first met with her on October second.'

'What did you do at that meeting?'

'I held a preliminary interview with Emily, and explained the results of the positive pregnancy test and her options.'

'When was your next meeting?'

'October tenth. We require a pre-abortion counseling session, and the abortion is paid for at that time. We also ask if someone will be there to help the woman through the procedure.'

'Like the father of the child?'

'Exactly. Or, in the case of a teen, her parents. But Emily indicated that her parents were not supportive, that she hadn't told the father about the baby, and that she didn't want to.'

'How did you respond to that?'

'I told her that she should tell the father, if only so that she had someone to lean on.'

'And when did the two of you next meet?'

'October eleventh. That was the date that the abortion was scheduled. The counselor is present to offer support before, during, and afterward.'

Jordan walked toward the jury box. 'Did the abortion take place?'

'No, something upset Emily and she decided against having the procedure.'

Jordan leaned both elbows against the railing. 'Was that strange?'

'Oh, no. It actually happens quite a lot. People back out at the very last minute all the time.'

'What did you do after she decided not to abort the baby?'

Stephanie sighed. 'I counseled her to tell the father.'

'What was her reaction?'

'She got even more upset, so I dropped the subject,' Stephanie said.

'When was the last time you met with Emily Gold, Ms Newell?'

'On November seventh, the afternoon before she died.'

'Why did you see her that day?'

'We had previously scheduled the appointment.'

'Was Emily Gold upset about something that day?'

'Objection,' Barrie said. 'Speculative.'

'Overruled,' Puckett said.

'Did Emily Gold seem upset to you?' Jordan rephrased.

'Very much so,' Stephanie said.

'Did she tell you why?'

'She said she felt like she'd run out of options. She didn't know what to do about the baby.'

'What did you tell her?'

'I reiterated that she should talk to the father. That he might offer more support than she expected.'

'How much time did you spend talking about whether or not she should tell the father?' Jordan asked.

'Most of the session . . . an hour.'

'In your opinion, when she left that office, was she going to tell the father about the baby?'

'No. Nothing I said could make her change her mind.'

'During the five weeks you met with her, did Emily at any time waver about whether or not she was going to tell the father about the baby?'

'No.'

'Do you have any reason to believe that she would have changed her mind after that last session?'

'No, I don't.'

Jordan sat down. 'Your witness,' he said.

Barrie walked toward the witness box. 'Ms Newell, you met with Emily on November seventh?'

'Yes.'

'What time?'

'She had a four o'clock appointment. From four to five.'

'Are you aware that Emily Gold's death occurred sometime between eleven and midnight that night?'

'Yes.'

'Between five and eleven is, let's see . . .' Barrie tapped her chin. 'Six hours. Were you with Emily during that time?'

'No, I wasn't.'

'Did you ever meet Chris?'

'No.'

'Were you party to any of their conversations together during the six hours before she died?'

'No.'

'So, Ms Newell,' Barrie said, 'is it possible that Emily did decide to tell Chris about the baby, after all?'

'Well . . . yes, I guess so.'

'Thank you,' the prosecutor said.

Michael Gold walked to the stand with all the enthusiasm of a condemned man. He kept his eyes trained on the judge, deliberately refusing to see either Melanie, on his left, or James Harte, on his right. As soon as he was seated, his hand on the Bible, he looked at Chris. And he thought, *I am doing this for you.*

In his heart, he could not imagine Chris murdering his daughter. The prosecution could have shown Michael a smoking gun with Chris's hand still on it, and he'd have had trouble believing it. But there was a small seed of doubt in his mind, one with the potential to grow to enormous proportions, which asked, *How do you know?* And he didn't. No one did but Chris, and Emily, and it was possible that Chris had done the unthinkable. Which was why he would not give Jordan McAfee what he wanted.

Michael and Jordan had met four nights ago to go over his testimony. 'If you tell the jury outright that Chris did not kill your daughter,' Jordan had said, 'then Chris will have a fighting chance.'

Michael had politely agreed to think about it. *But what if?* that little voice had said. *What if?*

He stared, now, at the boy his daughter had loved. The boy who'd made a baby with her. And he silently apologized for what he would not say.

'Mr Gold,' Jordan said gently, 'thank you for being here today.' Michael nodded. 'It must seem strange to be testifying for the defense,' he added. 'After all, this is a murder trial, and the defendant is accused of killing your daughter.'

'I know.'

'Can I ask you why you decided to testify today, for the defense?'

Michael licked his lips, his brain mechanically shuffling forth the answer he'd practiced with Jordan. 'Because I knew Chris every bit as well as I knew my daughter.'

'I'll be brief, Mr Gold, and I'll try to make this as painless as possible. Could you describe your relationship with Emily?'

'I was very close to her. She was my only child.'

'Tell us about Chris. How did you know him?'

Michael's eyes touched on Chris, sitting very still in his chair. 'I've known him since the day he was born.'

'What was the age difference between Chris and Emily?'

'Six months. In fact Chris's mother helped deliver Emily – I was a little late. Chris was in the hospital room with my daughter before I was.'

'And you watched them grow up together?'

'Oh, yeah. They were inseparable, from the first day they shared a bassinet. Chris used to be underfoot in our house just as much, I guess, as Emily used to be underfoot at the Hartes'.'

'When did they move from being friends to . . . something more?'

'They started dating when Emily was thirteen.'

'How did you feel about that?' Jordan asked.

Michael picked at the sleeve of his sportsjacket. 'How does any father feel about that?' he mused. 'I was protective; she was always going to be my little girl. But I couldn't think of anyone else I'd rather have Emily explore all that with. It was going to happen at some point, and I knew and trusted Chris. I certainly trusted him with the most important thing in my life – my daughter. In fact I'd been trusting him with her for years, by then.'

'What was your perception of their relationship?'

'They were very, very close. More so than the average teenager, I think. They confided in each other all the time. God . . . I can't think of anything Emily didn't tell Chris. He was her best friend, and she was his, and if that was moving onto a slightly more adult level, it was probably time for it.'

'How much time did she spend with Chris?'

'Hours.' Michael smiled faintly. 'Every waking minute, it sometimes seemed.'

'Would it be fair to say that Chris saw Emily more than you did?'

'Yes.' He grinned. 'I guess I saw her about as much as any parent sees a teenager.'

Jordan laughed. 'I know what you mean, I've got one of them at home. At least I hope he's at home.' He walked toward the witness stand. 'So you didn't see Emily all that often, time-wise, but you still felt very close to her?'

'Absolutely. We always ate breakfast together, and we'd talk the whole time.'

Jordan softened the edges of his voice. 'Mr Gold, did you know that Emily was sexually active?'

Michael turned red. 'I . . . maybe I suspected it. But I don't think any father really wants to know that.'

'Was it something Emily discussed with you?'

'No. I think it would have made her as uncomfortable as it makes me.'

Jordan reached toward the railing of the witness stand, bridging the distance between himself and Michael. 'Did she tell you she was pregnant?'

'I had no idea.'

'To your knowledge, did she tell your wife?'

'No.'

'She was very close to you and your wife, but she didn't tell you?'

'No.' Michael looked up at Jordan, offering the smallest gift he could. 'I think it was the sort of thing Emily wouldn't have told anyone.'

'So Emily didn't mention her pregnancy. Did she tell you she was depressed?'

'No, she didn't.' Michael swallowed, knowing it was coming to this. 'And I didn't notice it myself.'

'You didn't see her all that often because she was with Chris—'

'I know,' Michael said, his voice hollow. 'But that doesn't work as an excuse. She hadn't been eating very much; and she was under a great deal of stress, with college applications and everything. And I thought . . . I thought that there was just a lot going on in her life.' He reached for a glass of water set out for the witness and took a sip, blotting his lips with the back of his hand. 'I keep thinking,' he said softly, 'that I'm going to find a note. One that I can use to make myself feel better. But I haven't.

'It hurts to lose my daughter. It hurts more than anything else has ever hurt in my life. And because it hurts so much, it's very tempting to pass the blame. It makes it much easier for me, for my wife . . . for any parent out there who this might happen to in the future, if we say, "Oh, there were no signs to see. She wasn't suicidal; she was murdered."' Michael turned to the jury. 'A father ought to be able to tell that his daughter's suicidal, right? Or even depressed? But I didn't. If I can point a finger at someone else, then it's not my fault that I didn't notice; that I wasn't looking closely.' He raked one hand through his silver hair. 'I don't know what happened at the carousel that night. But I do know that I can't accuse someone else, just so that I won't feel guilty.'

Jordan let out the breath he'd been holding. Gold had given more than he'd expected, and – feeling optimistic – he decided to push a little. 'Mr Gold,' he said, 'we have two scenarios here: murder or suicide. Neither is something you want to believe, but the fact remains that somehow, some way, your daughter is dead.'

'Objection,' Barrie said. 'Is there a question before the witness?'

'I'm getting to the point, Your Honor. Give me some leeway.'

'Overruled,' Puckett said.

Jordan turned back to Michael. 'You say you knew Chris as well as you knew Emily. Having known Chris his whole life – and as a long-term witness to Chris and Emily's relationship – was it murder, or was it suicide?'

Michael held his head in his hands. 'I don't know. I just don't know.'

Jordan stared at him. 'What *do* you know, Mr Gold?'

There was a long silence. 'That Chris wouldn't have wanted

to live without my daughter,' Michael said finally. 'And that even though he's sitting over there, he's not the only one who should be judged.'

Barrie Delaney did not like Michael Gold. She had not liked him at her first meeting, when he seemed absolutely incapable of grasping the fact that all the evidence pointed to the boy next door offing his own daughter. She liked him even less when she'd found out that he was testifying for the defense. And now, after his self-flagellation on the stand, she absolutely couldn't stand him.

'Mr Gold,' she said, oozing false sympathy, 'I am so sorry you have to be here today.'

'So am I, Ms Delaney.'

She crossed in front of the witness stand, until she was aligned at the edge of the jury box. 'You said you were very close to Emily,' she said.

'Yes.'

'You also said you didn't spend as much time with your daughter as Chris did.' Michael nodded. 'You said you didn't know she was upset.'

'No.'

'You didn't know she was pregnant.'

'No,' Michael admitted. 'I didn't.'

'You also said she told Chris everything.'

'Yes.'

'You couldn't imagine anything Emily didn't tell Chris.'

'That's right.'

'So she would have told Chris she was pregnant, correct?'

'I . . . I don't know.'

'Yes or no?'

'Yes, I guess.'

Barrie nodded. 'Mr Gold, you said that you came here because you know Chris Harte so well.'

'That's right.'

'But this trial is about your daughter, and what happened

to her. Either she committed suicide, or she was murdered. It's a horrific choice, just as Mr McAfee said. It's terrible that it has to be your next-door neighbor who stands charged; and it's even more terrible that it's your daughter who is dead, but the fact is the jury has those two choices, Mr Gold. And so do you.' She took a deep breath. 'Can you actually see your daughter picking up a gun, holding it to her head, and pulling the trigger?'

Michael closed his eyes, doing what the prosecutor asked, for the sake of Emily and his wife and that strident voice inside his head. He imagined Emily's beautiful face, amber eyes drifting shut, the gun nuzzling her temple. He imagined a hand wrapped around that gun with confidence, with despair, with pain. But he could not say for sure that it was Emily's.

He felt tears streak from the corners of his eyes, and he curled slightly on the stand, as if to protect himself.

'Mr Gold?' the prosecutor prompted.

'No,' he whispered. He shook his head, the tears coming faster now. 'No.'

Barrie Delaney turned to the jury. 'Then what,' she asked, 'are we left with?'

The act of changing from his trial clothes to his prison uniform seemed to Chris a shedding of skin, as if in peeling off the blazer and natty trousers he also removed a layer of civility and social grace, leaving him raw and primal back in his cell. For the first hour after returning from the courthouse, Chris wouldn't speak to anyone, and other inmates were careful not to approach him. He had to breathe in the stale air of the jail until it was all that filled his lungs, cramp himself to his accommodations, and only then could he move with the sure footing and indifference he'd cultivated after seven months in prison.

He ventured into the day room of the medium security unit, aware of a buzz and disquietude. Several of the other men cast furtive glances in his direction, then looked at the TV or the walls or the row of lockers. Chris had been there long enough to know that people left you alone during your trial, but this went deeper. They were not *ignoring* him; they were keeping a secret.

He walked over to a table surrounded by men. 'What?' he said simply.

'Man, didn't you hear? Vernon hung himself at the State Pen last night. With a friggin' pair of shoelaces.'

Chris shook his head to clear it. 'He what?'

'He's dead, man.'

'No.' Chris backed away from the knot of inmates watching him. 'No.' He walked swiftly to the cell he'd shared with Steve a month earlier.

He could bring Steve's face to mind more easily now than he could Emily's. He thought of what Steve had said before he was transferred, about what they did in Concord to convicts who'd killed children.

By the end of the week, Chris could be heading to the state prison, too.

He burrowed beneath his blankets, shaking quietly with grief and fear until he heard himself being paged to Control to meet a visitor.

Gus threw her arms around Chris the minute he came close enough for her to do so. 'Jordan tells me it's going well,' she enthused. 'Couldn't be better.'

'You're not there,' Chris said stiffening. 'And what's he supposed to say? That you're not getting your money's worth?'

'Well,' Gus said, settling into her bridge chair. 'He has no reason to lie.'

Chris bent his head, massaging his temples. 'Saint Jordan,' he muttered.

There was nobody else in the visiting room. Usually Gus arrived earlier, but with the trial she'd had to get home to Kate and make dinner before she struck off again to visit Chris. Chris, who seemed awfully agitated. Gus peered at him curiously. 'Are you all right?' she asked.

He rubbed his eyes, and blinked up at her. 'Fine,' he said.

'Peachy.' He started to drum his fingertips on the table, and looked at the officer posted by the stairs.

'Jordan says I'm the star witness,' Gus said. 'He told me that the jury's going to ride my emotion all the way to a not guilty verdict.'

Chris jerked. 'Sounds like something he'd say.'

'You seem very edgy tonight,' Gus said. 'But from all accounts, Michael helped you tremendously today. Jordan's done a remarkable job up to this point. And certainly you know I'd do handsprings to get you free, Chris.'

'What I'm saying, Mom,' Chris answered, 'is that the jury may not want to see your handsprings. That they've already made up their minds.'

'That's crazy. That's not the way the system works.'

'What do you know about the way the system works? Is it right that I've been in jail for nearly a year, just waiting for a trial? Is it right that my lawyer's never once asked me, *Hey, Chris. What really happened*?' He leveled cold blue eyes on his mother. 'Have you thought about it, Mom? This trial's going to be over in a day. Have you thought about what color you're going to paint my room when they take me away for the rest of my life? About what I'm going to look like, at forty and fifty and sixty, when I've been living in a room the size of a closet all those years?'

He was quivering by the time he finished, and there was a wildness to his gaze that Gus recognized as the edge of panic. 'Chris,' she soothed, 'that isn't going to happen.'

'How do you know?' he cried. 'How the hell do you know?'

From the corner of her eye, Gus saw the officer take a step toward them. She shook her head slightly, and he resumed his post at the stairs. Then she gently touched Chris's arm, carefully masking her own fear at seeing her son red-faced and trembling. She realized what a strain it must be to be eighteen, and listening to strangers decide your life. It was just as James had told her: Chris was wearing a mask in the courtroom. Simply being able to sit there without breaking down spoke volumes about his determination, and his character. 'Sweetheart,' she said, 'I can understand why this is so frightening—'

'No you can't!'

'I can. I'm your mother. I know you.'

Chris's head swiveled toward her slowly, a bull about to charge. 'Oh?' he said. 'And what do you know?'

'I know that you're the same wonderful son I've always loved. I know that you're going to get through this, like you've gotten through everything else. And I know that the jury isn't going to convict someone who's innocent.'

Chris was shaking so hard at this point that Gus's hand fell away from his shoulder. 'What you don't know, Mom,' he said softly, 'is that I shot Emily.' And with a muffled cry, he turned and fled up the stairs to the guards who would safely lock him away.

Gus made it through signing out at the control booth, past the officer who unlocked the jail door, and all the way to her car before she fell to her knees in the parking lot and threw up. *I'm your mother*, she had said. I know you. But apparently, she hadn't. She wiped her mouth on the sleeve of her jacket and slid behind the wheel of the car, blindly fumbling the keys into the ignition before realizing she was in no condition to drive. Chris had said it, clear as day. He shot Emily. And while Gus had defended him from gossip and slander and even his father's indifference, she had been playing the fool.

Small darts stabbed at her mind: Chris's shirt at the hospital, covered with blood; Chris's reluctance to talk to Dr Feinstein; Chris admitting with relief that he'd never been suicidal. She rested her forehead against the steering wheel and moaned softly. Chris, oh, God, Chris had killed Emily.

How could she not have seen through him?

She put the car into gear and drove slowly out of the parking lot of the jail. She would go home and tell James and he'd know what to do . . . no, she couldn't tell James, because then he would tell Jordan McAfee, and even Gus's rudimentary knowledge of criminal defense told her that would be a bad idea. She would go home and pretend that she had never come to visit her son that night. In the morning, everything would look different.

And then she'd be put on the witness stand.

It struck Gus as strange that in the legal system, there was an immunity that could protect you from testifying against your husband, but there was nothing that you could hold up as a shield to keep you from testifying against your child. Odd, since a child was the one who had your smile, or your eyes, or at the very least, your blood running through its veins. Gus would have been ten times more likely to give evidence against James than Chris. And it was not a matter of perjury, in her battered mind, but motherhood.

She was wearing a garnet-colored dress whose gathered sleeves only set off the fact that she was trembling uncontrollably. Gus had fixed a smile on her face, certain that if she even let her lips relax from their rictus the slightest bit, she would blurt out what she knew. She stood outside the double doors of the courtroom, having been told by Jordan that she'd be the first – and only – witness called that day. The bailiff stood across from her, impassive.

Suddenly the door opened, and she was led down the courtroom aisle. She kept her eyes on her feet the whole way. As she sat down in the small box, she thought, *How much bigger is the one they'll lock Chris in for life?*

She knew that Jordan had wanted her to look at Chris as soon as she was seated, but she kept her gaze trained on her lap. She could feel her son, a magnetic pull toward her left, his nerves jangling nearly as loudly as hers. But if she lifted her eyes to his, she knew that she'd start to cry.

Suddenly a thick, worn Bible was thrust before her. The clerk of the court instructed her to place her left hand on it and raise her right. 'Do you swear to tell the truth, the whole truth, and nothing but the truth, so help you God?'

So help you God. For the first time since entering the court-room, Gus locked her gaze with her son's. 'Yes,' she said, in a voice that carried. 'I do.'

Jordan didn't know what the hell had happened to Gus Harte. Every time he'd seen her – Christ, even the night her son was carted off by the local police with an arrest warrant – she'd seemed self-possessed and beautiful. Slightly wild and natural, with that tumble of strawberry curls, but lovely all the same. Today, however, on the one day he'd needed her to be perfect, she was a total mess. Her hair was straggling from a hasty braid; her face was pale and pinched without makeup; her fingernails were bitten to the quick.

Being a witness affected everyone differently. Some people grandstanded. Some seemed in awe of the system. Most settled down to the task with a suitable amount of reverence. Gus Harte only looked like she wanted to be anywhere else but there.

Squaring his shoulders, Jordan walked toward her. 'Could you state your name and address for the record?'

Gus leaned toward the microphone. 'Augusta Harte,' she said. 'Thirty-four Wood Hollow Road, Bainbridge.'

'And could you tell us how you know Chris?'

'I'm his mother.'

Jordan turned his back to the jury and Barrie Delaney and smiled at Gus, hoping to loosen her up. *Relax*, he mouthed silently. 'Mrs Harte, tell us about your son.'

Gus's eyes darted nervously around the courtroom. On one side she saw Melanie, with her stone face, and Michael, his hands clenched on his knees. On the other side was James, who was nodding at her slightly. Her mouth opened and closed silently. 'Chris is – he's a very good swimmer,' she finally said, and Jordan wheeled about.

'A good swimmer?'

'He holds the school record for the two-hundred-meter butterfly,' she rambled, 'We're very proud of him. His father and I.'

.Jordan advanced on her before she could stray farther from their planned testimony. 'In your opinion, would you say he's responsible? Trustworthy?'

He could sense Barrie behind him, her confusion palpable as she considered whether or not to object to Jordan leading his star witness. 'Oh, yes,' Gus said nervously, looking into her lap. 'Chris always acted well beyond his years. I would trust him with my—' She stopped abruptly. 'With my life,' she finished.

'You knew Emily Gold,' Jordan said, baffled by now, but knowing he had to stop Gus from saying things the jury did not need to hear. 'For how long?'

'Oh,' Gus said softly. Her eyes sought Melanie's, in the gallery. 'I was Melanie Gold's labor coach. I saw Emily before her own mother did.'

Thank God, Jordan thought. 'How long did the Golds live next door?'

'For eighteen years,' Gus said. 'Chris and Emily spent most of those years joined at the hip.'

'By that, you mean they were never apart?'

'Yes,' Gus said evenly. 'They might as well have been twins.' *Then what happened?* she thought, the question reverberating in her mind. 'They used to have their own language, and sneak out of the house to see each other, and—'

Then what happened?

'—stick up for each other—'

Jordan nodded. 'You were close to Emily's parents, too?'

'We were very good friends,' Gus said thickly. 'Like an extended family. Chris and Em grew up like brother and sister.'

'When did Chris and Emily become boyfriend and girlfriend?'

'Chris was fourteen,' Gus said.

'Did you and the Golds encourage this relationship?'

'We asked for it,' she murmured.

'Do you think Chris loved Emily?'

'I know he did,' Gus said firmly. 'I know.' But she was

thinking of what she had felt with Michael, even as she was drawn to him – that need to pull away flaring just as strong. And she was wondering if maybe you could not go from brother and sister to boyfriend and girlfriend, add that much more love and commitment, without feeling too close for comfort. *Is that what happened?*

Jordan narrowed his eyes as he suddenly pinpointed what was the matter with this very odd testimony: Gus wasn't looking at Chris – in fact, she seemed reluctant to do so, which was something the jury would certainly notice. 'Mrs Harte,' Jordan said. 'Can you look at your son for me?'

Gus slowly turned her head. She took a deep breath and resolutely stared at Chris, quickly pinching away the tears at the corners of her eyes. 'This boy,' Jordan continued. 'This son you've known for eighteen years. Would he ever have hurt Emily Gold?'

'No,' Gus whispered, her gaze sliding away from her son. She swiped the tears away quickly with the back of her hand. 'No,' she repeated shakily.

She felt Chris's eyes on her, begging her to look at him. So she lifted her face to his, and saw what the jury could not: his eyes tortured and his mouth tight with pain, as he watched his mother lie for him.

'I know how hard this is for you, Mrs Harte.' Jordan walked over to the witness stand, his hand on her arm, tender and solicitous. 'I only have one more question. In your opinion—'

Gus knew what was coming. She'd rehearsed it with Jordan McAfee; she'd lived it a thousand times the night before. She closed her eyes, anticipating the actual words that would make her forsworn.

'*No.*'

At the rough, broken voice, Gus's eyes snapped open. Jordan turned, as did the judge and the prosecutor, to stare at Chris Harte. 'Stop. Just stop it.'

Judge Puckett's brows beetled together. 'Mr McAfee,' he said, 'would you control your client?'

Jordan crossed the courtroom and firmly grasped Chris's arm, his back to the jury. 'What the hell are you doing?'

'Jordan,' Chris said urgently, 'I need to talk to you.'

'I have one question left. Then I'll call a recess. All right?'

'No. I have to talk to you now.'

Jordan took a deep breath and raised his head, seemingly smooth, years of training giving him the ability to mask how absolutely furious he was. 'Your Honor, may I approach the bench?'

Barrie, completely in the dark, walked up to the judge beside him. 'Look,' Jordan said. 'My client is telling me he has to talk to me immediately. Could we take a short recess?'

Puckett frowned. 'This damn well better be crucial,' he said. 'You've got five minutes.'

Jordan found them a small room in the courthouse not much bigger than Chris's cell. 'Okay,' he said, clearly angry. 'What's this all about?'

'I don't want my mother on the stand anymore,' Chris said.

'Too damn bad,' Jordan spat. 'She's the best defense you've got.'

'Take her off.'

'There's only one question left, Chris. The jury has to hear your mother say that she can't possibly imagine her son killing Emily Gold.'

Chris glared at Jordan, as if the attorney had never spoken. 'I want you to take her off the stand,' he said, 'and put me on.'

For a moment, Jordan was speechless. 'You get on that stand, and you'll lose this case,' he said.

Defense attorneys did not, as a rule, put their clients on the stand. It was too easy for a prosecutor to trip up a defendant, or twist words around. Just one anxious misstep – one nervous glance – and even the most innocent defendant would look like a liar to a jury.

Putting Chris on the stand, though, was absolutely out of

the question for a different reason. By his own admission, Chris hadn't wanted to kill himself. Any half-decent prosecutor would be able to get that out of him. And Jordan's entire defense strategy had been predicated on an interrupted double suicide. Yet Jordan had a sick, sinking feeling that telling his own story was exactly what Chris wanted to do.

'You get up there,' Jordan said, a vein throbbing in his temple, 'you go to prison. It's that simple. You're a witness, you have to tell the truth. I've spent four days telling everyone you wanted to blow your brains out, and you're going to go up there and start telling everyone you weren't going to kill yourself and then what the hell happens to my defense?'

For a moment Chris did not say anything. Then he turned, speaking so quietly Jordan had to strain to hear him. 'Seven months ago, you told me the decision to testify was mine, and mine alone. You told me that if I wanted to go on the stand, you had to put me up there by law.'

They stared at each other, a stalemate. Then Jordan broke away, holding his hands up. 'Fine,' he said. 'Fuck it.' And he walked out of the room.

He almost collided with Selena. 'What the hell,' she asked, 'is going on?'

Jordan took Selena's arm and drew her a distance from some of the onlookers whose heads were turned their way. 'He wants to take the stand.'

Selena sucked in her breath. 'What did you tell him?'

'That I'd be the first to wish him well at the state prison.' He threw back his head. 'Jesus Christ, Selena. We had a fighting chance.'

'You had better than a fighting chance,' she said softly.

'I might as well just bring him in to Delaney and tell her it's an early Christmas present.'

Selena shook her head sympathetically. 'Why does he want to do this?' she asked. 'And why now?'

'He's discovered his conscience. He's seen God. Shit, I don't know.' Jordan buried his hands in his hair. 'He wants to tell the jury that he wasn't going to kill himself. He doesn't want his mother to do it for him. The fact that it makes me and the whole defense look ludicrous is beside the point.'

'You really think that's what he's going to say?' Selena asked.

Jordan snorted. 'For God's sake,' he muttered. 'What could be worse than that?'

He walked back into the room, where Chris was calmly sitting, and slapped a piece of paper onto the table. 'Sign this,' he snapped.

'What is it?'

'It's a waiver. It says that you're willingly about to screw yourself even though I told you not to, so that I don't get sued when you appeal to the Supreme Court for ineffective assistance of counsel. You may be willing to put your ass on the line, Chris, but I'm not.'

Chris picked up the pen that Jordan handed him and scrawled his name.

The court was a living thing, vibrating with rumors and questions as Jordan stood up to face Gus Harte on the stand for the second time. 'Thank you,' he said abruptly. 'No further questions.'

It was almost worth it, he thought, to see Barrie's face when he did that. The prosecutor knew – as did Jordan – it did no good to put the defendant's mother on the stand without trying to get her to state that Chris would never have killed Emily.

Stupefied, Barrie got to her feet. She'd been willing to bet her salary, however meager, that the reason Chris had leaped to his feet was because he had one terrific question for Jordan to put to his mother, or why else would he have stopped the direct examination right in the middle? She walked gingerly toward the witness stand, fully aware that she was treading through a minefield, and wondered what the hell she was supposed to get out of a cross.

Well, she thought, *I might as well do it for McAfee.* 'Mrs Harte,' she said, 'you're the defendant's mother?'

'Yes.'

'You don't want to see him go to jail, do you?'

'Of course not.'

'It would be pretty hard for any mother to imagine her son would kill anyone, don't you think?'

Gus nodded, and sniffed loudly. Barrie glanced up sharply, aware that one more question might send the witness off the deep end again, and make Barrie look like a dragon. She opened her mouth, and then closed it. 'No further questions,' she said, and quickly walked back to her seat.

Gus Harte was escorted from the witness stand, and Barrie busied herself with her notes. Jordan would say that the defense rested, and then it was up to her to drive home her verdict with a closing argument. Which, she had to admit, would be gravy after that last witness. She could hear her own voice, ringing with conviction. *And his own mother . . . Chris Harte's own mother . . . could not even look at him during her testimony.*

'Your Honor,' Jordan said, 'we have one more witness.'

'You what?' Barrie exclaimed, but Jordan was already calling Christopher Harte to the stand.

'Objection!' Barrie sputtered.

Judge Puckett sighed. 'Counsel, meet in chambers. Bring the defendant.'

They followed the judge into his offices, Chris hanging back. Barrie began speaking before the door had even fully shut. 'This is a total surprise, Your Honor. I was given no notice that this was going to happen today.'

'Yeah, well, you're not the only one,' Jordan said sourly.

'Would you like a recess, Barrie?' Puckett asked.

'No,' she muttered. 'But a little more courtesy would have been nice.'

As if she hadn't spoken, Jordan slapped the waiver down in front of the judge. 'I told him I don't want him to take the stand, and that it could ruin his defense.'

Judge Puckett glanced at Chris. 'Mr Harte, has your lawyer explained the full ramifications of what taking the stand means for you in your case?'

'He has, Your Honor.'

'And you signed this form here saying that your lawyer did indeed explain this to you?'

'I have.'

'All right,' the judge shrugged. He led the small entourage back into the courtroom.

'The defense,' said Jordan, 'calls Christopher Harte to the stand.'

Jordan moved in front of the defense table, advancing on his client. He could see the jury, sitting on the edge of their seats. And Barrie, who looked like the cat that had swallowed the canary, and why shouldn't she? She could cross-examine Chris in Swahili and still win this case.

'Chris,' Jordan said, 'are you aware you are on trial for the murder of Emily Gold?'

'Yes.'

'Can you tell us how you felt about Emily Gold?'

'I loved her more than anything in the whole world.'

Chris's voice was clear and steady; Jordan had to admire the kid. It wasn't easy to get up in front of a courtroom that had probably already sentenced you in their minds and offer up your own version of the story. 'How long had you known her?'

Everything about Chris softened: the lines of his body, the edges of his words. 'I knew Emily her whole life.'

Jordan wildly wondered where to go from there. His objective, for what it was worth, was to forestall the blow. 'What were your earliest memories?'

'Objection,' Barrie called. 'Do we really have to sit through eighteen years of this?'

Judge Puckett nodded. 'Let's get on with it, counselor.'

'Can you tell me about your relationship with Emily?'

'Do you know,' Chris said softly, 'what it's like to love someone so much, that you can't see yourself without picturing her? Or what it's like to touch someone, and feel like you've come home?' He made a fist, and rested it in the palm of his other hand. 'What we had wasn't about sex, or about being with someone just to show off what you've got, the way it was for other kids our age. We were, well, meant to be together. Some people spend their whole lives looking for that one person,' he said. 'I was lucky enough to have her all along.'

Jordan stared at Chris, stunned into silence by his speech, like everyone else in the courtroom. This was not the tone of an eighteen-year-old. This was someone older, wiser, sadder.

'Was Emily suicidal?' he asked suddenly.

'Yes,' Chris answered.

'Can you tell us, Chris, what happened on the night of November seventh?'

Chris lowered his eyes. 'It was the night Emily wanted to kill herself. I got the gun, like she asked me to. I drove her to the carousel. We talked for a while, and... whatever.' His voice drifted off, and Jordan watched him carefully, aware that he was back at the carousel again, back with Emily. 'And then,' Chris said quietly, lifting his gaze to his attorney's, 'I shot her.'

The courtroom erupted, reporters running for their cell phones and Melanie Gold shouting and pointing a finger as her husband, pale and silent, dragged her away. 'I need a recess, Your Honor,' Jordan said tightly, and physically hauled Chris off the witness stand and out of the courtroom. Barrie Delaney laughed out loud. Gus sat very still, tears running unchecked down her cheeks. Beside her, James was rocking slightly back and forth, whispering, 'Oh, God. Oh, my God.' After a minute, he turned to Gus and reached for her hand, but what he saw in her face stopped him. 'You knew,' he whispered.

Gus bowed her head, unable to admit it, equally unable to deny.

She expected to feel a slight rush of the air beside her as

James vacated his seat to pace, to think, to just get the hell away. But instead, she felt his hand, warm and firm, steal around hers. And she held on for dear life.

Back in the tiny vestibule, Jordan sat with his head in his hands. He did not move, or speak, for a full sixty seconds. When he began to talk, his head was still lowered. 'Is this about getting an appeal?' he said evenly. 'Or do you just have a death wish?'

'Neither,' Chris said.

'You want to tell me, then, what's going on?'

Jordan's voice was soft, too soft for the roiling emotions in his head. He wanted to throttle Christopher Harte for making him look like an idiot, not once, but twice. He wanted to kick himself for being such a smartass and not asking Chris ten minutes ago what he was going to say on the stand. And he wanted to slap the grin off the prosecutor's face, because she knew and he knew who was going to win.

'I wanted to tell you before,' Chris said. 'You just didn't want to listen.'

'Well, since you've fucked everything up royally, you might as well tell me everything.' At the very outrageousness of that, Jordan laughed. For the first time in ten years, maybe longer, he was going to be forced to salvage a case with the truth. Because it was absolutely all he had left.

He had learned long ago that the truth did not belong in a courtroom. No one – not the prosecutor, and more often, not the defendant – wanted it there. Trials were about evidence, counter-evidence, and theories. Not what had actually occurred. But the evidence and counter-evidence and theories had all just gone down the toilet. And the only thing Jordan had to fly with was this kid, this stupid kid, who felt honor bound to tell the world what had really happened.

Fifteen minutes later, Jordan and Chris left the small room, shoulder to shoulder. Neither one of them was smiling. Neither one of them spoke. They walked quickly, their strides parting the crowds who had heard the rumors and who stared after them with their mouths gaping. At the door of the courtroom, Jordan turned to Chris. 'Whatever I do, go along with it. Whatever I say, just play along.' He saw Chris hesitate. 'You owe me this,' he hissed.

Chris nodded, and together they pushed open the door.

It was so quiet in the courtroom that Chris could hear his own pulse. He was back on the witness stand, his hands sweating and shaking so badly he had to tuck them beneath his thighs. He had looked at his parents only once; his mother had been smiling weakly and nodding at him. His father – well, his father was still there.

He did not let himself look at Emily's parents, although he could feel their fury, poker-hot, all the way from the gallery.

He was very, very tired. The weave of the sportsjacket was scratchy through the thin oxford cloth shirt, and his new shoes had rubbed a blister on his heel. His head felt like it was going to burst.

And then, suddenly, he heard Emily's voice. Clear, calm, familiar. She was telling him everything would be all right, saying that she wouldn't leave him. Chris glanced around wildly, trying to gauge if everyone else could hear this, too, hoping to see her, even as he felt a stillness stroke over his heart.

'Chris,' Jordan said again, 'what happened the night of November seventh?'

Chris took a deep breath and began to speak.

Then

November 7, 1997

He kept his eyes on it, the gun, on the small dent it made on the white skin at her temple. Her hands were shaking as badly as his, and he kept thinking, *It's going to go off.* And on the heels of that, *But it's what she wants.*

Her eyes were squeezed shut; her teeth bit into her lower lip. She was holding her breath. She was expecting, he realized, great pain.

He had seen her like this before.

He remembered with great clarity a memory he had forgotten to tell Dr Feinstein, surely his earliest one, since he was barely walking. He'd been running on the sidewalk and had fallen down. Bawling, he'd been lifted into his mother's arms, and had sat on the porch while she kissed his seemingly unscraped left knee and spread a Band-Aid across it for good measure. It was after he'd been soothed that he realized Emily was screaming, too, and getting the same treatment from her own mother. She'd been right next to him on the sidewalk, although she hadn't fallen. But on her left knee was a brand-new mottled bruise. 'He cuts himself,' his mother had laughed. 'And she bleeds.'

It had happened other times when they were children – Chris would get hurt and find Emily wincing, or vice versa – she'd tumble off her bike and he'd cry out. The pediatrician called it sympathy pain, said it was something they'd outgrow.

They hadn't.

The gun slipped on Emily's temple, and he suddenly knew that if she killed herself, he would die. Maybe not immediately, maybe not with the same blinding rush of pain, but it would happen. You couldn't live for very long without a heart.

He reached up with his hand and grabbed Emily's right wrist firmly. He was bigger than she was; he could draw the gun away from her head. With his free hand he pried Emily's fingers from the butt of the Colt and carefully uncocked the hammer. 'I'm sorry,' he said. 'But you can't.'

It took a moment for Emily's eyes to focus on his, and when they did they darkened with confusion, shock, and then rage. 'Yes I can,' Emily said, grabbing for the gun, which Chris held out of her reach.

'Chris,' she said, after a minute. 'If you love me, give it back.'

'I do love you!' Chris shouted, his face contorted.

'If you can't stay with me, I understand,' she said, looking down at the pistol. 'Go, then. But let me do it.'

Chris's mouth tightened, and he waited, but she would not meet his eye. *Look at me*, he silently begged. *Neither of us is going to win.* And although he was not feeling the lead of a bullet, now that he'd opened himself up to it, he could clearly feel Emily's sorrow, which made it hard to breathe and impossible to think. He had to get out of there. He had to get far away from Emily, so that he would not feel anything at all.

He stumbled to his feet and crashed through the shrubbery that circled the carousel, his tears making the night curve crazy. Swiping the backs of his hands across his eyes, he started to run, until he reached the Jeep.

He didn't get into the car, and realized he was waiting to hear the shot.

A half hour passed, slow and viscous, and before Chris realized what he was doing he'd walked halfway back to the carousel. He saw Emily just where he'd left her, cross-legged on the floorboards with the gun cradled between her palms. She was stroking the length of it as she might have caressed a kitten, and she was crying so hard she could not catch her breath.

Emily glanced up when she noticed his feet at the edge of the carousel. Her eyes were red; her nose was streaming. 'I

can't do it,' she said, choking on her own words. 'I can tell you
to get the hell out of here, and I can yell and scream and say
I want to, but I can't.'

Heart pounding, Chris pulled Emily to her feet. *This is a
sign*, he thought. *Tell her what it means*. But as soon as she was
standing, she pressed the gun into his palm. The pistol was
slick with Emily's sweat, and as warm as her own skin. 'I'm
too much of a coward to kill myself,' she whispered. 'And too
much of a coward to live.' She lifted her eyes. 'Where do I go
from here?'

Anything Chris was going to say dried in his throat. He
knew that if he wanted to, he could wrench the gun away from
Emily and throw it so far that she'd never be able to find it.
He was stronger than she was . . . and that was the problem.
He could suffer; he always had been able to. It was why he
could swim such a brutal butterfly; why he could wait in a
duck blind in zero degree weather for hours; why he could
talk himself into letting Emily kill herself. But even when they
were tiny, when he saw the sympathy bruises rise beneath
Emily's skin, it had hurt Chris more than when he'd actually
fallen. He could stand pain, himself. He just couldn't stand
hers.

Chris was transfixed by the agony he saw on Emily's face.
Whatever this thing was that she could not tell him, it was
killing her. Slowly, and far more painfully than the Colt would.

Chris's mind cleared with a great buzz and burst of light,
the way it sometimes did when he broke the surface of the
water on a winning final stroke. Just like that, it made sense.
Emily was not afraid of dying. She was afraid of *not* dying.

In that moment, with the night shrinking around them, Chris
didn't think to run, to get help, to buy time. It was just the
two of them, and there was no alternative – for the first time
Chris understood what Emily had been feeling. 'Please,' she
whispered, and he realized that pleasing Emily was all he'd
every really wanted to do.

He picked up the gun in his left hand, and embraced her.

'This is what you want?' he whispered, and Emily, realizing, nodded. She relaxed in his arms, and that small degree of trust unraveled him. 'I can't do this to you,' he said, drawing back.

Emily put her hand on his and pulled the gun to her temple. 'Then do it for me,' she said.

She could not see his face in that position, but she pictured it. She imagined Chris the way he had been during a moment the summer before, on the tennis courts at the school. It had been a brutal ninety-five degrees, and God only knew why they'd decided to play tennis, but there they were, Emily with her wild serves going clear over to the adjoining court, and Chris running after the balls, his laughter bouncing as high.

She remembered him standing with the sun behind his back. His racquet was in his left hand, in his right he tossed a Wilson ball. He paused to wipe it across his forehead, mopping up his sweat, and then smiled wide at Emily. His voice was husky and deep, beloved. 'Ready?' he asked.

Emily felt the gun touch her skin, and drew in a breath. 'Now,' she said.

Now, Chris, now.

He heard the words, heard Emily's voice vibrating against his chest, but his hands were shaking again and if he pulled the trigger he'd probably shoot himself and was that really so bad?

Now. Now.

He was crying so hard at this point that when he looked at Emily from the corner of his eye, her face wavered, and he believed that he'd already begun to forget her. But then he blinked and she was beautiful and calm and waiting, her mouth parted like it sometimes did when she fell asleep. She opened her eyes and all he could see was her conviction.

'Oh, I love you,' he said, at least he thought he did, but Emily heard him either way. She brought up her right hand

and settled it over his, her fingers curving over his own to urge him on.

She pressed his hand, and it squeezed on the trigger, and then he was deaf and dizzy and falling, with Emily still in his arms.

Now

May 1998

Chris fell silent, and shock settled over the courtroom like a fisherman's net, drawing close all the questions that had been raised during the trial. Jordan moved, the first one to break the spell. Chris was bent over on the witness stand, arms crossed over his stomach, his breathing uneven.

There was just one way to save this case. He knew exactly what the State was going to say – he'd done it for years, himself. And the only chance he had to come out on top was to take the wind out of Barrie Delaney's sails: to prosecute Chris before she got the chance.

Jordan approached the stand, grimly preparing to rip into his own client.

'Why were you there?' Jordan asked cynically. 'Were you planning to commit suicide, or what?'

Bewildered, Chris looked up at the attorney. In spite of what had happened in the past hour, Jordan was still supposed to be on Chris's side. 'I thought I could stop her.'

'Really.' Jordan snorted. 'You thought you could stop her and you wound up shooting her instead. How come you brought two bullets?'

'I . . . don't really know,' Chris said. 'I just did.'

'In case you missed?'

'In case . . . I wasn't thinking very clearly,' Chris admitted. 'I just took two, is all.'

'You fainted,' Jordan said, changing the subject. 'Do you know that for a fact?'

'I woke up on the ground, bleeding from my head,' he said,

'that's all I remember.' And out of the blue he recalled something Jordan had said to him months before: *The witness stand can be a very lonely place.*

'Were you unconscious when the police arrived?'

'No,' Chris said. 'I was sitting up, holding Emily.'

'But you don't remember actually fainting. Do you remember what happened just before you supposedly fainted?'

Chris's mouth opened and closed around empty words. 'We were both holding the gun,' he managed.

'Where were Emily's hands?'

'On top of my hand.'

'On the gun?'

'I don't know. I guess so.'

'Can't you remember exactly where?'

'No,' Chris said tightly, growing more agitated.

'Then how do you know for sure that her hands were on top of yours?'

'Because I can still feel her touching me, now, when I think about it.'

Jordan rolled his eyes. 'Oh, come on, Chris. Cut the Hallmark Card garbage. How do you know Emily's hands were on yours?'

Chris glared at his attorney, his face reddening. 'Because she was trying to make me pull the trigger!' he shouted.

Jordan turned on him. 'And how do you know that?' he needled.

'Because I do!' Chris's hands clenched on the railing of the witness box. 'Because that's what happened!' He took a shaky breath for control. 'Because,' he said, 'it's the truth.'

'Oh,' Jordan said, falling back. 'The truth. And why should we believe this truth? There have been so many.'

Chris began to rock slowly on the seat of his chair. Jordan had told Chris he'd fucked up his own defense, and Chris realized that now the lawyer was making him pay. If anyone was going to leave this courthouse looking like a fool, it was going to be Chris himself.

Suddenly, Jordan was beside him again. 'Your hand was on that gun?'

'Yes.'

'Where?'

'On the trigger.'

'And where was Emily's hand?' he asked.

'On mine. On the gun.'

'Well, which is it? On your hand or on the gun?'

Chris bowed his head. 'Both. I don't know.'

'So you don't remember fainting, but you do remember that Emily's hand was on yours and the gun. How could that be?'

'I don't know.'

'Why was Emily's hand on your hand?'

'Because she was trying to get me to kill her.'

'How do you know?' Jordan taunted.

'She was saying "*Now, Chris, now.*" But I couldn't do it. She kept saying it and saying it and then she put her hand on mine and jerked on it.'

'She was jerking your hand? Did she jerk your finger on the trigger?'

'I don't know.'

The attorney leaned closer. 'Did she jerk your wrist to make your whole hand move?'

'I don't know.'

'Did her finger ever brush that trigger, Chris?'

'I'm not sure.' He shook his head hard, trying to clear it.

'Did her hand knock into your finger on the trigger?'

'I don't know,' Chris sobbed. 'I don't know.'

'Are you the one who made that trigger go off, Chris?' Jordan said, inches from Chris's face. Chris nodded, his nose running, his eyes raw and red. 'Chris,' Jordan said, 'how do you know?'

'I don't know,' Chris cried, covering his ears. 'I don't, God, I don't know.'

Jordan reached over the railing of the witness stand and gently pulled Chris's hands down to rest beneath his own on the wooden divider. 'You don't know for sure, Chris, that you killed Emily, do you?'

Chris's breath caught in his throat. He stared wide-eyed at his attorney. *You don't have to figure it out*, Jordan silently implored. *You just have to admit that you can't.*

He was battered from the inside out, and his heart felt as if it had been trampled . . . but he was at peace for the first time in months. 'No,' Chris whispered, accepting this gift. 'I don't.'

In her life, Barrie Delaney had never prosecuted a trial quite like this. Jordan had quite effectively done her job for her, up until the end when the defendant was an emotional wreck and basically recanted his confession. But he had given a confession. And Barrie was not one to quit that easily.

'A lot happened on the night of November seventh, didn't it?'

Chris looked up at the prosecutor and warily nodded. 'Yes.'

'At the very end of it all,' Barrie said, 'was your hand holding the gun?'

'Yes.'

'Was that gun pressed against Emily's head?'

'Yes.'

'Was your finger on the trigger?'

Chris took a deep breath. 'Yes,' he said.

'Was a shot fired?'

'Yes.'

'Mr Harte,' Barrie said, 'was your hand still on that gun, and on that trigger when the shot was fired?'

'Yes,' Chris whispered.

'Do you think you shot Emily Gold?'

Chris bit his lip. 'I don't know,' he said.

'Redirect, Your Honor.' Jordan walked toward the witness stand again. 'Chris, did you go to the carousel thinking that you were going to kill Emily?'

'God, no.'

'Did you go there that night planning to kill her?'

'No.' He shook his head vigorously. 'No.'

'Even at the moment that you held the gun to Emily's head, Chris – did you want to kill her?'

'No,' Chris said thickly. 'I didn't.'

Jordan turned, so that he was not facing Chris any longer, but staring at Barrie Delaney as he parroted her cross-examination questions. 'At the end of the night on November seventh, Chris, was your hand on the gun?'

'Yes.'

'Was that gun held up to Emily's head?'

'Yes.'

'Was your finger on the trigger?'

'Yes.'

'Was a shot fired?'

'Yes.'

'Was Emily's hand on the gun, with yours?'

'Uh-huh,' Chris said.

'Was she saying, "Now, Chris, now"?'

'Yes.'

Jordan crossed the courtroom, coming to rest in front of the jury. 'Can you say, Chris – without a doubt – that your actions, your motions, your muscles, were the only things that caused that shot to be fired?'

'No,' Chris said, his eyes shining. 'I guess not.'

To everyone's surprise, Judge Puckett insisted on having summations after lunch. As the bailiffs moved forward to take Chris to the sheriff's lockup downstairs, he reached out to touch Jordan's sleeve. 'Jordan,' he began.

The lawyer was collecting notes and pencils and documents that had been scattered around the table. He did not bother to lift his head. 'Don't talk to me,' he said, and left without a backward glance.

Barrie Delaney treated herself to a Häagen-Dazs ice cream bar. Chocolate inside, and chocolate outside. A clear celebration.

As an assistant attorney general, the only way to make a

name for oneself was to have the good fortune to be next on
the roster when a high-profile case happened to come up. In
that, Barrie had been fortunate. Murders were rare in Grafton
County; dramatic courthouse confessions were unheard of.
The whole state would be talking about this case for days.
Barrie might even be interviewed for the network news.

She carefully licked around the edge of her ice cream, aware
that a spot on her suit wouldn't be a good idea when she still
had a closing argument to give. But as far as she figured, she
could stand up after Jordan's summation and recite the alphabet,
and Chris Harte would still be convicted of murder. In spite
of Jordan's last ditch efforts, a jury knew when it had been
taken for a ride. All that crap about the double suicide attempt
which the defense had tried as a strategy, and which was just
that – crap – was going to weigh heavily on those twelve minds
when they retired to deliberate.

The jury had the memory of Chris saying he'd shot the girl.
The whole debacle with his mother on the stand. And the knowledge that for the first three days of this trial, the defense had
deliberately been lying.

Nobody liked finding out they'd been duped.

Barrie Delaney smiled and licked her fingers. *Least of all*,
she imagined, *Jordan McAfee*.

'Get away,' Jordan yelled over his shoulder.

'Tough,' Selena shot back.

'Just leave me alone, all right?' He stalked away from her, but
she was damn tall and those long legs ate up his stride. Seizing
the opportunity, he ducked into the men's room only to have
Selena throw the door back on its hinges and step inside. She
glared at an elderly man using the urinal, who quickly zipped up
his fly, flushed, and left. Then she leaned back against the door,
to prevent anyone else from entering. 'Now,' she ordered. 'Talk.'

Jordan leaned against the sink and closed his eyes. 'Do you
have any idea,' he said, 'what this is going to do to my credi-
bility?'

'Absolutely nothing,' Selena said. 'You got Chris to sign a waiver.'

'Which is exactly what no one's going to hear on the news. They're going to assume I'm as competent in a courtroom as one of the Seven Dwarfs.'

'Which one?' Selena asked, smiling slightly.

'Dopey,' Jordan sighed. 'God. Am I an idiot? How could I have put him on the stand without grilling him first about what he was going to say?'

'You were angry,' Selena said.

'So?'

'So. You don't know what you're like when you're angry.' She touched his arm. 'You did the best you could for Chris,' she gently reminded him. 'You can't win all of the time.'

Jordan glanced at her. 'Why the hell not?' he said.

'You know what?' Jordan began, facing the jury. 'Three hours ago, I didn't have the slightest idea what I was going to say to you all right now. And then it dawned on me – I wanted to congratulate you. Because you've seen something very unusual today. Something surprising that never, ever makes its way into a courtroom. You, ladies and gentlemen, have seen the truth.'

He smiled, leaning against the defense table. 'It's a tricky word, isn't it? Sounds larger than life.' He straightened his face in a good impression of Judge Puckett. 'Very serious. I looked it up in the dictionary,' he admitted. 'Webster's says it's the real state of things, the body of real events or facts.' Jordan shrugged. 'Then again, Oscar Wilde said that the pure and simple truth is rarely pure and never simple. Truth, you see, is in the eye of the beholder.

'Did you know I used to be a prosecutor? I was. Worked in the same office where Ms Delaney works now, for ten years. You know why I left? Because I didn't like the idea of truth. When you're a prosecutor, the world's black or white, and things either happened or they didn't. I always believed there was more than one way to tell a story, to see things. I didn't think truth even belonged in a trial. As a prosecutor you present your evidence and your witnesses, and then the defense gets a chance to put a different spin on the same stuff. But you'll notice I didn't say anything about presenting the truth.'

He laughed. 'Funny, don't you think, that I should have to take the truth and run with it to the end zone, now? Because that's all I have left, in defense of Chris Harte. This trial . . . unbelievably . . . has been about the truth.'

Jordan walked toward the jury and spread his hands on the railing of the box. 'We started this trial with two truths. Mine,' he speared his chest, 'and hers.' He jerked a thumb at Barrie Delaney. 'And then we saw a lot of variations. The truth, to Emily's mother, is that there's no way her daughter could have been anything less than perfect. But, then, we all see people the way we want to. The truth, to the detective and the medical examiner, comes from an arrangement of hard evidence. That isn't to say that the evidence might not lead them to their theory. The truth, to Michael Gold, means taking responsibility for something too horrible to imagine, even though it's easier to point the blame at someone else. And the truth, to Chris's mother, has nothing to do with this case. Her truth is believing in her son . . . no matter what that entails.

'But the most important truth you've heard comes from Chris Harte. There are only two people who know what really happened the night of November seventh. One of them is dead. And one of them just told you everything.'

Jordan skimmed his hand along the rail of the box as he surveyed the jury. 'That, ladies and gentlemen, is where you come in. Ms Delaney has given you a set of facts. And Chris Harte has given you the truth. Do you just blindly agree with Ms Delaney – see things the way she wants you to see them, through her black-and-white glasses? Do you say: There was a gun, there was a shot, a girl died; therefore it must be murder? Or do you look at the truth?

'You have a choice. You can do what I used to do – what

I like to do as a lawyer – just go on the facts and form your own opinions. Or you can hold the truth in your hands, and see it for the gift it is.' He leaned toward the jury, his voice softening. 'There once was a boy and a girl. They grew up together. They loved each other like a brother and a sister. They spent every moment together, and when they got older they became lovers. Their feelings and their hearts became so intertwined that they could no longer distinguish their individual needs.

'Then, for a reason we may never know, one of these young people began to hurt. She hurt so badly that she didn't want to live. And she turned to the only person she trusted.' Jordan walked toward Chris, stopping just inches from his client. 'He tried to help. He tried to stop her. But at the same time, he could feel her pain as if it were his own. And in the end, he couldn't stop her. He was a failure. He even went so far as to walk away.'

Jordan looked at the jury. 'The problem was, Emily couldn't kill herself. She begged him, she pleaded, she cried, she put her hand over his on the gun. She was such a part of him and he was such a part of her, that she couldn't even complete this final act by herself. Now, here's the question you face, as a jury: Did Chris do it by *himself*?

'Who knows, ladies and gentlemen, what made that trigger kick? There is physical power, and then there's the power of the mind. Maybe it was Emily jerking against Chris's hand. And maybe it was Emily telling him that she wanted to die, more than anything. Telling him that she trusted him and loved him enough to help her to do it. As I said, Chris Harte is the only person in this courtroom who was there. And by his own testimony, even Chris does not know for sure what happened.

'Ms Delaney wants you to convict Chris on a charge of first-degree murder. However, to do that, she has to prove that he had the time and opportunity for reflection. That he thought about what he was going to do, that he settled on his purpose, and that his mind was made up to take Emily's life.'

Jordan shook his head. 'But you know what? Chris didn't want to kill Emily that night – or any other night. It was the last thing he wanted to do. And Chris didn't have time to think about what happened. He never made up his mind to do anything. Emily made up his mind for him.

'This trial is not about Ms Delaney's set of facts, or about anything I said in my opening statement, or even about the witnesses I presented. It is about Chris Harte, and what he chose to reveal to you.' Jordan slowly moved his eyes over the jury, catching each of the twelve gazes. 'He was there, and he has some doubts about what actually happened. How couldn't you?'

Jordan started toward the defense table, pausing midway. 'Chris told you something most juries never hear – the truth. Now it's up to you to tell him you were listening.'

'Mr McAfee certainly has a future as a novelist,' Barrie said. 'I was getting caught up in the drama, myself. But what Mr McAfee was trying to do was draw you away from the clear-cut facts of this case, which he says are not the same thing as "the truth."'

'Now, we don't actually know if Chris Harte is telling the truth,' she said. 'We know he's lied before – to the police, to his parents. In fact, we've heard three different stories during this trial. The first story was that Emily was going to kill himself, and so was Chris. The second story was that Emily was still suicidal . . . but Chris was going to try to stop her.' Barrie paused. 'You know, that works a little better for me, because Chris doesn't seem very suicidal.

'Oh, but then Chris changed his story again: Emily couldn't manage to pull the trigger by herself, so he had to physically pull it for her.' Barrie sighed dramatically. 'Mr McAfee wants you to look at the truth.' She raised her brows. 'Which one?'

'For the sake of argument, let's stick to Chris's last story. Let's assume that's the truth. Yet even if it is, you have no choice but to convict him. You've seen the physical evidence

– which is the one thing that hasn't changed during the course of this trial. You've heard Detective Marrone say that Chris's fingerprints were on the gun; you've heard the medical examiner say that the trajectory of the bullet through Emily's head indicates that someone shot her; you've heard him give evidence of Chris's skin beneath Emily's fingernails and bruises on Emily's wrist incurred during a struggle. But perhaps more importantly, you've heard Chris Harte say that he shot Emily Gold. By his own admission, he killed her.

'A person is guilty of murder in the first degree if they intend to cause the death of someone else. If their actions are premeditated, deliberate, and willful.

'Let's think about this: Chris Harte weighed the pros and cons and then decided to bring a gun to the scene of the crime. That's premeditated. He loaded the gun. That's deliberate. He took the gun from Emily's hand of his own free will, held it up to her head, and was still holding it when the shot was fired. That, ladies and gentlemen, is murder in the first degree. It doesn't matter if he felt sorry for Emily. It doesn't matter if Emily asked him to do it. It doesn't matter if it hurt him to kill her. In this country, you can't just take a gun and shoot someone. Even if they ask you to.'

Barrie walked toward the jury. 'If we believe Chris now, where do we draw the line? Especially when the victim is no longer alive to testify. We'd have criminals roaming the streets, assuring us that their victims begged them to kill them, honest to God.' She pointed toward the witness stand. 'Chris Harte sat there and told you that he took the gun, held it to Emily's head, and shot her. No matter what else was going on around that – the emotions, the psychological mumbo-jumbo, the confusion – that is what happened. There is your truth.

'You have to find Christopher Harte guilty if the death of Emily Gold was a direct result of his actions. If those actions were premeditated, deliberate, and willful. So . . . how do you know without a doubt that Chris Harte's actions qualify?' Barrie crossed the courtroom, ticking off her points. 'Because he could have put down that pistol. Because he could have walked away at any time. Because he was not forced to shoot Emily Gold.' She stopped at the exhibit table and picked up the murder weapon. 'After all, ladies and gentlemen, no one was holding a gun to Chris's head.'

By six P.M., the jury had not returned a verdict. Chris was brought back to the jail to sleep. He sloughed off his clothes and crawled under the covers, refusing dinner, refusing to speak to anyone who banged on the bars of his cell.

A backbeat pounded at the base of his skull – the one thing that neither Jordan McAfee nor Barrie Delaney had mentioned. Maybe it wasn't important to them; Chris himself certainly hadn't thought about it until Jordan had jogged his memory of that night for what it really was. And it had to do with Emily.

She had loved him. He knew this; he had never doubted it. But she had also asked him to kill her.

If you loved someone that much, you did not lay that sort of burden on him for the rest of his life.

Chris had struggled with it, had decided that loving Emily meant letting her go, if that was really what she wanted. But Emily had been so selfish, she'd never even given Chris the choice. She had bound him to her irrevocably, with shame, with pain, and with guilt.

The sounds of an inmate fight breaking out one floor below and the jangle of an officer's keys were swallowed by a rage that swelled and roared in Chris's ears. In that moment, he was furious at Emily for doing this to him. For putting her own wishes before his, when he'd done the exact opposite.

For landing him in this stinking hole for seven months, seven months that he was never going to get back. For not telling him about the baby. For leaving him behind. For ruining his life.

And in that moment Chris realized that, had Emily Gold been present, he would have willfully killed her.

⋆　　　⋆　　　⋆

Selena pushed away her empty wine glass. 'It's over,' she said. 'You can't change anything, now.'

'I could have—'

'No,' she told Jordan. 'You couldn't.'

He closed his eyes and leaned back in his chair, the nearly untouched steak stretched on a platter in front of him. 'I hate this part,' he said. 'Waiting. It would have been cheaper for the taxpayers if they'd just handed me a hara-kiri sword and told me to do the honors.'

Selena burst out laughing. 'Jordan, you're such an optimist,' she said. 'One little glitch isn't going to ruin your career.'

'I don't care about my career.'

'What is it, then?' She studied him, her mouth rounding. 'Oh . . . Chris.'

He scrubbed the heels of his hands over his face. 'You know what I can't get out of my head?' he said. 'That part when Chris was on the stand, and said he could still feel Emily touch him sometimes. And I told him to cut the crap.'

'You had to, Jordan.'

He waved her words off, dismissive. 'It's not that. It's that I'm more than twice as old as Chris Harte, and I've been married, and I've still never felt that way. Gut feeling – do I think he killed that girl? Yeah, I do. Technically, anyway. But Jesus, Selena. I'm jealous of him. I can't imagine loving someone so much you'd do anything they asked. Even if that happened to be murder.'

'You'd do anything for Thomas,' Selena said.

'It's not the same, and you know it.'

For a moment, Selena was silent. 'Don't be jealous of Chris Harte. Feel sorry for him. Because the chances of him getting that close to someone again are very slim. You, on the other hand, still have everything to look forward to.'

Jordan shrugged, steepling his fingers. 'Whatever,' he said.

Selena sighed and drew him to his feet. 'Time to get home,' she said. 'You have an early day tomorrow.' And then, in the middle of the restaurant, she grabbed his ears in her hands and gently tugged his head forward so that she could kiss him.

Her mouth was hard on his, and her tongue slid easily between his lips. By the time Selena drew away, Jordan was fighting for breath. 'What,' he said, 'made you do that?'

She patted his cheek. 'Just wanted to give you something else to obsess about,' she said, and turned on her heel, leaving him to follow.

By nine o'clock, the Hartes were ready for bed. There was no other way Gus could think of to make the morning come more quickly. She shut the light off and waited for James to come out of the bathroom.

The mattress creaked and dipped as James got under the covers. Gus turned her head away, staring out the window, where the moon was fingernail-thin. By the time it was full again, her firstborn would be serving a life sentence at the State Penitentiary.

She knew why Chris had interrupted her testimony, just as well as she knew that she'd been doing a miserable job. He couldn't watch her on the stand, each lie splitting her heart into a set of Russian nesting dolls, growing smaller and smaller until there was nothing left inside. Chris had never been able to bear seeing someone he loved in great pain.

It was why he had shot Emily.

She must have made a sound, an involuntary sob, because all of a sudden James drew her against his chest. Gus turned into the solid heat of him, wrapping her arms around him.

She wanted to get closer, under James's skin; to become a part of him so that she wouldn't have her own thoughts, her own worries. She wanted his strength. But instead of speaking she turned her face up and kissed him, her mouth raining over his neck and her hips pressing into his.

The bed, the room, was burning up around them. They scratched at each other in an effort to come together. James entered Gus within seconds, her body convulsing around his, her mind blessedly, blissfully empty.

When it was over, James stroked her damp back. 'Do you remember,' she whispered, 'the night we made him?'

He nodded into Gus's hair. 'I knew it then,' she murmured. 'I could feel it was different from other times. Like you'd given yourself to me, to hold.'

James tightened his arms. 'I had,' he said. He felt Gus's shoulders quiver, and the slick of her tears against his chest. 'I know,' he soothed. 'I know.'

As the jury filed into the courtroom, Chris realized he could not swallow. His Adam's apple had lodged in his throat, and he could feel himself wheezing and his eyes watering. Not a single member of the jury looked his way, and he tried to remember what other inmates at the jail had said about that, from their own experiences – was it a good thing, or not?

Judge Puckett turned to one of the jurors, an elderly man wearing a stained broadcloth button-down. 'Mr Foreman, have you reached a verdict?'

'We have, Your Honor.'

'And is this verdict unanimous?'

'It is.' At the judge's nod, the clerk of the court approached the jury box and took a folded piece of paper from the foreman. He walked slowly – snail's pace, Chris thought – back to the judge and handed it to him. The judge nodded, and then sent the note back to the foreman.

Leslie Puckett glanced up, face blank. 'Will the defendant please rise?'

Chris felt Jordan come to his feet beside him. He had every intention of standing up, too, but his legs wouldn't work. They lay puddled beneath the bench, his feet block-heavy and immobile. Jordan looked down and raised his eyebrows. *Get up.*

'I can't,' Chris whispered, and felt his attorney grab him beneath the armpit and haul him upright.

His heart was pounding wildly, and his hands felt so leaden he could not even clasp them, no matter how hard he tried. It was as if all of a sudden this body did not belong to him anymore.

He could sense everything in that instant: the smell of soap that had been used to clean the woodwork in the courtroom the night before; the drop of sweat that streaked between his shoulderblades; the tap of the court reporter's shoe on the edge of her work station. 'In the matter of *The State of New Hampshire* versus *Christopher Harte*, on the count of murder in the first degree, how do you find?'

The foreman looked at the slip of paper he held. 'Not guilty,' he read.

Chris felt Jordan turn to him, a wide, astonished smile splitting his face. He heard his mother's soft cry a few feet behind him. He listened to the roar of the courtroom, exploding in the wake of the unexpected. And for the third time in his life, Christopher Harte fainted.

Epilogue

Everywhere Chris went, he opened windows. He drove with them rolled down, even though the air conditioning was on. He opened them in every room of the house. Even at night, when it grew cool, he piled blankets on his bed, preferring those to a small square of air that did not circulate.

But sometimes, even with all the fresh breezes, a scent would carry on the wind. He'd wake up suddenly from his sleep, fighting to get away from it, suffocating. And his parents would find him the next morning sleeping on the couch, or on the living room floor, or once even at the foot of their own bed.

What's the matter? they would ask. *What happened?*

But there was no way to explain it to someone who had not been there; for absolutely no reason, he had suddenly smelled prison.

It came one Saturday in June, a long white truck with the world on its side, backing into the Golds' driveway and spitting out six men who would carry away their belongings. Gus and James watched from the porch as boxes were hauled and mattresses settled, as lamps were noosed with their own cords and bicycles ridden into the belly of the truck. They did not say a thing to each other, but they both found outdoor tasks to occupy themselves, so that for the entire day they were able to bear witness.

Neighborhood gossip said that the Golds were moving across town – not a long-distance move, but certainly a necessary one.

The house had been put on the market and a new one purchased before it even sold.

People said that Michael had wanted to go far, Colorado, maybe, or even California. But Melanie had refused to leave her daughter behind, and where did that leave them?

The new house had an office, again, for Michael's veterinary practice, and was by all accounts a lovely, secluded place. It was a rumor, of course, but someone had heard that it had three bedrooms. One for Michael Gold, one for his wife, and one for Emily.

Before Gus could stop herself, she walked to the end of the driveway. She watched the long van slip over the crest of the road, followed by Melanie's Taurus. And then, some way behind, came Michael's truck.

The windows were open in the truck; it was too old for the air conditioning to work with any regularity. Michael slowed as he came to the Hartes' driveway. She saw that he was going to stop. She saw that he wanted to talk to her. To take her apology, to offer absolution, to simply say good-bye.

The truck rolled to a near stop, and Michael turned, his sober gaze meeting Gus's. There was a flash of pain; the weight of possibility; and on its heels, the flat, square stare of understanding.

Without saying a word, he drove away.

Chris was in his room when the moving van began to pull out of the Golds' driveway. Long and white, it groaned its way through the trees that lined the gravel strip, narrowly missing the mailbox.

Melanie Gold's Ford, and finally Michael's truck. A caravan, Chris thought. Like the gypsies – off to find something easier, or better.

And then the house was empty, a yellow clapboard monolith. The windows, bare of curtains, seemed like vague and distant eyes, willing to stare but unable to remember. Chris leaned out the sill of his open window, listening to the buzz of cicadas, the settling heat of summer, and the quiet crunch of the moving van making its way down Wood Hollow Road.

Curious, he craned his neck out the window, trying to see the edge of the sill that curved around the top. It was still there, the pulley that had been one end of the tin-can message system he'd had with Emily when he was a kid. There was another one, he knew, on the top edge of Emily's old window.

Chris stretched up his hand, twanging the fishing line that was moldy, but still intact. It had long ago caught in one of the pine trees between the properties, tangling up the can and whatever message had been inside it, and they'd never managed to get it loose.

Chris had tried, but back then he'd been too little.

He twisted himself so that he was sitting on the still, his hands stretching up along the shingles outside the house. He was able to snag the string with his fingers, and he felt a disproportionate amount of accomplishment, as if getting it on the first try meant something. As the rotted string gave way, Chris watched the rusty can fall from its threaded perch between the houses.

With his heart pounding, Chris ran down the stairs, taking them two at a time. He headed toward the spot where he'd seen the can go down, his eyes tracking back and forth until he saw a winking of silver.

The trees grew tall and narrow here, shading away the sun. Chris fell to his knees beside a high pine and jammed a finger into the can, drawing forth a piece of paper. He could not remember what this final message had been about; could not even remember whether he had been sending it to Emily or Emily had been sending it to him. His stomach knotted as the paper slid free of the tin.

Carefully, feeling the fragile folds give, he opened it.

The paper was blank.

Whether it had always been that way, or if years had erased

whatever was written, he did not know. Chris tucked the note in the pocket of his shorts and turned away from Emily's house, thinking that maybe it really didn't matter one way or the other.

A CONVERSATION WITH JODI PICOULT

Q: How do your ideas for books take shape?

A: Usually my ideas take the form of a what-if question: What if there was a mother who . . . ? I start mulling it over, and before I know it I've got a whole drama unfolding in my head . . . Interestingly enough, *The Pact* was not a big page-turner when it started to take form in my mind. I was going to write a character-driven book about the survivors left behind after an unfinished suicide pact between two teenagers, and I went to a local police chief to do some preliminary research. He was restating the facts of the plot for me – a plot in which I expected the teenage girl to be the one who lived. 'Huh,' he said. 'The girl? Because if it was the boy, who was larger physically, he'd automatically be suspected of murder until evidence cleared him.' And before I knew it I was leaning forward in my seat, saying, 'Really???' From there, I created the character of Chris . . . The story just began to unfold, and I could play around with the bigger questions of how well we really ever know the people we love.

Q: How much time do you spend researching a book and how much time on the actual writing?

A: It takes me the same amount of time to write a book as it does to have a baby. It's always nine months, give or take a couple of weeks . . . For some reason that's the length of time it takes for my mind to gel a batch of ideas into a cohesive book. I know that I write fast, compared to other authors, but if it took me much longer I'd probably get bored with the plot and want to move on . . . [And] I always do my research before I write a single word – I'm a stickler for getting things right in a book . . . Sometimes that means role-playing with a lawyer or observing cardiac surgery or speaking to astronauts or milking cows on an Amish farm . . . it varies from book to book . . . The most bizarre research I did for *The Pact* was go to jail – something my four-year-old gleefully announced in nursery school that day. It was like being in a zoo full of humans – very demoralizing – and the inmate who spoke to me during an interview was incredibly enlightening. You know all those little tidbits in Chris's jail scenes, the ones you figure had to be made up? They're not.

Q: You have three young children. How do you find time to write?

A: Well, to answer your question, I am currently typing these responses and simultaneously playing Trivial Pursuit Junior. I'm really a mom; I just moonlight as an author. I spend most of my daylight hours with my kids – ages seven, five, and three – and work when my husband gets home at night and does the bedtime routine . . . Because I have very little time to write, every moment is precious . . . If I didn't somehow make the time to write, I'd go crazy – it's something I need to do, like a compulsion . . . To many women, being a hands-on mother with a thriving writing career seems impossible, but to me they are complementary: I am a better mother because I see the world through a writer's eyes . . . and I'm a better writer because I see the world through a mother's eyes.

Q: In the process of writing, do you work in sequence?

A: In six novels I can remember only one scene I wrote out of sequence. However, I can start a book and discover that it goes off in a different direction from the way I expected. There is always a point in a novel where I believe it starts writing itself, and I'm along for the ride . . . Certain scenes stun me after they're written – I'll just stare at my computer screen in amazement and think, 'Good Lord, where do I go from here?' . . . It's a little unnerving, but I love it when there are moments where my characters almost walk away from me on their own feet – it makes me feel like I've really brought them to life.

Q: When you work on a book, do the characters inhabit your thoughts as if they were real people?

A: Oh, sure. I once had a dream when I was in the middle of my second novel; the protagonist came to me and said she didn't like what I was writing for her. And why shouldn't my characters be real? While I am writing a book, I spend more time with them than I do with my husband! Actually, when readers say they put down the book and the characters were still living with them for a few days, it is the highest form of praise to me . . . *The Pact* has brought a lot of interesting comments from readers – one woman wrote me to say she'd made peace with her mother's suicide after reading the book; one mother said it opened up a line of communication with her teenage daughter she'd never expected to have.

Q: In some ways, Emily is the main character of *The Pact*, yet we learn most about her through observations and recollections of others. Had you thought about writing through Emily's eyes?

A: As soon as I realized that the first image you have of Em is of a dead young woman, I knew that she would have to be pieced together by every other character. Part of the grand mystery here is that we never really know Emily . . . [but] we're struggling to make sense of her . . . . However, Hollywood has now optioned *The Pact*, and I was asked to co-write the screenplay, so the characters of both Chris and Emily have been expanded. That meant adding conversations and scenes between them, and really re-exploring her thoughts and her motivations. It was heartbreaking to clarify the words and thoughts that Em might have spoken which would make Chris ultimately decide to do what he did. There were moments when I was writing scenes for the script that I found myself crying all over again.

Q: On page 214 Emily tells Chris, 'Wanting isn't the same as loving.' Can you comment on Chris's answer?

A: When Chris answers and tells her that wanting only makes him love her more, I think it's at that point that we as readers realize that Chris envisions this relationship very differently from Emily. Chris has bought into his parents' expectations; Emily of course has not. For Chris, the sexuality that's coming into their relationship is growing out of their lifelong connection. For Emily, it's grafted on in a way that sticks out sorely. Chris tells Emily that he's always loved her, that the wanting part is new. But it's the part that's going to dissolve the relationship, in Emily's mind. I don't think we can say whether Chris and Em are right for each other, because that makes us as flawed as their parents. The only ones who can say this are

Chris and Em themselves, and when their opinions on the topic diverge, love suddenly isn't enough.

Q: The title refers to the pact between Emily and Chris. Are there other pacts? And what about the subtitle, A Love Story?

A: There are so many pacts in this story I lose count: the pact of each set of parents' marriage, the pact of friendship between Melanie and Gus, the pact that Michael and Gus nearly break about coveting a neighbor's wife. As for the subtitle, I've gotten some flak for that. Some readers think it's the anti-love story. I think it's really interesting to have a love story where one lover is dead on page 1. However, the love story between Emily and Chris follows a certain arc of infatuation, intimacy, betrayal, and resolution. Another pair goes through the same arc: Gus and Chris. To me, the parent/child love story is just as crucial to the novel as the romantic one.

Q: As you wrote The Pact, did you know what would happen at the end?

A: I knew it would culminate in a trial. I didn't know whether Chris would be convicted or acquitted. I actually think that he should have been convicted . . . but I didn't write it that way because the book was so full of heartache and sorrow that I envisioned readers sending me hate mail – the novel called for an uplifting ending, if you can call it that.

Q: What are you working on right now?

A: I just finished the first draft of a novel about a young Amish girl who is charged with murder after her newborn baby is delivered in secret and dies. And I've begun spinning ideas for the next novel I'll be writing, which is currently a messy set of hasty notes stuffed into a box in my office.

Q: Are you ever surprised by the reactions of reviewers and discussion groups? Do people ever not get the story as you intend it to be interpreted?

A: I learned a long time ago not to listen to reviewers because, after all, they're just one person with an opinion. Readers, though, are a different story. I set up a Web site (www.jodipicoult.com) when *The Pact* was published, and got over a hundred e-mails from fans. It was fabulous – usually, you don't get to hear from your readers, and this has been a gift to me . . . I also often go to book discussion groups when one of my books has been read . . . I love to meet people who are as passionate about my stories as I am . . . They ask questions about the characters and the plot and make connections that sometimes I never even saw . . . As an English major, I can only applaud different interpretations. What's fiction but a great starting point for discussion?

Book Club Discussion Questions
for *The Pact*

1) How do you feel the extended family environment created by the Hartes and the Golds affected their children? Did it contribute to Emily's suicide?

2) Is there such a thing as being too close to another non-blood relative family?

3) How do you feel Chris handled his guilt? Can he justify helping Emily commit suicide?

4) How did the marital relationships of the Golds and the Hartes contribute to Gus's and Michael's temptations?

5) Is Emily correct in believing she had no alternatives to suicide? Explain.

6) Is Melanie justified in her feelings and actions toward the Hartes following Emily's death? What might justify her behavior?

7) On page 43 is the following statement: 'Chris and Emily had grown up with love, with wealth, with each other. What more could they have needed?' Comment.

8) In what ways does jail change Chris? In what ways does he benefit from the experience, and in what ways does it hurt him?

9) Consider the personalities of the Hartes and the Golds. Do opposites attract? Does it make for the best communication in a marriage? How do the events of the book support or deny this thesis?

10) Where do you see these characters in five years?

11) Is the punishment meted out to Chris just? In your opinion, is Chris guilty of murder?

12) Which character in the book is the most adaptable? The least adaptable? Why?

13) Do you think Chris's trial will affect Jordan's view of the justice system? Explain.

14) What is the significance of the 'blank' piece of paper that Chris finds in the tin can at the end of the book?

Here's what I know about me as a writer: I would write no matter what – even if there was no one out there to read what I'd written.

But the fact that you are there? That's amazing.

I love to hear from you. If you want to let me know what you thought about the questions I raise in this novel, or find out more about what I'm doing next, here are some easy ways to stay in touch:

- Follow me on twitter @jodipicoult
- Like my Facebook page
  www.facebook.com/JodiPicoultUK
- Visit my website www.jodipicoult.co.uk, and sign up to my newsletter.

Thank you for reading!